PRAISE FOR *THE SECOND LADY SILVERWOOD*

'Hot stuff. I loved it!'
Fern Britton

'An exciting and thoroughly enjoyable new talent has
exploded onto the market. I absolutely loved it!'
Katie Fforde

'A delicious Regency romp'
Alan Titchmarch

'Heyer with spice! I adored it'
Liz Fenwick

'D-E-L-I-C-I-O-U-S . . . An absolutely glorious
Regency romance. I love love loved it'
Sophie Irwin

'Sensual and exciting! I loved it!'
Heidi Swain

'Witty, heartfelt, deeply emotionally authentic and
incredibly sexy, this is Regency romance at its finest'
Katy Moran

'Filled with wit and passion. Perfect for fans of
Bridgerton and Georgette Heyer'
Darcie Boleyn

'Witty, spicy, seductive ... a historical romance
full of raunch and wit'
Hannah Dolby

'Sexy, seductive and
Sarah Ben

T0002108

By Emma Orchard

The Second Lady Silverwood
The Runaway Heiress

THE SECOND
LADY
SILVERWOOD

EMMA ORCHARD

Allison & Busby Limited
11 Wardour Mews
London W1F 8AN
allisonandbusby.com

First published in Great Britain by Allison & Busby in 2023.

A CIP catalogue record for this book is available from
the British Library.

First Edition

ISBN 978-0-7490-2964-7

Typeset in 11/16 pt Sabon LT Pro by
Typo•glyphix, Burton-on-Trent, DE14 3HE.

Printed and bound by
CPI Group (UK) Ltd, Croydon, CR0 4YY

To all the Heyer ladies,
who kept me sane through lockdown

It must be very improper that a young lady should dream of a gentleman before the gentleman is first known to have dreamt of her.

Northanger Abbey – Jane Austen

PROLOGUE

1807

It all began so well.

Kate's first grand ball. She had been to small parties with dancing before, both here in London and at home in York, but this evening was entirely different. The Season was well underway, and this was one of the most coveted invitations, which had sat in gilt-edged splendour for several weeks on the mantel-shelf in her grandmother's rather dingy rented lodgings in Bloomsbury.

The Moretons had no particular pretensions to wealth or fashion, but they were clever, agreeable and amusing. Although it had been many years since she had last resided in London, Mrs Moreton maintained a wide and witty correspondence, and as a consequence had a quite surprising number of acquaintances at the highest levels of society, and was received everywhere. It was known that she was an intimate friend of Madame D'Arblay, and through her good offices had been introduced to the Queen, who had looked on her with favour. She was foreign, of course, which was unfortunate, but her birth was noble, and she spoke English perfectly, with the slightest hint of an Italian accent, which the *haut ton* was pleased to find charming. It would not do to be too exotic, naturally, but a touch of difference – just a touch, no more – lent spice. One might meet the vivacious widowed lady and her tall, statuesque granddaughter at the most exclusive entertainments, and tonight they would be among the hundreds of intimate friends helping Lord Ansell celebrate his lovely daughter Vanessa's debut into society.

Kate was in truth only a little acquainted with Miss Ansell, and could not presume to say she knew her well; she was always pleasant and polite enough when they met, but Vanessa was the acknowledged hit of the Season, from an aristocratic and wealthy family, while Kate Moreton was in the end just a provincial nobody. Perhaps it was only natural that they should not share confidences. What could they have to say to each other? Yet she was fascinated by the ease with which Vanessa seemed to move through the world, and would love to know what lay behind that flawless, exquisite face. Something, surely, must occasionally disturb that creamy serenity. Did she not have fears and doubts like any girl, however lovely she was?

But tonight Kate had little thought to spare for anything but excited anticipation. She had saved her most becoming new gown for this momentous event, and as she climbed the steps and entered the imposing Mayfair mansion at her grandmother's side, she was conscious that she looked her best. The pale pastel colours considered most suitable for young ladies making their come-out did not become her, and her grandmother was not so foolish as to insist that she wore them tonight; her gown was a deep rose pink, with an overdress of gauze in the same shade, and her abundant dark hair was studded with tiny silk rosebuds. Her fine, velvet-brown eyes were sparkling with pleasurable expectancy, and the rose of her gown found an echo in the slight flush of her cheeks. She was eighteen and, she thought, just possibly in love. And tonight, he would be here, and she would dance with him. Surely he would ask her.

She had met him first a few weeks previously, at a small, informal dance held by one of her grandmother's friends – another elderly lady bringing out her orphaned granddaughter into the world. The duennas sat around the room, chatting, fanning themselves languidly in the stuffy atmosphere, and under their sharp-eyed supervision Kate danced with any number of young gentlemen. For the most part she enjoyed the dancing, but as individuals the youths made little impression on her, except for the one who was sadly clumsy and stepped on her foot, and then overwhelmed her with awkward apologies. But then her hostess presented her with another partner, and introduced them, smiling and saying that she thought they would be well suited.

Benedict Silverwood. Captain Silverwood. Kate was tall – a defect, she knew, albeit one she could scarcely hope to mend – but he was taller. He was a little older than some of the other young men she had met, and perhaps it was that, along with his service as an officer in the army, that gave him the air of quiet confidence that set him apart. He was very handsome, of course. That was undeniable. His eyes were an arresting light grey, his face composed of strong, masculine planes: square chin; high cheekbones; finely sculpted, resolute lips. He might have been considered classically beautiful, except that his nose had been broken at some point and had set a little crooked. Perhaps a captious critic might have said that this irregularity marred his features, but Kate was not a captious critic, and she found she liked the imperfection. She might otherwise have found him too intimidatingly perfect. But it was his smile that truly captured her attention. It lit up his whole face, and made his eyes sparkle. It was impossible not to respond to it, as it betrayed an infectious joy in life that found an immediate answer in Kate. She had no patience for affectation, or for those who professed to find life dull. Life was anything but dull.

They danced, that first time they met – he was graceful, and she felt herself to be graceful in his company – and conversed a little. She asked if he was on leave from the army, and he explained a little reluctantly that he had been wounded in the shoulder the previous year, in the disastrous British expedition to the Río de la Plata, and then had taken a fever, from which he was only now recovered with his mother's tender nursing care. She liked the way he disclaimed any heroism, but made a joke of the misadventures of his military service, and she liked the warm affection he plainly held for his mother. Oh – she liked everything about him.

They met again, and danced again, at other parties, and liking, on her side at least, quickly, inexorably deepened into something more. He seemed to her an estimable young man, amiable, well-mannered, and full of ready humour, but never cruel or mocking. He treated everyone with an instinctive courtesy, and was as ready to partner the shyest, dowdiest debutante as the most beautiful: as Vanessa Ansell.

Now she would see him at Miss Ansell's ball – she knew the families were acquainted – and perhaps he would ask her, Kate, to dance the supper dance with him, so that they could spend precious time together afterwards while they took refreshments. They would not be alone, of course – no young lady could ever be truly alone with a man, and the thought of it made her shiver a little, although whether in fear or in a scandalous desire for what she knew was forbidden, she could hardly have said – but even in company they could talk . . . She had not the least reason to think him particularly interested in her, but still she could not help hoping and dreaming a little.

And it was – at first – so much better even than she could have hoped. The ballroom seemed to her a glittering fairyland, with crystal chandeliers reflected in a myriad tall mirrors, so that it was hard to see what was real and what was reflection. The room was decorated with towering flower arrangements, stunning pillars composed of white roses and pale blue delphiniums, and the scent of the roses was heavy, almost intoxicating, in the early summer heat. There was an almost dreamlike, magical air to the proceedings, a feeling that this evening was somehow outside time, and anything at all might happen. And so when Captain Silverwood appeared at her side, as if she had summoned him up like a genie by wishing for him, and, bowing very correctly to her grandmother, asked if she would partner him for the first dance – the first dance! – she did not betray her excitement, but merely smiled and accepted, laying her gloved hand on his strong black-clad arm. If her heart beat hard and fast in her breast at even this slightest and most innocent of contacts between them, he did not know it, and if her face was flushed and her eyes shining, why, any young lady might be forgiven for betraying a little animation on such a thrilling occasion.

It was so wonderful, to be moving in perfect harmony with the rhythms of the dance and with each other, as they met, and parted, and met again, and turned. Kate had never been so happy in her life, and knew she would remember this moment for ever: the music, the lights, the ladies in elegant silks and sparkling jewels, the men in evening black, and the heady scent of roses. Benedict. He had smiled down at her, too, and it was perfect.

And then it wasn't. It was the strangest sensation: as though there had been a thread tying them together, and then suddenly – it snapped. She felt it snap. She stumbled and lost her way in the dance a little, the instinctive harmony between them lost, and when she looked at him, she saw that she no longer held any of his attention. He was gazing over her shoulder, as if transfixed, at someone else, and she turned a little too, to seek the object of his regard.

Vanessa. Tiny, delicate and flawless, a shimmering fairy princess, an ice queen from a children's story. Her gown was celestial silk, and over it she wore a gauze half-slip of white embroidered with dozens of tiny brilliants, which sparkled as if enchanted. Her silver-gilt curls were threaded with glittering stones too, but they were all dimmed by the brilliance of her lustrous blue eyes, as she smiled radiantly up at her partner and twirled gracefully in the dance. Her dance.

Kate saw, she saw Benedict's heart go out to her, she saw the arrested expression in his eyes as he fell headlong in love with Vanessa Ansell. No one else perceived it, but she did, and she felt as though he had taken a blade, sharp and thin and deadly, and stabbed her in the breast.

The music, the lights, the movement and the glittering company, even the suddenly overwhelming scent of roses, all lost their savour and became dull and lifeless, as though some malicious sprite had waved a wand to banish the enchantment and reveal the true, base nature of the world. Kate realised her error now, because all of this splendour belonged exclusively to Vanessa. The exquisite ballroom had been designed with breath-taking extravagance entirely as a setting for her, the flowers had been chosen with enormous care to match her gown and her blue eyes, and Kate – tall, plump, ungainly Kate, a nobody from nowhere – was an interloper here, with her ridiculous, tawdry pink gown and her ridiculous, deluded hopes that Benedict Silverwood might love her. Of course he could not love her, when there was Vanessa.

The music, mercifully, came to an end, and Kate murmured some broken words of thanks; it did not matter what she said, because he was not attending. He stood like a statue, gazing at Vanessa, and when Kate left him, she thought that he did not even notice her departure.

CHAPTER ONE
Seven years later – 1814

'Race you to the river!' Lucy did not wait for Kate's answer, but set off running down the broad lawn as fast as her short legs could carry her. Kate laughed, and followed her, though her longer skirts and constricting stays impeded her progress. A lady was not supposed to run, of course, but Kate cared little for such things, and ran as well as she could, delighting in the movement and in the beauty of the summer day. When she caught up at the river's edge, the child had clambered, agile as a monkey, onto her favourite perch on a tree branch, and sat there, swinging her bare, muddy legs and grinning triumphantly at her pursuer.

'I won! And you did not finish your story!' she said

now. 'I want to know if the cat rescues the girl, and if he tells her about the magic well!'

'I have no breath for it!' she panted, exaggerating her distress to tease Lucy. 'You have killed me, Lucy Silverwood, and now you will never know how the story ends. And besides, it must surely be time for you to go back to the house and change. Your father is returning this afternoon!'

Lucy's face lit up. The little girl was wildly excited at the prospect of seeing Sir Benedict, and could talk of little else. Although she was lively by nature, and venturesome, she was above all a deeply affectionate child, and she adored her father. Kate did not know if he would be annoyed if his daughter were not ready to greet him in her best muslin, but she would not like to be the cause of the child's getting into trouble, and it would be no easy matter for her nursemaid, Amy, to set her to rights, remove all the mud that plastered her from head to foot, untangle her wild silver-gilt curls and coax them into some sort of order.

Kate Moreton, like Lucy, was an only child, and her heart ached in sympathy for the lonely little girl, surrounded by elderly people, most of whom fussed excessively over her. Kate was a newcomer here, but she understood that Sir Benedict was in general to be found in residence at the Hall, now that he had left the army, and that when present he spent a great deal of time with his daughter, and rode with her, and engaged with her in more active pursuits than his frail mother and her elderly governess-companion were able to pursue.

But he had not been here for more than a day or so since Kate had arrived to stay at the Vicarage, and she had not once encountered him. He had gone to London, for the Season, and she had heard it whispered that he was on the look-out for a bride once more. And why should he not be? He was handsome, charming, eligible and rich; he must want an heir, since his older brother's tragic death and that soon after of his own young wife, Vanessa.

'Lucy!' a deep voice called. They looked up, and suddenly there he was, a tall, broad figure silhouetted against the sun on the riverbank, dazzling her.

Kate had supposed when she arrived in Berkshire that she would meet him eventually, now that she lived in the village where his estate was situated, and all the more because she had somehow found herself – she could hardly say how – on friendly terms with his mother, and teaching his daughter Italian, of all ridiculous circumstances. But weeks and weeks had passed, and she had persuaded herself that, since she had not seen him, she would be able to avoid seeing him for ever. Even though she had known he was to return today, she had relaxed her guard completely. She was shocked to see him so unexpectedly now, and quite overset.

She knew that vanity in her case was preposterous, but she would certainly have wished to make a better show on her first meeting with him, if meeting there must be, instead of being at her very worst: hatless, her hair all anyhow, her face pink and perspiring, and mud liberally splashed about her person. And that was the least of it, for she was in charge of his daughter, and Lucy looked as though she had been rolling in river mud, probably because she had. She stammered out some words of apology, she knew not what.

He came closer, and she could see him better. Their previous acquaintance, if it could be called that, had been conducted in ballrooms, at dances, and of course now he was dressed in riding clothes. She knew it was a truism that gentlemen looked their best in evening wear – and regimentals, of course: thank heaven she had never seen him in regimentals – but she could not in all honesty say that he looked any the less appealing in buckskin breeches and top boots than he had so long ago in evening black. She thought there might be a few more lines carved by time and suffering upon his face, around his striking grey eyes and beautiful, firm mouth, but they suited him; they gave him gravitas. His hair was still a soft honey-brown, his shoulders were still broad, his frame well-built, straight and tall, he was still the handsomest man she had ever seen, and her heart still leapt – stupidly, pointlessly, cruelly – at the sight of him. If she had ever deceived herself that she had overcome her infatuation with him, she knew better now. She might as well still be a girl of eighteen, not a spinster of five and twenty.

He knew her name, because Lucy had said it, and he addressed her kindly, concerned, clearly, to put her at her ease. She could not flatter herself that he recollected her in the least, and she would *not* be bitter; there was no reason why he should, nor could she expect him to recognise her in these very altered circumstances. When last she had seen him, at the end of the Season of 1807, she had been one debutante among many, not a penniless spinster, and he had been in love – gloriously, wholeheartedly, publicly, and above all requitedly – with Vanessa Ansell. While he had danced, and smiled, and been pleasant and kind to other young ladies, including Kate, for his manners were generally acknowledged to be all that was pleasing, he had had eyes only for Vanessa. It still hurt to think of it.

Kate could not have said how she extricated herself from the encounter, but she did so, and she was sure he noticed nothing amiss. He barely looked at her, after all. She bade him farewell, and Lucy, in an outwardly composed manner, and walked up the lawn, but when she reached the trees at the edge of the park, she ran wildly among them, careless if branches caught at her gown, until she could not be seen, and sank into a damp, miserable huddle on the ground, and sobbed her heart out, just as she had on that night at the ball seven years ago.

CHAPTER TWO

Benedict stopped dead, hearing cheerful female voices close by. He realised that he was still unobserved, and stepped back under the hanging branches of the huge old weeping willow that stood on the riverbank.

The child – a girl of six or so – was balancing on a branch at the water's edge, dangling her legs and bare, dirty feet over the river. Benedict's heart caught in his mouth for a second, but the danger was illusory; the branch leant out over a shallow pool, divided from the main current, the drop was tiny, and surely the worst she could suffer if she did slip was a partial dunking; the state of her gown suggested that it would not be the first of the day. She was not alone, in any case. Her companion, a tall, buxom young woman in her twenties who was unknown to him, was almost equally dishevelled; her dark brown curls were coming down and she had a smear of mud across her brow. If either of the pair had sported bonnets at the start of the afternoon, they had long been discarded.

Their faces were flushed with laughter, and with the heat of the summer day. It seemed that the young woman had been telling the child a most thrilling story – something to do with a girl, and a talking cat, he gathered. She was begging for more, but her companion refused her. 'Your papa is arriving this afternoon, and I am sure that you would wish to wash and put on your best gown to greet him. Your grandmama would be vexed if you presented yourself to him in such a condition.'

Lucy's face lit up, and Benedict's heart squeezed a little. 'Papa! Of course, you are right, although I am sure Grandmama would not care so very much, for she is not stuffy like Amy. But I do not want to be late – let us go!' She jumped lightly down from the branch to the edge of the pool, and scrambled up towards her companion; reaching her, she seized her hands and cried, 'I am so excited to see Papa! It has been weeks and weeks. I wonder if he will think that I have grown, for I am sure I have!'

It was not correct to remain thus concealed, nor to overhear any more of this conversation. Benedict stepped forward, out of the shadow of the great willow, and called out, 'Lucy!'

She swung round, and her face shone with pure delight as she cried out, 'Papa! Papa, you are here!' and ran to fling her muddy arms around him, and they hugged each other fiercely.

The young lady – he held some vague recollection that his mother had mentioned her in one of her indecipherable letters – previously so animated, froze, and a shutter seemed to descend across her face. She stood, irresolute. It was plain that she would much have preferred to efface herself, and not intrude upon his notice at all, but that she felt herself obliged to do so in common courtesy. He was, after all, in some sense her employer, he supposed, although they had not met.

'Lucy, I will leave you now; you will wish to be alone with your papa. Sir Benedict . . .' She dropped a very correct curtsey, which inevitably looked somewhat ridiculous in the informal circumstances, and the awareness of it showed on her expressive face. 'I am sorry you find Lucy in such a dreadful state, but the fault is mine, so pray do not blame her for it.'

'Oh, Kate – Miss Moreton, I mean – will you not come with us?' said Lucy, tugging on his arm. 'I am sure Papa would like to hear your story, and he does not regard a little mud, do you, Papa?'

Benedict bowed. 'Miss Moreton, I am delighted to make your acquaintance. Pray do not reproach yourself. No, the fault is mine for arriving before the hour I had intended, and preventing Lucy from performing her toilette. I am sure that, if you apply to her, my mother would be very quick to tell you how I drove her quite to distraction in my childhood by appearing in the same state, or worse, on an almost daily basis.'

'Thank you, sir, you are very kind. Lucy, I will see you

later in the week for your next lesson. If there should be any alteration in the timetable, I am sure your grandmother will send to let me know.' She curtsied again, and was gone, and vanished from Benedict's mind just as quickly, lost in his pleasure at seeing his daughter again after their separation.

Some hours later, he sat with his mother on the broad stone terrace at the back of the great house, watching the sun dip low over a bend in the broad Thames. It was good to be home. The Dowager Lady Silverwood wore a modish cap tied under her chin, covering her grey curls, and was well wrapped in colourful shawls; she declared that she was not in the least cold, as it was summer and her bones did not trouble her so very much at present. They were alone, as Miss Dorothea Sutton, who served both as governess to Lucy and companion to his mother, was away visiting her brother and his family in Bristol.

Lucy had finally been borne, protesting, off to bed, only persuaded to retire by her father's promise to take her out on her pony on the morrow. 'She is not generally so ill behaved; it is merely that she is excited to see you. She missed you,' Lady Silverwood said with a smile.

'I missed her.'

'And?'

He sighed. 'I have attended more balls, routs, breakfasts, concerts, masquerades and I know not what else than should be expected of any man of sense. I do not know how people endure it; I am sure they cannot like it. I have danced, I believe, with every debutante who has made her curtsey to the Queen in the last five years and remains as yet unwed. If I have missed one by some chance, it certainly cannot be said to be Maria's fault.'

'And yet she writes me that none of them pleases you. Are you so very particular?'

'Ma'am, it seems I am. I recall I said to you that I was prepared to marry almost any young lady who fulfilled my very reasonable conditions, and yet when it comes to it . . .'

His mother said quietly, 'Is Vanessa's loss still so very raw?'

'I do not say that it is. Days will go by when I do not think of her. But when I dance with a young lady of eighteen or so, full of life and hope, and she reminds me in that moment of Vanessa as she was when I met her, I do not feel that I can ask for her hand. I certainly cannot in good conscience ask for her heart, for I do not have a heart free and whole to give any young lady, which she surely deserves. And then there is Lucy to be thought of – is it wise or even rational to expect a green girl, a debutante, to be the mother that she needs?'

Lady Silverwood was silent. It seemed to him that he had distressed her, and he said swiftly, 'My dear mama, you have been so much more than a grandmother to her. Please do not think that in—'

His mother cut him off. 'I have done my best, Ben, but it is not enough. I am well, now that it is summer, but in the winter my wretched bones prevent me from attending to her as I should, and it will only be worse as I get older. As she grows, she will need more of a woman's love and care, not less. There should be no foolish talk of replacing me, for that is not at all the issue; the child needs a mother. And let us not forget that you need an heir.'

'That is the real problem, is it not – how to combine the two? I could marry any one of these eligible young ladies in a month, I dare say, assuming she would have me . . .' His mother snorted in a most unladylike fashion. 'Assuming she would have me, and in a year she might bear me a son, and I would have my heir, but what of Lucy? How can I ever be sure that this hypothetical young lady would care for her as I would wish? At best she might disregard her, and give all her love to her own children, as would perhaps only be natural; at worst . . .'

'At worst she could be cruel to her,' the Dowager sighed.

'I would rather stay unmarried for ever and let the title and estate go hang – or go to Cousin Felix, which is much the same thing – than that. But then what is to become of Lucy, should I die? I know I am only two and thirty, Mama, but after all the losses we have suffered in the last few years, we both know that that is no guarantee of anything.' He reached out and took his mother's gnarled hand in a strong but careful clasp, and squeezed it gently, and she returned the pressure, and could not contradict him.

It was true enough. Not long since, they had been a larger family, and a happier one. Lady Silverwood had been widowed somewhat prematurely, it was true, and her eldest son in particular had felt the loss of his father deeply, but in 1807 all had looked fair. Captain Benedict Silverwood was newly wed to Miss Vanessa Ansell, one of the most brilliant debutantes of her Season, after a whirlwind romance while the captain convalesced from wounds and a fever contracted in South America. Benedict's older brother, Sir Caspar, had been a sadly wild youth, but had reformed upon falling in love with a woman of character; he was not long married too, and his wife, Alice, was in the family way. Certainly, the captain's service in the army, to which he was obliged to return not long after his wedding, his health being fully restored, gave his fond relations cause for worry, but as for the rest, surely the title was secure, and the succession.

But now, seven years later, Caspar was dead in a curricle accident, and Vanessa dead, and Caspar's new-born son too, along with his mother, Alice, and all that was left was the Dowager, crippled by arthritis, little Lucy and Benedict, and the weight of all of it on his shoulders.

He had stayed in the army after his wife's death to do his duty to his King and country, hardly caring in his shocked state if he survived or not. He had made major – there had been no shortage of dead men's shoes to fill, as they had fought their agonising way up the peninsula into France. It sometimes seemed to him that there could not be an inch of the soil of Portugal, Spain or France that was not soaked in blood, and he had had every opportunity to observe that men – and women and children too, for that matter – bled the same, whatever their nationality or professed loyalty.

By the time of the Battle of Orthez he had had enough, the thought of the responsibilities waiting for him at home weighing heavier on him each day, and he had resigned his commission promptly after Napoleon's defeat, citing pressing family reasons. He had retreated to his estate and his daughter; the daughter he had hardly seen in the weary years that had passed as he chased Bonaparte half across Europe, and barely knew. He had come through it all relatively unscathed, he supposed, and 1814 was a summer of victory celebrations – the Corsican despot was exiled to Elba, and at last there was to be peace. Benedict could see that peace was something to be celebrated; he supposed that after being at war so long he could hardly be surprised if for him it still seemed so elusive.

But one thing he could be sure of: it was time and past time now to be thinking of marriage, of the responsibilities of the estate, and Lucy's future, and his own. He had put himself in his older sister Maria's hands, and said 'Find me a wife', and she had done her energetic best, but something was wrong; he could only imagine it to be him. It would not surprise him in the least. He had long feared that there was something broken inside him.

The Dowager looked with loving, anxious eyes at her son. Of course any lady in possession of her senses would be happy to have him, not just for the title and the estate, and Benedict's substantial private fortune, inherited from her own father, but for his handsome face and person, and, if they came to know him well enough, for the sweetness of his disposition and the goodness of his character. Once she would have added, for his wicked sense of fun, and the mischievous light that danced in his grey eyes, but she had not seen that side of him in a long while, and sometimes feared that it was gone for ever, driven away by all that he must have seen and done in the army, and most of all by the dreadful losses he had suffered and the cares he had been forced to assume while still in his twenties.

She said slowly now, 'Ben, of course I agree that it is necessary you marry, and that beyond the concerns of the estate you must consider Lucy most particularly. I am sure that not all young ladies would be unkind to her, and many would come to love her as their own, dear child as she is, but I quite see that it is impossible to be assured that you had made the right choice until it was too late. I know how severely you would reproach yourself if you chose wrongly.'

She hesitated for a second, and then said, 'It seems to me that the answer has been staring me in the face, and I have not seen it. You should marry someone who is already acquainted with Lucy, and loves her.'

'And where shall I find this paragon, Mama?'

'Why, I believe you met her this afternoon!'

CHAPTER THREE

The Dowager had not needed her son's confirmation to know that his plan to seek a bride in London had not come to fruition. She had been in constant correspondence with her daughter, Mrs Singleton, and her latest letter, delivered only a few days ago, had been a most uncharacteristic admission of utter failure.

Mama, she had written in her bold, decisive hand, *I throw up my hands and admit defeat. I had great hopes of Miss Fanshawe, as I think I told you – Ben danced with her twice at Almack's last week, she was in high beauty, all in blue, so becoming with her fair colouring, and even Lady Jersey very justly remarked that they made a most handsome couple. A substantial marriage portion, Mama, and of course a highly eligible connection, with the dear Duke her uncle. Such an accomplished young lady, too, and so charming, and very pretty – I have even thought sometimes that she resembles Vanessa a little, so you cannot say that Ben might not like her looks, or any nonsense of that nature.*

Upon reading this, Lady Silverwood looked up from her letter, frowning unconsciously, so that her companion, Miss Sutton, asked her what the matter was, but she merely sighed and made no answer, returning to her reading, and so Dorothea shook her head and continued her packing.

I made up a party to attend the victory festivities in Hyde Park, inviting her and her mother Lady George Fanshawe along to view the celebrations – I did it all for Ben, you know, as I felt sure that, on such an informal occasion, he would find no difficulty in taking the young lady aside a little and becoming better acquainted. I am not suggesting anything improper, of course . . . The word 'improper' was underlined three times and the Dowager smiled a little wryly as she read it. *Only that it is so very difficult to converse when one only meets at balls and so on. I thought perhaps he just needed a little push from me, in order to make an effort to attach her affections! But when I told him of my plans, he said –* Mama, I was so angry I could have boxed his ears! *– he said, 'Miss Fanshawe? WHICH ONE IS SHE?'*

At this point Mrs Singleton's missive became

somewhat incoherent with natural frustration, and her pen had blotted sadly. The Dowager put the note down entirely, with an expression on her face that caused Miss Sutton to leave off her chores and say gruffly, 'Trouble in Town? Nobody ill, I hope, Charlotte?'

'No, dear, it's merely Maria, complaining that Ben seems to care nothing for the latest debutante she is dangling under his nose. She says – and really I wonder sometimes at her lack of sense – that this one reminds her a little of Vanessa, and seems to think that that should be a point in her favour as far as her brother is concerned.'

'Vanessa was a diamond of the first water,' said Dorothea dispassionately. 'Obviously he liked her style well enough. Little fragile thing, and he wanted to protect her, I dare say. Fell in love with her when he barely knew her. I expect Maria thinks he may do the same again. Hard to fault her reasoning.'

'I do fault it! He needs someone quite different from Vanessa.'

Miss Sutton frowned. 'Say what you like about Maria, she's always been thorough. Remarked on it often when I was her governess. Most diligent child, painstaking. I don't suppose she put all her eggs in one basket, did she?'

The Dowager sighed again. 'No, indeed. She's written to me of several young ladies in succession, all of whom she had great hopes of, until Ben found fault with them or – worse – failed to recollect them from one day to the next. And yet it is vital he marries. You know it as well as I do. What is to be done?'

'No idea,' said Dorothea. 'You put your mind to it. I have faith in you, Charlotte. Sure you'll come about. Ben deserves it, after all – not just a bride, I mean. Happiness.'

'He does. Of course he does, Dotty. But where is he to find it?'

CHAPTER FOUR

Benedict set down his glass now. 'The young woman who accompanied Lucy today? Really, Mama? I did not pay her any particular attention, but I know that Lucy has mentioned her with great enthusiasm in her letters to me. You said something of her yourself, I think – some sort of paid companion?'

'Men!' said the Dowager in exasperated affection. 'I wrote to you at length of her, Ben! She is Mr Waltham's granddaughter, and I engaged her to teach Lucy some rudiments of Italian, but that was a mere ruse.'

'Of course it was,' he said, smiling fondly at her. 'Pretend you have not written me of her at all, or that your handwriting is not nigh on illegible, and Lucy's near as bad, and explain it all to me, Mama.'

'She is, as I say, Mr Waltham's granddaughter,

his daughter's only child, and she came to live with him some months ago. She is very well educated, and speaks perfect Italian, and so I was able to suggest the notion that she give Lucy lessons, for you know that Dorothea is entirely unacquainted with the language, and cannot be expected to learn it at her age. And thus Lucy has some young, lively company, and runs about the park with her, rather than staying cooped up with two old women from one week to the next, and Miss Moreton besides has a little money for herself, which she sorely needs. She is very proud, and by no means wished to be paid, but between us her grandfather and I insisted.'

'Is she really teaching Lucy Italian?' he said, in a desperate and probably futile attempt to divert his mother from her purpose. 'When I saw them, they appeared to have been jumping in puddles, rather than declining verbs.'

'It is possible to do both at once, dear, you know. Yes, in fact, the child seems to be doing well enough at it, and what is more to the point they have grown excessively attached to each other, as you must have observed. I did write and tell you of my scheme, dear, for of course I would not dream of introducing anybody into Lucy's life without consulting you.'

Benedict opened his mouth as if to speak, but his mother was not done.

'I do not think she had yet arrived when you left for London, so you had no occasion to meet her then. Poor girl, she is all alone in the world, her parents long dead, and Theodore Waltham not likely to last more than six months, if as long. The Vicarage will go to the next incumbent, of course, and she will be homeless, living on less than a hundred pounds a year, I should think. I do not know what is to become of her. But if you marry her, all will be well.' She beamed at him, her eyes shining, and he was conscious of a sinking feeling that was all too familiar. No one could describe his mother as a managing female; she was gentle, and reasonable, and wanted only the best for everyone, but it was remarkable how often she did seem to get her own way. Yet this was a wild start, even for her.

Perhaps misinterpreting the expression on his face, she said, 'It is not as though I am suggesting you marry someone of low birth, Ben. I know she has no fortune, but her family is perfectly respectable. Mr Waltham's mother was a daughter of Lord Fitton, and the Walthams themselves are a cadet branch of the old Essex family. She made her come-out, you know, under the aegis of her grandmother, Mrs Moreton, and was presented to the Queen. Why, you danced with her more than once during her Season; she told me so herself.'

'I have not the slightest recollection of it,' he said repressively.

'I do not wonder at it in the least. I believe she made her debut in '07, when you met Vanessa, so I expect you had no eyes for any but her, and that explains it. But she remembered *you*.'

He felt himself to be at a disadvantage. It all seemed so eminently sensible: a young woman, but not too young, and so not likely to be foolishly romantic, who cared for Lucy – he had seen for himself even in their one brief encounter that she did – and whom Lucy plainly liked and trusted. Of sufficiently good birth to satisfy the opinion of the world, if that mattered. Of no fortune – that was of no importance. If there were rational objections, he could not in this moment call them to mind, and yet he felt sure that he should, all the while aware that it would be as well to try to argue with an avalanche in the Pyrenees.

'Mama!'

'Yes, dear?' She was smiling at him, as though it were quite a settled thing.

'Mama, please! I have scarcely set eyes on this young lady. She made no impression on me. I cannot hold that against her, as my attention was all on Lucy, and I scarce looked at her. And I know I have said that my requirements are not unreasonable. I do not think they are. I am not looking for a great beauty, and I do not hold out any hope that I shall love the woman I marry as I once loved Vanessa. All that is behind me now. But you must accept that I need to be able to . . . to . . .'

Her heart ached for him, though she showed not the least sign of it on her face. She merely said sedately, 'I have always considered her a most attractive girl, and I am sure that there is nothing in her face, person or manner that could give you the least disgust of her.'

'I am very glad to hear you say it. But surely I may be allowed to judge for myself?'

'I suppose that is sensible enough,' she said with the air of one making a great concession. 'I shall invite her to take tea with me tomorrow, and you may see her when she has not been playing with your daughter half the day, and her hair – you might observe tomorrow that it is very pretty hair – all down her back, and her petticoats six inches deep in mud, I dare say. You may come in, quite naturally, and she shall have no idea that anything is afoot, so that you will not be in the least embarrassed, and nor shall she, if you find you cannot like her. So, it is settled: good.'

Benedict was not quite sure how he had come to agree to this, nor, indeed, exactly what it was that he had agreed to, but tea seemed innocuous enough. So it was that a message was written, to be taken early on the morrow by the younger footman, Philip, and Miss Moreton, if she accepted – and there could be little doubt she would – was to come and take tea at the Hall, in quite a natural fashion, all unconscious of the grand scheme that the Dowager was brewing.

CHAPTER FIVE

Kate sat with her grandfather that evening, and read to him as he dozed. When she was sure of his being deeply asleep, she set down the book, folded her hands in her lap, and allowed her troubled thoughts to overwhelm her. The events of the day – the sudden meeting with Sir Benedict – had quite overset her, and besides that it had revived an internal debate that she had thought she was done with.

She could not have avoided coming to live here in Berkshire for such a foolish and selfish reason as an old infatuation – her grandfather needed her, and there was no one else. She had visited Mr Waltham quite frequently, in fact, over the past years, but Benedict Silverwood had been away in the army for most of that time, so she had had no apprehension of meeting him then. They moved in very different social circles, after all. And she had a perfect right – a clear duty – to be here now, and could not reproach herself for that. If it should prove to be awkward, the awkwardness was hers alone, unknown to another soul here, and she would deal with it alone, as she dealt with everything.

But she had asked herself a thousand times in the past few months if her motives in involving herself as deeply with the Silverwood family as she had were innocent, and the sad truth was, she did not know.

She cared deeply for Lucy. She had struggled with her conscience, but she acquitted herself of any ulterior motive. The twin truths that years ago she had envied the little girl's mother and pined after her father like a mooncalf were irrelevant, she truly believed – the child's friendlessness and her innocent, open-hearted pleasure in her company could not but speak to her. They neither of them had a sister or a brother, nor a mother, and they understood each other on some deep level where lonely people meet and recognise their like.

But she could not deny that there was a strange, hurtful pleasure in being friendly with the Dowager, and hearing her speak fondly of her son, and seeing the youthful Lawrence picture of him standing with his brother and sister that hung in her sitting room. Kate was not a liar; she had told his mother that she had met him, and danced with him, all those years ago. The Dowager had sharp eyes, despite her comfortable, grandmotherly exterior, and it was just possible that

41

she had divined Kate's secret. If she had, she had never spoken of it.

Kate Moreton had no hopes of any kind. She must and would acquit herself of any accusation by the nagging voice of her conscience that she had inveigled herself into the Silverwood family with any dishonourable purpose in mind, other than perhaps to hear his name spoken occasionally. Was that dishonourable? Surely not, though it was certainly foolish. She had not – she hoped – even expected or wanted to meet him. It was not as though her stay here would be very long.

She knew her grandfather would die soon, and it would be heartless to wish it otherwise, for he was so very tired, and had so little pleasure in his life. And she supposed that, when that sad day came, and the funeral was done, she would bid farewell to Lucy with regret on both sides, and go to Italy to re-join her grandmother, and the great-grandmother she had never met, and the great-uncles, and cousins, and all the many wives and children. She loved her vivacious, outspoken grandmother, and missed her, and she was sure that there would be laughter, and sunshine, and pleasure in daily existence – more than there was here, in a quiet house with a dying, frightened man – but she had no illusions about her noble but impoverished Italian family and their life there, scrabbling for a living at the edge of the court of Parma, where Napoleon's second wife was soon to arrive to preside over her tiny domain.

And if she decided not to go to Italy, but somehow

eked out an existence here in England, taking in pupils, living in a tiny cottage or a rented room? She feared that her relationship with Lucy could then only cause her pain – Benedict would surely marry soon enough, and she would be faced at best with a choice: to watch him with his new wife, and Lucy's new mother, from the position of a dependant, on the fringes of their lives, or voluntarily to break the connection, which would, she thought, hurt the child, and certainly would hurt her. She had done this to herself, ensured this unnecessary distress for herself, and now he had come back and she would surely be obliged to see more of him, which anyone but an idiot could have predicted. She might tell herself – had told herself a thousand times – that the ridiculous infatuation she had permitted to overwhelm her as a girl was done with long since. She might indeed say that it was so, must be so, but after her instinctive reaction to him this afternoon, and the storm of tears that had overtaken her and left her drained, she was by no means sure that she could trust herself where he was concerned. It was mortifying to reflect that seven long years had come and gone and left her no wiser than she had been at eighteen.

She sighed, and rose silently, tidying away her things and making sure that her grandfather had all he needed if he should wake. She left the door slightly ajar, and retired to her own chamber; the Vicarage was small, and if he should call out in the night she was sure to hear him.

In the morning, the footman Philip came with a note for her from the Hall, as he sometimes did; she had thought it would be notice that her next lesson was to be postponed, but when she opened it she saw that Lady Silverwood bade her to come to tea with her that afternoon. She had by ill luck been sitting with her grandfather when she opened the missive, and she had not the presence of mind to lie to him, nor did she care to do so. She told him of its contents, and he was very glad, and insisted that she go. He had had a tolerably good night, he told her, though she did not believe him, and was feeling better than he had in days. The news that she should leave his bedside and have some congenial company was just exactly what he liked to hear, so that it was entirely impossible to do anything to destroy his pleasure, when there were so few things that made him happy now and all his concern was for her.

She fortified her spirits by telling herself sternly that there was no reason – no reason at all – to suppose that Sir Benedict would be present. He had been away for weeks, and that with harvest time almost upon them; he would surely have a thousand matters urgently requiring his attention on the estate, and would not be wasting a sunny afternoon sitting indoors taking tea with his mother and his daughter's dowdy Italian teacher. At the same time, she need not wear the limp grey gown better fitted for domestic chores that she had put on this morning; she could at least arrange her hair becomingly, and shake out her best yellow muslin. It had been purchased last year, from one of the modistes in York, for she had had little leisure for shopping since she had arrived in Berkshire, and it was probably sadly outmoded, but what did that matter? At least she could be respectable in her outward appearance, if she were not sure that she could trust her innermost feelings to be so readily tamed.

Kate set out along the sunny village street, slowly, so as not to arrive unbecomingly overheated, and tried to silence the small voice in her head that kept repeating, *Perhaps he will be there, perhaps he will be there!*

CHAPTER SIX

Kate was admitted into Silverwood Hall by the stately butler, Thompson, and followed him up the sweeping marble staircase to the Dowager's private apartments. Her hostess, who was sitting alone in her charming pink and gold sitting room, greeted her with her usual warmth, and asked after her grandfather. Kate could give no very good account of him – indeed, she said, she had not liked to leave him, but when he had heard that the Dowager had asked her to tea he had been so insistent that she went that she could not refuse him without causing him distress, which would in itself have been injurious to him. Charlotte Silverwood was all too aware that the vicar very much disliked the fact that Kate was obliged to nurse him, and was always very eager to see her engaged in other occupations, such as visiting their neighbours, as today, or spending time with Lucy. His concern for his granddaughter's future was a torment to him, and he was stubborn in maintaining a fiction that he was not so very unwell at all, since to confront the fact that he was dying would be also to confront the fact that he left her very ill provided for. She would inherit every penny he possessed, but that was little enough. He had not by any means been extravagant, but his living was a poor one, and it was by malign chance not in the Silverwoods' gift, or they would have made sure to do better by him. He had been unlucky in life; his wife had been an invalid for many years before her death, he had been unable to save, and since his illness he had been obliged besides to pay a curate, an earnest young man named Newman, from his modest stipend, to carry out his duties.

Lady Silverwood was very sorry to hear that her old friend was so unwell, but she knew that to dwell on it could only give her young guest pain. It seemed to her that Miss Moreton was rather quiet this afternoon, not just her usual self, no doubt because of her worry for her grandfather and the strain of caring for him when there could only be one outcome, so she turned the subject skilfully to matters more agreeable, and spoke of Lucy, and of how pleased she was with her progress. Kate smiled and said, 'I fear you flatter me, ma'am! I have not taught her so very much Italian, after all, but she has picked up something of it, with great quickness, and seems to like it, and we have fun while she is learning, which I know was a great object with you.'

At that moment the door opened, and Lucy burst into the room, crying, 'Miss Moreton! I did not know you were here!'

She was followed in more sedate fashion by her father, and he was able to observe that his first impression had not been wrong; the young lady was decidedly attached to Lucy, and the feeling was reciprocated. The child hugged and kissed her, despite having seen her the day before, and Miss Moreton returned the embrace with affection, and greeted her with a pleasure that appeared to him to be entirely genuine. That aspect of the matter must be regarded as settled; he could, of course, have no notion as to how she might treat Lucy if she were to find herself her stepmother and then subsequently mother to a child of her own, but that was not something that could ever be known, he supposed, of any woman, in such a delicate situation.

The young lady, whom he had not the slightest recollection of ever having met before yesterday, though his mother was adamant he had, was not as animated as he had observed her to be when she had been alone with Lucy; she saluted him, quite correctly, with a small smile, but no particular attention. Perhaps his presence caused her some little constraint, since he understood that she went about in society scarcely at all. But he could not fault her manners, which were elegant. She was not effusive, and made no attempt to curry favour with him, nor to engage him especially in conversation, neglecting the others present, as he had observed other young ladies to do during his time in London. There could be nothing further from her mind, clearly, than any attempt to flirt with him or attract him by any arts she might possess. He could have no doubt that she was entirely ignorant of the Dowager's schemes, and he was glad of it, for it allowed him to observe her freely, without any self-consciousness on either side.

He was forced to concede that he liked what he saw. Vanessa had been divinely fair, and delicate as a fairy, but he would not think of Vanessa. Best he put her entirely from his mind. Miss Moreton was tall, and generously built, with a good, even a voluptuous figure; he supposed he was allowed to notice her figure in such delicate circumstances, if he noticed that it was good. Her complexion had rather an olive tone, and she was dark – her eyes were a rich velvet brown, with long, thick lashes, and she had clouds of dark brown hair, softly curling, and very simply dressed. Pretty hair, indeed, as his mother had observed. There was a wild rose colour in her cheeks.

Her style of beauty – he found himself thinking with some surprise of her as beautiful; some deeper part of his brain, or perhaps not his brain at all, seemed to have decided that she was, without his being conscious of making such a decision – was not of the kind that looked its best in the pastel muslins worn by young ladies. Today she was wearing a pale yellow gown with long sleeves and a high neck – very correct, no doubt, but surely not a colour nor a style that showed her to complete advantage. She would look her best in the kind of gowns worn by young married ladies: rich, dark silks and velvets, cut low to show her fine shoulders and splendid bosom . . . He shifted slightly uncomfortably in his seat. He had, before he had become aware of the direction of this thoughts, gone a great deal further down this road than he had intended. He supposed, somewhat to his surprise, that *that* was another question answered. Could he imagine himself married to her, with all the intimacy that that implied? Well, it seemed he could, without the least difficulty in the world. And he must stop imagining it, this very minute. It was preposterous; they had barely exchanged two words with each other, and here his cursed imagination, which had hardly troubled him in the last few months, would have them . . . He stopped, resolutely.

Miss Moreton rose to take her leave, and Lucy said, 'We could walk with you, could we not, Papa?'

'We could, of course, my dear, if Miss Moreton cares to have our company,' he said.

CHAPTER SEVEN

Kate's wretched heart had lurched when he had entered the room in Lucy's wake. He looked so very handsome, once again dressed in breeches and top boots and a beautifully cut coat. She blessed the self-control that allowed her to make polite conversation with him, and with his mother, and she blessed too Lucy's affection for her, and her touching excitement at her papa's presence, which caused her to bubble over with delight at what to another child would merely be a dull tea party with older people and nothing at all out of the ordinary. The child was in high spirits, and talked a good deal, and Kate perceived that her father watched her with love, and responded to her with a fond smile, and was plainly glad to see her so happy.

It was seven years since she had spent so long in his

company, and it was a kind of exquisite torture. When she had realised herself infatuated with him all those years ago, she had at first upbraided herself as a silly, shallow chit who knew no more of Captain Silverwood than that he had a handsome face, excellent manners, and came of a good family. As well to fall in love – of course she was not in love, that was quite ridiculous, but let it pass – as well to fall in love with an actor upon the stage, playing the part of a handsome prince. But even then she had known that this was not true, and that she had done herself, and him, less than justice. He was no made-up figure of a cavalry captain in a novel, who set young girls sighing over his gallantry and his flashing eyes; he was a fine young man, who treated everybody he encountered with instinctive courtesy. He was intelligent, and quick of perception, and she had heard that he was spoken of as a promising young officer, courageous and audacious, likely to go far, and she saw that his many friends regarded him with respect and affection. Even her grandmother, the highest of sticklers, had noticed him, and remarked on him with approval, as the sort of young gentleman whom these cold, stuffy English (this from a woman who had herself fallen in love with and married an Englishman, and lived in England for near fifty years) so rarely produced.

When he had fallen headlong for Miss Ansell, he had been open, honest in his love, delighted when he found it quickly reciprocated. He played no tricks, put on no foolish airs to gain his beloved's attention, displayed no jealousy, and another man might have done, for Vanessa Ansell was the acknowledged diamond of the Season, and she had a dozen suitors, all of higher rank than he. He had merely loved her wholeheartedly, and delighted in her company, happy to do anything he could to please her. And still his love and absorption did not lead him to ignore others, or treat them any less well; he was as happy to dance and converse in a friendly fashion with any less favoured debutante – with Kate herself – as he had ever been. Even in her pain, Kate had been able to acknowledge him worthy of any woman's love, and she could see now that she had been correct.

She knew nothing of his private life, of course, since his wife had died. He might for all she knew be a rake, a libertine – he might have a dozen mistresses, and drink to excess, and gamble, and live a dissolute life when he was in London. But she saw no sign of dissipation in his face, and somehow she did not think it. Perhaps she did not want to think it, and, after all, what concern was it of hers, or of anyone's, if he did? He had no ties to any woman alive. She could only say that she knew him to be a conscientious and diligent landlord, respected and even loved by his tenants, and always concerned for their wellbeing, a kind master to his servants, and a loved and loving son and father. She might have wished that her youthful fancy had lighted on a less worthy subject, for she feared, watching him as he smiled down at his daughter, that time spent in his company now was more likely to revive her fascination than to kill it.

She waited for a break in the conversation, and declared her intention to leave; she had stayed quite long enough, a correct half-hour or a little more, and could – should – now go. She had met him, and talked with him, and maintained her composure, and surely the next time, if there was one, would be easier, and presently he would hardly affect her at all.

CHAPTER EIGHT

Miss Moreton did not seem to be transported with delight at the prospect of Benedict's escort home, and protested that she was entirely accustomed to walking across the park alone, that she did it three times a week, and would not for the world put them to the trouble. But Benedict was not obliged to say anything, nor to urge his company on her in a way that might seem odd to her, for Lucy was insistent, and soon won the day. Bonnets and hats were fetched, and shawls, and the small party soon set off. As they left the imposing, pillared front of the house, and struck out across the broad lawn, a foolish-looking spaniel with one ear turned inside out came hurtling from the direction of the stables, and began dancing and leaping up around Lucy, emitting shrill, excited barks. She greeted him with pleasure, and it seemed he was to form one of the expedition. Child and dog raced ahead, and back, circling the adults and then chasing off again.

'I collect my daughter has claimed Juno's smallest pup for her own,' he said drily. 'I believe she wrote me something of it. She has named him Wellington, has she not? I am sure His Lordship should be flattered.'

Miss Moreton smiled. 'I should think he would be, if he knew of it, for it was meant as a great compliment. They are inseparable, and it is good for her, I think, to have such a lively companion for once.' Then she seemed to pull herself up short, and flushed, and said with some constraint, 'I am sorry, sir. I would not have you think that I wish to imply any criticism – or, indeed, any opinion at all – of your arrangements for Lucy. I have no right to do so, and would deserve the severest censure.'

He said a little abruptly, 'Nonsense. You implied no such thing. You have grown fond of her, I think, since your arrival here.'

'I have, sir. I do not see how it could be otherwise, for she is delightful. It is a pleasure to me to spend afternoons with her, and I promise you, I would not take payment for it, if Lady Silverwood had not been so very insistent, and my grandfather supporting her, so that it was impossible to refuse without showing discourtesy to them both. But if you should dislike it—'

'I by no means dislike it. On the contrary, I am grateful to you. My mother and I were discussing Lucy last night, and she told me – as indeed she had already informed me by letter – that you have been good enough to instruct her in Italian, and, more than that, to bear her company. My mother considers that it is not healthy for her to spend so much time with what she is pleased to describe as elderly people – herself, Miss Sutton, and the bulk of the servants. And I own that it is true. The arrangements I have made for her are less than ideal, and could easily be criticised.'

He sighed and ran his fingers through his hair in a gesture of frustration. 'When my wife was alive, the case was of course different – it was entirely appropriate that they should chiefly live here with my mother while I was abroad, and after her death it seemed cruel to me to remove Lucy from the only home she had ever known, and those who loved her. And where would I have placed her, in any case? I was fully occupied in Spain, and then in France, and glad enough to feel that Lucy was safe and happy. I know that Miss Sutton is too old, really, to have charge of a child of six, but she is as much a companion and friend for my mother as a governess, and how could I ever pension her and send her away? Yet to employ a younger lady as governess while Miss Sutton remains in the same establishment would be impossible. She is a good woman, a member of the family by now, but she is not easy, and she and another governess who "supplanted" her would surely fall to pulling caps, and Lucy and my mother would be upset. But I am told that she accepts your presence, which I am sure has involved the exercise of no little tact on your part. So you have been heaven-sent, Miss Moreton, and I am in your debt.'

She said in a low tone, 'There can be no question of debt between us, but I am honoured by your frankness, sir. I do understand your dilemma, and if I may be allowed to venture a comment, I do not think you have so very much to reproach yourself with. Lucy is healthy and happy, and despite the very sad loss of her mother she knows herself to be loved. How many children, even of the highest degree, can say as much?' Her voice was musical, and a pleasure to listen to, he observed – he had the greatest dislike of a sharp, grating voice in man or woman – and she spoke with sound common sense, and with feeling, upon a topic that was very close to his heart.

They were nearing the edge of the park now, and Lucy was waiting for them. Her canine companion had possessed himself of one end of a long stick, and Lucy held the other, and feinted to take it from him: a most delightful game for both of them. Her father said, 'My dear, we shall go out through the gate into the village, and there will be wagons with horses, and other animals too, I dare say. I will accompany Miss Moreton to the Vicarage, and you may choose to come, if you leave Wellington here, or you may choose to stay here with him, inside the demesne. Which shall it be?'

Lucy grumbled for a moment, but she could see the justice of it, for Wellington could by no means be relied upon to behave himself, if there should be a cat, or anything of that nature, as certain painful episodes from his recent history showed all too well. He looked up at her, with large, tragic brown eyes, head on one side, seeming to know that she was contemplating leaving him, while Miss Moreton's eyes, of much the same rich velvet colour, were amused, and she said, 'I shall not be offended, Lucy, if you should decide to stay with Wellington. I should think we would have the greatest difficulty in getting through the gate without him, if you do not stay to restrain him, and even if we do so somehow, he will probably set up howling for you, in a most distressing manner.'

'It is true that I might throw a stick, and distract him, so that we might get through,' said Lucy seriously, 'but I cannot like to deceive him, and he would be so very sad, and I would be sorry for it, for he is only a baby, really, you know.'

And so it was decided, and Lucy and Wellington hared off towards the river, where there were sure to be ducks to be barked at, and Benedict and Miss Moreton passed through the trees to the weathered old wooden door that led so surprisingly but so conveniently directly into the village street, making sure to close it securely behind them.

He offered her his arm, and she took it, and they made their way past the neat red-brick cottages towards the Vicarage. 'I was so very sorry to hear that your grandfather is ill, ma'am. Is he able to receive visitors?'

She smiled a little sadly. 'He should be, if he would but consent to accept that he is an invalid, and might receive them in his chamber. But he prefers to maintain a fiction that he is not by any means as unwell as in truth he is, and so he will have it that he must be dressed and brought downstairs to the parlour if anyone should call upon him, and the exertion of the stairs, going down and then up again, is too much for his heart, and like to carry him off before his time, Dr Crew says. And so he receives very few visitors, and is the worse for it.'

He saw that his words had distressed her, or reminded her of an ever-present distress, and was sorry for it, and made haste to turn the topic. 'I regret then that I may not call upon him and pay my respects, as I would like to, for we are old friends. I understand you have not lived with him so very long; where did you reside before?'

'I lived in York, with my father's mother, until quite lately; I spent almost my whole life there with her, as I lost my parents when I was very small.'

'And now your grandmother has died? I am sorry for it.' Although she did not wear mourning, he noticed; perhaps the death was not so very recent. But decidedly she was left sadly alone in the world, and he could see why his mother was so concerned for her.

He was surprised to hear her chuckle. 'Oh, no! Nonna Albina is very much alive. She is Italian, you see, and now that Europe is at peace at last, she decided to return home. She has an enormous family in Parma, any number of brothers and sisters and nephews and nieces, whom she had not been able to see for many years, and her mother Contessa Luisa is still in good health – can you imagine? – at almost ninety years of age.'

'Oh, now I understand your mastery of Italian. You did not think to go with her?'

'I should have liked it, and planned to do it, for I have

grown up with stories of my family there and never met them, but when we last came to visit my grandfather we discovered that he was so very much more unwell than he had let us suspect, and it was agreed that I should remain with him . . . for the present.'

So she had a family after all, although they were near a thousand miles away. He was glad for her, that she should not be entirely alone and friendless, as his mother had described it. He did not think it at all the thing to ask her what she meant to do when her grandfather should have taken his leave of this world; it would be an indelicate, callous question, and it was in no sense his business. But he was beginning to think that his mother was right, as she so often was, and that it might perhaps become his business, the solution to all his difficulties lying so close at hand, and in a form that he acknowledged to be highly attractive to him, so that duty, practicality and personal inclination might perhaps be combined to the benefit of all.

They took their leave of each other at the door of the Vicarage, and he made his way home, deep in thought.

CHAPTER NINE

Kate had been distressed when Lucy had insisted upon their accompanying her home, but there had been no means that she could devise to prevent it, without displaying a sort of egregious incivility that would have been upsetting to the child and to her grandmother, and likely furthermore to provoke a close attention and scrutiny from Sir Benedict that she by no means wished to incur, and was not at all sure that she could easily support. And so she was obliged to acquiesce, and accept his escort with a show of pleasure that she wished were feigned, but was not, for she felt a thrill of guilty joy at the prospect of walking with him, and hearing his beautiful, deep voice, even if it were only uttering the merest of commonplaces.

But it seemed that commonplaces were not to be the subject of their conversation at all. Kate felt that she had made a grievous misstep almost at once, in appearing to take on herself a right to address Lucy's situation that she by no means possessed, nor should appear to want to possess, but he did not take offence, and instead began to discuss his dilemma with her quite gravely, with obvious sincerity and a respect for her opinions that set her heart to fluttering in her chest. They had never had a serious discussion before, but instead had conversed of the merest trifles, as one did at a ball. To hear him express his deepest feelings and concerns for Lucy she must consider the sincerest compliment he could pay to her, a virtual stranger. When besides he spoke with such good sense and touching emotion, she was almost overset, and had to call on every shred of self-possession that she could call her own to answer him in a rational manner, and make plain her own feelings of appreciation and intelligent interest, without betraying how deeply his words and actions affected her. It was a brief moment, too soon interrupted, but she felt in that instant that a spark of true connection had been shared between them. She supposed that in her usual way she would lie awake at night and wonder if it had been real, or if she had instead imagined it, or made a foolish show of herself in some manner and not realised it at the time, but for now she felt a small flare of contentment, almost of happiness, and she held it to her as long as it should last.

They left the park, and Lucy was persuaded to remain inside it with her little dog; Kate was pleased to see how her father did not put his foot down, but gave her a choice, so that she was obliged to consider what would be best, and use her intelligence to decide that to expose the puppy to all the dangers of the village street would by no means be sensible. Lucy made the wiser choice, rather than having it forced on her by paternal diktat, and scurried off with her companion.

And Kate's happiness was by no means diminished when they began walking slowly along the street, and he asked her some question intended to lead her to talk about herself; she knew it for common courtesy and nothing more, but what exquisite pleasure to converse with him as equals for a brief time, and to see the kindling of interest, however fleeting it might be, in his eyes when she spoke of her Italian family. It was over soon enough, but she hugged it to her, and when she lay abed and thought of it, she refused to let it be spoilt by anything at all that her disagreeable inner voice might suggest.

CHAPTER TEN

Lucy and Wellington were waiting for him when he returned to the demesne, and demanded his attention with the tale of their adventures, and so it was not until after dinner that Benedict was able to have private conversation with his mother. The evening had turned chilly, with a sharp breeze blowing off the river, and they were seated in her parlour, in front of a small but welcome fire.

'Well?' the Dowager said, raising one eyebrow.

He stretched out his long legs and gazed into the depth of the flames. 'I . . . will not say that you are wrong, Mama,' he said at last. 'There is plainly a strong bond of affection between the two of them. It is a pleasure to observe them together, and I cannot think Miss Moreton anything but an excellent influence in every respect. Her manners and her bearing are good, and she converses like a sensible woman.'

'Such tepid praise!' she said teasingly, though she might as well have broken down and cried to hear her son, once so lively, so passionate, describing an attractive young woman thus. She supposed that it was no wonder, after all he had suffered, but how it hurt her heart that it should be so.

'I do not mean to be tepid. From what little I have seen of her, I consider her a young lady of distinction, intelligence and sensibility. I believe that you may be right: that she would be well suited to be Lucy's mama-in-law, and my wife and the mother of my children, and – not the least of it – that she may be fit to follow you in due course as mistress of these estates. That in itself is no small thing, you know, my dear.'

She blinked away a sudden tear. 'I stand corrected! This is praise indeed. But do you like her, Ben? Do you think that you could perhaps one day – I do not say now – come to love her? You are looking for a wife, an intimate companion, someone with whom you will, God willing, spend thirty or forty years, not interviewing an upper servant or a governess, however well qualified.'

'I know it. Yes . . . I like her. I like her very much. I cannot say more than that at present.' He would not deny that he did like her. He enjoyed her company, and he found her appearance sufficiently pleasing, even without giving licence to his cursed imagination to . . . Enough of that. Setting that aside, he had felt oddly comfortable as he walked with her; she was tall, and matched his stride, and there had been an elusive sense of connection between them; they had not talked of the weather or any such nonsense, but of real things, real feelings. It had been long since he had had such a conversation with a young woman. He did not care to think how long.

'Well, then!'

'It is easy to say, "Well, then." Have you any reason to suppose she would welcome an offer from me, or from anyone? And she is not as alone in the world as you assume, you know – she has a grandmother, and I dare say a score of uncles and cousins, in Italy. Not that I should at all wish her to accept me to avoid destitution, but her situation is not as desperate as you led me to believe, and she may well choose, once poor Waltham is dead, to go to stay with them, and make her life there, and no doubt find a husband. I wonder that she has escaped matrimony so long.'

She pounced. 'You think her so attractive, then?' He nodded, smiling a little, and she thought it enough for now, and did not press him more on the matter. 'I agree with you: she is a very well-looking young lady. I have conversed occasionally with her over the past few months, and I believe that she formed an attachment when young, which for some cause or other did not prosper, and although she received several respectable offers when she lived in York, she refused them all. And as for these Italian relatives, Ben, they are all very well, and charming people, I am sure, but I do not understand them to be persons of substance, despite their noble birth. Theodore Waltham has spoken of them in the past. The head of the family is her great-uncle, the current Count – why should he care for a great-niece he has never met? – and he has a dozen or so children and grandchildren to support, in some crumbling castle or other, living hand to mouth. Should she join them, she will be a dependant, a poor relation, probably set to teaching their children English without benefit of a wage, and she must know it. Such a prospect cannot compare with the life that you could offer her.'

'I suppose it cannot. I can offer her much, if I cannot offer her all that I once laid claim to, but I think I might still have the best of the bargain. In fact, I am sure of it. And so how are we to proceed? I like her very well, Mama, but I can make no show of having fallen in love with her, or going down on one knee, or any such stuff. You surely know that those days are behind me.'

'Of course, dear,' said his mother, although her hand was at her eyes, perhaps to shield them from the glare of the fire, and so he could not see her expression. She continued, 'I think it best if I pay a visit to Mr Waltham, and we discuss it together.'

'She tells me that he will insist on getting up and dressed, if visitors call, and that it is very bad for him.'

The Dowager sighed. 'I know. And thus I have not seen my old friend for weeks, because of his foolish pride. But if I present myself without warning, when she is out, and bully my way upstairs before he knows that I am there, I may bring it off. I know he is excessively worried about her, and esteems you highly, and so I think your proposal will be acceptable to him. I hope he will know best whether he should raise it with her, or I should, or you should address her directly yourself.'

'Understand me, Mama, I will not have her compelled – I have no taste at all for a reluctant bride. And I will not have poverty constrain her, either. If, once he is dead, she desires to go to Italy and cannot afford it, I will pay for her passage, without a word of complaint, if she refuses me. She must be free to choose, and I must know that she is. I insist upon it.'

CHAPTER ELEVEN

Lady Silverwood took advantage of Miss Moreton's next lesson with Lucy to pay her momentous visit to Mr Waltham. It was raining a little that afternoon, and like to set in heavier, and the Italian lesson was being conducted in the schoolroom. Benedict was closeted with his estate manager, and so his mother called up her carriage, and was set down in front of the Vicarage, asking her coachman to return in an hour.

The door was answered by Mr Waltham's maid Polly, who was granddaughter to the butler at the Hall, and the Dowager had no difficulty at all in overwhelming her and making her way upstairs, wincing and clinging to the polished banister as her hips and knees pained her. Shortly she was seated beside the vicar's bed with a restorative cup of tea, regarding her old friend sadly. He had deteriorated substantially in the weeks since she had seen him, into a shadow of his former vigorous self, and she was not sure she entirely succeeded in concealing her shock from him.

'My dear Theodore,' she said, 'forgive me for forcing myself in on you in such a rag-mannered way, but I have a matter of the greatest importance to discuss with you, and there is no time to lose.'

He moved his thin hands fretfully over the sheets. 'I expect you think I am dying, Charlotte, and have come to say goodbye, or some such nonsense.'

'And are you not?'

'Well, yes, damn you for an interfering woman, I suppose I am,' he said in most unclerical fashion, but although his words were forceful, there was no heat or anger in them, just a bone-deep weariness and anxiety. 'And I am tired, and would be glad enough of it, and the prospect of re-joining my dear Mary at last, if it were not for the fact that I worry so about that granddaughter of mine. What is to become of her, Charlotte, tell me that?'

'And that,' she said, 'is precisely why I have come to see you, Theodore. I think I may have a solution to all your worries, and to mine, too . . .'

When Polly curtsied Lady Silverwood out to her carriage an hour later, she was shocked to see that the Dowager had been crying, although she thanked her pleasantly enough, as ever, and promised to send over a basket of hothouse fruit in case Mr Waltham might fancy it. And when she went upstairs to remove the tea things, as an excuse to see how he did, it seemed to her that he too had tears on his face, but for all that he spoke to her more cheerfully than he had done in an age, and asked her to send Miss Kate up to see him when she should return from the Hall.

Putting off her serviceable bonnet, stout boots and pelisse and shaking out her umbrella, Kate was very surprised to hear from Polly that the Dowager had been to visit her grandfather in her absence, and even more surprised to see how cheerful he looked when she went up to see him. Clearly a visit from such an old friend had been a tonic for him, but it was more than that; he seemed easier in his mind, less fretful, than had been in a long while.

He said, 'My dear, come and sit beside me, for we need to have a serious talk, you and I.'

She seated herself in her usual shabby armchair by the casement window and looked at him expectantly.

'Kate, it has been a pleasure having you to live with me, and I am very glad to have come to know you better than your visits in the past permitted. You have always been very dear to me – my poor daughter's only child – but I think it is only lately that I have come to value you as you deserve, and to be truly anxious about your future. I am grateful for your loving care, and painfully conscious that I have failed you. When I am dead, Kate, what do you plan to do?'

She stirred in instinctive protest, but he raised a frail

hand to stop her. 'Hush, Kate, I have been weak and foolish, but I am determined to be so no longer, and it is not quite too late. You know that I am dying; do not trouble to deny it. What will you do?'

It would be dishonest to pretend that she had not thought of it, and he deserved better from her. This was no time, clearly, for polite fictions. 'I suppose I will join my grandmother in Italy. There is always a home for me with her.'

He huffed in exasperation. 'I thought as much. Kate, I am fond of the ridiculous creature myself, and I do not deny that she loves you, and has always somehow contrived to keep the pair of you afloat, along with the income from your teaching and the pitiful help I could give you, but I understand her to be living at the charge of her mother – a woman of ninety – who herself depends on the support of the head of the family, your great-uncle the Count. And he in turn supports the whole boiling of them on what little his estate provides, and I suppose what he may in future be able to scrape from the leavings of the Austrian woman in what will surely be an *opera buffa* establishment at Parma. Is any of this untrue?'

Kate could not help but smile slightly as she acknowledged the justice of this. 'Of course it is all too true! I imagine Nonna Albina will enjoy herself excessively, as *opera buffa* is exactly what she likes, and if as it is rumoured the former empress is no longer perfectly respectable, I am sure you do not mean to tell me that Nonna is the same. At her age, Grandfather – you should be ashamed of yourself!'

He snorted with laughter, which set him coughing, and she helped him to a sip of cordial; it was a moment or two before he could speak again. 'I am sure she is as respectable as she ever was. I do not mean to criticise Albina's character, only her circumstances. She is very well able to take care of herself, and always has been, I make no doubt. But such a court is no place for you, and what could you do there? If offers were to be made to you by any of its habitues, they would not be offers of marriage, my girl. And say you stay there unmolested, which is by no means certain, what is to become of you when those two old women are dead, even assuming that Albina has the poor taste to live to be a hundred, as I expect she fully intends? You will by then be fifty or so, which is not by any means a comfortable thought. You will be a poor relation and you know it. *La zitella inglese* – do I have that right?'

She blinked a little at his cruelty, and he saw, and reached out his hand to her. 'I am sorry, my dear. I no longer have time for the word with the bark on it. I would like to die knowing you are secure and provided for, in a way I cannot accomplish. A hundred pounds or so a year is all I will be able to leave you, and how will you live? Do not, I beg you, raise the foolish scheme of going as a governess. It is a wretched life for anyone, and your youth and beauty render you entirely unfit for it.'

'My youth and beauty? Such stuff. I am already a spinster, dear Grandfather, and have never been in the least beautiful. And I do not disagree with anything else that you say, except for your reproaches to yourself, for we both know you have done all you could, and I could ask no more. But what is to become of me, after all, if my choice lies only in which country I should live, poor and unmarried as I must be in either place? There is the word with no bark on it for you, indeed.' She was agitated, and her breath came quickly; it was not so very pleasant to have her bleak future set out for her so brutally, for all that she held no illusions about it.

'That is the heart of it, is it not, Kate? What if I have another solution for you? Will you hear me out?'

'I cannot imagine what it might be, but of course I will.'

'Charlotte Silverwood came to see me today – I expect the girl told you? We too had a very frank discussion about the future.'

She frowned in confusion. 'Is she proposing I should replace Miss Sutton as Lucy's governess? But I thought you could not like such an idea, after what you just said? And besides, I was talking to Sir Benedict yesterday of Lucy's situation, and he did not mention it, and in fact said that engaging a younger governess while Miss Sutton remains in the household is not to be thought of. Unless he means to marry and set up his own establishment, I suppose, but he did not indicate . . .'

Mr Waltham was laughing again, and set to wheezing afresh. 'My dear silly girl, it is not as a governess that he wants you.'

She looked at him, her face blank. 'Grandfather, I think that I do not perfectly understand you.'

'You are correct, he does mean to marry. He means to marry you, if you will have him.'

CHAPTER TWELVE

S he had flushed, but now her face drained of all colour. 'If that is a jest, sir, it is not one I care for in the least. I wonder that you should make it.'

'It is no jest, Kate. I am sorry if my laughter misled you; I should not allow my unfortunate quirk of humour to intervene on such a serious matter. It is quite true; Sir Benedict intends to make you an offer.'

She had risen to her feet, and stood with her hands at her face, as if in horror. 'Oh, no, no, no . . .' she said softly, her eyes blank.

He was concerned to see her so overset, and said, 'Sit down, and drink some of my cordial. I am sorry that my news has shocked you so.'

Hardly knowing what she was about, she sank back into her chair, and looked at him in frank disbelief. 'I do not . . . I do not comprehend you. Surely there is some misunderstanding between you and Lady Silverwood – she cannot, she *cannot*, have intended to suggest anything so ridiculous.'

'Shall I tell you what she said, and you may judge for yourself?'

She nodded, and poured herself a glass of liquid, and gulped it down.

'She told me that Sir Benedict is resolved to marry again, and not before time. You must know his situation – he needs an heir, if the estate is not to go to that rackety cousin of his, and he wishes besides that young Lucy should have a lady standing in the relation of a mother to her, who will care for her. Charlotte is all too conscious that her own health is not good, and that as the child grows older she will struggle more and more to provide all that she needs. She does not press her son to wed – there is no need; he is aware enough of the necessity of it himself.'

'I can see that all this is true, and yet I do not see what any of it has to do with me. I still feel sure that you have misunderstood her.'

'You do not let me finish, child. Sir Benedict went to London for the Season with the express intention of finding a bride; he set Mrs Singleton the task, but she failed.'

'I do not see how that could be true. Surely he is everything that is most eligible, and his sister could have had no difficulty in suggesting a thousand young ladies who might suit his purpose admirably.'

'Perhaps not quite a thousand, but yes. If the problem were only to find someone who might bear him an heir, I am sure he might take the plunge once more like any man, and be as certain or uncertain of his success as another. But he is equally concerned for the child he already has.'

She puzzled it out, and stammered at last. 'You mean . . . you mean seriously to say to me that he wishes to marry me because I am fond of Lucy! That *that* is what his mother told you? I never heard anything so ridiculous in my life.'

He sighed. He was very tired, and in pain, but he had begun this, and he could not stop now. 'It is not so ridiculous, my dear. He is a young man of proper feeling, and he worries – and who shall say that he is wrong? – that any young lady he marries may be kind enough to Lucy in the first instance, but prove to be careless or even unkind when she has a child or children of her own. He cannot endure that any choice of his should make her life unhappy, when she has already endured the most grievous loss a child can suffer. Whatever you feel about the rest, I know that you of all people must see the justice of this.' She was not able at that moment to speak, but nodded, her eyes shining with sudden tears.

He went on wearily, 'He has observed for himself that there is already a bond between you and his daughter. He has met and talked with you, and has the highest opinion of your good breeding and good sense – and I should think so, too, or I should like to hear why! Your lack of fortune is a matter of complete indifference to him, and, though I think he cares little for such things, he knows your birth to be as good as his. He admires you, as well he might, and wishes that you would do him the honour of becoming his wife.'

She opened her mouth to give utterance to she knew not what whirling thoughts, but he forestalled her. 'Kate, do not think that I have given him – via his mother – leave to pay his addresses to you. I have not. I was by no means willing to do so, because I had not spoken to you of the matter, and knew you to be entirely ignorant of it. You are of age, and can make your own decisions. I have no power to force you, and would not if I could. I ask only that you will think on it: think on it very seriously.'

He took her hand again, and his voice was weak, his breath short, as he said, 'It is not merely that your worldly position is so very precarious, my child. I hope you know that I would not urge you to any match that would be distasteful to you, or with one who was in any way unworthy of you, just to assure your position in life. I would like to think no gentleman in holy orders would do such a thing. But I have known this young man since his birth, and I can look you in your dear face and say with all honesty that he is everything I could ever have wished for you in a husband. I believe that he would try his utmost to make you happy, and I have every hope he might succeed. And as for him, he is an estimable man who has endured a great deal of undeserved pain, but you could make him happy too, I think, and forge a life and a family together. To bring life and joy out of misery, that would be something indeed.'

She sat silent for a long moment, looking at something or someone surely not in the room with them, and then she said, 'I must consider. My head is spinning so . . .'

'I can only ask that you do give the matter very serious consideration. You will not be importuned. Charlotte has asked me to tell you that she would like to call on you tomorrow, to discuss the matter, but if you do not wish it, we need only send and let her know, and she will not come. And she also begged me to say that she does not consider your agreeing to talk to her as any more than that; you do not bind yourself in any way by doing so, nor raise any expectations, and may of course still refuse the match without any consequences whatsoever. She was most insistent that you do not feel any pressure upon you to agree. And Sir Benedict himself will not speak a word of any of this to you unless you explicitly say that he may.'

She said in a hollow voice, 'She is all consideration. I . . . I will go to bed. I will send Polly so she may make you comfortable.' And then she fled.

CHAPTER THIRTEEN

If Kate slept at all that night, it could only have been for a few wretched minutes, and those minutes racked with vivid nightmares that made them worse than her waking hours. She felt as though her head might explode, it was pounding so, and it was only by forcing herself repeatedly to recall the precise words that her grandfather had spoken that she convinced herself she was not trapped in some fever dream.

At one point in the most desperate hour of the night she found herself sitting up in bed in her nightgown, laughing immoderately, tears streaming down her face, while she endeavoured to smother the sound of her hysteria in a pillow. To think that for seven years she had cherished a foolish infatuation – she refused to call it more than that – for a man she scarcely knew and whom she had always accepted to be entirely beyond her reach, and now, now, when she was months at best away from bereavement and looking in the cold face of poverty, it was suddenly proposed that she marry him: a prospect that she had dreamt of a thousand times as a silly girl, even then knowing it was impossible. It was surely the most bitter trick that fate could play – to taunt her with all she had ever wanted: to say, *Take him, you can have him after all, but on such terms.*

She must refuse him. Surely it would be a form of refined torture to marry him, feeling as she did, when he did not, could not, love her? Good God, he was marrying for an heir. She would . . . He would . . .

Kate's grandmother had made sure she was fully aware of the facts of life; she had no patience with the English way of keeping girls in ignorance, considering it foolish and dangerous. So she knew that he would come to her bed. He would lie down with her and touch her body, and put his seed in her. She knew all the details, in theory, but she did not know how such things were managed in the absence of love. Would he kiss her? Try to give her pleasure, to share pleasure with her? What did a gentleman do, in such circumstances? Were there rules? She thought she knew what a lady did, an English lady: nothing. She lay there, and did nothing.

To have him make love to her – the words were a mockery. She must refuse him. Every feeling revolted at the thought.

But oh, she was so very lonely.

And he had spoken to her, looked at her, seen her. Listened to what she had said, taken her words seriously. She thought now that *that* was the real temptation. The thought of his hands and his lips on her body was something to torment herself with in the dark, as now – it could not be entirely real to her. But she had walked with him in the daylight, had put her hand on his arm, his real, solid arm, and he had smiled at her. She could have that; she could have that every day. Him, and perhaps a family. Lucy, whom she already cared for deeply, and could love, if she were allowed to, and other children. She felt she had enough love to give any number of children, and if he could never love her, they surely would. She thought what it would be, to hold a child of hers in her arms – Lucy, or another from her own body – and now she did cry in earnest.

She did not spend so very long dwelling on the material advantages of his proposal, for they were obvious. She should not allow herself to be swayed by them, and she did not think that she would be. No, it was the sneakingly seductive prospect of company and warmth that was so tantalising, so very hard to refuse.

And yet she had refused them before, or something like them. She had refused Mr Melkinthorpe, which had been easy enough, even though she could see that he sincerely admired her, and he was a kind and decent man, who had laid all that he possessed, metaphorically, at her feet. (It would not have been possible for him to lay his possessions before her physically, as a large and prosperous wool manufactory in Sheffield employing several hundred persons is not so easily taken up like a toy and set down before a young lady.) But despite his many sterling qualities and undoubted wealth, he was so very much older, and so very red in the face, and so very prone to spray his interlocutor with spittle when he was agitated, that Kate had felt she could do nothing but turn him down as gently as she could.

She had had another offer too, from a threadbare young Italian musician, and that had been more of a temptation, for though he was near penniless, he had put before her a life of travel, music and adventure – laughter, too, and perhaps passion, for he had been handsome, with liquid dark eyes that sparked a fugitive response in her, and when he had kissed her one evening in the dark shadows by the minster she had been so tempted to respond, to let him touch her and give her the comfort and pleasure that her body craved. But once again something had stopped her – she did not know, looking back, if it had been fear of the unknown, or something else – so she had told him no, and he had shrugged gracefully and moved on to the next town and the next girl. And now she was alone, and older, and the choice was so much harder.

It occurred to her all at once that she had one very pressing reason for acceptance: her grandfather. She knew that the very uncertain future that lay in store for her was making his last months of life ugly, and even standing in the way of the calm Christian acceptance of his fate that he aspired to, and had striven for all his life, despite the premature loss of his beloved daughter and the long, painful illness his dear wife had suffered. He was a kind and loving man, and with a word she could relieve him of all anxiety on her behalf, and allow him to prepare to meet his maker with an open heart. It was like his goodness not to press this on her as a reason, not even to suggest she thought of it. But now she had, and it could not lightly be set aside.

And then she turned over restlessly, and punched her pillow into a more comfortable shape, and wondered if all these fine and rational arguments – had she not just almost convinced herself that it was her Christian duty to marry Sir Benedict, surely a fine example of sophistry? – were so seductive, so very appealing to her, just because she wanted him. Plain and simple. She wanted him to be hers, not another woman's. The most beautiful, most accomplished, most loving, most intelligent, kindest and moreover the richest, wittiest woman in England, whoever she was, might want him – might very easily want him; she could have no difficulty in believing it – but she could not have him, because she, Kate Moreton, a nobody, a spinster and teacher of Italian, would have him. She was not so noble and self-sacrificing as to say, *I hope he finds love with another, more worthy than myself.* She did not want him to find love with anyone but her. And surely that way lay terrible hurt, for even she knew that to marry a man was one thing, but to know him yours was quite another. And she could not believe that he would make her any such promise.

She must refuse him . . . To marry him when he did not love her, and never would love her, was surely to lay herself open to the most terrible pain; the searing pain she had suffered when she had seen him fall in love with Vanessa, and afterwards when she had seen them together so happy, would be as nothing to the agony she would invite if she married him now. He would probably not be faithful to her, she thought suddenly: why should he be? What man was faithful to a bride he cared nothing for? He would be hers in every conventional way, and yet not hers at all in any way that really counted. A parody of what she had always dreamt of. Torture, torment. It was not to be thought of. Better to live and die alone. Surely.

And yet, and yet, and yet . . .

It was no wonder that Kate presented a pale, woebegone face, eyes ringed with dark circles, to the Dowager when she arrived at the appointed hour the next day. Kate had asked Polly to show her guest into the garden when she arrived, and awaited her there, on a bench set under an old oak tree, once again in her yellow muslin. She had no desire that anyone should overhear this conversation.

The day was fine and fresh after yesterday's rain, but somewhat breezy even in this sheltered spot. Lady Silverwood was, however, well wrapped in a pelisse and shawls; Kate offered to fetch rugs, but she brushed the words aside. 'I am very well, thank you, my dear. I see by your face that your grandfather has passed on my son's proposition to you, and that it does not cast you into transports of joy.'

Kate blushed, and looked down at her hands, clasped in her lap. 'I have been awake all night, ma'am, considering what I should do.'

'So I see,' said Her Ladyship drily. 'And I have come to help you, if I can.'

'Please, ma'am, do not think that I am ungrateful, nor that you find me unaware of the honour that Sir Benedict does me, an honour I did not expect—'

'Stuff and nonsense!' said the lady forcefully. 'May we be honest with each other?'

'I hope so,' said Kate warily.

'I will not insult you by speaking of Lucy, nor of your situation, nor your grandfather. I have a great deal of respect for your good sense, my dear, and I know that you will weigh all the arguments for and against my son's proposal as they deserve; indeed, only you can say how much weight each should have in your mind and in your heart. And it is of no consequence to say that I would be very happy if you could see your way to taking him; why should you care for that? But if you mean to refuse him, or if you cannot come to a decision, I know why, and it is of that that I wish to speak to you.'

'Ma'am?' Kate did not trust herself to say any more.

'You think you should not have him because you love him, and he does not love you.'

Kate had occasionally suspected that Lady Silverwood might have divined her feelings, but she was still shocked to hear it spoken of so openly, her deepest secret laid bare. She feared she gasped; she was almost sure she did so.

'I beg your pardon for having discerned your feelings, my dear, and for speaking of them openly when I am sure you would rather I did not, but I have come to ask you – no, to beg you – to see if you cannot find it in your heart to make that a reason to marry him, rather than a reason not to do so.'

'I do not understand you, I am afraid, ma'am.'

'He has been so terribly lost, since his brother died, and then Vanessa. I beg you to understand: the nature of the double blow shook the foundations of his world. He had never imagined for a second that he would inherit the title and the responsibilities of the estate, and then when he did, suddenly he found himself bearing the responsibility all alone, and with Lucy to consider too, a motherless baby as she was. He threw himself into his military service; I do not think he would greatly have cared if he lived or died. I believe he was entirely reckless for a time. He was as one frozen. But he did live, thank God, and now he is slowly coming back to life. At long last, I feel that he is.'

Kate said helplessly, 'Of course I understand why you should want him to marry, and why you should wish so earnestly that he find happiness again. But why me?'

'My daughter Maria tells me he showed not one scintilla of interest in any of the poor young creatures she thrust under his nose; she said at the end of the Season she did not believe that he would have known the one from the other, let her be as beautiful or as witty as you please. He might have said, "Oh, she is the redhead, I think," or, "I believe she might be the one with the annoying laugh." But no more than that. And yet he knows who you are, my dear.'

'I am his daughter's Italian teacher.'

'You are more than that. I see a spark of something in him when he looks at you, or speaks of you. It is only a tiny thing, but it is there. And – I am sorry if this shocks you, my dear, and I hope you will forgive me the indelicacy – he desires you.'

Kate spluttered, resolutely ignoring the treacherous little flame that ignited deep inside her at the thought of his desire for her, 'He cannot possibly have spoken to you of such a thing!'

'Of course not.' The Dowager smiled. 'But a mother knows; one day I hope you will be the mother of my grandson, and you will see if I am right.'

'I do not . . . I am not . . . His wife was a great

beauty, an incomparable – I was acquainted with her, so I know that it is true! – and I am nothing of the kind. I am sure you must be mistaken.'

'First of all, my dear, that is more nonsense – you are of a different style of looks, no doubt, but you have it in you to be a great beauty too, if only you were happy, which I hope you may be. And secondly, it would not matter if you were as ugly as sin, if he desires you, which I tell you he does. Men are such strange creatures where that is concerned. Of course I am glad you are not as ugly as sin – think of the poor children – but if you were, I would accustom myself to it.'

Kate could not help but laugh. 'Oh, ma'am, I do not know how to answer you! This talk of . . . of desire is a mere distraction, and I should not let you run away with the idea that I love him, just because I admit I set up a foolish infatuation for him, when I was a girl, for what has that to say to anything now?'

'I am making a sad affair of this, am I not? What I intended to say to you was that I do not believe for a second that you became infatuated with my son, if that is what you choose to call it, just because he has a handsome face and a winning smile. I choose instead to think that a young woman of your quality perceived the like virtues in him, even if you did not know him very well. Tell me truly, Kate Moreton – have you wasted seven years of your life pining for a hero from a storybook?'

'No,' she said at last with painful honesty. 'No, even then I was aware of his many excellent qualities, and could only admire them.'

'And do you find that this admiration was in any way mistaken, now that you meet him again?'

'You must know that I do not. He is everything that is—' She broke off, but it was too late, and the Dowager pounced.

'Call it infatuation if you wish, then: as though your feelings have no value because they have so far led to nothing. But really, my dear child, how well acquainted do you suppose Benedict was with Vanessa, or she with him, in the whirlwind of their courtship and marriage? I will tell you – not very well at all. Three weeks betrothed, I dare say, and then a month or so married, most of it spent making sheep's eyes at each other, and then he was off to war. Do not be setting them up as a great love affair with which you can never compete. It is not so. If he is pining for her, which I am by no means sure he is, then he is pining for a girl he barely knew, and who barely knew him. And you are real, and alive, and here, and he wants you.' Lady Silverwood stabbed the daisy-strewn lawn emphatically with the sharp ferrule of her parasol as she made each point. 'And you want him too, oh yes, you do, you are a woman with blood in her veins, not a paper doll. I am not so foolish as to expect you to confess it to me, so do not look at me like that.

'If you want him, and are in love with him, or half

on the way to it, and you are prepared to be a little patient – for all men require patience, my dear, if you have not learnt it yet – and he respects you, and is interested in you, and desires you, it is my very earnest hope that it will do very well.' She looked up, and her face was suddenly crumpled, appearing very serious, and older somehow. 'I cannot promise he will come to love you, for I do not suppose he could promise that himself. But I think he might. I hope that he might, with all my heart. And that is what I want for him – at least a chance of love. I could not bear to see him slip away again; I want him to come back to us. I have lost enough, I think.'

'Oh, ma'am . . . I do not think you know what you are asking of me!'

'Believe me, I do know. I am very well aware that it is not an easy thing. It will take a great deal of courage, to dare so much. And another thing! Do not speak or even think as though he is your superior, and does you some great favour if he condescends to marry you. I will not have it so. His advantage is material, no more. If you will risk your heart to love him, and risk your life to give him a child, he should kiss your feet in gratitude, I am sure. I do not know what more there is to be said, and my old bones ache, so I would like to go home. What do you say, Kate Moreton, now you have heard me out? Are you brave enough, or do you mean to spend the rest of your life wondering what might have been?'

Lady Silverwood looked at Kate, her eyes sharp, and Kate met them straight on. It had been an extraordinary conversation, and it seemed they were at the end of it, and she was obliged to take a decision. How could she possibly decide, when she was so torn? And yet she must. She took a deep breath.

CHAPTER FOURTEEN

Benedict resisted the impulse to straighten his neckcloth, and rapped smartly on the Vicarage door. Polly opened it to him after a few moments, her eyes bulging slightly at the unexpected sight of him, and so formally dressed, too, for he had honoured the occasion with dove-grey pantaloons and shining hessian boots. His mother had in the last two days paid not one but two visits to the Walthams, which was unprecedented, and now here he was, in all his finery; he could practically see the cogs whirring in Polly's shrewd brain, and watched as a solution to the puzzle – the correct solution, he would wager – presented itself to her, and she gazed at him in avid speculation. But he greeted her without the slightest sign of self-consciousness, he hoped, and asked her how she did, and she was forced to overcome her confusion, answer him, and show him into the garden, where Miss Moreton awaited him among the old roses. Polly showed a disposition to linger, but Kate smiled at her, and said that they did not need any refreshment, so she was obliged to take herself off and leave them alone.

She was wearing simple white muslin today, and she looked very cool and unconcerned, but he observed that a pulse beat in her throat, and she was having difficulty meeting his eyes as she asked him in her low, pleasant voice to be seated beside him on the bench. This interview was deuced awkward – he would rather face a cavalry charge – but would not grow any the less so if he delayed like a callow boy. It was not the first time he had proposed marriage, after all, though he dared not, would not, think of the other occasion, and all that had come after it.

He sat beside her, and said, 'Miss Moreton, let us not beat about the bush. I know that my mother has spoken to you, and I apologise if there was any embarrassment in such an unconventional approach. I am a man of two and thirty, and should not need my mama to do my wooing for me, but I was not at all sure how a direct overture would be received, and I did not wish to be the cause of any distress, should my offer be unwelcome.'

'No, you have been most considerate, sir. I would have been . . . taken by surprise if you had addressed me on such a topic yourself, for naturally I had not thought of such a thing.' She was looking down at her hands, her lids lowered, and he could not read her face.

'My mother tells me that I have reason to hope that you will accept my proposal. I would be very glad if you could. Miss Moreton – I hope I may call you Kate? – Kate, will you do me the honour of becoming my wife?'

She looked up at him now, and he saw that her brown eyes were sheened with tears. He supposed that these highly unromantic circumstances were not how a young lady might wish to receive an offer, or at least, not an offer that she intended to accept. She had received offers before, he knew, and had rejected them, which must mean that she had looked for love, and had not found it, and now here she was, poised to accept him, when he did not love her, and she did not love him. No wonder she had tears in her eyes. He might weep himself, if he dwelt too long on their situation, and the past hopes that lay dead for them both.

But she said, 'Yes, sir, I will accept your very flattering offer. I will marry you.' He thought that perhaps a solitary tear trembled on the edge of her thick lashes, and then fell.

He took her hand in his – it was cool, like her – and he raised it to his lips. 'Thank you! Please believe that I will do everything in my power to make you happy.'

'And I will try to do the same for you, sir.'

'Please call me Benedict.' He thought her hand trembled in his grasp, and he said suddenly, not considering his words before he spoke, 'Kate, they are not somehow forcing you, are they – my mother and your grandfather between them? I should not like to think that you are in any way unwilling.'

She smiled ironically now, and slid her hand from his grasp, saying, 'Are you trying to persuade me to retract my acceptance now that I have given it? Do you regret it suddenly, now that the words are uttered, and you truly face the prospect of marrying me?'

'No!' He rose to his feet, and stood looking down at her. 'No, I do not regret it in the slightest.' It was true: he did not. He felt oddly light of heart at the thought of marrying her. A fresh start. It was time.

'I think you would feel yourself obliged to say as much. But I would have you be honest. If you wish now that this conversation had never taken place, it can be so.'

He thought perhaps that he had hurt her with his clumsiness; it would be no wonder. He ran a hand through his carefully arranged hair in exasperation with himself, and sat beside her again, a little closer this time. 'I am no hand at this, so I will have to ask you to forgive me, and I hope you will. I am very glad that you have accepted me. I would prefer to be honest, too, and I shall be. One cannot control one's sensations, however one might try, and when you said yes to me, I was conscious of a great feeling of relief, as though a weight had been lifted from me, and of . . . pleasure.'

She was blushing; he had observed before that it became her. But she had not answered his question, he realised suddenly; she had instead diverted his attention with questions of her own. He took her hand again, and held it in a firmer clasp. 'Kate, I would like it very much if you would marry me, but I would prefer to be perfectly sure that you wish to do so. I know that you can only experience a natural apprehension about so serious a step, and all the changes in your life that it will involve, but I hope to convince you that these changes will be for the better. And I was particularly anxious for my mother to tell you that, if you should desire to re-join your grandmother in Italy, and could not afford to do so, I would gladly pay for your passage, and wish you well, rather than have you accept me from such dire necessity.'

'That was a very kind thought, sir. In fact, your mother did not mention it.' She saw his expression of sudden consternation, and explained hastily, 'Do not blame her, sir. I am sure she discharged her mission with quite as much delicacy as you could expect. We did not discuss . . . financial considerations, and she placed no such pressure on me. She paid me the compliment of saying that she knew I would not be unduly influenced by such concerns. If I must say it plain to you, I will – nobody forces me, I am quite willing.'

'Very well. I am glad of it, and glad to be reassured that you have not been bullied. And please, if I am to call you Kate, I will insist that you call me Benedict.'

'I will try to remember . . . Benedict,' she said with a small smile.

An awkward silence fell between them, and began to stretch. She was looking down at her lap again, and biting her full lower lip. He became aware that he would like very much to kiss her, and not just to seal their bargain or because he thought he should, but he did not know how to broach the subject. He could not just lunge at her and claim her mouth like a clumsy oaf, and yet if he could not manage such a simple thing as a kiss, how was he ever to . . . ?

She broke the silence. 'Perhaps we should go and tell my grandfather. I know he has been anxious, and I am sure he will be very happy to hear the news.'

'By all means let us do so,' he agreed. They rose together, and she turned to leave the garden, but he did not follow her, and she looked back at him questioningly. 'Kate,' he said. 'I would like to kiss you. Will you permit me to do so, now that we are betrothed?'

'Oh . . . yes, of course.' The wild rose colour had flared in her cheeks again, and she came back towards him, and stood close. He reached out, and touched her cheek, very gently, and then he lowered his lips to hers.

CHAPTER FIFTEEN

Kate did not know how she had maintained a calm exterior during his proposal, when her blood was pounding hard in her veins and she felt ready to swoon. She felt as if she were standing on the brink of a precipice; it was not yet too late to turn back, to choose safety. She could have run from the garden, from his presence; he would not have pressed her. But she had not. She had allowed him to continue.

He had shown her every consideration, and could not have been more respectful. He had not told her of his feelings for her, such as they were, before he made his offer, but she could not expect that; he had told her that he was relieved that she had accepted, and – more – that he was pleased. Relief could merely be that a disagreeable task was done, and that the anticipated result had been achieved; relief was nothing. But pleasure – that was something, was it not? She thought of the tiny flicker of flame that the Dowager had described, and hoped that nothing that she had clumsily said or done when she had challenged him had snuffed it out. It seemed all too likely.

But it appeared that she had not so sabotaged her hopes, for he wanted to kiss her. How could she refuse? She said something, she scarcely knew what, and then he reached out and touched her burning cheek, a butterfly touch, and then his lips were on hers.

She did not know what to do. This was not safe. She dared not show herself to be over-eager, yet it would be disastrous to show excessive coldness either. If there was an acceptable level of response, she did not know what it was. She did not even know what she felt as he kissed her this first time, so caught up as she was in her warring thoughts. She must have made some small movement of distress, for he at once withdrew his lips from hers and said, 'Did I hurt you? I am so sorry!'

'No!' She would be honest. 'Sir, Benedict . . . I do not know how to respond, and it is my wretched nature that I will always think too much. I do not want to be cold to you, and repel you, and yet I do not want to appear too . . . too . . .'

He was still standing disturbingly close to her, and he smiled down at her now very warmly. 'Now, that is the kind of honesty I can appreciate, and I thank you for it. I understand exactly what you mean, for I am cut from much the same cloth. I will always be worrying if I have made a misstep; it is a curse, and sometimes makes it nigh on impossible to behave naturally.'

'Exactly!' she said breathlessly.

'So,' he said, and as he spoke he put his arm about her, and pulled her closer, though he did not hold her tightly, 'shall we agree to set that aside, and silence the nagging voices that tell each of us we are bound to make perfect fools of ourselves, and merely say: we should like to kiss each other; we have a perfect right to kiss each other, and we shall do so, and enjoy it?'

'We can try,' she said doubtfully.

He cupped her face in his hand, and brushed her lips with his. She was overwhelmingly aware of his nearness, of the strength of his arms and the warmth of his body. 'We can do better than that. Stop thinking!' he said against her mouth.

She did. Unable to resist him, she opened her lips a little to his, and his opened to her, and after a moment he pulled her closer, his arm tightening about her. His lips were soft, deceptively unthreatening at first, and she gave herself up to them, and melted into his embrace.

It was everything she had ever dreamt of.

After some time had passed – it might have been a few moments, or much longer, she could not have said – she felt him pull away from her slightly, and heard him: no, she felt him sigh against her cheek. She stiffened, and he was aware of it; how could he not be, holding her so close? He said, 'And now you are thinking and doubting again! Do not! I am releasing you because I must, and not because I want to. I would very happily stay here and kiss you all day long, but I know that we had better defer that pleasure. And it would surely be a pleasure.'

He smoothed a wayward curl back from her brow, and said, 'I shall not ask you if you liked it; I know you did, and so did I. And I very much look forward to doing it again. Often.'

'Oh . . .' she said, and she felt her body swaying involuntarily towards him.

He smiled, taking her hand in his and pressing his lips to it, then turning it in his grasp and seeking the pulse at her wrist. He brushed it lightly with his thumb and then kissed it, and she gasped. 'Yes, you feel it too, don't you? Kate, I feel compelled to say something to you. You know the reasons why I marry; it would be tedious to rehearse them. One of them, you must be aware, is that I am lonely, I have been lonely for a long time, and seek a wife for companionship. Companionship in my daily life, of course, but also in my bed. I have been beaten down by life rather, I admit, and I have become accustomed to think that the least of the reasons, but now that I have held you in my arms, I realise I was mistaken.'

She did not know what it was that he meant to say to her, and so did not speak. It seemed the implication of his words was flattering, and hopeful, but she dared not assume that it was so. He said, 'I think, I hope, that we will find that we can give each other a great deal. Companionship certainly, but I think there will be passion too, and I had not looked for it. I do not suppose that you had either.'

'How could I?' she whispered very low. 'How could I know . . . ?'

'I want us to enjoy each other. And I think for that, you need to trust me. It is important that you should know I have not been a promiscuous man. I wish I could say that I have been celibate since . . . since I was widowed, but it would not be true. I had a mistress a while since; that is over. I have always been careful, very careful to take no risks with my health or that of others. Do you understand me, Kate?'

'I think so. You are telling me that I am in no danger from you.' If only that were true.

'I am. I suppose there are many kinds of danger, but that at least I swear you do not face. We could be married very soon, if you agree; I see no reason to delay. Can we make a pact? If I tell you that I want you, and that I think you want me, will you agree once we are wed not to be a correct lady who is always worrying about the proprieties? Will you set aside your doubts and let yourself feel passion?'

She gazed at him, her mind whirling. It was not as though he asked her to risk any more than she was already staking. He was asking her to be bold, but she was already far bolder than he could know. He had her heart already, and she was pledging him her body too by marrying him. She had stepped off the cliff; she was falling. What possible difference could this make?

She said slowly, 'If you are indeed serious, I believe I will. It is not in my nature to choose half-measures.'

'Somehow I did not think it was. Thank you, Kate. I will do my very best to make sure you do not regret it.' He bent to kiss her again, quickly but harder, as if sealing a promise, and her lips tingled afresh at his touch. 'Now let us go and speak to your poor grandfather, who can only be in a fever of impatience, which cannot be good for him. Then I shall go home and tell my mother, and Lucy, too, and everyone will be delighted.' He took her by the hand, and drew her into the house.

CHAPTER SIXTEEN

B enedict made his way back through the village and the park in something of a daze. They had told Mr Waltham their news, and he had cried, and they had pretended not to notice it, and drunk the toast to their health and happiness that he had insisted upon. Polly had been called to fetch a dusty bottle of Madeira and three glasses, and so it was to be assumed that the news was out, or soon would be. Kate's abundant, silky hair had quite come down during their passionate embrace in the garden, and was in considerable disorder – he supposed he must have been running his fingers through it – and it would take an understanding very much duller that Polly Thompson's to miss the significance of it all.

Kate! He had kissed her, and it had been wonderful. Good God, but it had been. Perhaps it was because it was months since he had held a woman in his arms – he would have liked to have been able to tell her that the last woman he had embraced was Vanessa, but he would not begin by lying to her – but when he had felt her glorious mouth open to him, and held her warm, rich body close, it had been so intensely, almost painfully pleasurable, it had taken all his self-control not to run his hands all over her and explore the curves that her demure muslin did very little to conceal. Her big, luscious breasts pressed against him, his hands in her soft hair, her arms wound about his neck . . . And when he had looked down into her face, and seen it flushed, her brown eyes dark with desire and her lips parted as if begging him to kiss her again, as if begging for much more than that, her body curving towards him by instinct . . . He was like a man who had been marching for hours, weary, dusty hours that felt like days, under the hot Spanish sun, parched, and then he had been offered cool water. Of course it tasted delicious. That was all it was. But she was to be his wife, and she had, brave girl, made him a promise of passion. Passion received and passion given. Shoot him for a liar if he did not hold her to it. Christ, that was a train of thought, what he might hold her to . . .

He had agreed with Kate that he would send his carriage for her, and she would come to dine with them that evening, so that they could begin to make plans. She would need clothes, no doubt, and all manner of feminine things; his sister could help. And there was the matter of her grandfather to be arranged, but nothing was insurmountable. A short engagement was perfectly usual, and perfectly regular. No reason at all to wait.

His mother was sitting with Lucy on the terrace; Lucy was reading from her chapbook, frowning in concentration, with Wellington lying sleeping at her feet, twitching as he chased ducks in his dreams. The Dowager raised an eyebrow in interrogation, and Benedict nodded. He imagined that he might be smiling in an idiotic fashion; he imagined his neckcloth might well be disarranged. 'My dear!' she said, her eyes filling with tears.

'Lucy,' he said, 'set down your book, for I have something of great importance to tell you.'

She put it aside gladly, and jumped up to greet him. 'Yes, Papa? What is it? Is it something nice?'

'I hope you will think it so.'

He took her hand, and they walked together across the lawn that sloped down to the river, which sparkled in the sunlight and made a sufficiently attractive picture. Wellington had stirred at the sound of voices, and waved his feathery tail languidly, but not awoken to accompany them. There was a bench set near the edge of the water, and he sat on it, and his daughter perched beside him, swinging her legs. 'My dear,' he began, 'I know it must have been hard for you, not having a mama . . .'

'Well, I do not remember her, and that makes me sad, sometimes. Grandmama tells me stories of her, and you do, of course, but it is not the same.'

'No, it is not the same. I am sorry, Lucy.'

'It's not your fault, Papa. I know you miss her too and you are sad sometimes because of it. I wish you were not sad. Perhaps you should like to get married again, so that you could be happy again? I believe sometimes grown-ups do that. I should not mind it, if it were someone nice. Not if it were someone nasty, who would be unkind to Wellington, but I do not think you would marry someone nasty, would you, Papa?'

He laughed. 'No, I would not! What if . . . what if I were to marry someone who you know already, and like very much?'

'That would be sensible, Papa. Who could it be?'

'Can you not guess?'

'Well . . .' She considered, head on one side, a gesture she had inherited from the Dowager. 'I do not think it can be Miss Sutton, for although she is very good really, she can sometimes be a little cross, and she does not like dogs at all. Or cats, even.'

He could not help but laugh. 'She was your aunt Maria's governess, twenty years ago, and mine, before I went to school. She is a very warm-hearted lady, for all her oddities, but I think she is perhaps somewhat advanced in years to be my wife.'

'Is she? I did not know. You are quite old too, Papa.'

'I know I am, but think of someone rather younger, my dear child, if you can.'

'I do not think it can be Amy, or Margaret, or Molly, or Susan, because although I am sure they like you, all they do is giggle when they see you, and I think if you were to marry one, the others would be upset. Though they are all very nice, mostly.'

Benedict did not think that this was the time to try to explain why he was not considering marrying either of his mother's housemaids, or the kitchen maid or the nursemaid, and he wondered why Kate had not instantly sprung to his daughter's mind as a prospective bride for him. 'Can you really not think of any young lady of your acquaintance?'

'Oh, Papa! Is it Kate? Please say that it is Kate!'

'Yes, it is Kate. I am surprised, though, that you did not think of her at first. I hope you are pleased.'

'Of course I am pleased, silly! I suppose I did not think of her first because she is quite young, and we have such fun together, and jump in puddles.' She saw the expression on his face and misinterpreted it, saying hastily, 'We do learn Italian too, of course. "Mud" in Italian is "*fango*" – is that not a funny word? So you see that I know things already.'

'Oh, my dear, I do not care so very much if you have not learnt a great deal of Italian. I was just a little sad that you did not think that a mama would be someone who would have fun, for I am sure your mama would have loved to do all manner of enjoyable things with you, if she could.' He was struggling to keep his voice even as he spoke, desperate not to communicate his sudden, piercing distress to Lucy.

'Would she? I did not know.' She sounded wistful for a moment, but then she brightened perceptibly and said, 'Does this mean that Kate, Miss Moreton, would be my mama?'

'If you would wish her to be, yes, she would be. I believe she would be very glad if you considered her so.' He had command of himself now; it had merely been a moment, and he had overcome it.

'Truly?'

'Truly.'

She flung her arms around him and hugged him fiercely, and he held her for a moment, comforted by her joy. It was happy news, after all, and as a family they deserved a share of happiness after all the pain. 'Thank you, Papa!' It seemed she was so excited she could not keep still, for she jumped up and said, 'Does Grandmama know? And Wellington?'

'I believe your grandmama has some idea, but she does not know for sure, and I do not think that Wellington can have the least idea of it. Would you like to tell them?' She did not answer him, but dashed up the lawn at great speed, and before he could reach the terrace at his more sedate pace he heard excited barking, which he took to be Wellington's approval of the thrilling news.

The little dog became so infected with his mistress's mood that he would not let off barking and allow the adults to speak, so that Benedict was obliged to tell Lucy to go and run about with him until they were both more able to control themselves.

He sank into a seat beside his mother, and she smiled

at him somewhat mistily and said, 'I gather that Lucy was pleased, since I see her so in alt?'

He grinned at her boyishly, quite recovered now. 'She was, and Wellington too, plainly. I think she would have been near as glad to have me marry Margaret, only that Susan and Molly, not to mention Amy, of course, would be jealous. But no, I am funning. She asked if Miss Moreton would be her mama, and that, I think, was what delighted her the most.'

The Dowager was busy with her handkerchief for a moment, but then said briskly, 'My dear, I think you have made an excellent decision, and I am sure you will be very happy – all three of you, and one day, God willing, more than three.'

'Indeed, I hope so. Kate is coming to dinner this evening, Mama – it is time we began making plans.'

'An excellent idea,' she approved. 'Will you allow me to talk to her a little, privately, so that we can fix on a date that will suit her?' She saw his puzzled expression, and said, 'Women's business, you foolish boy. One does not merely choose a wedding date at random, without knowing if it will be . . . convenient for the lady.'

A slight flush of colour crept up into his cheeks as he apprehended her meaning. 'Of course you are right.'

'I often am. What is to be done about poor Theodore, Ben? Have you discussed it?'

'We have discussed almost nothing.' He feared he had coloured yet more deeply, as he recalled that they had kissed more than they had talked. But his mother, if she

113

saw, did not acknowledge it by any more than a twinkle in her eye. 'I must be guided by Kate, but I would think it a sad thing to wait for him to die – for that is what it would amount to – before we married. He is very gratified by our news, and although I imagine he will not attend our wedding, nor officiate as I am sure he would wish, I can only think that he would prefer it to be soon, so that he may see his granddaughter settled.'

'And you too would prefer it to be soon, I collect, dearest?'

'You are a wicked old woman. I refuse to be embarrassed by you. Yes, Mama dear, I would.'

She chuckled. 'I was born in a less mealy-mouthed age, and I have little patience with you young people and your refined sensibilities. But I will say nothing – nothing to *you*, at any rate. We must instead consider how we may provide for Theodore's comfort, so that Kate feels easy leaving him. Thank goodness Polly is a sensible girl with some experience of nursing, and Theodore likes her. I think it might be best if she is set to care for him, and we send someone else to look after the house, and we shall pay their wages, of course. I will put my mind to it.'

'Thank you, I think that will be a relief to her, and to him.'

'And before I forget, Kate's bride clothes will be my wedding gift to her. I think she will pay for dressing, as the saying goes – I cannot wait to see her outfitted becomingly, and I am sure you are in complete agreement.'

'I am, thank you, Mama. I had thought to set Maria to work, as shopping is what she enjoys above all things. I will write to her this afternoon, of course, as I expect will you, and then perhaps I can take Kate up to London as soon as may be arranged. While Maria is bankrupting you at her modiste's, I shall bustle about and obtain a licence, and set old Kinghorn to drawing up marriage settlements, and I know not what else. A wedding band, certainly, and a wedding gift for Kate.'

'What will you buy her, Ben?' He smiled again, considering the question, and her heart rejoiced to see it.

'Rubies, I think. You may tell Maria that I intend to buy her rubies, and to dress her accordingly.'

'Very good, I shall.' She hesitated for a moment, then said, 'Have you thought where you will live? I know you have had no chance to discuss it.'

'I do not mean to turn you out of doors, Mama.'

'I know you do not, but Kate should be mistress of her own household, and if I live with you, Dorothea must live with you, and then you cannot make better arrangements for Lucy.'

'Let me think on it further, and lay my suggestion before Kate. It is not fair that I should speak of such an important matter with anybody – even you – before her.'

'Of course it is not,' she said, regarding him with warm approval. 'And now I think you should go and find Lucy, for it is past time for her bath, which I expect she will sorely need, and we need to change for dinner. You have done a good day's work today, my dear.'

'Thank you, I believe that I have.'

'This time it will be different, and turn out happily, you will see.'

'I hope so. This is my last throw of the dice, Mama. I could not endure . . .'

'I know, my dear. Believe me, I know.'

CHAPTER SEVENTEEN

Kate was more than a little nervous as the tall, liveried coachman handed her into the elegant Silverwood chaise, and she smoothed out the skirts of her one silk gown around her. It was olive green, and she had last worn it at the grand Assembly Rooms in York when she had attended with her grandmother, in what seemed like another life.

After she had left her grandfather, who had been worn out by the emotion of the afternoon and had fallen asleep in mid-conversation, she had sat down to write to Nonna Albina, to tell her of her betrothal. She prevaricated a little, by choosing to write first to various friends from York to give them her news. Somewhat conventional letters, for the most part, and easy enough to write. There was a pupil of hers, though, who was like a younger sister to her – Cassandra – but this was like writing into the void. Cassandra Hazeldon had left Yorkshire to live with family in London after her father had died six months ago, and since then all Kate's letters had gone unanswered; she could not think that this one would be any different. It was entirely out of character for Cassandra to ignore her so, and the worry for her friend was a constant niggle at the back of her mind, but presently it was swept away in the effort of writing to Albina.

Kate could not so easily afford paper that she could be writing versions and tearing them up because they revealed more than she meant to say, so she proceeded very slowly and carefully, considering her words as she went. She did not by any means think that Albina would disapprove of her decision, for she knew her to be eminently practical beneath all her fine words and love of drama, but she found it oddly difficult to set down the thing in cold ink: *I know he does not love me, but I have decided to marry him anyway. Perhaps I am being foolish; perhaps I will regret it bitterly. Am I wrong, Grandmama? Am I making a terrible mistake?* She wanted to be calm and rational, or appear to be so; the last thing she desired was to write a letter that would betray the confusion in her heart and set a woman of near seventy storming back halfway across Europe – and Albina was quite capable of it – because her foolish granddaughter needed her. It was strange to think that she might well be married before this letter reached

Parma; almost certainly she would be before any reply could come.

She leant back against the coach's silk squabs and shook her head. She would be married . . . It was as well, she reflected drily, that the journey from the Vicarage to the Hall was such a very short one, for she hardly had time to start worrying afresh about Benedict, and the seductive pleasure of his kiss and the promise of much more, and all of her uncertain future with him, before she was pulling up by the house's imposing Palladian front, and the steps were being let down for her to alight. Benedict, looking very handsome in his evening clothes, was waiting for her, with Lucy at his side in her dressing gown and nightcap, her nursemaid hovering awkwardly a few paces away.

The little girl ran directly up to her and hugged her, crying, 'Kate, Miss Moreton, I am so glad!' and Kate returned the embrace with a full heart. 'I am supposed to be in bed,' Lucy confided, 'and I will go presently, if I must, but I am *not* being naughty, whatever Amy says, because Papa himself said that I could stay up just to greet you. I thought it was important, so that you knew directly that I am very happy that you are to be my mama, or otherwise you might think I was not, and be worried.'

'That was very thoughtful of you, my dear Lucy. I am very glad to hear it, for I can think of nothing in the world I would like better than to be your mama, if you will have me. Now I see that Amy is waiting to take you up, for it is very late, so may I kiss you good night?'

'You may, ma'am,' said Lucy in a very dignified, grown-up way, 'and I will kiss you, and Papa too, of course, so that he is not jealous.'

After a round of slightly sticky kisses, Lucy was borne inside, still protesting slightly for the sake of pride, and they were left alone. He offered her his arm, and she placed her gloved hand upon it. She felt suddenly bashful in his company, all the more because he was smiling warmly at her, and saying, 'You are in great good looks this evening, Kate. That colour is most becoming to you.'

'Thank you,' she murmured, and found herself suddenly tongue-tied.

He led her around the side of the house to the terrace – a walk that took several long minutes and which they accomplished in a somewhat awkward silence – where Lady Silverwood was sitting wrapped in her usual shawls and cap. 'Come and kiss me, my dear,' she said, and Kate crossed to her side, and dropped a shy kiss on her soft cheek. 'You look quite charming tonight. Sit by me. I shall not congratulate you, for I think that Benedict is rather to be congratulated on his good fortune than you, and that I have already done. I am very, very happy to welcome you into our family.'

'Thank you, ma'am!' she said, almost overcome. 'I do not seem to be able to say anything but thank you, but I do not know how else to express my gratitude for your kindness.'

'Stuff and nonsense,' said the Dowager. 'Sit down, Ben – do not loom over us so. We have a great deal to discuss.'

Lady Silverwood revealed her plans for Kate's bride clothes, and she could do nothing but stammer inadequate thanks again, for she did not have the means to fit herself out in the style that she knew would be necessary for her to do Benedict credit. She could see the sense of putting herself in the hands of Mrs Singleton, although when she had met that lady briefly some weeks ago she had found her quite intimidating, so very fashionable, brisk and bright-eyed as she was, and so very talkative and emphatic in her manner. She hoped that Benedict's stylish sister would be as ready to welcome her as the rest of her family had been; she feared she would not.

She had been puzzling over what should be done about her grandfather, and was very glad to hear of Lady Silverwood's plan, which she thought eminently sensible. She too did not care to think of herself as waiting for him to die, and said so; he was, she told them, very anxious to have the peace of mind that would come from seeing her wed, and this would do him more real good than any nursing care she could provide. As for his being lonely afterwards, the Dowager declared stoutly that she was not prepared to countenance any more foolishness about Mr Waltham being too proud to receive her in his bedchamber; she had been there once, and they had both survived it, and so she meant to be a regular visitor from now on, and she was sure that Dorothea would do the same when she returned from Bristol.

Benedict said, 'I am glad that we are all in such agreement. Kate, I have another matter I would like to discuss with you – will you allow me to accompany you home after dinner, and we can talk of it while we walk?' Perhaps she looked a little anxious, for he said reassuringly, 'It is no great matter, and I do not think it is anything that you would dislike, but it is something I should discuss with you before I speak to anyone else of it.'

She could do nothing but assent, and then it was time for them to go in to dinner. They were an awkward number, and so Lady Silverwood had directed that they should dine, as she and Sir Benedict often did when they were alone, in the small breakfast room; the table was round, and not very large, and so they were able to converse in a comfortable manner, without any stuffy formality as would be, the Dowager said with a smile, so ridiculous on what was, after all, a family occasion. 'And a celebration, too!' she said, raising her glass of champagne to each of them in turn.

CHAPTER EIGHTEEN

Benedict looked across the table at Kate, who sat smiling at something his mother had said and then made a reply that set the Dowager chuckling in her turn. She had been rather shy and conscious of some embarrassment when she had arrived, he thought, but she was easier now – perhaps the champagne had helped, for he hardly thought that she could be very accustomed to it.

He had not flattered her when he had told her she was in looks tonight; the dusky green gown did become her. Its dull sheen complemented her lustrous dark hair and glowing olive skin much better than pale muslins did, and it flowed in some places and clung in others in a way that he had observed immediately as she descended from the carriage. It had small, puffed sleeves, but they were covered by full oversleeves to the wrist in thin gauze dyed green to match the silk. There was something particularly tantalising about the glimpses they afforded of her round, bare arms beneath the filmy fabric. He had not seen her in evening dress before – or if, as his mother told him, he had seven years ago, he did not recall it – and heartily approved of the lower neckline it permitted, though that was modest by London standards; he supposed it would be lower when she was married, and he approved of that too, in anticipation.

She saw him watching her, and looked down, blushing under his regard. The wild flush crept down her neck and across her chest, and he wondered suddenly how far it went, and where exactly it stopped, and pictured it, and found himself hard as a poker all at once, and short of breath.

It was as well that the ladies chose at that moment to withdraw and leave him to sip his port in solitary splendour. He half-rose, and bowed more awkwardly than was his wont, encumbered as he was by his unexpected and most unwelcome erection. He subsided into his chair in relief as the door closed behind them, and set his mind to regaining his composure. Once again Kate's proximity had affected him as if he were a clumsy schoolboy rather than a grown man, a man of experience. He had been married, albeit briefly, he had taken what comfort he could from willing women's bodies after his wife had died, and not so long ago he had briefly set up a mistress. He was no rake, but neither was he a green boy. It was ridiculous to be so aroused, merely at the sight of Kate and the idea of touching her bare skin, and he must overcome such wild desires immediately. But then he thought of what the women were discussing – the date of the wedding – and the implications of it, and it scarcely helped. He leant back in his chair and stretched out his long legs, taking deep, calming lungfuls of air.

In her drawing room, the Dowager patted the sofa beside her and said to Kate, 'My dear, let us decide the most important thing – the date you are to be married! I have taken you aside to do this because in large part it depends on your situation.' Seeing that she looked confused at this statement, the Dowager laughed and said, 'Since the timing of the event is within your control, you need not choose to arrange it for the middle of your courses, or two days before they are due!'

Kate choked slightly at her frankness, but a moment's reflection convinced her that she was quite correct, and they bent their heads over the little almanac that Lady Silverwood carried in her reticule, and settled on a date in three weeks' time; far enough away to allow for all the necessary arrangements to be made, and close enough so that Mr Waltham (to say nothing of anybody else) should not become too impatient at the delay. Kate would of course be married in the village church, her grandfather's parish for so many years, so that if he could not be there, he could at least picture it quite clearly. Lady Silverwood had been married there herself – but not her son, who had married Vanessa in Town, though this was left unspoken – and it was in all respects very suitable.

So that was decided before Benedict joined them, and he was glad to hear it, and give his approval, although he quite understood that in such matters he had scarcely anything to say, as a mere man.

After a little while he said, 'Perhaps I should escort you home, Kate, so that we may have our discussion. I think it is not at all cold this evening, if you should not object to walking.'

'Of course not,' she said. 'I have my shawl.'

'A very good notion,' said the Dowager. 'Good night, my dears. Do not hurry your "discussion" in the slightest, for I shall not wait up, Ben!'

'My mother is quite impossible,' he murmured as he led her out of the grand door and down the front steps.

Kate laughed. 'She does not put me to the blush as much as she might, for my grandmother is far, far worse. My only consolation has always been that although her remarks are often made in public, and at no small volume, they are generally in Italian, which I hope may not be understood by most people.'

'If only my mother's were!' He hesitated and then said, 'The matter I wished to discuss with you was that of where we shall live.'

'Oh! How foolish of me – I had not given a thought to it. Everything has happened so quickly . . .'

'I know that you and my mother are disposed to be great friends, and believe me when I say that I am very glad of it, but she believes – and I agree – that you should be mistress of your own establishment.'

She made a sound of instinctive protest. 'I cannot be responsible for driving Lady Silverwood from her home! I could not countenance it!'

'No, I did not think you would. I am glad in one respect that there is no dower house on the estate, because the strain of the move would be injurious to her health, and yet she would insist upon undertaking it, if such a house existed.'

'What is to be done, then?'

He stopped, and turned, and gestured vaguely at the Palladian grandeur behind them, and she turned to consider it with him. The centre of the house was porticoed, and greatly resembled a Grecian temple constructed in white Portland stone; four huge Ionic columns supported a pediment, and in order to reach the grand front entrance on the first floor it was necessary to pass under an archway, and ascend a flight of steps. Perhaps if you had grown up here it might be possible to become accustomed to its magnificence; Kate could not imagine ever viewing it without a little shock of surprise and awe. It was beautiful in its classical symmetry, and it was so very large. It was built in the same classical style as the Assembly Rooms in York, which she had as a child considered the most magnificent building in the world, and a great source of pride for her hometown, but it was bigger. Much bigger. It was, in truth, a palace.

It seemed that Benedict was thinking along similar lines, for he said now, 'As you can see, we cannot be said to lack for space. I had thought that we might with very little labour bring some of the rooms in the west wing back into use, and my mother and Miss Sutton could remove there – something that could be done by degrees, so as not to place an undue burden on her constitution – and we could have what would amount to two separate establishments, with separate dining rooms and separate entrances. We should not then all need to live in each other's pockets each and every day. Miss Sutton could at that point retire on a pension, with no loss of face to her, and we could employ a younger and more suitable governess for Lucy, who would remain with us and yet still have her grandmother close by as she has been all her life. We would need a few extra staff, but many of my mother's more senior servants are too elderly, really, for their positions, and stay on through pride, and love of her. They could be pensioned off too, or go with her to lighter duties, depending on their wishes. What do you think?'

She frowned, and considered it. The main façade of the house was large and impressive, and the wings on each side were lower, balancing each other, but still of quite a substantial size. She had never entered either, but she knew that the one on the east side contained a ballroom that had lain unused for years; the western side she had no knowledge of at all, but any rooms there would surely be spacious enough, and at the rear would offer a fine prospect down the lawns to the river.

'It certainly would be less of a disruption for Lucy, and for everybody. Would it really not be too difficult to achieve?'

'Not at all. Such plans were drawn up in detail after my brother married, and the work was all but done, and then . . . sad events intervened, and they were set aside. I was not here to see it, and was not fully acquainted with what was done, but I went over the rooms this morning with Mr Luke, my steward, who was, and we were both of the opinion that it is mostly a matter of some decoration and cleaning, and should not take longer than a fortnight or so, if set to with a will.'

'I am sorry that you should be reminded of such sad things, Benedict.'

'It cannot be avoided. It is certainly not your fault.'

'So it is true that your mother agreed to the removal once?'

'She did, and the bedchambers there are upon the ground floor at the back, thus saving her the effort of climbing the stairs, which is a great nuisance to her in the winter, when her arthritis is very bad.'

'It seems ideal, then.'

'I am very glad that you approve it – I shall discuss

it with her on the morrow, and set everything in train. She will need to broach the matter with Miss Sutton when she returns from Bristol, but I think she can hardly object, as all is made new on the occasion of our marriage. Dorothea is very stubborn, but even she will not care to look like the bad fairy at the feast, and so I am sure that my mother will bring her about. I think in truth she is weary of teaching, and no wonder after thirty years of it, and her pride only requires a reason to stop.'

Kate could not help but laugh at the image of the gruff, eccentric Miss Sutton as any kind of fairy, and this inspired Benedict to tell her of Lucy's alternative suggestions of a bride for him, and her novel objections to the various candidates, and they were both chuckling as they walked on across the park.

When they reached the weathered door in the high brick wall, he turned to her and said, 'Of course I shall not leave you here, but escort you home. I am halting because, if I should be lucky enough to be able to kiss you again, it must be here, not on the Vicarage doorstep in full view of half the village.'

'Do you wish to kiss me?'

'I cannot allow that to be a serious question, so I am forced to the conclusion that you are flirting with me, Miss Moreton!' His voice was warm, and it was delicious for her to stand so close to him in the twilight, and know that he wanted to embrace her. She privately admitted herself eager to embrace him too.

'Flirting? I think I must be. I am sadly out of practice, I fear.'

'As am I!' he said, and took her in his arms.

She turned up her face to him, and their lips joined hungrily. It seemed that their bodies had decided opinions about their kiss earlier in the day: had very much objected to its being cut off so soon, and strongly approved of its being resumed. If there was a captious little voice in Kate's head that, despite her promise, still tried to prevent her surrendering herself to enjoyment by detailing the myriad ways in which this was a bad idea, it was drowned out by the pounding of the blood in her veins.

Benedict's tongue darted into her mouth, and, after a moment of surprised stillness from Kate when he feared he had gone too far, hers came to meet it, tentatively at first and then with a passion to match his own. Their mouths were wide open, and after a while he pulled away slightly, but only so that he could suck on her full, sensual lower lip, and nip at it gently with his teeth. She moaned deliciously against him, and he deepened the kiss once more, thrusting into her warm wetness with his eager tongue. Good God . . .

He found that he was cupping her face in both his hands, and had pushed her back against the wooden door, pressing her against it with the full length of his body. He was aroused again, as hard as he had ever been in his life, and the knowledge that she could surely feel it through the thin fabrics that covered her excited him all the more. Her hands were tangled in his hair, holding him to her, as if there were any need. He feathered tiny kisses along her cheek and the line of her jaw, and murmured, 'Sweet Kate!' into her silky curls.

'Benedict . . .' she gasped, and her voice brought him back to his senses. Was he, Benedict Silverwood, father, baronet, magistrate, bloody churchwarden, really going to anticipate his marriage and have his bride – the Vicar's virgin granddaughter, no less – up against the door of his estate? Pull up her skirts to bare her lush thighs and . . . *Stop it, Silverwood!*

He groaned, and buried his face deeper in her hair, releasing the pressure on her body just a little. 'I do not want to let you go,' he groaned at last. 'I think you are able to tell that all my desire is urging me to quite another conclusion. But we must not do this.'

'I suppose we must not,' she whispered. 'It would be very wrong.' He liked that she was not coy; she did not pretend that she did not understand him. But her soft breath against his skin inflamed him all the more, and he ran his thumb over her kiss-swollen lips, and shook his head ruefully.

'It would be very right. It would be glorious – for me, at least. But no, I shall have you first in a bed, Kate, when we are properly married, and take my time to make it wonderful for you, and such dangerous amusements as this may come later. I hope they may.'

She buried her face in his coat, and he held her loosely, resisting the strong impulse to pull her closer again and take up where he had left off, inhaling the intoxicating scent of her hair and trying not to regret that he must always be so damn sensible and dutiful. Where had being sensible ever got him in the past?

CHAPTER NINETEEN

The first thing that Lady Silverwood had done when Benedict had told her his news was sit down and write a missive to her daughter, Maria Singleton, and her son had done the same. The notes had both been taken by the fast mail coach, and the following afternoon brought not a reply, but Mrs Singleton herself, by private conveyance, with her husband to bear her company. A journey of some thirty miles was not to be undertaken lightly, and so their arrival could be seen as ominous. Presumably she had not come so far merely because she was eager to offer her felicitations to the affianced couple in person.

It might be considered fortunate for family harmony that on her arrival Maria should find her brother gone out on business about the estate, so that she was able to speak to her mother alone, Mr Singleton being firmly adjured to amuse himself, which he chose to do without any grumbling – perhaps he had heard quite enough of his wife's views on the subject of her brother's nuptials already – by going into Sir Benedict's library, sitting in the most comfortable chair, putting the newspaper over his face, and falling instantly asleep.

Mrs Singleton greatly resembled her mother, being a small, bird-like woman, with sharp blue-grey eyes and a sharper tongue. She was very fashionably dressed in a Pomona-green pelisse with elaborate braided decoration, and she was engaged for a few moments in removing this garment, along with her enormous Oldenburg bonnet and kid gloves, and handing them to the hovering butler, while her mother waited patiently, an ironical quirk of the lips the only sign that she was aware of what was coming. It was not until the door closed behind the servant that the younger lady said, 'Mama! What is this nonsense that you and my brother have been telling me?'

'Do sit down, Maria. You know I have the greatest dislike of people standing over me.'

Her daughter huffed impatiently and subsided into an elegant pink satin chair.

'That's better, dear. I hope you are quite well, and Singleton, and all the children? These hot days can be so trying.'

'Mama!'

The Dowager smiled and said, 'It is not nonsense,

Maria. You had your chance; you had a whole Season to find Benedict a bride, and you did not do so.'

'Only because he would not co-operate! I told you, he was excessively vexing! He attended every event I asked him to, that is perfectly true, and danced every dance, and made polite conversation, and even smiled, but he was not . . . he was not really present. You know how he can be!'

'I do indeed,' sighed her mother. 'But he is present now, I think. Really, Maria, I suggested Miss Moreton as a bride for him out of desperation, because when he laid out again his concerns for Lucy it suddenly occurred to me that she would answer admirably, in a way that no one else would, and he must marry somebody, after all. But honestly, my dear, I think I have hit on the very thing. He sees her – do you understand me? He looks at her and actually sees her in front of him, in a way that I do not think he has really seen a woman since Vanessa died.'

Her daughter snorted. 'I understand from the gossip in Town that he had until a few months gone been "seeing" plenty of a bold, bouncing young woman with brassy golden hair – surely dyed – who drives about the park in a vulgar yellow barouche, so I have not the least idea what you mean!'

'I dare say you may be right, Maria, but you surely know that that is not the same. You would scarcely expect him to marry her!'

'Of course not, unless he had run mad!'

'Well, then.'

'Well, then?! I can only think that you have run mad yourself, to have decided that he should marry a spinster governess – do not split hairs, Mama, she might as well be a governess – with not a penny in the world and nothing to recommend her!'

'Kate Moreton is a young woman of intelligence, sense and good feeling. Lucy adores her, and she adores Lucy – you know how important that is to your brother. Her birth is unexceptionable, her manners are excellent, and when she is properly dressed she will be a beauty. It is true she has no money; Ben has enough for both of them. Do you really think it wise, besides, that he should marry a girl who reminds him in any way of Vanessa? He plainly has not the slightest wish to do so, and no wonder. Your objections are frivolous, Maria.'

'Frivolous?!' that lady spluttered.

'Yes, frivolous. If you had induced him to be interested – even just a little interested – in one of the many pretty debutantes whom I am sure set their caps at him, I would have stifled my doubts about the wisdom of such a match, and my worries for Lucy and for him, and been all complaisance. But you could not, or he would not; it amounts to the same thing. You told me he could not distinguish one of them from another, and well do I believe it. And yet here he is, all afire with plans for the wedding and for how we shall live, and speaks of how he will buy rubies for Kate's wedding gift. Rubies, Maria! Tell me truly if you could imagine the man you say he was in London talking of buying rubies, with a foolish smile on his face that reminded me for a moment of how he used to be years ago!' Lady Silverwood fanned herself vigorously, for she had become quite heated in her agitation.

Her shaft hit home. 'Rubies, you say!' mused Mrs Singleton, with an arrested look in her eyes. 'But Mama, he has only been home three days or so. You cannot mean to tell me that he has fallen in love with this girl in that time, for I would not believe it.'

'No, he has not done that, yet, though I hope he may, but he is interested in her, and he desires her, too.'

Mrs Singleton all but rolled her eyes in exasperation in a most unladylike fashion. 'Must you always be talking in that vulgar way, Mama? So he desires her; what has that got to say to anything? I am sure he does! I dare say she may be laying out all manner of lures to catch him and keep him. She can never have dreamt of such a prize, at her age, and in her circumstances.'

Her mother laughed. 'No, dear, she lays out no lures. She is a perfectly respectable young woman, though I do not know how long she will stay respectable, the way your brother looks at her; luckily the engagement is to be a short one. And as for being vulgar, I would rather be vulgar than ridiculous, and I imagine you would not wish him to marry a woman he does not desire, if you want him to be setting up his nursery without delay? I am sure I do not know how you contrived to have your children, dear, without being a little vulgar with Singleton every now and then.'

'Mother!' Maria looked suitably shocked, but met her mother's eyes and suddenly burst out laughing. 'Mother, you are terrible! I own there may be something in what you say. But I shall reserve judgement for a while, and see for myself. I still cannot think it a good match, whatever you say. He could do so much better, you can surely see that!'

The Dowager brushed aside her objections, as a gnat. 'It greatly depends on what you mean by "better", does it not? You will come to own that I am right, dear, you will see. But now I am glad that you are here, for you can stay the night – I assume you intended to, and have brought valises, as the afternoon is well advanced already? I shall have Mrs Smith make your room up – and carry Kate back to London with you tomorrow and take her to your modiste to order her bride clothes.'

Mrs Singleton opened her mouth and then closed it again; there was no point arguing with her mother when she got the bit between her teeth, whatever her continuing reservations. 'Very well, Mama,' she said with artificial patience. 'Do you have any commissions for me?'

'Dear girl, I most certainly do . . .'

Benedict had small objection to make when he returned home and the idea was put to him. 'A very good notion,' he said approvingly. 'I will go over and see Miss Moreton now to make sure that she can be ready in time, and that Mr Waltham will manage without her, for I assume that it will mean an overnight stay for her at the least, perhaps two. Oh, and you need not trouble to make room in the chaise for her, Maria; I mean to come too and carry out my urgent business in Town, so I will take her up in my curricle.' And he was gone in haste, striding out the door, before his sister could reply.

The Dowager gave her daughter a very speaking look. '*Now* do you understand what I mean, Maria?'

Maria waved her hand dismissively. 'Oh, it is certainly true that I have not seen him so animated this age, for he walked through the Season like one in a dream. It is excessively provoking, and I am still cross with him when I think of it! If only I had known that all I needed to do to capture his attention was to find an impoverished governess at her last prayers and dangle him in front of her, I might have done so myself, and saved you the trouble! Well, I hope you may be right, Mama, and we shall see, shall we not?'

'When have you ever known me to be wrong, dear child?' said her mother with unruffled placidity.

CHAPTER TWENTY

Kate approved the London plan, for she knew she would be obliged to meet Mrs Singleton and enlist her aid in assembling her trousseau, so it might as well be now as later, but she could not help but feel nervous when Benedict suggested that she dine yet again at the Hall in order to properly make the acquaintance of his sister and brother-in-law. She could not refuse him, though, whatever her private fears regarding his sister's attitude. He argued – and she could see the force of his argument – that it would present a very odd appearance indeed for her to arrive to stay with Mr and Mrs Singleton when she had hardly met her, and him not at all. 'It will mean the green silk again!' she said a little despairingly.

'I have no objections to the green silk,' he said with a wicked smile. 'Perhaps Polly should iron it directly? For

I imagine it may have become somewhat crumpled when last you wore it.'

'Oh, you are as bad as your mother!' she said, blushing and laughing, and he seized her about the waist and kissed her swiftly, and then left her to her packing. Her grandfather was very pleased to give his assent to the scheme, and to know that she would soon be outfitted as she deserved, and Polly was quite willing and able to take particular care of him while she was away.

Benedict did not send the carriage this evening, but arrived himself, walking across the park again. He seemed to be taking every opportunity that he could to spend time with her, and Kate tried not to dwell too much on what this might signify. Tomorrow they would be several hours close together in his curricle, although there would be a groom behind them, she supposed.

They walked along the village street arm in arm, and a quite surprising number of people seemed to find occasion to emerge from their cottages as if by accident, and greet them with a raised cap or a bobbed curtsey. 'I see Polly has been busy,' he said, as he acknowledged quite the twentieth salutation with a smile and a word.

'It need not have been Polly, though I expect it was,' replied Kate ruefully. 'I am sure all the servants at the Hall know too, for there has been such a number of visits between us, and dinner last night, and again tonight, and your meeting with Mr Luke . . .'

'Does it make you uncomfortable, Kate? I am sorry, but I cannot see how it is to be avoided. I shall tell the servants formally tomorrow morning, for the announcement will appear in the *Morning Post* and the *Gazette* in the next few days, you know, and then it will be in a sense official.'

'It does not bother me. Nobody has said anything unkind.'

'I should think not!'

She shook her head; that was easy for him to say, from his secure social position. But it was true; she had met curious stares as she walked through the village, but nothing more. She did not know if Benedict's status protected her, or the respect in which everyone held the vicar. It could be nothing to do with her, surely, for she had spent almost all her time either teaching Lucy or with her grandfather, so that she was barely known to anybody, apart from having seen them in church every Sunday. She had led such a very quiet life in the past few months that it was strange now to be thinking of going to London on a shopping expedition. Miss Moreton of York had been lively and gregarious once, with a reputation for a pleasing wit and a wide circle of friends and acquaintances, besides her pupils, and she supposed that she might be so again when she became – it was hard to accustom herself to the thought – Lady Silverwood.

He opened the door to the park, and allowed her to precede him through it. Closing it behind him, he said with a perfectly straight face, 'Sadly we must not linger here, Kate, no matter how much we might wish to, for my sister will be waiting impatiently to meet you!'

She was beginning to take his measure now, and to see that he took wicked pleasure in causing her confusion, and so she snorted in an unladylike fashion, and said, 'I see that you are trying to provoke me, sir, and I think it most ungentlemanlike of you. I suppose I will never be able to pass through this door again without you putting me to the blush.'

'Oh, Kate, I hope not, for putting you to the blush . . . is so very enjoyable!'

'Disgraceful!' she said, laughing, and walked away from him in a determined fashion, and he followed her meekly enough, slightly to her disappointment. She supposed in all truth that she did not wish him, right at this moment, to shove her in an ungentle manner against the weathered wood and commence kissing her till she swooned, pausing only to whisper endearments in her ear. Well, no, she did wish it, of course, but it would not do. Polly had had a terrible time getting the creases out of her gown, and she could not appear at dinner looking a fright. Possibly he might accompany her home again tonight; she wondered if he would think of it.

Benedict caught up with her, and presented his arm with a little bow, and she put her hand on it. 'Perhaps I might escort you home once more, Kate, if the evening is fine,' he said, as if echoing her thoughts, with the smile that wreaked such havoc on her precarious composure. She tried to preserve an impassive countenance, but her lips curved in an anticipatory smile against her will, and she licked them involuntarily. 'Quite so,' he said outrageously.

It was fortunate that a heightened colour became Kate, as it did not often become ladies with a paler complexion, for when she arrived on the terrace with blushing cheeks and bright eyes it merely made Mrs Singleton think her, grudgingly, a handsome enough girl. If Mr Singleton's views diverged from his helpmeet's in any way, he was not such a fool after fifteen years of marriage as to make them known to her.

Kate found her prospective sister-in-law civil enough – her welcome was correct, but little more, and there was a certain stiffness in her manner, and an absence of warmth. Her heart sank, for she could see that Mrs Singleton was by no means reconciled to the match, and on reflection she could not wonder at it. It made for a little awkwardness, but Benedict and his mother were at great pains to make her feel at ease, and it seemed to her that even Mr Singleton smiled on her kindly, and attempted to convey a certain sympathy for her, albeit without the use of actual words. Perhaps, she thought, Maria would relent towards her in time; she could see that she was a woman of decision, and strong opinions, and it had been Kate's experience that such people were never quick to like ideas that were not of their own devising.

The evening was not one of unclouded ease, then, but still, there were plans to be discussed. Kate had tried all her life not to be shallow, but she had often feared that she might be, and the talk of velvets, lace and silks, gowns and pelisses and spencers, bonnets and shawls, which commenced once the ladies had withdrawn to leave the gentlemen over their port, could not fail to be delightful to her.

The Dowager looked at her thoughtfully and said, 'I can well imagine the colours that will become you, Kate. That green is perfect, and a darker green too, I think. Dull gold, and deep pink, and red. All shades of red. And rich brown, too, and ivory. No pastel colours.'

'No,' agreed Kate. 'It has been a sad trial to be obliged to wear them. You cannot conceive what a perfect fright I look in pale blue or pale green. When I was a little girl,' she said wistfully, smiling at her own foolishness, 'I always wanted a red velvet gown above all things.'

'And you shall have one, my dear,' said Lady Silverwood warmly, 'and I am sure that nothing will suit you half as well.'

'Unless it might be the dull gold,' insisted her daughter.

'She shall have both.'

'She shall have both, and Benedict shall say which becomes her best,' said Mrs Singleton a little maliciously.

'What shall I say?' asked her brother as he came into the room with his brother-in-law.

'You shall say which new gown becomes Miss Moreton best,' said Maria, 'for Mama thinks that red will be most becoming, and I think dull gold, and we shall soon see who is right.'

'Oh, no,' said Benedict, 'I am not such a fool as all that, I thank you. Do you think that I am wet behind the ears? I shall say that all gowns suit Kate equally, and I am sure it will be true, and she will look delightful in all, or why else would ladies of such excellent taste have chosen them? What do you think, John?'

'Quite right,' Mr Singleton said stoutly. '"Agree with everything, admit nothing" is my motto, Ben!'

'And one that I shall follow to the letter,' said Benedict with a smile.

Mrs Singleton said suddenly, frowning, 'Oh, I had meant to ask you – where do you intend to go for your honeymoon? For you will find no lodging in Brighton at such short notice at this time of year, you know, yet you would not wish to go to anywhere dowdy and depressing, I am sure. And I presume you do not mean to take Lucy with you, but will leave her here with us?'

'Yes, I think it would be better if she remains here with her cousins. She has been looking forward to your coming to stay ever since it was first projected, and is delighted at the prospect of playing with Jane and Anna. It would be cruel to deprive her of it, and it will give us more freedom in where we go and what we choose to do, if we do not have to concern ourselves about keeping her amused all day.'

The Dowager seemed to make a slight choking noise, but declared herself perfectly well when her son enquired solicitously if she were ill, and needed her vinaigrette.

A honeymoon! Kate had not thought of it, but she supposed that it was quite usual, and that it might be easier to begin their married life together with some time alone. Entirely alone . . .

Benedict said now, 'I do not know what you would prefer, Kate – perhaps we should discuss it in private?'

'I do not think I have any very strong views on the topic – I had not previously considered it at all,' she said, determined to ignore the wicked glint that she thought she saw in his eye. 'I suppose it would be tedious to go very far afield and have a long journey to get there, and I do not think I would greatly care to be visiting very many sites of historical interest, unless you should particularly care to do so, Benedict?'

'I would not,' he said firmly. 'Trailing around an historic cathedral and being instructed by some dull book to admire the flying buttresses, whatever they may be, is not at all to my taste.' He hesitated and then said, 'I had wondered if we might not consider going to Somerford House.'

'Why, that is a capital idea!' said the Dowager, her eyes bright with approval.

'Is it not let still?' said Mrs Singleton. 'Surely it has always been let?'

Benedict smiled at Kate and explained, 'Somerford House is the manor house in which my mother was born, and spent a very happy childhood. It is near Cirencester, so a little more than fifty miles from here – not so very far. It had been let for many years to an elderly gentleman who was a notable historian and scholar – there are many interesting Roman remains in the area,

Kate, but we need not trouble ourselves with them unless we wish to – who died some three months past. As he had allowed the place to fall into sad disorder, I took the opportunity to do some refurbishment before we looked for new tenants. It is not a large house, but very old and full of character: cosy, I should call it, and the countryside around it is very fine.'

'It sounds perfect,' Kate said. 'Could it be made ready in time?'

'I think it could, but I will enquire further into the matter. The furniture is still all in place, I know, so I do not see why it should not be possible. I spent a night there when I went up from London last month to look it over, and it was comfortable enough. It was not set up to receive a lady then, but I believe that could be achieved without too much trouble.'

The Dowager said comfortably, 'I am sure you would like it enormously, Kate, and what is particularly pleasing is that there would be no need to be burdened with a great number of servants. I expect that, if you should decide to go, Mrs Thompson might be persuaded to come out of retirement to accompany you and cook for you, for she was born there too and has any number of relatives in the village that she is always happy to visit. I should think she would be able to find extra maids or gardeners for you, too, if you should need them.'

'That is an excellent notion, Mama!' Benedict smiled.

Maria grimaced. 'Well, for my part, I cannot imagine what you would find to do in such an out-of-the-way place to keep yourselves amused, but it is quite your affair, of course.'

There was a short, electric silence, which Mr Singleton broke in heroic fashion by saying stolidly, 'Fishing. Excellent fly fishing in those parts, if you should care for it, Ben. Do you fish, Miss Moreton?'

'I have never done so, sir,' she replied gratefully, refusing to meet her betrothed's eye or even glance in his direction, 'but even if I did not care for it, I am sure that I should not object to sitting on a riverbank reading a book while Benedict fished, and if he should happen to catch anything, I will promise to eat it.'

'I will make sure to bring a wide selection of reading material with us,' said Benedict with a perfectly straight face. 'I should not wish you to be bored.'

'You are all consideration, sir!' she replied with tolerable composure.

'I hope you will always find me so, my dear.' Their eyes met, and held, and a tiny, charged moment stretched between them.

The Dowager cleared her throat. 'I am sure that Mr Waltham will be anxious about Kate, as it grows so late,' she said untruthfully. 'So I think it is time for you to escort her home, Benedict. You will all have to be up betimes for your journey to Town.'

Kate bade Lady Silverwood and the Singletons good night, and Benedict escorted her away.

When the door had closed behind them, Maria asked her mother incredulously, 'Does he really walk across the park with her as if they were a parlourmaid and footman on their half-day, and kiss her in the shrubbery?'

'Oh, my dear, I do hope so!' her mother said.

'And why not, I should like to know, Maria?' agreed Mr Singleton unexpectedly, for he was not in the normal way of things a sparkling conversationalist, and sometimes his wife forgot that he was there at all for minutes at a time. 'Dashed fine girl, young fellow, engaged couple, wedding in a fortnight or so, fine balmy evening, park full of shrubbery – if they can't have a kiss and a cuddle now, when can they do it, eh?'

'I am sure I have always remarked most particularly on your excellent good sense, John,' said the Dowager, and her son-in-law looked startled, but gratified, as they all made their way to bed.

CHAPTER TWENTY-ONE

"A wide selection of reading material"! I suppose
you think that you are extremely amusing,
sir!' said Kate as they made their way across the lawn
in front of the house.

'Do not you, Kate? That is a sad thing for a man to
hear his betrothed say when it has barely been a day
since their engagement was agreed upon. I am sure
that it takes longer, in the normal way of things, for a
young lady to begin to find her husband dull! At least
let them actually be married before such a discovery
is made!'

'I do not think you dull, sir, merely incorrigible!'

'That is a fortunate circumstance. Only let us reach
what I am already resolved to call *our* door, and I shall
show you how very right you are. I will one day point

out the hallowed place to children of ours, and say, "It was in this very place that your mother and I—"'

'You will do no such thing!' she said, while thinking that it was exactly the sort of thing that he might do.

'I shall not, of course, my dear, if you should not like it,' he replied promptly, and with suspicious meekness. She eyed him warily, wondering what next he might say to tease her, and, if he could not see her regard quite clearly in the dusk, he seemed to feel it, for he chuckled, and took her hand, and drew her swiftly on to their destination.

They paused by the door, as if by mutual agreement, and its very proximity and the recollections that it called up had already set her blood throbbing in her veins. He reached out and traced the line of her lips with one finger. 'You have such a kissable mouth, Kate,' he said huskily. 'Your lower lip particularly, so full and sensual . . . It stirs all manner of thoughts in me that I should be very sorry to be forced to share with anyone, except perhaps you, soon enough.'

He lowered his lips to hers, and she met them gladly, but this time he did not hold her face or stroke her hair, as he had always done when he kissed her before. His hands were on her body. They ran down the curve of her back, and reached her buttocks, and cupped them, lifting them to pull her against him. She could feel the warmth and strength of his hands through the layers of thin silk and linen that covered her. She was emboldened to touch him too, and she slipped her

153

hands inside his coat – he was no dandy; it was loose enough to permit her to do so – and allowed herself to explore the corded muscles of his back though his shirt and waistcoat.

He took his lips from hers, but only so that he could kiss her neck, his breath hot on her skin. He found the pulse that beat so hard in her throat, and pressed his mouth to it. His thigh nudged hers apart, and he lifted her to settle her against him; her shoulders were pressed against the door, but her lower body was supported by his. If he had released her, she thought in some corner of her brain, she would have fallen, but he did not release her. His hands gripped and squeezed the soft flesh of her bottom, and she felt the hardness of his thigh against her most sensitive places, the thin fabrics between them very little barrier. His lips traced lower, trailing fiery kisses across her shoulders and down to the upper slopes of her breasts, pushing down the silk that covered them, and all the while he was pressing her against him – his lips, his exploring hands, his thigh – and she became aware that she was gripping him back in a shockingly wanton manner, something that seemed to be quite beyond her conscious control, the muscles in her inner thighs clasping him by some deep instinct, riding him, the slippery silk of her gown aiding the delectable motion. And she was pressing her shoulders back against the door, thrusting her barely covered breasts up at him, offering them to him shamelessly. And moaning. She was moaning.

'Benedict!' she gasped.

'Yes, sweet Kate?' he murmured against her skin between kisses.

'You said you would not . . . You said that when you . . . had me, it would be in a bed. When we are married. Not here. Dangerous amusements, you said.' Perhaps her words would have carried more weight if she could have stopped herself from gripping his hard thigh between hers, or stilled her instinctive motion, or if she had the strength to push his head away. At least she had not wound her fingers in his hair and held his hot mouth to her breasts, urging him on, but then, he did not seem to need any urging.

'And I swear that that is still my intention. Trust me for that. But that is not a reason to deny you a little pleasure . . . May I pleasure you, Kate, with my mouth and my fingers? I promise I will do no more.'

His words hung between them in the warm, still evening air for a moment. Another woman might have pretended not to understand him, might even genuinely not have apprehended his meaning. But not Kate. She knew exactly what sinful temptation he was offering her. And she wanted it. She wanted his hands touching her most secret places; she wanted the release that he promised her.

'Yes,' she heard herself moan, most shockingly. 'Oh, Benedict, yes!'

And then he loosened his hold on her, but only so that he could, outrageously, wonderfully, pull up her skirts, and slip one hand beneath them. His fingers skimmed the soft skin at the top of her stockings, a fleeting caress, but did not linger there; he continued on in delicious exploration, tangling in her curls, seeking and finding the taut, swollen nub between her lips and stroking it. 'Ahh! There, sweet Kate? Should you like it if I touch you there?'

'Yes!' she gasped. *I am truly dead to all shame*, she thought, and then she did not think anything at all, but only felt, as he pressed his clever fingers against her, finding a rhythm and slipping to and fro in her wetness. She was already wet for him.

He groaned, 'I do not have enough hands for everything I want to do to you!' but he seemed to be managing well enough, for he used the hand that was not so scandalously occupied to push her gown down from her shoulders and free her breasts completely from her bodice. He murmured in satisfaction, 'My God, you are spectacular!' and then he could say no more, for his lips were on her erect nipple, brushing it gently, tantalisingly at first, and then sucking on it hungrily, pulling it deep into his mouth. She moaned in encouragement, and his hand went to the other breast, and cupped it, finding the nipple and rolling it between his fingers. It was wonderful, all of it.

She gave herself up to him and to sensation, her hands clinging to his back – somehow she had found his warm bare skin under his shirt – her head back, gasping, her breasts thrust forward for his kisses and caresses, her sex pressing into his hand as he stroked her with clever fingers. She felt the pleasure building inside her, moving towards release, and he must have sensed it too, for his caresses became more urgent, the pressure firmer, his mouth and his fingers more demanding, more insistent.

It was too much. She came in glorious waves, moaning his name.

He pushed his thigh back between hers, and dragged her skirts up even higher, so that she was naked and wet against the knitted silk of his pantaloons. 'Ride it out on me,' he commanded her, and then both his hands found her bare buttocks, and his fingers splayed across them, squeezing them together, pulling them apart a little, squeezing them together, and he ground his body urgently against her, while his mouth plundered her breasts. She freed her hands from his coat, and tanged her fingers in his hair, and held his head to her, as he sucked her harder, and she rode his silk-covered thigh in intense waves of pleasure, and he gripped her, and held her, and thrust himself against her softness, harder and faster.

'My God!' he gasped against her at last. 'My God, Kate!'

She whimpered, and he laughed shakily. 'Kate Moreton, I have just come in my drawers like a schoolboy, and it was wonderful! Thank you!'

She shook her head, unable to speak, and he dipped his mouth to her breasts again, murmuring, 'One last kiss . . .' and trailed his lips across her sensitised skin to capture one swollen peak for a moment and swirl his tongue around it. 'I cannot let you go!' he groaned against her wet, tingling flesh. 'But I know I must!' Then regretfully he adjusted her gown to cover her, and pulled down her skirts, smoothing them over her legs, holding her firmly all the while, as he seemed to know that she was she was weak and boneless, and had lost her sense of balance.

He took her in his arms, and she buried her face in his shirt. They stood together in the darkness, while he stroked her hair and she trembled in his hold.

At last she said, 'I should go.'

He sighed. 'I suppose you should. Let me look at you.'

She moved away from him, though it cost no small effort to do so. 'Do I appear . . . ?'

She could see that he was tempted to make her a scandalous answer, but he did not. He merely arranged the folds of her shawl a little more securely about her shoulders, the tips of his fingers brushing her skin, but not lingering, and said, 'I think you – we, for I can only imagine the state of my neckcloth – will pass casual scrutiny. Besides, there should be few people about at this hour, and those that are about are probably also up to no good, and in no position to judge us.'

They passed through the door, and made their way along the silent street with only the waning moon to guide them. Most of the cottages were dark and shuttered, as he had said; it was grown very late. There were a few cats out about their secret nocturnal business, but nothing else stirred.

'I would not have believed three days ago that I would be "up to no good" in the woods and creeping through the village fearing observation, as if I were a poacher,' she whispered ruefully. 'What have you done to me, Benedict Silverwood?'

'I could say the same, Miss Moreton. I have always been eminently respectable, so I can only presume that you are a bad influence.' His voice was low and warm with laughter.

She felt giddy with pleasure, saying shakily, 'I? You may ask anyone in York, and they will tell you that I have a spotless reputation, and am highly esteemed for my learning, my musical abilities and my proficiency in teaching the Italian tongue. I am, too, the granddaughter of a gentleman in holy orders: a spinster whose name has never attracted a breath of scandal.'

'A spinster, you? I think not! Ah, Kate, I wonder when I shall next taste that Italian tongue of yours?' he said softly, as they arrived at her doorstep. 'We shall be together for hours in my curricle, thigh to thigh, and Sykes up behind us, and me unable to lay so much as a finger on you. Torture, my dear, I assure you!'

'For me too . . .' she breathed, and took her key from her reticule to put it in the lock, and opened the door. She looked back for a last glimpse of him, and saw that he was standing smiling, his hair and neckcloth sadly disordered, kissing his fingers to her; a charmingly courtly, old-fashioned gesture, it would have appeared to any observer, if they had not known the forbidden, delicious use to which those fingers had been put, just a few moments ago.

CHAPTER TWENTY-TWO

Kate looked up to see Benedict watching her, his eyes glittering in the candlelight. 'I can't take my eyes off you,' he said huskily.

She was wearing one of her new gowns – dark red velvet, embroidered on the bodice, such as it was, with deeper red silk – and rubies, the magnificent rubies he had bought her as a wedding gift. Surely she was ridiculously overdressed for a dinner *à deux* in the country, but when she had said as much to him during dinner, he had merely chuckled and said that that would be remedied soon enough. She had to admit to herself that she had known that he would say that; it seemed that she was flirting again. With her husband.

They had married early that morning. Kate had gone into her grandfather's chamber in her ivory silk wedding gown before she had left for church; he had grasped her hand with all his feeble strength and said, 'You look beautiful, my dear! You remind me of your grandmother, and your poor mother on her wedding day.'

She smiled down at him. 'I am only sorry that you cannot officiate, Grandpapa. It seems wrong to see Mr Newman standing where you should be standing, more than ever today.'

'He will do well enough, for all his voice does not have the carrying quality one might wish for. He is a good fellow. But Kate . . .'

She sat on the bed beside him. 'What is it, dear?'

'I hope you will be truly happy. I know . . . I hope that you do not enter into this marriage only to ease my mind. I would be sorry to think that.'

'If I am to be truthful with you, I might have thought to use you as an excuse, even to myself. Does that make sense to you?'

His tired, old face looked concerned, and the lines carved by pain deepened. 'Yes, my dear, but that is not—'

She shook her head to stop him. 'I might have done, but I did not. I lay awake all night puzzling it out, when you told me of what Lady Silverwood proposed, and in the end I was forced to admit that I wanted to marry Benedict, and any other justifications I might use were shams. So once I had admitted as much to myself, it was only a question of whether it would be right after all to do it. And then when the Dowager came to see me, she gave me so many good, unselfish reasons – reasons entirely unconnected with my own inclinations, which might still be selfish – that I thought I could see my way to it. She told me that the real question was if I was brave enough, and she was right to put it so, for all life is a risk, is it not? To marry, to care for someone, is to risk losing them. Who should know that better than you? But now it is time, and if I do not leave directly I will be late for church, dear Grandpapa. We will come back and see you before we leave.'

She rose to her feet, and kissed him gently on his wrinkled cheek, and he kissed her hand, and watched her go.

It had been agreed that Mrs Singleton and her husband would walk across the park and accompany her to the church; it was only a few steps away from the Vicarage. Maria was very smart in a blue silk pelisse, and Mr Singleton offered Kate his arm, smiled at her reassuringly, and told her she looked fine as fivepence. They stopped in the church porch so that Maria could look her over; that lady twitched at her Brussels lace veil to bring it into more graceful folds, until she pronounced herself satisfied at last. 'You look splendid,' she said a little abruptly. She was not a woman who often displayed the softer emotions, but it almost seemed as though her eyes were bright with tears now, and her voice was certainly slightly constricted. 'I cannot say when I have seen a lovelier bride. My brother is a very lucky man, and I hope he knows it! Be good to him, will you, Kate?'

Kate was surprised, and touched, for she had thought Maria still somewhat hostile to her marriage, but she had no time to make her any sort of answer other than a stammered yes, for Miss Sutton arrived at that moment with Lucy and her cousins, Jane and Anna, who were all to be her bridal attendants. They were very fine in new gowns, which matched, as Lucy excitedly pointed out to her, and Kate's heart was glad to see the child so happy. It took some time to marshal the elated little girls into order, and then Mrs Singleton and her old governess slipped inside, and Kate took Mr Singleton's arm, and it was time. It was a true family affair: Mr Singleton would give her away, and his eldest son, James, a tall boy of fourteen, would stand as Benedict's groomsman. She was at the last moment sorry only that her grandmother could not be there by her side, but was a thousand miles away.

The ceremony was something of a blur; she could recall scarcely more than Benedict's beautiful deep voice making his responses. She knew that she had looked at him, and he at her, when they had both promised to worship each other with their bodies. Perhaps that was a shocking thing to be thinking of, in a church, during one's wedding ceremony, but then, she reflected, they could hardly be the first. The words were there for a reason.

The wedding breakfast was brief, and chiefly notable for the girls becoming thoroughly overexcited, and having to be sent out, to change out of their best gowns before they should be ruined and to run off their excess energy by haring up and down the lawn with Wellington, who had, despite Lucy's entreaties, not been invited to attend the event, although he had a rather bedraggled bow about his neck to honour it.

Kate changed into her new travelling clothes in Mrs Singleton's bedroom, with her help and the help of her maid. She had an abigail of her own now, Polly's cousin Sarah, but she had gone on ahead to Gloucestershire with the other servants and the baggage, to make all ready to receive the newly-wed pair.

Lucy flung her arms around Kate on the steps of the Hall, and hugged her. 'I will miss you!' she said. 'But do not think that I shall be too sad, because Jane and Anna are here, and we have all sorts of plans. Let me whisper in your ear . . .' Kate bent her head obediently, and Lucy hissed, 'Midnight feasts! I am sure you did not observe, for we were very crafty, but we have taken food from the breakfast, and concealed it, and will eat it tonight in bed, at midnight! I know that you will not tell anyone, and in any case you cannot, for you are leaving!'

Kate could only laugh, and hug her in return, and tell her to be good. Benedict swung the child up in his arms, and she kissed him, and clung to him, but only a little, and she seemed happy enough as she waved them off, with Wellington jumping around her, barking agitatedly.

'I am excessively glad that I do not have charge of those children tonight!' said Benedict as he tooled the curricle down the drive and out between the gateposts topped with pineapples.

'Oh, so am I! But I am sure your sister and Miss Sutton between them will have no trouble in managing them. Do you know that they plan to hold a midnight feast, with food smuggled from the breakfast?'

'It would be wonderful if they did not. I only hope that no one will overindulge themselves and become unwell – least of all Wellington. But I am happy to say that it is not our concern tonight, Kate.'

They were at the Vicarage in a moment, and the groom Sykes sprang down from behind them to the horses' heads. They went upstairs together, and, once they had tapped on the door and entered, Benedict crossed over to the vicar's bed, shaking his hand and saying with a smile, 'Sir, may I present Lady Silverwood to you?'

'Oh, my dear!' he said shakily, as she bent to kiss him. 'I was listening to the bells earlier, knowing that they were ringing out for you, and it made me so glad to hear them. I am aware that you have a long way to travel, so I will not detain you, but I am very happy to see you together. You be sure and take good care of her, Benedict Silverwood, or you will have me to answer to!'

'I give you my word I will, sir,' Benedict said.

They had left him then, Kate struggling to compose herself, and set off on their journey. Even in a modern curricle with a regular change of fast horses, it would take a good while to reach Gloucestershire.

They had made quite good time, and arrived not long since. Kate had been very curious to see the house that held such fond memories for the Dowager, and found it to be an old manor, not large, as Benedict had said – it was hard to imagine a house he would consider large; the Palace of Versailles, perhaps? – and built from golden stone, with a slate roof and many small, irregular windows, nestled deep in a lush, overgrown garden. It seemed, inevitably, more homely and welcoming to her than the grandeur of Silverwood Hall. There would be time to explore tomorrow, perhaps. Not tonight.

She had gone up to wash off the dust of the road and change for dinner; they had stopped for nuncheon at one of the changes, but that seemed long ago, and Kate was hungry. She found her new maid waiting for her, with hot water and towels set out ready. Sarah – or Thompson, as she would learn to call her – had already laid out an evening gown for her: dark red velvet. 'I hope that will be acceptable, milady. I was told that Sir Benedict requested especially that you wear this gown tonight.'

Kate had raised an eyebrow, but said nothing. She had no idea what he was about, but she was too shy to question her maid on such a subject, and she did not suppose the girl knew any more than she had said.

She made her way down to the drawing room, and found Benedict waiting for her in evening dress, the black coat setting off his dark honey hair to perfection, his linen crisp and white. He took her hands and kissed them when she entered the room, saying, 'You look beautiful, Kate. Spectacular, in fact.'

She shook her head, blushing, but she knew that she looked as well as she ever had, perhaps better. Sarah had dressed her hair in a new style taught to her by Mrs Singleton's abigail: piled up on her head, with one shining ringlet falling over her bare shoulder. The rich hue of her gown, a deep red that she had never worn before – it was not really suitable for an unmarried lady – flattered her Italian colouring and her dark hair in a way that nothing else had ever done. The puffed sleeves just skimmed her shoulders, and the embroidered bodice was very low, much lower than any other gown she had ever worn. The upper slopes of her breasts were entirely exposed, pushed up as they were by her short stays, and, from the look in Benedict's eyes, he fully appreciated the effect.

He said, 'I am sorry to be so mysterious and dictatorial in insisting you wear that gown; I hope you did not mind too much? It is merely that I have a wedding gift for you, which will, I hope, go perfectly with the gown.' He handed her a large, flat box, and when she opened it she found a magnificent ruby necklace, long teardrop earrings and elegant bracelets cushioned on white velvet.

She looked at him. 'Benedict! It is too much!'

'Nonsense, my dear. Will you not try it on?' He took the necklace from the case and unfastened it. She thought there must be quite thirty smaller stones, cabochon cut, set in gold and linked to each other simply with tiny gold loops, and in the centre two larger stones, one above the other – the upper an oval, the larger a teardrop depending from its setting – and both set in gold and surrounded by small pearls. He laid it about her neck and stood behind her to fasten it, the tips of his fingers just brushing her skin and making it tingle, and when he had done up the clasp, and the delicate gold safety chain, he kissed her neck above the fastening. 'I think you had better put in the earrings yourself,' he said, stepping back, 'for I would fear hurting you.'

Her hands were trembling slightly as she pushed the gold wires through the holes in her earlobes, and trembling a little more as she undid the tiny buttons and stripped off her satin gloves – she was intensely aware of him watching her with hunger in his eyes – to put on the bracelets, which echoed the design of the necklace. 'Look at yourself – there is a glass there,' he said.

She looked, and saw an elegant, voluptuous stranger. The largest jewel nestled just above the deep valley between her breasts, and the stones caught fire from the candlelight as her bosom rose and fell; she was slightly breathless. The rubies in her ears sparkled as she turned her head, and she had to admit that they looked well indeed against her dark hair. 'What can I say but thank you?' she murmured. 'They are beautiful, Benedict, and so well chosen.'

'They are mere baubles; you are beautiful,' he said, and in the old, silvered glass she saw him move to stand behind her once more, and bend his head to kiss her neck and bare shoulders. Her gown was very low at the back, too, and he pressed tiny kisses down her spine and along her shoulder blades until he reached the edge of her bodice. 'I like your hair in this new style,' he whispered against her skin, and the feel of his breath on her made her shiver suddenly. He saw it, felt it, and his eyes grew darker. 'I think if we are ever to eat dinner tonight,' he said wryly, 'it must be now, for it is ready, and although I have no particular appetite – for food – just at the moment, it would be unkind to send it all back untasted to Mrs Thompson. I am sure she has exerted herself greatly, and that it will be very good, even if it is wasted on me.'

They had eaten – she could not in truth have said precisely what – and the servants had cleared the table and left them, and here was Benedict, lounging back in his chair, telling her that he could not take his eyes off her, and she knew it without him saying so, for he had scarcely looked away from her all evening, as she had not from him.

He rose and reached out his hand to her. 'Shall we take the air a moment, before we go upstairs?' he asked. 'As long as you do not fear that you will take cold?'

'I think I will survive it,' she replied drily. 'I should be glad of a breath of air, for the room feels very warm to me.'

'As it does to me,' he said with a perfectly composed countenance. 'I am sure I cannot account for it. I have been conscious all evening of a feeling that I am wearing too many clothes, and you too.'

'I hope you are not beginning with a fever.' She was flirting again.

'I began with a fever some three weeks ago, I think,

Kate. You are both the cause and the remedy, I hope. But let us go outside and see if the night air can do anything to cool us, or if, as I suspect, it serves only to make us worse.'

They passed out into the hallway, and then through a small door onto a stone terrace that looked out over the garden. It was getting dark, and bats swooped fast above their heads. The air was heavy with the scent of old roses, lavender and jasmine: heady, intoxicating. She said as much to him, but he shook his head. 'The scent that intoxicates me is yours.'

'I do not wear any perfume.'

'I know you don't. It's you.'

And then she was in his arms.

CHAPTER TWENTY-THREE

They kissed in the warm darkness, her velvet crushed against his hard body, his hands pulling her tight against him and caressing the bare skin of her back that was revealed by the low bodice of her gown, but after a few heady moments he whispered ruefully, 'I think that on this momentous occasion you should go upstairs and have your maid ready you for bed, and I will come to you. You can be very sure that I will come to you.'

'Why, Benedict? Do you not want to undress me?' This was beyond flirting; she did not know what she should call this. Shameless invitation, perhaps. She had had a little wine and she wondered if it was that that made her reckless; she thought it was not. Perhaps it merely gave her courage to say what she otherwise could not, and voice her deepest desires. No half-measures. She had thought he might undress her himself; she had thought he might strip her of everything except the rubies. His eyes had been doing so all evening, after all.

He groaned against her neck, 'Because, my temptress, I do not, just at this moment, have the patience to undo a thousand tiny, no doubt fiddly buttons, and take your lovely new gown and lay it very carefully aside as it deserves, and then remove your many petticoats, and unlace your stays, and carefully take off your delicate chemise to reveal the glories beneath. I am sure one day soon I will do this, and more, exquisitely slowly, and you may do the same to me, with any variations that occur to you. But at this moment, at this precise moment, Kate, if I take you upstairs into your chamber, and you turn to look at me, beautiful breasts heaving, your cheeks flushed and your delicious lips slightly parted, I will – I warn you – throw you on the bed and have at you without either of us removing a single item of clothing.'

'Oh!'

'I am sure you would say "Oh!" My hope is that if we both undress like civilised people, I will have time to collect my senses as much as I am able, possibly by pouring cold water over myself, and approach you with more . . . finesse than I could achieve right in this instant.'

She knew she should be shocked, horrified at his words – a true lady surely would be – but she found instead that a treacherous spark of excitement was kindled deep inside her at the thought of being thrown on the bed and . . . and ravished. In her confusion she could not find the words to argue with him. What would she say: *Please ravish me*? She was not quite so far gone yet.

And so they climbed the old wooden stairs together, and parted for a while. Kate rang for her maid from her dressing room, and was helped to undress. So many buttons, he had said, and he had been right. All the stages of disrobing that Benedict had listed just a few moments ago, even removing her stockings . . . As she took them off, she quivered at the thought of his fingers untying her garters and tossing them aside, then very, very slowly unrolling the flimsy silk down her thighs.

She relieved herself, washed, and put on her new nightgown. A little regretfully, she took off the rubies and put them back in their case. Sarah brushed her hair for her, so that it fell in a great shining curtain over her chest and down her back. She had been about to plait and coil it primly, as she always did for sleep, but Sarah stopped her by saying, blushing furiously, 'Milady, it is not my place to tell you what to do, but . . . you have such pretty hair. Perhaps you should leave it down, just this once.'

Kate took her meaning, and flushed with colour too. 'You are quite right, of course. Thank you.' The girl curtsied and left, and Kate went into her bedchamber. It was quite sparsely furnished, and what furniture there was were antiques: a big carved four-poster with a deep new mattress and lovely, fragile tapestry hangings, a big chair by the carved stone fireplace, an ottoman chest and a huge cheval glass in one corner. There were wax candles in silver sconces set here and there, and a scent of lavender in the air. It was very quiet, so deep in the countryside as they were; the old house creaked as it settled, as old houses will, and an owl hooted outside, but in the distance. She found she was trembling a little.

She was barefoot, and she walked across the faded rug to the cheval glass, and stood looking at her reflection. Once again, she seemed a stranger. She was not accustomed to see herself with her hair down and flowing free like this, except when she was busy washing it, and she was certainly not accustomed to seeing herself in one of the nightgowns that Maria had insisted she purchase. It was made from the finest Dhaka muslin and had cost a truly extraordinary sum, but when she had protested Mrs Singleton had snorted and said that her mama had particularly insisted upon it, which silenced Kate very effectively. She had then been informed that it was of the highest quality, which was used to make the intimate garments of the favoured wives and concubines of the richest rulers of India; she had not the least difficulty in believing it.

There was no fastening on the bodice; it simply plunged to the high waist and tied there, and it had more fabric ties down from waist to hem. No fiddly buttons, she was pleased to note. She felt as she looked at her reflection that the omission was probably deliberate, and some thought had gone into its design: she was not sure that this was a gown that was intended for sleep at all. It had tiny sleeves and a little shawl collar. No doubt it was ideally suited for the heat of summer and would be deliciously cool. But this was to avoid its most notable feature, which she could hardly miss as she stood and stared at herself in the glass.

It was transparent. She had known it to be very thin when she had seen it before, but she had not been in it then. She could see every detail of her breasts and her erect brown nipples quite clearly through the fabric. She could see her navel and her belly. She could see the dark curls at the junction of her thighs. More to the point, he would see them. If she had had a book, she could have read the finest print through it, she was sure. She did not have a book to hand, and was besides in no mood for reading, and trusted that he would not be either. There would be something very wrong if she was mistaken, unless, she supposed, it might be a very particular kind of book. And even then, she mused, running her hand over the full curves of her body, he should scarcely need instruction or inspiration. The gown would have been daring on any lady, whatever her endowments; on a woman of Kate's statuesque build, it was . . .

'Indecent!' she said aloud.

'You should see it from behind,' said a warm voice at her back.

She gasped, 'Benedict! I did not hear the door open!'

'I have been standing here for a moment, admiring the view. Worshipping, you know. As I promised I would.'

She did not know if she were more embarrassed that he had seen her looking at herself in the glass, or touching herself, or that he had seen her in this gown. Which thought was surely ridiculous, in such a situation. If she had not meant him to see it, why had she put it on? The point seemed in any case moot, as he crossed the room to her side in three long strides.

'I see from your face – and it is not every man who could spare the time to look at your face in such a situation, so I hope you are suitably impressed – that you are thinking again, Kate, and I desire that you stop immediately. And certainly if you are thinking that this gown is anything other than vastly becoming, you can leave off thinking *that* immediately.'

'Maria made me buy it. I did not realise it was so very . . . It is scandalous,' she insisted.

He took her in his arms and spoke against her ear. 'I agree, madam, it is. I have been in this room close on a minute, it is our wedding night, and we both remain clothed – barely clothed, in your case, but still – and standing on our feet. Very pretty feet, yours, Kate, I perceive, but they should be up in the air by now. Scandalous is a very well-chosen word.'

She could not help but laugh, and he said, 'I see that you imagine I was jesting, my lady. You will soon discover your mistake.'

'Will I, sir?'

'Oh, yes . . .' And then he had found the ties that fastened the gown and was undoing them, and pushing the wispy material from her shoulders, and she – she! – was finding the belt of his silk dressing gown, and fumbling to unknot it. He murmured approvingly as it pulled apart in her hand, and fell away.

Luxurious fabrics slithered to the ground, and they were both naked. She did not have time to feel conscious of embarrassment, or discover if she was indeed still capable of it, for he scooped her up easily in his arms – it seemed he was equal to the task, which was happy news – his hand warm and caressing against the back of her thigh, and carried her over to the four-poster bed, and laid her down on it.

He stood looking down at her for a moment, smiling. 'Kate, you are a goddess! Do you know it?'

She did not answer him, for she was looking at him. He had a deep, puckered scar on his right shoulder – a bullet hole, she supposed, from his wound taken in South America. The fact that his body was not perfect somehow made him more real to her. And he was very real, standing here naked. His chest was strongly muscled and scattered with whorls of soft brown hair, as were his powerful legs and arms; his torso was extraordinarily well defined, like that of a Greek statue, and on it a trail of hair led down and drew the eye . . . She blushed and looked away.

'Oh, no,' he said. 'You promised me not so long ago that you would discard the proprieties. No half-measures, you said. Here I am, Kate, such as I am, and I am hard for you. Do not be shy to look. I hope you like what you see. God knows I can never have enough of looking at you.'

He was magnificent, she thought, but she was still a little shy, and told him so, and he relented, and came to lie close beside her, brushing her dark, silky hair back from her brow. 'Your hair is so beautiful – I have wondered what it would be like when it was down,' he murmured. He gathered a great mass of it in his hands, and buried his face in it where it lay against her shoulder. She reached out and touched his head, stroking his honey-brown locks with a loving hand, enjoying his closeness. If her hand should find that it ceased stroking after a while, and instead urged his face to her breast, what harm? 'Is that what you want, Kate?' he said, his voice muffled in the cloud of her hair.

'Yes,' she whispered.

'You want me, if indeed I can find them through your wonderful curls – for I can feel them, but not see them clear, it is beyond tantalising – to hold your beautiful breasts, and kiss them, and suck on them? That is what you would like?'

'Yes.' It was not quite, *Please ravish me*, but it was close enough.

He used his lips and his fingers to push aside the silky strands, laughing a little as they tickled his nose, and he uncovered her, until she was bare to him. She wound her hair in a great hank and threw it over her shoulder, then lay back, and he cupped her in both his hands, feeling the weight of her, and told her that she was glorious. And then his lips were on her, teasing at first, licking, brushing across her hot skin, then sucking each nipple in

179

turn deep into his mouth and feasting on it. She held his head and wound her fingers deep in his hair.

He moved to lie across her, his mouth still on her, and she could feel the heat and hardness of his body against hers, his thigh pushing hers apart, the hair on it rubbing against her soft skin, sensitising it. She ran her hands down his smooth back and clung to him.

'I want to kiss you now,' he said at last against her taut, wet nipple. 'I want my tongue in your mouth and yours in mine.' And he moved higher over her and took her mouth. He was hot and wet and urgent, and she matched him, and she found now that she could reach his buttocks, and grasp them, the better to pull him closer against her.

Her breasts were tingling from his caresses, and the hair on his chest rubbed against them, a delicious torture. She wanted him to touch her, why did he not . . . ? But he was there. He did not take his mouth from hers, but he slipped one hand between her thighs, and found the swollen bud, and stroked it as he had before, and as she had before, she moaned and pressed herself against him, eager for the release that she knew he could provide.

He dipped a fingertip into her wetness, and then out again, and slid back and forth, and his other hand found her erect nipple again, and he rolled it between finger and thumb, and tugged on it, hard, not too hard, and all the while his tongue was tangling with hers, their mouths wide open, and his hardness pressing into her belly, rubbing against her. She arched her back and came in great waves of intense pleasure, raising her hips from the bed, digging her fingers into his buttocks, moaning into his mouth.

He moved over her and slowly slipped his fingers from her sex, saying, 'I need to be in you, my sweet Kate, and feel those waves of pleasure you are feeling. Will you let me show you how you can take me?'

'Show me!' she demanded shamelessly. 'Show me right now!'

'Wrap your legs around me. I will guide myself into you . . .' He reached down between their bodies with one hand, and found her wetness, and was inside her.

She flinched at the sudden unfamiliar sensation – stretching, discomfort – but he said, 'I will not move. I will not do anything until you are comfortable. You will move, you are in charge. Clench on me there, hold me tight. You have me . . . Ah, God, you have me, Kate. Clench on me, and release me. Can you feel it? Can you pull me deeper into you?'

'Yes!' she gasped. She was full of him, but she felt calmer now. No, that was wrong, that was nonsense, she was anything but calm. She tightened herself on him once more, and as she did so she moved her hips slightly, settling herself against him, around him, and he groaned. She did it again, experimentally, gyrating a little more, and once again he groaned.

'I think perhaps, if you will allow it, I might move too now. I do not think I am mistaken in saying that you are beginning to get the idea of it.'

'I think you should move. I believe I am . . .'

And he began to move slowly, and she with him, tentatively at first, and then not so, and together they found a rhythm. In a moment he was thrusting into her, harder, and she met him, and he kissed her, deep and urgent, and she understood now what the tongues signified, and why it was so erotic.

Then he was rolling her over, still joined to him, so that she straddled him, and he said, 'Ride me, Kate! And if you lean towards me, you will see what I can do to please you!'

She leant forward, and found the headboard of the bed and gripped it, bracing herself. Her breasts were in his face, and as she rode him he tongued her nipple once more, and she teased him with it, pulling away a little and then pushing it back on him, into his wet, eager mouth, feinting to deny him entirely as he moaned in frustration and then offering him the other. He reached down and took a firm grip on her buttocks with both hands, and spread his fingers wide and pulled her, ground her, against him. Their pace increased and she clutched the headboard tighter and pushed against it harder, harder, and then suddenly he buried his head between her breasts, gasping her name as he convulsed inside her, lifting her up into the air with his powerful thighs and then bringing her down again, rolling her onto her back and thrusting into her until he was spent, and lay on her for a moment, panting.

'Kate, good Christ, Kate . . . I did not hurt you, did I?' He pulled away from her, out of her – she moaned instinctively at the separation – and he raised himself up on an elbow so that he could take his weight off her body, looking down at her in concern.

'You did not hurt me. I promise you did not. Did I hurt you, though, Benedict? I was afraid I might smother you, and then I did not care if I did or not. Is that very shocking?'

'Excessively shocking,' he said, and lay down beside her, scooting down the bed so that he could pillow his head between her breasts once more. 'I wish you might smother me in your magnificence. Kill me now. I cannot think of a more splendid way to die.'

She put her arms around him, and cradled him tightly to her, their bodies as close as they well could be. 'Like this?'

'Just like this.'

CHAPTER TWENTY-FOUR

Kate stirred a little, and stretched, but found herself in an unaccustomed position, with a weight upon her. She was hugging a pillow, as she always did in sleep, but there was a warm body pressed to her back, and an arm flung across her body.

Benedict.

They surely could not have slept like this all night, but at some point he had spooned against her and wrapped his arm about her, burying his face in her hair. He was still sleeping, she thought; she could feel his deep, regular breathing against her neck. The novelty of his strong body so close to hers was extraordinary to her, and she nestled back into his embrace, and enjoyed the sensation of being held. She might easily have fallen asleep again, and would have said – in the most unlikely event of anyone asking – that she felt safe, comfortable, were it not for one circumstance. He was hard. His member lay snugly between the cheeks of her buttocks, as if the place had been devised especially for it, warm and heavy against her sex. And hard. It was impossible to mistake it.

She wondered how sensitive it was: if she moved a fraction, would he – it – react? Remembering how she had clenched on him last night, she repeated the motion. He was not inside her now, so he might easily not feel it. She was not moving her body externally at all, just her . . . Oh. An instant reaction. Again – another reaction. She settled her bottom more deeply into his groin, an action that was received with enthusiasm.

A whisper in her ear: 'Kate?'

'Mmm?'

'Are you doing this on purpose?'

'Yes.'

'That is useful to know.'

He adjusted his position a little, and his left hand slipped beneath her body to cup her breast; his right hand slid between her legs. 'Better, no? Please do continue.'

She pressed herself against him, and he pressed back; she wriggled, he groaned. He teased her nipple between his fingers, while his other hand stroked her clitoris, and all the while his enlarged member slid to and fro between her thighs, a delicious friction against her entrance.

It was delightfully pleasurable, but it was suddenly not enough. She altered the angle of her body instinctively, thrusting her buttocks back and her breasts forward.

'Do you think you might be ready for me, Kate? Do you want me inside you?'

'I do.' *Please ravish me.*

He released her breast for a moment – he seemed to know that she needed his other hand to stay exactly where it was – and guided himself into her. She gasped, and clenched around him once more, and ground her bottom into him, and he pressed his fingers harder against her nub. He was kissing her neck, biting it gently, and thrusting into her, slowly at first then faster, harder. His hand gripped her breast, his other worked between her legs, and he was thrusting deeper, deeper. She felt held, possessed, overwhelmed, and she loved it. She buried her face in her pillow and moaned into it, and gave herself up to sensation.

She felt the waves building within her – the dual pleasure of his hand on her and him inside her was irresistible, and she arched her back and ground herself harder against him as she came. He felt it, and it pushed him over the edge, and he spent himself in her, gasping into her neck, biting her, pressing her hard into the pillow, and she adored the pressure.

They lay joined, panting, their bodies slick with sweat, as the waves of satisfaction subsided. 'Lady Silverwood,' he whispered in her ear, 'you are a wanton creature!'

'Mmm . . .' she said, and settled herself more comfortably against him, and slept.

When she awoke, she was alone.

CHAPTER TWENTY-FIVE

Kate was puzzled, and a little hurt, but she was also ravenously hungry, so she washed, and called for her maid to dress her in one of her new muslin day gowns, and went in search of breakfast. She found it, but not him. After she had eaten, she established quite quickly that he was nowhere in the house, unless he were hiding in the kitchen or the servants' quarters, which seemed unlikely.

She could search for him in the grounds, of course, but should she? She was at a loss. If only theirs had been a love match, she might have been justified in seeking him out and upbraiding him with neglect, discourtesy; what kind of man left his wife's bed on the morning after their wedding, and vanished without a word? *A man who was not in love with his wife*, came the answer from the nagging voice inside. A man who had made her no promises apart from passion. And he had had passion. *Twice*, said the little voice, *in point of fact, and the second time most definitely initiated by you.*

Perhaps she had done something wrong. Perhaps when he had said that they should disregard the proprieties and enjoy each other's bodies, he had not meant it, or perhaps there was some unspoken line that she had crossed without even knowing it was there. He had called her wanton, and she had thought he was teasing her, but perhaps he was not. Perhaps there were things that ladies did not do, and she had done them. Twice. He had certainly seemed to like them at the time – *Deny that if you can, infuriating voice* – but perhaps on sober reflection he did not want a wife who acted in such a way. How could she tell?

After all, he did not know that she loved him, that she had yearned for him for seven long years, the hated voice insinuated. *Maybe he thinks you are a hussy, a creature in heat who would rub herself against any man.*

That would be grossly unfair. It should not matter to him, she argued, *if I love him or not. He does not love me and has never pretended to. We are married. I have only given him what he asked for: no half-measures.*

When were men ever fair to women? the relentless voice sneered. *Perhaps last night – and this morning, if we're counting – was the only happiness that you will get, that you deserve, and perhaps even that was an illusion. Still, do not be too down-hearted: it could well be that you are already with child. It certainly would not be your fault if you aren't, with all your wriggling about and your moaning. And it could be a boy, couldn't it? So there will be no need to do . . . that again. Any of it. Possibly ever.*

She did not look for him.

Eventually she found herself a book – she avoided dwelling on the bitter irony of it: Benedict had promised her reading matter, so that she would not be bored, and though it had been a jest, he had provided it – and curled up on a bench in the garden with a cushion to pretend to read it. In other circumstances, she might have been intrigued to learn that a single man in possession of a good fortune must be in want of a wife; it had certainly been her experience that this was so. But the question for her today was, *How will he treat her, once he has married her?*

She had no appetite for nuncheon, and did not go in to eat it; she did not know if Benedict had done so, but he did not seek her out. She was thoroughly miserable. She forced herself to read by sheer willpower, and was against her will drawn into the story, and so the afternoon passed.

At last she went in and ordered some tea, and drank it thirstily, and then went to change for dinner. Her horrid inner voice told her to choose the dowdiest thing she had – preferably something grey, woollen, with very high neck, and perhaps a matching wimple. But she had no dowdy evening gowns, Maria had made sure of that, and she would not wear a morning gown and give herself an odd appearance. Defiantly, she chose instead one of her loveliest gowns. It was changeant silk, a deep brown shot with gold, and she pinned it to her chemise with a topaz brooch that had belonged to her grandmother Waltham. Her neck and shoulders and the upper slopes of her breasts were bare. If he were to reject her, she could not bear that he should do it while she wore his jewels. She would be all too tempted to fling them at him, like some ridiculous creature in a melodrama.

It occurred to her that he might not appear at all, and what would she do then? But he was there, when she came down the stairs, and bowed, and escorted her in to dinner almost in silence. He looked as miserable as she felt, she thought; his face was a mask, and he was pale, and drawn about the mouth. While the servants were in the room handing them the dishes, he made polite conversation about nothing at all, drinking steadily all the while, and she replied in kind, although she refused the wine, wanting to keep her head clear, or at least as clear as it could be. Obviously he was troubled by no such concern. It was horrible. If this were to be her life now, she was not sure how long she could endure it. Especially as she had no idea why.

The servants cleared the dishes and left them alone, She would not, she would not, rush into speech. Let him talk. Her little voice could go to the devil; she had nothing with which to reproach herself. He too was silent. He did not look at her, but gazed down unseeingly into his glass, swirling the dark liquid in it. She rose abruptly to her feet. 'I will leave you to your wine, sir,' she said coldly.

'Kate?' he whispered.

She turned to look at him, brows raised.

'I'm sorry. I'm sorry I left you alone.'

'I think you need to explain.'

He set his glass down and ran his fingers through his hair. 'I do owe you that. I should not have left you without a word, and certainly not after you gave yourself to me so generously, last night and then this morning. Will you not sit down?'

She said, 'No, you should not have done that. I do not think I have deserved it.' But she sat, and looked at him, waiting.

He sighed and said, 'I knew I wanted you, you know, the second time I saw you. The first time I was all intent on Lucy and not attending to anything else. But when you sat having tea with my mother, so cool and prim in your yellow muslin . . . I was supposed to be looking on you as a prospective bride, to see if I could like you, and I went far beyond what I had expected, for all I could think of was taking you to bed. And after that, after I first kissed you . . . you know what happened then, and those other times afterwards.'

'You said you would try to make me happy, and I said I would do the same for you. And you made me a bargain – you said that we should set aside our doubts and worries and enjoy each other, and the passion we could share. I think I have kept my side of the bargain, Benedict.'

'God knows you have.'

'You did not promise me love, but I did not expect coldness; I did not expect to be deserted on the day after my wedding without a word.'

'I know. I'm sorry.'

'But why?'

'I can't . . . I knew that I desired you from the first. And in the days before our wedding, I found myself entirely obsessed with making love to you. Unable to think of anything else. When I pulled up your skirts and pleasured you in the darkness . . . My God, Kate, I have never done anything like that before! I know you have no reason to believe me, but I swear it is true. I have been laying hands on myself every night and thinking of you. I thought . . . I thought when we were married, and I had made love to you, I thought my desire, my need for you would lessen. Become manageable, just a part of life, and by no means the most important part. As it has been before, Kate, with other women I have known. But it has not. It is worse. Much worse. Now I know how wonderful you are, I truly cannot think of a single other thing I want to do but bury myself in you.

'I left you this morning because I knew that if I stayed I would want to take you again. And again after that, just as soon as I was able. I have been walking for miles instead, attempting to exhaust myself so that I would not think of you, of your irresistible body, and failing miserably. If I had followed merely my own inclination, we would not have left the bedchamber at all today.' He drained his glass and looked across the table at her, his grey eyes glittering hungrily.

'I know I should be explaining myself better – I am struggling to do so, Kate – but that's not what I want to do. I want to lay you across this table right now and fuck you – not make love to you gently, as a husband should his bride, but fuck you. I should not use such words, I know, but I was a soldier for so long, and a gentleman's vocabulary does not come close to expressing all that I want. I'm hard thinking about it now. I'm hard all the time. I barely know myself. It . . . disturbs me. I did not look for this.'

She should have been shocked at the crudeness of his language, and the stark animal desire it revealed, but instead she shivered and licked her lips at the thought of what he wanted to do to her. If he stood now and held out his hand to her, she would not refuse him. He saw, and understood, and cursed again, and she said, 'How do you think I feel?'

He looked a little startled. 'What do you mean?'

'I had barely kissed a man before I met you. No man had ever touched me before you did. If you are not accustomed to behaving in this way, I most certainly am not.'

He laughed mirthlessly. 'I am very glad to hear it!'

'But I thought . . . I thought newly married couples on honeymoon were expected . . . Otherwise why did Maria and your mother make me buy indecent nightgowns, if not to tempt you? Is it not always like this?' He shook his head, a wry smile twisting his lips, and she exclaimed in frustration, 'How am I supposed to know what is usual and what is not?'

'I have been married before, Kate. It was not like this.'

'I did not ask you— I would not ask you that.'

'I was . . . It was different. I wanted, burnt to make love to Vanessa, of course I did. It was inevitably awkward at first, she was shy, and I was not very experienced. We found our way, we enjoyed it – I think she enjoyed, I hope she did, I tried to make sure she did. Sometimes I have tormented myself since in wondering if I let her down; if I took my pleasure selfishly with her, and that is why—' He broke off abruptly. 'Perhaps I did. It is far too late now to tell, or to set it right. But all I know is, it was not like this. Nothing like this. I feel almost as though I am losing my mind. I've never known anything like this before.'

'But does that mean that it is wrong? I'm not being facetious, Benedict. It is merely that I do not see why it disturbs you so, or why you are so certain that it is wrong.'

'The things I want to do to you . . .'

'Do you intend to hurt me?'

His face was a picture of shock. 'Of course not! I have seen enough of pain and suffering, and God knows I have been responsible for plenty myself, since I got my commission. I would never wish to hurt you. I know there are such men, men of all ranks in society who take pleasure in abusing women, but I am not made like that, Kate, I swear to you. There is enough hurt in the world already – I would never wish to add to it.'

'I believe you.' He looked instantly relieved. 'But, Benedict, this is no way to go on. You have left me alone and prey to all manner of fears all day long, and just because you would not talk to me and tell me what you were feeling. That was not kind. I thought at first that something I had done had given you a disgust of me . . .' He stirred and made an inarticulate protest. 'You must surely see that I had no way to know. I cannot look inside your head.'

He rose to his feet and came to kneel awkwardly before her. 'Forgive me, Kate? I have been foolish, and selfish, and I have distressed you. That was the last thing I wanted, and yet I have done it. Please try to forgive me.'

She was silent for a moment – not to torment him, though he perhaps deserved it, but considering. She was sorely tempted for a moment to tell him how she felt about him, but she dared not reveal herself so, she dared not risk his shocked response, and yet she talked to him of honesty. She was a hypocrite, then. She wondered if someone who did not love him would be able to forgive him for the way he had treated her today; she imagined many women in her situation would not by any means let him escape so easily, but would make him suffer through coldness and continued recriminations to which he would have no answer. She could not do it – her heart would not let her – but equally she could not tell him the truth. She was as bad as he, therefore, and so she could not be angry with him. They both had their secrets.

She said, 'I do forgive you, Benedict. Truly.'

'Thank you!' he groaned, and lurched forwards, burying his face in her lap. She stroked his hair, and held him, and they remained so for a moment in the candlelight. After a little while something occurred to her, and she could not help but begin to laugh rather wildly. He looked up at her questioningly.

'When she first came to see me,' she explained at last, 'your mother told me that, if I did not know it already, marriage would teach me that men required a great deal of patience. I am not sure that this is the sort of thing she was referring to, but she was quite right.'

He smiled ruefully up at her. 'She so often is. She will tell you so herself.'

'But, Benedict, how are we to go on?'

'I think that depends on you.'

'And I think you should make yourself perfectly clear. No more misunderstandings.'

He hesitated and then said with some difficulty, 'It seems to me that I will . . . make love to you as often as you let me. In every way you will allow. I have admitted it to myself, and to you. So it will be up to you to call a halt. I cannot tell where that should be, for I am lost. You can trust me not to hurt you deliberately, but beyond that, I have no self-control at all where you are concerned. I would hate myself if I hurt you without knowing. And so you shall be the one to call a halt. I promise you I will obey you in that second, if you say "stop".'

'Very well.'

'Very well? I think now you are the one who needs to make yourself perfectly clear, Kate.'

'I do not know what I might like, or not like, or how often I might like it. How could I? I do not know . . . how much I want. How much of you. I do not know where my limits may lie. All I know is, I have not reached them yet. If you had woken me this morning, touched me, wanting to make love again . . .'

'Would you have done it, Kate?'

'I would. Gladly. Not merely to please you. Because I wanted it.' *Because I wanted you.*

He looked up at her, and his eyes were full of hunger once more. He laid his hand on her thighs, and smoothed the rich, changeable silk over them. 'Kate, may I come to you tonight, in the same manner as I did last night? I do not think I can trust myself to undress you yet, though I would very much like to do so. And will you wear that nightgown?'

'I do not see why I should not wear it. After all, I can scarcely have been in it for ten minutes last night, can I?'

'But they were very memorable minutes,' he murmured. 'I for one will never forget them. And tonight perhaps it will stay on your glorious body a little longer, or perhaps it will not. Shall we try, and see?'

CHAPTER TWENTY-SIX

Kate, hair loose about her shoulders, stood in her scandalous nightgown in front of the mirror once more, and waited for Benedict. It was the same as last night, and yet it was different. Last night she had been aroused, thinking of their previous encounters, but still nervous, as any bride might be. Tonight she was not nervous in the least. Tonight she ran her hands over the curves of her body and did not care if he should come into the room and see her doing it. More – she hoped he would.

He had told her with words that set every inch of her body aflame that he was obsessed with making love to her, could think of nothing else; she could not doubt his sincerity, and she saw now that this had set loose something inside her. She was free, if only for a little space, to be the same as he. There was nobody here to judge her for her desires, or to counsel caution. She would push away for as long as she could any thoughts of love, or of the future and all its uncertainties, and let their mutual passion take them where it might. Whatever happened after, she would always have that to cling to. And at this moment, if its flames should consume them both and leave only ashes, she did not care.

This time when the door opened, she heard it, and she watched him cross the room to her side. He was wearing his silk dressing gown again, but he unfastened it and let it drop to the ground. She drank in the sight of him, and this time did not look away or lower her lashes.

He came to stand close behind her, and met her eyes in the tarnished glass. 'It is an extraordinary thing,' he said, his voice not quite steady, 'that this garment somehow manages to make you look more naked than you do when you are actually naked.'

'I thought last night that it would be possible to read a book through it.'

'I am sure it would, although I have no desire to do so just at this moment. Even *Aretino's Postures* would be redundant.' She raised an eyebrow in enquiry, and he said, 'It is a very shocking book, my dear, with outrageous illustrations depicting classical personages in . . . various amorous attitudes. I expect the old reprobate who rented this house from us had a copy in his library; many men do. But I do not find myself in need of any such inspiration when I see you like this.'

He stroked her hair aside and kissed her neck. 'You have a mark here, from where I bit you this morning, I think. I am sorry.'

'Do not be sorry. I liked it.'

He groaned into her hair, and in sudden impatience pulled up her gown to bare her bottom, and pressed the full length of himself against her, skin to skin, lifting her up a little so that his member sat between her thighs as it had that morning. She stood on tiptoe and leant back into him, his body supporting her weight. His hands reached round to cup her breasts, and tease her taut nipples through the thin fabric. His lips found her earlobe, and he sucked on it, and bit it gently. 'Mmm . . .' she murmured.

'Kate,' he whispered in her ear, 'will you permit me to lay you across the bed and pleasure you with my mouth?'

She gasped at the thought; it set her tingling with anticipation. 'Tell me exactly what you mean to do . . .'

He was hard against her softest places as he spoke, and while he played with her nipples he whispered his words against her skin. 'I mean to bend you over the bed with your splendid bottom in the air, and then I mean to kneel behind you and kiss your spectacular cheeks. I may bite them, perhaps, as I would the ripe peach that they greatly resemble, but only very gently, if you do not object, of course. And then I shall worship your cunny with my mouth, and lick it, and put my tongue in you, and lose myself in you, and when you come in my mouth, as I hope you shall, I will carry on licking you until you beg me to stop or you will die of pleasure. And then, sweet Kate, I will hold your hips and slip my cock into your delicious wetness and fuck you as you lie there in your naked glory until I in my turn die of pleasure, or come inside you, whichever should be first. Do you have any objections, madam?'

'None whatsoever,' she moaned, 'as long as you mean to do it straight away.'

They stumbled over to the high old bed together, his hands still on her, and she bent over it, raising herself to him and pressing her upper body into the covers. 'Like this?'

'A little higher.' She wriggled. 'There!' He dragged up the transparent muslin further and smoothed it over her back with hands that shook slightly. 'My God, what a picture.' He dragged the ottoman across the floor and knelt on it between her legs, his hands either side of her hips. 'Are you quite comfortable?'

'No,' she said. 'Why do you delay?!'

'Oh, Lady Impatience!' he chuckled. And then he bent and kissed her bottom, butterfly kisses at first, but she growled, and so he laughed, and bit her, and she found she liked it. And then he said, 'Spread for me!' and she spread her buttocks wider. He murmured approval, and splayed them with his big hands, and lowered his face to her. She reached out and grabbed handfuls of the bed covers, as his tongue found her most secret place, and licked around it, and then dived into its wetness.

She moaned and arched her back, pressing herself into his face quite shamelessly, and he took a firmer grip on her cheeks, his fingers digging into them, and his tongue darted in and out of her, and then she could no longer tell exactly what he was doing with his mouth, except that it was giving her the greatest pleasure that she had ever known in all her life, and she came, powerful convulsions spasming through her whole body. And then he had two fingers working inside her, so that she could clench on them, and he was licking along her, between her cunny and her nub, and sucking on it, and she was crying out, and then it was all too intense, and at last she had to beg him to stop, as he had said she would.

He stood up, she supposed – he was gone from her and she felt cold air on her hot, wet skin – but then she heard the ottoman being dragged away, and his hands were on her, and his . . . his cock was at her entrance; she could feel it, nudging into her.

'Kate?'

'God, yes!' And he slid into her, a delicious friction, filling her up, and she gasped and raised herself up to meet him, wanting to take him deeper yet.

He groaned, 'I do not think I can be gentle!' and gripped her hips and began thrusting into her, hard and fast, and she pressed up against him, bunching her fists in the bed cover, taking it between her teeth and biting at it too. He held her and pounded into her, and once again she felt herself entirely possessed and filled by him.

He was too aroused; it could not be long. As he

came, his hands urged her body more upright, one hand steadying her against him, the other finding her breast and clasping it as he convulsed and spent himself deep inside her. 'Kate, Kate, my sweet Kate!' he groaned.

They fell together onto the bed, and he kissed her neck and hair, and murmured endearments. He was a heavy weight on her, but she did not dislike it in the least. At last he said, 'Let us lie down properly and hold each other.' So they stood, and found their way to the head of the bed, and collapsed onto it, panting, embracing still.

After a little while she struggled upright, and went to relieve herself, his seed trickling out of her. When she returned, she found him lying on his back, his hands behind his head, watching her and smiling. She looked down ruefully at the crumpled nightgown, and began to unfasten the ties, so that she could remove it, meeting his eyes boldly as she did so. 'Oh, yes, do!' he said. Naked, she climbed into bed beside him, and lay down with her head on his chest, dragging her long hair over her shoulder so that she did not lie upon it. He put his arms about her and she snuggled against him until she was entirely comfortable. He reached down with one hand to cup her bottom and caress it languorously.

'I do not have any words, Kate – that was glorious. You were glorious. Wonderful. Did you . . . ? Am I being unforgivably arrogant in presuming that you liked it? All of it?'

'I think you must know very well that I liked it. Much more than liked it. Are you fishing for compliments, sir?'

'I may be. Although I think the greatest compliment you could pay me was just now, pressing your delicious cunny into my face for me to feast on, thrusting your beautiful arse up so that I could take you deeper, moaning and gasping as I pounded into you. Have you reached your limit yet, Kate?'

'I do not believe I have.'

'What do you like most? Honestly, now?' He was kneading her bottom gently as he spoke, and she was still tingling deliciously, and felt as though she could purr with contentment. She reached out a lazy hand and began to explore the whorls of soft hair on his chest, tracing a pattern through them, finding his nipples and circling them with her finger, brushing her fingertips across them. He made a small sound of pleasure.

Her voice was low. 'I liked your tongue in me, on me. I liked that very much. And I like it when you grip me so tightly with your hands, and thrust into me. I am very conscious of your strength as you hold me. I feel . . .'

His voice was very deep. 'What do you feel?'

'Possessed.'

'Oh, Kate . . .'

'I feel that I have given myself to you utterly, held nothing back. I like it. I think it is in my nature to like it. No half-measures, remember?' As she spoke, she realised that she had come perilously close to declaring her feelings for him once more, but had not quite done it. Perhaps he would think she meant physically: that he had possessed her physically, no more than that, and that she had given herself to him physically. God knows that was true enough too.

'I don't know what to say to you. I feel it too; that I have possessed you completely. I have never known such intensity of feeling. In this moment I feel that I have given and taken all I could, all anybody could. And yet I know that my imagination will persist in finding new ways to have you.'

'I told you that I had not yet reached my limit, Benedict.'

'You take my breath away. Do you . . . have you any ideas yourself, my lady?'

She did.

CHAPTER TWENTY-SEVEN

She said, 'I wonder . . . I do not know if you realise that girls are not always as ignorant as men think them. Girls talk. We gather scraps of information wherever we can find them. Partly it is for our own protection; I hope you understand. Ignorance makes us weak and vulnerable – I suppose I should say, more weak and vulnerable. But partly it is . . . curiosity. I think it is natural, this curiosity. I am sure boys are the same, but it is easier for them, for no one truly grudges them the knowledge.'

'You are right. At a certain age boys' entire existence is dedicated to the pursuit of this information. But I'm sorry, I interrupted you. Go on . . .'

'Of course, my grandmother does not believe in keeping girls unaware of what passes between men and women when they are intimate, so she told me the truth of it when I was fourteen: of how children are conceived, at least, and what it is that men want from us. And those facts were very different from some of the wilder stories circulating in my school, believe me. So we knew, but we were still fascinated. We knew that there were other things that people did, that no one would tell us about, not even my grandmother. We knew that there were pictures of such things, as you said earlier, and we wanted to see those pictures.'

'And did you find them?'

'We did. Two of my friends crept to their family's library every night for a month and searched through hundreds of dusty old books until they found what they were looking for. And then, when they had the opportunity, they stole it. Or borrowed it, I suppose I should say, as they knew they had to put it back in case it might be missed. I believe it was a French book.'

'It seems quite likely,' he said with a smile in his voice.

'It showed all sorts of things. Positions. Men . . . doing to women what you just did to me.'

'My mouth on your cunny, or taking you from behind?' he whispered. He was still caressing her bottom, but less languorously, more firmly; she was still toying with his nipples, caressing his chest, but less idly. He still seemed to like it, all of it; she knew she did.

'Both. And women . . . touching men's . . .'

'Touching men's cocks. I believe I would enjoy hearing you say it, Kate.'

'Touching men's cocks. Grasping them. And sometimes, putting their mouths on them.'

He gulped and said, 'Oh . . . That. Do you think it possible that you might like that, Kate?'

'The women in the pictures seemed to like it. And the men certainly did.'

He let out a crack of laughter. 'I am sure they did! Are you saying . . . ? Do you want to touch my cock, Kate, and perhaps take it into your mouth, then? Because if you did, it would give me a great deal of pleasure. But only if you enjoyed it too.'

'I might. Your mouth on me was . . . wonderful. And you liked doing it to me too, did you not?'

'That's too mild a word. I adored it. To give you such pleasure, to feel the pleasure in you and know that I have caused it . . . To look at you now – or perhaps even more at another time, when you are fully dressed and in public – and think: *I made her helpless, nearly swooning; I licked her most secret places and made her scream with pleasure.* You did scream, you know.'

She could well believe that she had screamed. 'Perhaps I might feel the same? I cannot know . . .'

'Unless you try it?'

'Yes.'

He went to wash himself, and she stretched out on the bed, enjoying the feel of the sheets on her naked skin. It seemed to her that all her sensations had been enhanced, but particularly touch. She was aware of her body as she had never been before, and all the more when he came back into the room and stood watching her. She had no thought of covering herself, but looked back at him, enjoying the desire that darkened his grey eyes. She had always felt men's eyes on her, but she had not asked for or welcomed their regard; it had been a threat, or an embarrassment at best. She had been all too aware that her precarious position in society, not to mention her physical safety, had depended on her reputation, on being seen as respectable. She supposed it still did to some degree, and always would, but not in this room, not in this bed.

He said, 'I know I have said it before, Kate, but it bears repetition: you are a queen, a goddess. Venus, I think. Venus in her bed, by candlelight.'

'I have never felt myself so before. To have a body like this as an unmarried woman, not wealthy, of no position in society, has been more of a curse than a blessing.'

'I can understand how it might be so. I am sorry that life has not been easy for you, but I hope it will be better now. All I can say is that society has not changed, but your position in it has.'

She chuckled wickedly, and extended her arms up behind her head so that her breasts thrust forward, stretching out her limbs sensuously against the sheets and wriggling luxuriously. 'Indeed, I feel my position to be . . . quite different now.'

He crossed the room in two long strides to join her in the bed. 'Minx! This talk of positions is making me hard again . . . But I want to kiss you and run my hands over your glorious body for a while, Kate. I do not feel that I have kissed you properly since we married – we have been too busy doing other things. Let us slow the pace and take some time. We have all night.'

She reached up her arms to him, and he lay down beside her and cupped her face in his hand. They kissed very softly at first, mere whispers of contact, brushes of the lips, teasing each other, but then inevitably deeper, tongues tangling slowly, while she ran her hands over his muscular back and taut buttocks, and pressed her body against his, breasts, belly, thighs, and he captured her buttocks and pulled her hard against him. Then he released her lips, but only to trace them with one finger. 'Luscious Kate . . .' he said huskily, as he ran his finger back and forth across her full lower lip, opening it to him so that he could stroke the soft wetness inside. He pushed his finger in a little further, and she touched it with the tip of her tongue. 'Oh yes!' he groaned, and she pulled it into her mouth, and sucked on it. He slowly pulled it out after a while and said, 'If you would truly like . . .'

'Tell me what to do, Benedict,' she whispered.

'Come . . .'

He took a pillow from the bed and went to sit in the big chair by the empty fireplace, dropping the pillow on the floor between his feet. 'Come and kneel here, Kate, and let me look at you and enjoy the anticipation for a moment.'

She sank down between his knees and pushed her hair back over her shoulders. His strongly muscled thighs were spread wide, and he was erect. He smiled down at her and leant forward to caress her breasts, tweaking the erect nipples, murmuring, 'So beautiful, so damn erotic . . .'

Then he took her hand and placed it on him, and his sensitive member jumped a little at the contact. He released her hand and leant back in the chair, watching her, and she held him, wondering at how soft and silky the skin was, warm and taut in her fist. She moved it experimentally, up and down, and he reacted. 'You could do that, and God knows that would be good for me, Kate, or you could lick it. Lick the head, run your tongue across and around it. No teeth, my sweet, or you will hurt me. Taste me, as I have tasted you.'

She bent her head, still holding him in her fist, and licked the glistening head, across the slit and round. It was salty, she found, but not unpleasant, and he moaned in a most gratifying manner. 'Lick up and down the shaft, Kate!' he murmured, and she did, letting go of him and gripping his thighs instead, so she could lave up and down the full, engorged length, sometimes returning to the head to tease it with her tongue. She opened her lips wide so that she could slide up and down, lubricating the motion with the wetness of her mouth.

'Do you like it, Kate, or shall we stop?' he rasped. 'I swear I do not mind!'

'Liar! I think you would mind a great deal if I stopped. But I do like it,' she whispered against his hot, silky skin. 'What I think I would like more is for you to tell me what to do next – no, beg me to do what you would most like. And perhaps I will.'

'Christ! Well, then, Kate, I must say first of all – while I still have the power of speech – that I will not come in your mouth. When I am near, I will ask you to stop, and then I hope you will straddle me and mount me so that I can come with your breasts in my face. But now . . . please take me in your mouth and suck me, up and down. Hold me in your hand, too.'

She looked up at him with a wicked smile but did nothing. 'Is that what you really want, Benedict?'

He made a strange involuntary noise, something between a laugh and a moan. 'Please, Kate? Please take me in your beautiful mouth. Don't tease me, I beg!'

She bent forward again and put her hand on him once more, and he leapt in her hold, and then very slowly she took him into her mouth, hearing him gasp as she did so. She settled herself more comfortably on the pillow, put her other hand on his thigh, and began to suck at him, her curtain of hair falling across her face. She could not have seen him very well through it, but in any case her eyes were closed. A moment later his hand came to hold her head, his fingers tangling in her hair, but he did not press down on her or force her to take him deeper. She set the pace, slowly at first and then a little faster, and once again she had the sensation of being filled that she had found affected her so much. She was trapped between his strong thighs, and by his hand holding her, but she liked it – much more than that, in truth. Her breasts were tingling, her secret places too, and he was beginning to thrust into her mouth, and grip her head more tightly.

It was not long before he ground out, 'Kate, please stop!' and slowly, reluctantly, she pulled away from him, though she did not remove her hand. He was swollen, glistening wet from her mouth, fluid leaking from his tip, and he was breathing hard. 'Straddle me!' he said.

She released him, then rose to her feet and manoeuvred over him, setting her knees either side of his thighs in the big old chair. Her chest was flushed and her breasts ached for his touch, for his mouth. She reached down and took hold of him once more, and guided him into her, and he moaned yes, and gripped her bottom with both his hands, digging into her softness with his splayed fingers, thrusting up into her as he had thrust into her mouth a moment ago, but harder, no longer exercising the strict self-control he had before, but letting go of all restraint. He was kissing her breasts, licking them, and then sucking hard, hungrily, feasting on her swollen nipples. She put her hands on his shoulders, grasping them tightly, and rode him, pulling him deep into her, arching her back, clenching her buttocks in his hands.

He came, groaning and spasming, lifting her into the air and pressing his face between her breasts. She wrapped one arm around his shoulder and the other about his head, holding him to her as he gasped and thrust, the strong muscles in her thighs gripping him as he spent inside her. 'Kate,' he panted at last between her breasts, when his spasms had subsided, 'let me carry you and lay you down and make you come. I feel you were so close.'

In a moment they were on the bed. At his direction she raised her hips, and he put a pillow under her and knelt between her thighs. He slid his fingers between her legs, slipping in the wetness that came from both of them, and gripped her buttock in his other hand, spreading his fingers wide and kneading it. She angled her body up towards him, offering all of herself to him once more without any embarrassment, they were past embarrassment now, and he said raggedly, 'Kate, will you touch your breasts while I pleasure you? I think it would be glorious to see you do that, if you should like it.'

'I have been liking it any time these ten years!' she whimpered. She cupped the full globes in both hands, lifting them, and then took each nipple between her thumb and forefinger, and rolled and tugged them, harder than he would yet dare for fear of hurting her.

'My God!' he said, and pulled her closer, pressing on her nub and rubbing over it until she was moaning and starting to come, pushing herself against his fingers. When she climaxed, he slid his fingers into her, and stroked them in and out of her, prolonging her pleasure until she could bear no more. At last he stopped, and pulled his fingers free of her, and licked them as she watched him.

He lay down beside her then, and stroked her wild, disordered hair from her face so that he could kiss her. They were both covered in sweat, flushed and panting, spent. 'You have worn me out. I am a little sore, Kate – are you? I should think you are.'

'Yes,' she said, 'but, Benedict, I like it. I like the feeling that reminds me you were in me. I think I shall one day do as you said you would: I shall look at you in a public place, in your finest clothes, and I in mine, as men kiss my hand and call me Lady Silverwood, and all the while I will be thinking that my cunny – is that the word? – is tingling from you taking me.'

'From me fucking you.'

'From you fucking me. Do you like to hear me say it?'

'I love to hear you say it. Say it again.'

'From you fucking me, with your cock and with your tongue and fingers.'

'My God, Lady Silverwood, I swear one day I will take you to a ball – the grandest possible affair, held by the stuffiest people in society, and watch you dance with other men, in that dress you wore tonight, the one that barely covers your breasts and changes colour as they rise and fall, and I will see half of the *haut ton* growing hard for you, and know they cannot have you, and then I will take you into an upstairs room while they are still dancing downstairs and lock the door and fuck you standing, while you bite my shoulder so that no one can hear you screaming as you come.'

'Is that in the nature of a promise?'

'Madam, it is!'

CHAPTER TWENTY-EIGHT

They slept late the next morning, and ate a substantial breakfast in bed, for they were hungry, and, scandalously, stayed there. They dozed a little after breakfast, and when they woke towards noon he lay back and said, 'I have a question, Kate. I feel that I have recovered my strength, so that your answer to it will not necessarily carry me off – but if I am wrong, so be it. You may put it on my headstone: "Here lies Benedict Silverwood. He asked his bride of two days a question, and her answering of it killed him. He would not have had it any other way."'

She was sitting propped up on pillows beside him, the sheets at her waist, her unbound hair still spilling wild about her breasts and shoulders. It was very likely true that no lady should ever sit uncovered in such a scandalous, wanton manner, even when alone with her husband, but should instead be modestly clothed at all times. She did not care. She said, 'I do not understand you. How can a mere response of mine to any question you pose me possibly cause you grave injury?'

He took her right hand, and idly began to trace invisible patterns on it, and on her palm. The light touch was oddly erotic, and she felt the hairs on her arms stand on end, and her nipples tighten beneath their veil of hair.

'Ah, but you see, your answer will have two parts: a verbal explanation, which I may be able to bear, and something in the nature of a practical demonstration, which might carry any man off before his time, albeit with a smile upon his face, and no regrets.'

She began to understand him, and she felt her lips curve up involuntarily into a smile that, she was almost certain, did not make her appear any more respectable. She was probably a lost cause by now, and if she were not, she would be soon.

'Last night,' he said, 'I very tentatively – afraid that you might be shocked at the suggestion, concerned for your tender sensibilities; I have no idea why you are laughing, Kate – I very tentatively ventured to suggest that you might touch your breasts, and that you might enjoy it. Your quite unexpected response, my lady, led me to believe that it was not the first time you had laid hands on yourself. May I say in passing that you looked utterly magnificent while you were doing it?'

'You may.'

'Thank you. And this led me to reflect, while I was pleasuring you with my fingers and watching you, and very much enjoying doing so, that perhaps you have been in the habit of exploring your luscious body and giving yourself pleasure in other ways, with this delicate little hand that I now hold in mine.' He raised the hand to his lips, and began to kiss it, to bite on the soft pad of her thumb, and then to take each finger in turn into his mouth and suck it.

'I have,' she said breathlessly, as he sucked on her. 'With that hand, Benedict, I have done so, a thousand times, I dare say.' *Do not ask if I have ever thought of you while doing it; please, do not do so. If you ask me that now, I will tell you, and I do not know how you might react. I must not speak of love and spoil everything.*

He did not ask. Instead he said, 'If you would care to do that while I watched you, my sweet wife, I would be very grateful. I would consider it a privilege. It might help me, too, to know how better to pleasure you, if I see how you do it yourself, you know.'

She laughed. 'I have not observed that you have struggled to do that so far.'

'I am glad to hear it, but one can always learn in life, and improve. Would you show me, Kate? I am sure it would be . . . entertaining for us both, as well as instructive for me.'

'Would you like me to do it now, Benedict?'

He swallowed. 'I would!'

She cast the sheet back and kicked it aside, so that she was entirely uncovered, and settled herself lower against the pillows, pushing her hair away and piling it behind her head so that it did not obscure an inch of her flesh. She wanted him to see, and she did not close her eyes, as she generally might, for she wanted to see him too, and know herself supremely desirable in his eyes.

She reached down and toyed with her breasts, stroking them, lifting them and enjoying their weight. Then she began to play with her nipples, gently at first, for she was not yet as aroused as she had been last night. He lay close beside her, but he did not touch her yet; it seemed he did not mean to. His hand was on his cock; he was hard, and he stroked himself slowly, never taking his eyes off her.

Her nipples were taut, and she began to tug on them a little harder, biting her lower lip and throwing her head back, pushing her chest up and spreading her legs wider across the sheets. She reached down – no, she thought of a better thing and took her hand, the one he had kissed and sucked, and sucked on her fingers herself, wetting them, looking at him all the while as he handled himself, and then she slid her hand across her breast and belly and tangled it in between her legs. She found her clitoris and circled it with her wet fingers, then began to slide between it and her entrance, opening her lips and dipping in, using all her wetness to lubricate the passage of her fingers to and fro. She was tugging at her nipple much harder now, finding the edge between pleasure and pain, arching her back. She found the pillow and bit on it, and he saw, and took his unoccupied hand and gave it to her, pushing two of his fingers into her mouth so she could suck on them. She took them in gratefully, and sucked them hard, and pinched her nipple, and came as he watched her, gasping against his fingers, biting them, raising her hips off the bed, thrashing her head from side to side, plunging her fingers deeper.

When she slipped her fingers out of herself and rested them lightly on her mound, he took the hand and sucked on it once more. He was kneeling beside her on the bed, erect, engorged, and she whispered, 'I see you enjoyed the demonstration, and have survived it. What will you do with me now?'

He said, 'Now that you are wet and ready for me? Get on your hands and knees at the edge of the bed, Kate. I have observed before that you enjoy being taken from behind.'

'Possessed,' she said. 'Possess me, Benedict.'

Again some little part of her mind screamed caution, and warned her that if he cared really to listen to her he would surely realise that there was a deeper meaning to her words and her actions, but in her reckless need for him she paid it no mind. She did as he commanded her, and he came and stood behind her, and slipped into her at once, and again she gasped at the delicious feeling of being full of him, and raised herself up a little so that the angle was better, deeper. He took hold of her hips in a fierce grip and began pounding into her, hard and fast from the very start, and she buried her face in the sheets and lost herself in the sensation. He came swiftly, grinding into her, pulling her hips hard against him, crying out, 'Jesus, Kate!'

When they lay together afterwards, he said, 'I cannot imagine any more erotic sight than you with your hands on yourself. Thank you for letting me see it. I wish I had the words to tell you how spectacular you are, and what a lucky man I am.'

She shook her head wordlessly, and pulled his head down so she could kiss him, saying in the touch of her lips all the things she could not, dared not, put into words.

He kissed her, and stroked her skin very lightly, and after a while he said, 'My dear, you like to be held, don't you? Constrained, almost, though that's not the right word, because you are willing, so gloriously eager and willing. You like to feel my strength claiming you, holding you down. And once you are fully aroused, you don't like me to be too gentle, I think? You are not so very gentle, when you touch yourself.'

'It seems you are right,' she said in her low, musical voice. 'I do not know why.'

'Why do we like what we like? I do not think anyone really knows. I like your breasts smothering me, you have surely noticed, and your thighs, too, and your buttocks, your magnificent ample flesh all around me. That's what makes me come.'

'I had observed, yes.'

He said hesitantly, 'I wondered . . .' He bent his head to her ear, and whispered a suggestion, and her eyes widened as she listened, but she was not shocked; she felt a little curl of dangerous, forbidden excitement inside her.

'Tell me what you mean, Benedict, so that I am sure I understand you perfectly . . .'

CHAPTER TWENTY-NINE

The days of their honeymoon slipped away, and they managed to quit their bedchamber and spend some of them outside in the glorious Cotswold summer sunshine, although the Roman remains still went unvisited, and seemed destined to remain so. Mrs Thompson put up picnics for them, and they took a blanket and sat by the river, and sometimes they ate, and sometimes they read to each other of the trials of the Bennet sisters, or talked, or merely enjoyed the slow pace of their days, and sometimes Benedict took Kate into the woodland and held her tight against a tree and possessed her, and sometimes she sank to her knees, his hands locked in her hair as she took him in her mouth to pleasure him, and sometimes she lay back lazily in the dappled sunlight and exposed her breasts to the air and caressed them while he pulled up her muslin skirts and petticoats, buried his head between her lush thighs and drove her to ecstasy with his tongue and his clever fingers. And at night the same, but a little darker, a little more extreme, as they explored what brought them both pleasure with the mirror, and the silken ties, the blindfolds, and the other pleasurable, naughty tricks they devised for themselves in private.

But it was not all idyllic, except perhaps upon the surface. There were shadows. It was all very well to commit herself wholeheartedly to passion, and to push all thoughts of love aside, but Kate had not been entirely honest with herself, she realised now. Some part of her, it seemed, had naively imagined that their intimacy, so much greater than anything she could have anticipated, would lead inevitably to perfect confidence and openness between them in all things. It did not. She was coming to realise that Benedict was not a man who showed his feelings very openly, and she could not help but notice that he talked very little of his past; oh, he was ready always to speak of Lucy, or his mother, or tell an amusing story of his military service that presented him in a ridiculous light – she recalled now that he had done this upon the very first occasion they had met, seven years ago – but apart from that he said very little of his time in the army, and nothing at all of the dreadful things that she knew he had seen, and, perhaps, done. How could she know?

He was always perfectly courteous towards her, except upon occasions where passion rather than courtesy was required, and he never absented himself from her physically as he had done on that first dreadful day, but there were moments when he could have been a thousand miles away from her, although they were in the same room, the same bed. Although he was inside her. There were whole areas of his life, she thought, that remained closed to her. And, apart from that one night when he had been drunk and bared some portion of his soul, he never mentioned Vanessa.

Kate could not force him to speak of things if he did not wish to do so. The bond between them was still fragile, she thought, and she feared to strain it. For all she knew, it might break, and then where would she be? She would not soon forget the aching sense of bewilderment and abandonment that she had suffered that day when he had left her all alone, a prey to countless fears. And she had no one with whom she could discuss such things, no one she could write to for counsel. Once again, she dared not pour out her heart to her grandmother, so far away, and she hesitated to write to any of her childhood friends in such terms. Once again, she missed Cassandra, and wondered afresh if all was well with her. Although Cassandra was younger, and unmarried – she presumed she must still be unmarried – and therefore she could hardly tell her everything, could hardly explain how it seemed so wrong that one could be so very intimate with a man, and yet still feel a cold certainty that you barely knew him.

It could not be said that they lacked for

correspondence, even if Kate still heard nothing from Miss Hazeldon. She had letters of congratulations from her other friends, who said they had received nothing from Cassandra either, but wondered if perhaps she was too caught up in the pleasures of society to think of writing. And they had frequent news from Silverwood Hall – she would be obliged to learn to call it home. They heard of Lucy's wellbeing, and her games with her cousins, and the refurbishment of the Dowager's new rooms in the Hall, and Wellington's adventures, and how her grandfather did. He was in tolerable health, said the Dowager; between Miss Sutton and herself he received visits every day, and was well cared for, and glad when he got her letters, and Benedict's, as indeed were they all.

Her mother-in-law too was glad to know that they were getting along well, and hoped upon their return to hear of all the fascinating historical sites that they must have visited, and their impressions of them, in detail. Perhaps, she enquired, Kate had found time for sketching, and the production of watercolour vignettes of the local beauty spots? She was sure it could not be otherwise, and very much looked forward to seeing her accomplished efforts and admiring them.

Benedict chuckled as he read this out to her, and said, 'I would say that it would serve her right if you told her that you had seen hardly anything but the hangings of our four-poster bed, and nothing at all that you felt able to put into a sketch or watercolour, or certainly not one you could show her, except that I doubt you could shock her by anything you said; I have never managed it in two and thirty years.'

'On the contrary, I am sure that she would be excessively pleased if I told her that, and write directly to tell Maria that it was all because of the nightgowns that she insisted I had!'

'She probably would at that, and, having seen the night-rails in question, who is to say that she is wrong? Not I, certainly.'

Kate was hugely relieved to receive word at last from her grandmother, and to know that her own letter announcing her marriage had reached her safely. It was a chancy business, sending news half across Europe: the ship from London to Genoa, and then the hope that a courier could be found to carry the missive across the width of the Italian peninsula to Parma, or to the castle deep in the Apennine hills, if her *nonna* should chance to be there instead. But her letter had made that perilous journey without any mishap, and another had returned in the same manner, and Kate now read that her grandmother was very glad to hear that she was married so well, and to such a fine man, whom she well remembered from the Season of 1807. Albina spoke of Benedict's previous marriage, of how his heart could not be whole and undamaged, and there were wise words of love and caution, which Kate did not share, and would not share. And there then followed a great deal of rather startlingly forthright advice about the best manner of handling husbands, which made Benedict cry with laughter when she translated it for him, and many less respectable recommendations, some of which he insisted she carry out upon the instant.

The weeks passed, the month appointed for their honeymoon near gone, and it was almost time to return to Berkshire, and real life, and other people about them once again. Would it be different there? She wondered. Better? Worse? Here there was passion, always, and often laughter, but deep underneath it all a slight current of unease, as if it might be a glimpse of something or someone – a flicker of a blue dress, a woman's laugh, a toss of silver-gilt curls – out of the corner of one's eyes, which disappeared as soon as one regarded it directly. And Kate's courses, due a fortnight or so after the wedding and generally so regular, had not arrived.

If she should be with child, it could scarcely be a matter of wonder and amazement. Were her breasts a little tender, which she had heard might be a sign? Well, in truth they were, but then . . . She blushed as she thought of last night. It was no surprise her breasts tingled and felt heavy; it would be extraordinary if they did not. Perhaps it was the effects of their lovemaking, perhaps it was a sign of her courses coming late, or perhaps indeed she was already carrying his child inside her.

That current of unease, that sense of walking on eggshells . . . She still had not spoken to him of love, nor he to her, and why should he? He did not love her, but she knew he liked her, and found her amusing, respected her good sense, and took pleasure in her company. He thought she was beautiful – he told her often, and she did not doubt that it was true; she could see it in his eyes, the warm appreciation and admiration when he looked on her, and not only, or not always, when his eyes were dark with desire and the anticipation of imminent satisfaction. There could at least be no doubt at all that he wanted her: that sating his lust for her, in her, every day had not lessened his craving, but made it instead grow stronger with the feeding, all the more as they discovered the innumerable ways in which their wants and needs complemented each other's, and confessed secret urges that it was hard to imagine either of them sharing with another. She wondered if he had shared them with his lost Vanessa, the first Lady Silverwood – from the few words he had said of their brief time together, she believed that he had not, but if he had dared to do so, how might she have reacted? Kate had barely known her except by sight all those years ago, and it was all too easy and too tempting to think of her as a golden-haired doll in a sprig muslin gown, with empty blue eyes, like Lucy's best china doll, and a rosebud mouth pursed in shock, but that would be unfair. She had been a woman with her own thoughts and dreams and wishes, not a puppet, and she had married him and loved him, whatever that had meant to her and whatever would have come of it. It was not her fault she was dead and cold, and Kate in her place, in the bed that should be hers, in the arms of her husband. Not in his heart, perhaps, but in the heart of his child and hers. She pushed her unease aside, forced it down. She refused to be jealous of a dead woman, or blame her memory if he could not find it in his heart to love her now. Perhaps he never thought of his dead wife any more, or rarely, or perhaps when he did think of her it was of one long gone, a faint, ghostly memory that could no longer cause him pain. Or perhaps he thought of her and missed her dear presence every day, and still deeply regretted her loss, and wished her back, and Kate gone. How was Kate to know? Still he did not speak of it, and she could not ask him.

CHAPTER THIRTY

Benedict drove his curricle through the open wrought-iron gates of Silverwood Hall with deeply divided emotions. He was glad to be home, he supposed, and certainly anxious to see how Lucy did, for as always when he was absent from his daughter, he missed her. It had undoubtedly been the right decision not to have her accompany them on honeymoon; she would have been bored at Somerford House, and surely had a more enjoyable summer with her cousins, first here and then in Weymouth, where his sister had taken all the children for a fortnight and from where they had only just returned, but he was still eager to see how she was. His prolonged absence for the greater part of her childhood had left a residue of corrosive guilt that always rose up again when he was obliged to be parted from her, however much he might be reassured by letters from his mother and from Maria that she was having a perfectly splendid time. And now his uneasy feeling was made worse by the fact that he had not in truth missed her as much as he might have, should have, while in Gloucestershire, for he had been entirely preoccupied with Kate. And a very large part of him indeed was wishing that he could have stayed there, with nothing whatsoever to occupy his days but Kate. He feared that it was wrong to have such strong desires and regrets, to wish to neglect Lucy so; yet another weight of guilt to add to all the past actions for which he had to reproach himself.

Perhaps, he thought as he tooled up the gravel drive, with his wife silent and a little apprehensive, he thought, beside him, he would find that a return to normality, to home and to his ordinary preoccupations with the business of his daily life, would lessen, even banish, the fevered, heightened state of perpetual sexual desire in which he had found himself for the last six or seven weeks. He was quite sure that a person of an ordered mind would want such a restoration of his equilibrium, would welcome it. In which case, his mind must be disordered, for he did not. Not in the least.

He drew up outside the columned front of the Hall, and his groom jumped down and went to the horses' heads. Lucy waved from the portico above, and came running down the steps to meet them, with the Dowager and Miss Sutton following her more slowly. In a moment she was in his arms, and he was swinging her around as she squealed in delight. When he set her down at last, for fear of making her dizzy, not to mention himself, she ran to Kate and flung her arms about her, crying, 'Mama!' He realised suddenly that it was the first time in her life that she had been able to say such a thing, to greet someone she loved in such a way, and his eyes prickled with tears. At least he could congratulate himself on having chosen a bride very much to Lucy's liking, whatever other private turmoil he might be suffering as a result of his choice.

Kate was returning her embrace enthusiastically, and listening with every appearance of intelligent understanding to her outpouring of excited chatter, which jumped from her cousins to sea-bathing to Wellington to playing on the beach in a way almost impossible to untangle; he supposed it did not matter overmuch as long as the overall tenor of it was positive. At length Miss Sutton drew the child aside with a stern injunction not to chatter on like a rattle, but to let others speak, which admonition did not seem to distress her in the slightest, but slowed the flow just enough so that they could greet the Dowager and her companion and make their way inside to put off their travelling coats and take tea.

The Dowager was insistent that Kate preside at the tea table, and she did so, blushing a little. He was amused to notice that this simple request that she take her rightful position as mistress of his house caused her more embarrassment than some of the quite outrageously naughty things he had asked of her – and she had performed with gusto – in the past few weeks. This train of reflection, however, was clearly unsuitable for the sitting room, and should be quashed. Until later. He was already resolved to be quite done-up by the journey, so that an early night would be necessary.

His mother was telling them of the progress of the work on her new apartments in the west wing; all was done, and their things had been conveyed there, so that she and Dorothea would sleep there tonight. Kate enquired with concern if they would not sooner delay a while, but her mother-in-law shook her head, smiling, and said, 'We could have gone before, my dear, but when it came to it I had a foolish fancy that I would not care to leave Lucy all alone with just Amy in the main part of the house. I don't suppose that Lucy would mind in the least, but I thought Amy might be nervous, and so she was. The rest of the maids are there too, but their rooms are upstairs, of course, quite a distance away. Now that I have thought of it, I have arranged for two of the smaller chambers in our wing to be made up comfortably for them, so that if you should both happen to be away again she can stay close by us without the least trouble.'

'A very sensible notion,' said Benedict. 'Luke wrote me that everything is quite in order for your occupation. He tells me that your dining room and sitting room look quite splendid, and that the food reaches you from the kitchens just as hot as it is in the dining room here.'

'Indeed it does, and we mean to take advantage of it. We shall breakfast in our rooms always, and only dine with you when you invite us.'

Both Benedict and Kate cried out at this, but the Dowager was adamant. Miss Sutton chipped in in her abrupt way in support. 'Dare say we shan't bother to dress, but eat all anyhow, with books on the table, and that blasted cat of Charlotte's stealing tidbits off her plate. Liberty Hall, it will be. Quite looking forward to it, to be plain with you, Benedict. Your mother is too, you know. Stays, and so on. Absence of. Footmen fussing around, likewise. Men, generally.'

'Present company excepted, naturally, ma'am?' said her interlocutor with a grin, not in the least offended.

'Hmph,' she said, not disconcerted in the least, 'You're better than most of 'em, I will allow. But still, point stands. Men, stays, fuss, gloves, stairs. Deal of nonsense.'

Miss Sutton's manner of speech was eccentric, perhaps, but always perfectly comprehensible, and everyone present was quite accustomed to it, and perfectly able to ascertain her meaning. It was clear that she was entirely sincere in what she said, and that there would be a certain relief in the alteration in their circumstances, for her and also for the Dowager. Lady Silverwood would have far fewer servants under her direction, and fewer responsibilities, and she would no longer feel that Lucy was her charge. Benedict was glad of it.

On one of their last days in Gloucestershire, they had made an expedition into Cirencester, in search of a gift for Lucy – and also in truth so that they could say at least that they had been there, and spare their blushes, if the Dowager should ask – and had found for her a charming little tea service in a shop that sold all kinds of curiosities. This was now produced and unwrapped, to a rapturous reception, and they were all served tea from the thimble-sized cups, and obliged to drink it very gravely. Lucy was then given permission – and the assistance of Philip the footman – to take the service up to the nursery so that she could hold a party for her dolls.

In short order, the Dowager and Miss Sutton were escorted to their own door with great ceremony, the Dowager saying with a straight face and twinkling eyes that she was sure that they must be excessively fatigued from their journey and in need of rest, and recommending them to go instantly and lie down upon their bed, upon which comment Miss Sutton visibly poked her in the arm and said distinctly, 'Charlotte! Spoke about this! Leave the girl alone!'

Kate could only laugh, and accept the Dowager's invitation to take tea in her sitting room tomorrow afternoon; she foresaw a grilling, which she would far rather undergo in her husband's absence, since it seemed she could not escape it.

After they had left, Benedict took her hand, and said, 'May I conduct you to your new bedchamber, my lady? I think you have not yet seen it.'

'You may, sir,' she said demurely.

They climbed the broad, curving staircase together, and he directed her down the corridor to her right, and through a door at the end of it, into a large and pleasantly sunny chamber at the corner of the house, with sash windows looking out over the river on two aspects. He closed the door behind him rather firmly, and leant back against it, regarding her as she looked about her with interest.

'This has not of late years been my mother's room,' he answered her unspoken question. 'It is the suite proper to the mistress of the house, with its own sitting room and dressing room, and she gave it up to my brother's wife, Alice, upon his marriage. She never did move back to it after Alice died, and it has been unoccupied ever since. There has not been time to think of redecorating it to your taste, but you must certainly do so, if you wish. My room is next to it, and connected through that door.'

She understood that he was telling her that it had never been his wife's room, that he had never shared it with her, so there would be no lingering memories of Vanessa here for him, and she was glad to know it, and resolved not to enquire too deeply in his reasons for telling her so. It might be concern for her sensibilities; it might equally be concern for his own. Once more she was conscious of all that lay unspoken and unexplored between them.

But she said only, 'It's lovely. Perhaps I may think of changing it in time, when I have lived in it and thought what would suit.' It was decorated in shades of pale straw, not a colour she greatly cared for, but it was homely and attractive enough, and she would see how it looked by candlelight before she made up her mind. In truth, when she found herself alone in a room with her husband, interior decoration was rarely foremost in her thoughts.

He locked the door behind him, and came to stand close to her, putting his arms about her waist. 'Would you like to see the sitting room, my dear, or would you like to wash and – as my mother so thoughtfully suggested – rest for a little while?'

'I think I would like to get out of these dusty travelling clothes, certainly, Benedict. I shall ring for my maid,' she said, moving out of his embrace and crossing to the bell pull by the bed, but he was there before her, and put his hand on hers to prevent her.

'Let us not trouble her.'

This was a fresh start. 'Only wait while I go to the bathroom for a moment!' she said, and made for the door he indicated. Once there, she stepped out of the pantalettes she wore for travelling, and washed swiftly.

When she returned, he had stripped off his coat, waistcoat and shirt, and was standing by the bed bare-chested in his breeches and boots. She had not seen him like this before, but thought that it became him greatly; the combination of bare muscular torso, leather boots and tight buckskin breeches could only be highly pleasing to the eye. To her eye, at least.

She gave him her back, and he commenced undoing the dainty buttons that fastened her cherry-red travelling dress. 'You see how good I am?' he murmured against her neck as he did so. 'I have learnt a little self-control – just a little – and now intend to explore the pleasure of undressing you. It occurred to me just now that I have never seen you in your stays, and that this was an omission that should immediately be rectified.'

Her gown dropped to the carpet, very soon followed by her petticoats, and she stood before him in her stockings, chemise and corset. Many a fashionable lady had reason to be grateful for the design of the stays, which, by lifting the bosom and presenting it to the interested observer as a sort of delightful shelf, could create the illusion of a generous endowment from a relatively modest one, but for Kate, whose bosom was exceedingly ample already, the garment produced an effect that was nothing short of astonishing. This was sufficiently apparent under her gowns, but much more so now. 'My good Lord in heaven!' he said reverently, and pulled her close, intent upon releasing the drawstring of her fine lawn chemise so that her breasts might be fully exposed.

A few breathless moments later, he freed his lips from hers to whisper against her mouth, 'Shall I remove this garment, Kate – will it make you uncomfortable if I do not?'

'I suppose that depends on what you have in mind,' she gasped. He had backed her against the silk-covered wall of the bedchamber, dragging up her chemise and lifting her so that her naked and most sensitive flesh slid against his hard, leather-clad thigh, a contact she welcomed avidly; her legs were locked about his body and his hands were at her breasts, teasing out the most delightful sensations. She was sure that they had toppled several small pieces of furniture and made a great deal of noise in their frantic rush across the room; just at that moment, she did not care a jot.

'If you are ready for me . . .' She moaned assent and felt his lips curve in a wicked smile where they touched her cheek. 'If you are wet and ready for me, my wanton Kate, I suggest we repair to that sturdy armchair, and you unbutton my breeches and climb onto me and take me in, where I need to be. But I would not for all the world cause you any discomfort; shall I unlace you first? I am sure it would only take a moment.'

'Do you not like the way my stays present my breasts to you?' she teased, running her hands up his back. She could feel that he liked it excessively; the evidence was hard against her belly even through the leather of his breeches.

He tweaked one swollen nipple, tugging it and twisting it as she liked, and ground himself into her, and she clenched her thighs about his leg and pressed herself against the slick leather. 'You must know that I do, madam.'

'And so do I, sir. I like it for itself, and for the effect it has on you. And as for the stays, you have good reason to know that I do not at all object to a little . . . constraint when you are pleasuring me.'

Before she had finished speaking, they were in urgent motion again, staggering across the room to the chair, collapsing into it, her hands fumbling with the buttons at the fall of his breeches, freeing him. He pulled her onto his lap and she settled herself above him; in a sudden dizzy, delicious thrust of movement he was inside her; she shuddered and cried out at the feel of him, and seized his head roughly between her hands, twining her fingers deep in his silky hair, pressing his hot, hungry mouth to her breast. She was not alone in enjoying a little constraint, she had discovered. In this position she seemed to overwhelm him with her body and its demands, and he could do nothing but obey her; she was in control, not he, and just now she would not let him take his time. As to who possessed, and who was possessed, at such a moment it was impossible to know, or to care.

His hands were on her buttocks, gripping them hard as their bodies thrust together urgently, and his mouth plundered her breasts, obedient to her direction. Her need for satisfaction was almost painful in its wild intensity, and she clenched her internal muscles on him as tightly as she could. There were occasions when finesse was required in lovemaking; this was not one of them, and after a few more almost desperate, fierce lunges they came together in a great surge of glorious release, bodies slick with sweat, grinding together. He buried his face in her flesh and she held him there as he gasped and spent himself in her, smothered by her. A month or so ago she would have been shocked to know that their union could be like this, an animal expression of primal need – shocked, too, to think that she could so assert herself in seizing pleasure from him, in giving them both the climax they needed. She was far beyond such concerns now. They both were. In moments like these, nothing in the whole world mattered except the ecstasy they could share.

At last she settled back on his thighs and took his sweat-beaded face between her hands, pressing her open mouth to his and plunging her tongue deep into him. He responded eagerly, still caressing her bottom, reaching down and stroking her soft, damp skin, tracing the edge of her stockings.

When at last their mouths separated and they sat panting in each other's arms, he brushed his lips over her flushed cheeks – the sudden gentleness of his touch a startling contrast with the violence of the passion they had just experienced – and murmured, smiling, 'You liked that, I take it, Kate? It seemed to me that you liked it excessively.'

She ran her hands over his bare chest and arched her back; his hands were still moving on her, still evoking tingles of pleasure, and so she said, 'I am still liking it, since it seems to me that we are not by any means done.'

'I think you may be right, at that. Tell me what it was that aroused you so – the stays?'

'The stays, certainly. But also you, Benedict, dressed like this.'

'The leather breeches please you, do they, you wicked creature?'

'The leather breeches, and the boots, contrasting with

your naked chest. The . . . urgency of it, of how much you want me.'

'God knows I do, my sweet. So you think that you might enjoy it, then, if I threw you down across the bed and took you from behind, you still in your stays and stockings, I still in my breeches and boots? All hot from the exertion of riding or driving, perhaps, and too eager for each other to undress?'

'I am almost sure that I would enjoy it very much indeed, Benedict.' They kissed again, long and slow this time, their tongues tangling, her wet, sensitised nipples brushing the hair on his chest. His hands were still busy about her bottom and thighs, stroking, caressing, touching her in ways that he knew she loved until she was almost purring, and then the tip of one finger – oh, Lord – was doing something quite outrageous, something that made her moan and stiffen in his embrace.

'Shall I stop?'

'Good God, no!' she gasped out, and he chuckled, and persisted. 'Do you think it might please you too, to pull up my skirts and have me in such a way as you describe?'

'Not in the slightest,' he said gravely, his grey eyes darkening with desire once more and giving the lie to his words, his clever finger still working, sliding in and out of her now, as she began to quiver in his embrace, 'I would only be doing such a shocking, abandoned thing to make you happy, dutiful husband that I am. I have not the least thought to my own pleasure.'

She laughed, a deep, sensual sound, putting one hand on his shoulder to steady herself as his finger pushed deeper within her, igniting sensations that had her writhing in his grip and trailing the other hand down his muscular torso, and lower yet, until she found him, hard and engorged again already, and grasped him, his flesh leaping at her touch. 'I think you lie!'

'Well,' he ground out, his breathing uneven, 'we could put it to the test, of course. I am sure the thought of you sprawled lewdly across the bed, chemise flung up to display your magnificent bare thighs and arse above your stockings, is a matter of the completest indifference to me.'

'Is it so, indeed?' He nodded. She was moving her hand upon him, and his breath was coming in little gasps now. Not that she was in much better case, with his finger still working deep in her. But still she wanted more. She had a free hand; she ran it over her breasts, touching herself as he watched her. The sensations she was experiencing were becoming ever more intense, crying out for release once more.

She licked her lips, and bit the lower one in the way that aroused him so, whispering, 'What a pity. So you would not care, then, if I clutched the covers in my fists' – she illustrated the action – 'raised myself up and spread wide to you, and begged you to claim me in whichever way you should desire?'

'On the contrary, I am sure I should smack you soundly on your naked bottom for your wanton talk!

I think it is my duty to do so.' He bent his head to her other breast as he spoke, and ran his tongue around her taut, swollen nipple, then took it in his mouth and sucked on it, hard, just as she liked it.

She whimpered at the thought, and at the touch of his lips, and pressed down a little upon his finger, working him more strongly with her fist all the while. 'I have not the least objection if you make me all pink and tingling, as long as you do not stop there!'

It seemed they had teased each other enough. He groaned against her breast, 'A man can only bear so much. Shall it be now? Please say it shall be now, Kate!'

'I think it must!'

CHAPTER THIRTY-ONE

Kate had washed and put on her dressing gown, calling for her maid to help her change into a simple day gown and dress her disordered hair informally; it was a little too soon to dress for dinner and she wanted to go up and see Lucy in her nursery, and say good night to her. 'I shall be back in a short while to change again, Sarah – there is no point in you going all the way downstairs only to come up again. Will you lay out an evening gown for me?'

Once she was dressed, she set out to find Lucy. An easy matter, she had thought, for Sarah had given her directions, and so she knew that she needed to cross to the other side of the grand staircase, but she had not bargained for the size of the house, and was soon lost. Ridiculous to be lost in what was now, she supposed, her home. Certainly she had no other any longer.

She opened door after door, and saw bedchamber after bedchamber, the furniture all shrouded in Holland covers – beautiful rooms, each one, decorated in shades of rose, and faded red, and delicate green. And finally blue. Pale, icy blue. There was little doubt whose chamber this had been, for the distinctive colour told her – Vanessa's colour. Suddenly Kate shivered, as if the room were perceptibly colder than the rest of the great house. She felt all at once like Bluebeard's wife, and like her wished she had never opened the door, never looked inside. Because she was here. The shock held Kate transfixed, frozen, an interloper once again in Vanessa's world of icy perfection.

A portrait: she had not known there was a portrait. Mr Lawrence again – did the man never rest? Presumably it had been painted just after her marriage in 1807, Kate supposed, for it showed the girl she remembered. Beautiful, always so beautiful, in a blue silk gown, her silver-gilt curls elaborately dressed and piled on her head, and sparkling diamonds encircling her slender white throat. *This might well*, thought Kate with a pang of burning, irrational jealousy, *be her wedding gown. Benedict might have undone those tiny crystal buttons for the first time with shaking fingers, and pushed the silk from her perfect shoulders, and bent to kiss her perfect skin* . . .

There was no purpose in allowing such thoughts to take possession of her. Vanessa had been his wife. They had kissed and caressed each other, made love, conceived a child. Kate knew this. Had always known this. And still the woman remained an enigma to her. She was irresistibly drawn to move closer, to stand as if in interrogation, to see if she could come to know the first Lady Silverwood better than she ever had in life.

It was a curious painting, she realised now as she scrutinised it. Vanessa did not face the viewer head on, as was the convention of portraiture. Instead her back was to the watcher – the better to see the pure line of her neck and the fragile wings of her shoulder blades. Those tiny crystal buttons ran down her graceful silken back – perhaps they were diamonds, Kate thought with what she recognised as a touch of hysteria. Perhaps she had had diamond buttons. *Why not? She had everything else.*

The diamond girl looked back over her shoulder at Kate, a tiny smile just turning up the corners of her rosebud lips. Her eyes were celestial blue, but they were just flat paint and they held their secrets. She looked as though she were leaving: leaving the room, leaving the world, leaving Benedict. Merely an accident of the pose that the painter had selected, Kate supposed. Because she was, after all, still here.

Did Benedict visit the portrait still – talk to it, share his feelings with it, as he never truly had with her? Yet another question to add to the long list of things that Kate could not know, and dared not ask.

All at once she could not bear the smug painted gaze for a second longer, realising suddenly that, if she had presumed to interrogate it, it in turn was interrogating her. Despising her. *He married* you? it seemed to sneer. *He had me, and lost me, and all he could think to replace me with was* you? Kate hurried from the room, and fought the urge to slam the door behind her. Instead she closed it very carefully, and stood with her back against it, shaking.

It was a long moment before she could compose herself, and slow her panicked breathing, and set out again to find Lucy's nursery. She would not allow herself to be diverted from her purpose by foolish fears and fancies; none of this was Lucy's fault. Vanessa was dead – long dead – and Kate was all the mother Lucy had now.

At last she took the correct turn, and found that Benedict was ahead of her, sitting by the little girl's bed; she had bathed and eaten her supper, no doubt said her prayers, and he was reading her a fairy story. She hesitated in the doorway, wondering once more if she was intruding, but they both smiled up at her warmly, and he made space for her on the bed beside him.

When he had finished, Lucy was plainly sleepy, but refused to let them go until Kate held her hand and told her 'one of her special stories, about the girl who lives in the castle and her adventures'. These were the heavily embroidered tales of Albina's childhood in her father's castle in the hills near Parma, which Kate had been told as a child and never forgotten. They featured highly intelligent talking animals, which, Lucy drowsily observed to her father, who was hearing one of the tales for the first time, she was very well aware did not exist in England, for she was not a baby, but might still in Italy, for all they knew, as they had none of them been to that country. By the time it was done she was heavy-eyed and only murmured, 'Good night, Papa, good night, Mama,' when they rose and left her, closing the door softly behind them.

'Thank you for coming up to see her, my dear – it means a great deal to her, as I am sure you observed,' he said softly as they descended the stairs and reached the landing below.

'It was my pleasure, Benedict.' Kate was aware that her eyes were brimming with tears at the little girl's words; they had touched her deeply in her still shaken state. She saw that he too was affected, and her hand went up of its own volition and touched his cheek. He cradled it for a second in his, and then drew her into his arms, burying his face in her hair and whispering, 'My dear sweet Kate, we are all so lucky to have found you.' His words and embrace were full of affection, without a hint of passion, and she realised that it was the first time that he had held her thus, not appearing to want anything from her but human contact, perhaps even comfort, apart from in the aftermath of lovemaking. She stood in the circle of his arms, and dared to hope, all the while aware of how dangerous such hope might be. And in a tiny corner of her mind as they embraced she still pictured Vanessa, looking over her shoulder and smiling her mysterious, pitying little smile, as if to say, *You foolish, foolish woman.*

They dined alone, and as they sat together in the candlelight Kate made a deliberate effort to achieve a sense of calm, even if it should be an illusion. They spoke of their plans for the coming months, and she lost herself in the distracting details with relief: they must find a new governess for Lucy, and Maria had invited them to London to stay with her for a week or two, and go about in society with her; Kate hoped this meant that she was now fully accepting of Benedict's marriage. It should be quieter in Town by the time they arrived, the frenetic activity of the Season and the summer victory celebrations long abated, and it would, they hoped, be possible for the new Lady Silverwood to make her debut as a married woman without attracting too much vulgar attention. Mrs Singleton had boxes at the opera and at the theatre, and would besides hold a small, select evening party in their honour.

'I confess I greatly look forward to the opera,' said Kate, eager to talk lightly of pleasant topics, and keep the shadows at bay. 'I always enjoyed attending the touring performance I have seen in the summer in York.'

'I look forward to the opera and the theatre with you, and even a few parties, although I did not care very much for my experience of the Season this year.'

He hesitated for a moment and then said, 'I expect my mother told you that I went in search of a wife. I think I can only now count myself very fortunate indeed that I did not find one there.' He raised his glass to her.

Kate blushed and raised hers in response, but could think of nothing to say that would not sound foolish. *Foolish, foolish woman*, was the refrain still echoing in her head, as those flat blue eyes mocked her. She could not be anything other than delighted at his words, and the implication of deeper feeling that seemed to underlie them, but her composure was a fragile thing, and always would be, she feared, while so much still lay unexpressed between them.

And then he added, with a wicked gleam in his eyes, 'Perhaps we will attend a ball, or some other event that is a sad crush, so that we are able to slip away and keep a certain appointment that we once made.'

She perfectly recalled the reference, and the smile she gave him in response to it made him drain his glass and rise to his feet, saying, 'I think it is time for bed, Kate.'

Kate rose too, and put her hand in his. Even such a light touch of his bare skin made her shiver with anticipation. It seemed they could sate themselves in each other, and yet this urgent desire would reignite at the slightest of touches. In this respect if no other, she knew him hers. At least they had this – this was not nothing – and surely no painted dead woman, however beautiful, however perfect, could take it from them. 'I'm sure you are right. I expect you are tired after driving so far, and all your . . . other exertions.'

'Perhaps a little. We shall see. Come, Lady Silverwood.'

CHAPTER THIRTY-TWO

Kate was shown into the Dowager's new sitting room, and was able to express genuine admiration. It was freshly papered with fine Chinese scenes and held all of her favourite paintings and objects, with the Lawrence portrait – Kate resolved with a tiny shudder that her thoughts would not dwell on portraits today – of the carefree young Silverwood siblings above the mantel in the place of honour, and shelves groaning with well-used books in the alcoves either side of it. There were French windows looking out over the lawns, and the river below, placid today and flowing quietly, was looking especially lovely with the reflections of the trees in it. Some of the leaves were beginning to turn gold; autumn was coming. There were beautiful new thick brocade curtains that could be snugly drawn when it should be cold, and altogether it was a very pleasant room in which to take tea, and be interrogated about the details of one's honeymoon by a lady whose sharp eyes missed nothing.

Kate enquired after Miss Sutton – she felt that her gruff but kindly presence might well have protected her from the Dowager at her most alarmingly frank, but was informed that she had gone to visit Mr Waltham. 'You must have observed, my dear, how fond they are of each other beneath their bluster; he is one of the very few men in the world that she has the least regard for, along with Benedict, of course. She absolutely loathed my husband and disliked poor Caspar even more, I think. How did you find your grandfather this morning?'

Kate sighed. 'In very good spirits, and delighted to see me, but weaker, I thought, than he was a month ago. He claimed to be perfectly well, of course, but he is . . . fading away. He has lost weight since I last saw him.'

The Dowager said, 'He has, and I am sorry it distresses you, but I hope you will agree that he is in good spirits. Your marriage was an enormous weight off his mind, and now that he no longer worries about you, he is quite tranquil, and has no regrets. I am sure he would be glad to hear any happy news you might have to give him' – and here she looked at Kate beadily, and Kate feared very much that she blushed and looked sadly conscious – 'but all in all I think that he is as content and hopeful as any sincere Christian could be as he approaches the end

254

of his life, and that is more than many of us will ever be able to say, you know.'

There was a great deal of truth in this, Kate knew, and it was moreover kindly meant, and she thanked her mother-in-law for it with some warmth. That lady looked her up and down, her blue eyes sharp as ever, and said, 'Well, on a more pleasant note, I hope I need not enquire if my son is treating you as he should, for I see that you are in great beauty. Blooming, one might almost say.' She cocked her grey curls on one side in enquiry, and smiled innocently at her daughter-in-law.

Kate shook her head. She was not deceived, being all too aware that the Dowager had with her usual cunning made sure to acquaint herself with the timing of her own courses, though Kate had been ignorant of her purpose then; she could not suppose for a moment that Charlotte had forgotten when they should have made their last appearance. However much she was pressed, she had absolutely no intention of informing her mother-in-law that as yet they had not done so. 'We have only been married a month, ma'am; you know that it is too soon to say.'

'But not for want of trying, I hope?'

It was impossible to do anything but laugh at such outrageousness and be conscious that she was blushing to the roots of her hair. 'Certainly not for want of trying! I think I can say in all honesty – if I am then permitted to say no more on the subject afterwards – that I do not believe that two newly married people could have tried any harder.'

'I am very pleased to hear it, my dear Kate. And Benedict looks well too, I thought, and happy.' This was phrased as a statement, not a question, but there was a question lurking there, all the same. The crucial question.

Kate understood perfectly well that her mother-in-law had now moved in her enquiry from the physical realm to that of feelings, and it was here that she still felt herself to be desperately unsure, and could offer no reassurance. 'I hope he is, ma'am. He does appear to be. He enjoys my company, I am sure. I cannot . . . I do not know what more I can say. He has not spoken of his feelings; I have no reason to think them unchanged from what they were when we married.' *I have no reason to think that he loves me. Foolish woman.*

The Dowager regarded her thoughtfully. 'I am sorry, my dear. I know it cannot be easy for you. And yet I perceive that there is a closeness between you.'

'Yes. Yes, there is, but that may be just . . . We find ourselves compatible in certain ways. Excessively so. I believe that I need not say more, nor should I wish to do so.'

'That is certainly something. It might not have been the case, after all. I do not think . . . I wonder how many couples find such a bond?' She looked down, and Kate understood her to be saying without words that she had not found a similar bliss in her own marriage. 'I suppose it is early days yet, as you say. And I am sorry for quizzing you. I should not be so impatient, nor so intrusive.'

Kate smiled at her. 'I can only imagine what my grandmother might be saying to me if she were here. The questions she would ask! Her letters are bad enough. I find you quite forbearing, in comparison. My embarrassment comes only from the fact that you are his mother, which makes for a certain awkwardness.'

'I can see how that might well be so,' said the Dowager drily. 'I am grateful for your frankness, dear Kate, and for your confidences. I certainly never had such a conversation with Vanessa, nor with poor Alice, for that matter. But then, they were so very young and naïve when they married, both of them, and Alice at least had a mother living to advise her, though Vanessa did not, of course, which perhaps . . . In my ignorance I believed that there was time for delicacy and patience. For closeness to grow between us naturally over the course of years. I know better now.'

Kate had not the least idea what to say. At last she ventured hesitantly, 'But if you had spoken to them, either of them, would it have made any difference? They both conceived children, did they not? And Alice died in childbirth, and her son did not survive. How could anything you said to them have affected such an outcome in the least?'

The Dowager nodded sadly when she spoke of Alice, and Kate suddenly realised something. She had no real idea how Vanessa had died; she had assumed it must be in childbed too, as it was a constant and very real threat hanging over all women who bore children, hanging over her too now, but she did not recall that anyone had ever told her so directly. It suddenly seemed important to know. 'Ma'am, what happened to Vanessa? I am sorry to distress you, and I know it can only be painful to discuss such a tragic time for your family, but . . .' She trailed off, unwilling to say that she thought she now had a right to hear details that surely were excessively unpleasant to recount.

Her mother-in-law patted her hand. 'Do not apologise, my dear. It is your family too now. She did not die bearing Lucy. She was killed in a terrible accident, a carriage accident. She survived it for a while, but . . .' Charlotte put her hand up to her face, and Kate realised that she was weeping, and struggling to conceal it. Any words that she could find to say, any comfort she could think to offer, would surely be wholly inadequate, and yet she could not sit in silence.

'Oh, ma'am, you have all suffered so much. Such a succession of terrible, undeserved events. This family has been so terribly unlucky.'

'I suppose it must seem so,' said her mother-in-law somewhat enigmatically, as she found her fine lawn handkerchief in her reticule and wiped her eyes. Her face was grey now, and she seemed understandably drained by the conversation they had had, but she leant forward with a sudden burst of frail energy and said, 'My dear, I hope that one day Benedict will feel able to share this tragedy with you himself. When once he does so, I think you will know yourself secure. I hope that that day will be soon. But if it does not come, please do not tell him what I have told you. I may be wrong, but I think it should be he who raises this topic with you.'

Kate could see the justice of that, but wondered dully if that day would ever arrive. He had endured so much; was it any wonder he would not open his heart to her now? She could do nothing but be patient, however hard it was.

CHAPTER THIRTY-THREE

Benedict leant towards his wife slightly and said in a low voice, 'You are in high beauty tonight, Kate.'

She smiled and thanked him, blushing charmingly. It was entirely true; she was looking quite at her best, he thought, and her best was nothing short of magnificent. Her hair was dressed in her favourite style with one dark, shining ringlet lying across her bare shoulder. For the trip to the opera that she had so longed for, she had chosen to wear the changeant silk in rich brown shot with gold. Thinking of it and how much it became her, he had recently surprised her with the gift of an unusual necklace of tiger's eyes in a golden setting, and it sat around her throat now, the lowest stone just dipping into the deep valley between her breasts. A valley in which a man could lose himself and never regret it for a moment.

The stones gleamed tawny against her olive skin, and complemented the rich, changeable hues of the gown. He would have said that the necklace drew the eye to her splendid breasts, but in truth they needed no such framing. He knew he could not be the only man here tonight who looked on her with hunger and grew hard as he looked. How could he be? But he was the only man who would take her home and make love to her. A vision of her lush body naked in his bed, writhing against the white sheets as she panted with desire for him to take her, to possess her, intruded itself into his thoughts with startling vividness, and he wondered how long this opera would be. Too long for his liking, he was quite sure. But she was thrilled to be here, and he would be patient, though it was a struggle, and entertain himself by watching her pleasure play out on her expressive face, even if it did torment him with reminders of the greater pleasure he hoped to see there as soon as they were alone.

Her eyes were bright with delight and her cheeks flushed with wild rose, her lips slightly parted in anticipation as she waited for the music to begin. Her breasts rose and fell with her slightly agitated breathing, and the stones gleamed with the movement. He could so easily reach out his hand and . . . Christ, this was no good.

He looked away from her at the theatre around them, desperate to distract himself from the urgent throb of his desire. He perceived that the box in which his sister's party sat was the object of general interest, that many of the occupants of the boxes opposite were regarding them with avid curiosity, some of them through quizzing glasses, some of them whispering behind fans as they stared. He supposed it was understandable, though it was not pleasant. The auditorium was full of the people he had met during his recent time in London. He had, after all, made his fixed intention to find a wife this past Season perfectly plain – else why would a man of his age and disposition have been attending balls and dancing with debutantes? He had signalled that he was on the hunt for a bride, but had found none on the marriage mart, and now here he was, barely two months later, with a wife by his side. A wife who was plainly not a green girl at the end of her first Season, but a mature woman, fashionably dark and voluptuous, strikingly attractive, impossible to overlook. Some of them, no doubt, would have seen the announcement of their marriage, and be aware that she was, as they would no doubt have it, a nobody. Both men and women would find their first sight of her quite sufficiently titillating, a worthy subject of gossip and speculation. Damn them for a pack of worthless, chattering fools.

And by some distance the worst of them was his cousin Felix, and there he was – of course malign fate would have arranged for him to be present tonight. His heir caught Benedict's eye, and bowed in the ridiculously affected manner he favoured, indicating with his finicky, dandified gestures that he would visit their box in the interval and make the acquaintance of Benedict's bride. One might be quite sure he would. Felix's delicate nose had surely been put out of joint by the news that his cousin was to wed; no doubt he would lose no time in coming to inspect the woman who would – God willing – very soon be the means by which he was supplanted.

Benedict checked himself; he was perhaps unfair. There was no denying the fact that the fellow was a dandy, but that in itself was no reason to condemn him; so was many another, his own friends along them. Some of the best soldiers he had known had been members of the dandy set in another part of their lives, and fought none the less bravely for it, and died in the heat of South America, the dust of Spain and the mud of France along with the rest. A deep concern for the set of his cravat and the shine of his boots did not automatically make a man a fool or a popinjay. If he thought Felix a jack-at-warts and a wastrel, he must find a better reason for it. He certainly could not snub him, but was obliged to receive him with cordiality and introduce him with due ceremony to his bride as a member of the family, which after all he was: he was a Silverwood too, his first cousin. And Caspar had liked him well enough – but then, that was no kind of recommendation, but rather the reverse. Perhaps indeed that was why he disliked the fellow so. Perhaps he resented the closeness that the two had shared as adults, when he and his brother had had little to say to each other once they were grown. An uncomfortable train of thought, and one not to be dwelt on. Were no safe topics whatsoever available to him tonight?

He realised that Kate was entirely oblivious to the sensation she was causing, caught up as she was in the excitement of her first visit to the London opera. Another woman must have noticed the myriad eyes on her, whether through shy self-consciousness or through its opposite, a love of attention, but not she, in her absorption in the moment. She had such a boundless capacity for enjoyment, for losing herself in pleasure, whether it be the passion they found in bed together, or the simple joy of jumping in puddles with Lucy, or her deep love of music, as now. As she had said to him once, before he knew her properly, it was not in her nature to live by half-measures. He found this quality in her admirable, and oddly touching. She was talking with his sister, smiling at something she had said, and suddenly he felt a surge of affection for his wife, of an intensity that surprised him, and it impelled him to reach out and take her gloved hand in his.

She turned to him, a hint of a question in her eyes. 'I was observing how delighted you are to be here, and how much you look forward to the music tonight. I hope it lives up to your expectations – do you know the opera well?'

'Oh, yes! I love Mozart's work, and this is one of my favourites. It all takes place over the course of one frenetic day, you know. I have sung the arias myself often enough, and coached my pupils in the pronunciation of the Italian if they desired to sing them, although many of them, of course, are not appropriate for the repertoire of young unmarried ladies.'

'That sounds decidedly promising. Which one of the more inappropriate ones would you sing for me, if I asked you to?'

She laughed, and looked up at him saucily through her long dark lashes. 'I suppose my choice would be "*Deh vieni, non tardar*"!'

'Will I survive you telling me what it signifies?'

Her voice was rich and seductive as she murmured the Italian words of the aria, and then proceeded to translate them for his ears alone. He closed his eyes, and held up a hand for her to stop, but with a wicked chuckle and a wickeder emphasis she continued, '"Come . . ."'

'My goodness,' his sister's unwelcome voice interrupted sharply, 'what are you talking of so intently? They are about to begin, but you are neither of you attending!'

'I'm sorry,' said Kate demurely, 'I was merely translating some of the Italian lyrics for Benedict, so that he might take more pleasure from them.'

'Very commendable, I am sure,' said Maria drily. 'How lucky you are, brother, to have found a wife so accomplished.'

'Well do I know it,' he replied. As the overture began, he raised Kate's gloved hand to his lips, and whispered for her ears only, 'You may display your many accomplishments for me later!'

'My mastery of the Italian tongue, you mean, sir?'

He groaned softly. It was undoubtedly going to be a long evening.

CHAPTER THIRTY-FOUR

Benedict was much more affected than he had expected to be by Kate's absorption in the opera. It was in many ways a ridiculous farrago of nonsense, involving a great deal of disguise and hiding in cupboards and behind sofas, but even he could tell that the music was sublime, and as for his wife, she was transported. He had mused earlier that she took equal pleasure in a variety of mundane experiences, but he saw now that this was untrue. She had a great deal of zest for life in all its aspects, but there was only one other activity he knew of that could entirely carry her away from herself in such ecstasy, and it was an odd and not entirely comfortable experience for him to see her like this now. It was not that he disapproved of her losing herself in the music to such a degree, tears streaming down her face, though he could well imagine that others might. He expected that those censorious persons would also very strongly deplore the passion that he and Kate shared. Neither thing was proper, nor genteel; both might be thought to display an excessively ardent nature. He did not give a fig for that, and saw no reason why women – ladies – should not be every bit as passionate as men. He had every cause to know that life was short, and he did not suppose that anyone – unless their marital relations had later proved to be most unfortunate – ever lay on their deathbed regretting making love to their wife or husband and enjoying it excessively. He could well imagine a person might well regret not doing it more, and he resolved not to be one of those unfortunate gentry. No, he revelled in her intensity of feeling; how could he not, when he was such a beneficiary of it? But it was a little disconcerting, to put it no more strongly, to see that his lovemaking was not the only thing that could bring her to such a pitch of enthusiasm.

Was he jealous of music? How preposterous. He could surely not be jealous of Herr Mozart, near thirty years dead, nor of the portly fellows disporting themselves on the stage before him. He did not imagine that his wife was likely to run off with either of the gentlemen in the ill-fitting wigs, however well they sang, and as for the pretty young fellow, so popular with all the women, who seemed to be going for a soldier, he strongly suspected that he was in fact a girl; he must ask Kate, later. Was it perhaps true then that he was jealous that Kate had the capacity to be totally absorbed in anything but himself? If that were so, it raised some rather interesting and not entirely welcome questions in his mind.

He was distracted from his uneasy musings by the arrival of the interval, and, hard upon it, the appearance of his cousin Felix Silverwood in the box. The fellow had address, he had to give him that, he thought grudgingly, as he watched his cousin make his bow over Kate's hand and profess himself charmed to meet her.

Mr Silverwood was near as tall as Benedict himself, and resembled him somewhat in colouring and in the lineaments of his face, but he was of a much less athletic build, his shoulders by no means so broad, nor his frame so powerful; he was indubitably a dandy, a Pink of the Ton, rather than a Corinthian or any kind of sportsman. His frame was willowy and graceful, and his attire exquisite in every respect, from his snowy neckcloth, tied in complex folds, to his form-fitting coat and pale waistcoat. His hair, much the same honey brown as his cousin's, was pomaded into fashionably disordered waves, he smelt like a damn perfume shop, and his handsome face was wreathed in delighted smiles that made Benedict, if no one else, feel decidedly queasy. Would the creature never let go of Kate's hand?

Felix was addressing him now. 'My dear cousin, I congratulate you! I knew, of course, that you were married, for your revered mother wrote to inform me of the happy news.' *I'll wager she did*, thought Benedict with grim humour, *and greatly would I love to have observed your reaction to her letter.* 'But I had no notion that you had carried off such a beauty. What a sly dog you are, Benedict, to be sure. Tell me, Lady Silverwood – or may I call you dear cousin? – where have you been hiding your light? For I am sure I would have remembered you, if I had ever had the great good fortune to encounter you before.'

Benedict gritted his teeth, and hoped that Kate would not be taken in by so much flummery. To him, at least, there was spark of malice in Felix's gaze, and in his honeyed words. He did not care in the least for the way he ran his insolent eyes over Kate's body, and, after all, to say that his 'dear cousin' was quite unknown to him was almost as much as to say that she was not a member of polite society – to imply perhaps that she was of obscure birth, even of ungenteel origins.

Kate did not appear to be discomposed, and he could not tell if she perceived the hint of a slur, if slur there was in the affected, lazy drawl. She only said coolly, 'I do not believe that we have met before, sir. But that is hardly to be wondered at, for I have passed the greater part of my life in York, where my grandmother resided until recently, and have only been living in Berkshire for a few months.'

'I am sure that the north's loss is our gain,' said Felix amiably. 'Dear Benedict's gain, chiefly, of course, but any new ornament in society is always to be welcomed.'

The way in which he pronounced the word 'ornament' as he looked at her made Benedict long to plant him a facer, and Maria must have seen some hint of it, for she rushed into speech, asking Felix some question about the mutual acquaintances whose box he graced this evening, and a moment later some military gentlemen arrived, welcome visitors this time, old companions from South America and the peninsula who were eager to be introduced to Kate, and the impulse passed, but the uneasiness lingered.

CHAPTER THIRTY-FIVE

'I suppose I will be obliged to invite Cousin Felix to my rout party, though he is a wretched, disagreeable creature, and I cannot feel quite easy in his company,' said Maria pettishly. 'Indeed, I think I have no choice but to ask him, unless we are to be quite at outs with him, and although I would not mind in the least, I admit it would present a very odd appearance, and would be bound to cause comment.'

Benedict had stirred in instinctive protest, and his sister responded before he had a chance to voice his objections. 'I know you dislike him very cordially, and so do I, but he is such a close relation that I have no option but to send him a card. I would be seen as snubbing him, otherwise, and he is very well connected, you know, and invited everywhere.'

The two couples were seated in Mrs Singleton's carriage, making their way home from the theatre. Mr Singleton had had to be roused from deep, refreshing slumber in order to make their exit, having slept through the greater part of the evening's entertainment, although when shaken briskly awake by his wife he had declared the opera to be capital entertainment, very jolly stuff, by Jupiter! He seemed only half-awake now, and made little contribution to the conversation, beyond an occasionally resonant sound somewhere between a snore and a snort.

Kate said hesitantly, 'Mr Silverwood is very handsome and elegant, there can be no doubt, but I own he made me feel somewhat uncomfortable; I cannot say why. Did I imagine that he intended some satirical meaning in what he said to me?'

'You did not imagine it, my dear,' Benedict replied. 'There is always an undertone to what the fellow says. And in this case his reason for it is not far to seek. He is my heir, and it cannot at all suit him to see me married.'

Maria laughed. 'Suit him! I will swear it does not. I am sure that he is very expensive – imagine his tailor's bills alone! – and I never heard that our uncle Henry's fortune was large, so I cannot conceive how he manages to live as extravagantly as he does. To have Silverwood Hall, the estate and the baronetcy fall into his lap would be a gift from heaven. But still, it would be quite ridiculous for him to be banking on inheriting from you, Benedict. Why, he is only four or five years younger than you, and so you might very easily outlive him, even if you had never married again, which he must have expected that you would one day.'

'All that you say is quite true,' her brother said. 'And no man of principle would bank on such an inheritance, let me be twice the age I am. But then I have no reason to think him a man of principle; he may be received everywhere, thanks to his birth, his air of fashion and his dashed ingratiating manners, but he has some deuced odd friends, he is a reckless gamester, and I would go bail that he is deep in debt and barely outruns the constable. I can only suppose that he has come to count on stepping into my shoes, or at least has been dwelling on it more than he should. I thought there was real malice in his words, and in the way he looked at you, Kate.'

She shuddered. 'I do not disagree with you. I thought so too, even though I do not know him at all. But surely he can intend us no actual harm? Let us agree that it was pique and jealousy speaking.'

Mr Singleton must have been half-following the conversation, for he muttered, 'Damned loose screw! Ugly customer!' but then gave a sort of gusty snort, and was lost in the arms of Morpheus again.

His wife ignored his interjection, but said, 'I expect that you are right, Kate. It would suit his envious nature to whisper disagreeable things about you, and cut up your tranquillity, but that must be the extent of it. And if he does so in too egregious a manner, everybody will know that he is motivated by nothing more than jealousy, for it is quite generally known that he is Benedict's heir. If he is not excessively careful, his reputation will suffer rather than yours. And I am sure he would dislike nothing more than to be a laughing stock. He is very proud, you know.'

'And yet we are obliged to entertain the fellow and smile at him, and be all complaisance!' grumbled Benedict. 'I know it has to be so, Maria, you need not say so again, but I cannot like it. I am sure he would do us a mischief if he could.'

'But what can he do?' asked Kate. 'If he were to noise it abroad that I have no fortune, and have earned a living by teaching, that is nothing more than the truth, and no secret from anybody. If he were bold enough to ask me, I should tell him so quite openly. I have made no false claims and have nothing disreputable to conceal.'

'Of course you have not,' said Benedict, his voice warm in the darkness. 'Do not lose a moment's sleep over him. And I pray you will not permit him to affect your enjoyment of Maria's party, either. It is to be in your honour, you know, to celebrate our marriage, and such a frippery fellow cannot be allowed to spoil it for you.'

Kate and Maria plunged into discussion of the arrangements for the rout and the crucial matter of what they should wear, and Benedict leant back, frowning a little in the darkness. He had to concede that his companions were right: even if Felix might intend genuine harm, which was by no means certain, there could be nothing that he could in sober reality do to affect Kate, beyond some unpleasant gossip. Benedict did not greatly care if tongues wagged over his choice of bride, as long as she was not put out of countenance by them; he did not mean to spend his married life in society, but was only in Town now to do the minimum required to introduce Kate to the polite world. Let Maria throw her rout, let Kate refurbish her wardrobe for the winter, and then they could be off to Berkshire, and Felix and the shallow, fashionable world he inhabited could go hang. By the time the Season rolled round again, he might be a father once more; perhaps there would be a brother for Lucy. Then Felix might gossip all he liked, for he would no longer be the heir to Silverwood. And if there was no child, or Kate's first child should be a girl, they would keep on trying. There was certainly no hardship in that.

CHAPTER THIRTY-SIX

Town was a little thin of company, as much of the *haut ton* was dispersed across the land at various country estates, engaging in desperate flirtations, if not full-blown affairs, and shooting a variety of unlucky creatures, but Mrs Singleton had had most satisfactory responses to the cards she had sent out for her rout party; she thought that her acquaintance must be in a fever of curiosity to meet the second Lady Silverwood. Those present at the opera, and at the theatre when they had attended it a few days later, would surely have spread the word that the bride was a beauty, and they would not want to forgo the opportunity of meeting her and judging for themselves.

There was not to be dancing, but there would be music. Music of a very high order. Maria was determined to avoid anything insipid and commonplace, or any impromptu scrambling for turns at the pianoforte, but had asked certain ladies and gentlemen of her acquaintance who were genuinely talented to favour the company with their most brilliant pieces. There was to be a printed programme, so that no young lady of inferior talent – nor her over-proud mama, as so often happened – might force herself to the fore and inflict her indifferent accomplishments upon those present. And Kate was to sing.

The Dowager had told her daughter that Kate was reputed to be an extremely accomplished singer – presumably Mr Waltham had told her so – and one afternoon when they were alone, Benedict and Mr Singleton having taken Lucy and her cousins to the Tower to view the menagerie, Maria had asked her casually to perform, offering to accompany her. She had at that point not yet revealed her plan to have musical entertainment at the party, and would certainly not suggest that her new sister-in-law take part if she should prove to be only adequate. She would triumph, or not involve herself at all. But as soon as Kate opened her mouth to sing the first line of the well-known country song she had chosen, Maria realised that her grandfather's report had not exaggerated the extent of her gift. Maria had been well taught and regarded herself with all due modesty as rather better than the normal run of ladies when it came to playing and singing, but she was happy to acknowledge that Kate was vastly superior, with a vocal range and purity of tone that few amateurs could match. She presented an enchanting picture, too, as she sang, her cheeks rosy and her vivid face mirroring the emotion of the words. When Maria had furthermore ascertained that her brother had never yet heard his wife sing, she was all the more resolved that Kate should perform for him and for the rest of her guests. She would be a sensation, and all the world – including Benedict himself – would see that Sir Benedict Silverwood had won a bride that others might envy, despite her lack of fortune.

She had thought that Kate might be a little reluctant and in need of persuasion, but she discovered that she was entirely accustomed to performing at select gatherings, had often done so in York, and was hardly nervous. It seemed to her hostess that Kate too was eager to display her talent in front of Benedict. She did not doubt that the general audience was of scarcely any interest to her sister-in-law, but that she was desirous above all things of impressing her husband. The Dowager had hinted before the marriage that Kate's affections might be engaged, that – on her part at least – this was no mere marriage of convenience, and Maria, alerted to the possibility, had observed her sharply since the pair's arrival in London, and had concluded that her mother was quite correct. As to how her brother felt towards his new wife, she could not yet venture to say. There was clearly affection and respect between them; he treated her with consideration, spoke to her with warmth, and was at ease in her company. Provokingly – for her mother's unshakeable belief in her own omniscience could occasionally be trying to even the most dutiful of daughters – the Dowager had clearly also been right when she had said that he desired her. It was obvious that he did – it burnt in his eyes and in his every gesture when his wife was present – and obvious too that the weeks since their wedding had served only to deepen this desire rather than to lessen it. Plainly, whatever his emotions might be, the intimate side of their marriage at least was proceeding in an excessively satisfactory manner; there was no mistaking the little shared glances, the blushes, the way in which his hands brushed her skin – her ungloved hands, the exposed flesh of her shoulders or arms – at the slightest opportunity when they thought themselves unobserved. His hungry gaze followed her about the room; his sister thought that he was himself unaware of it. But did all that amount to love on his part? Maria did not know. She thought that perhaps he did not know himself. He had not entered into matrimony seeking love, and it might well be that his past most unhappy experiences would make love an unwelcome guest. To be so vulnerable once more to the mercy of the uncertain fates might indeed be the very last thing that he wanted.

Maria, after all her initial hesitation, was of her mother's party now, resolved therefore to aid the progress of this relationship in any way she could. She too had been devastated by the circumstances of Caspar's and then Vanessa's deaths. Her heart had ached for Benedict in the months and years that followed, and like her mother she now saw faint sparks in him that led her to hope that what had been broken in him might be mending. But he had never discussed Vanessa with her – had barely ever spoken a word about his dead wife in her hearing – and she believed that similarly he had not spoken of her with Kate. He had built a sort of protective wall around himself, and whether he was willing or even able to allow that wall to be breached by love for his bride, Maria did not know. She feared very much that he had deliberately and understandably put himself out of reach of the softer emotions, and if this was so, she feared for Kate, and for their future together.

CHAPTER THIRTY-SEVEN

It was the evening of Mrs Singleton's rout party, and the elegant rooms were filling up with fashionably dressed people. It was an intimidating prospect, meeting and inevitably being judged by so many, but Kate had Benedict at her side, and Maria, and even Mr Singleton smiled warmly at her and told her that she would do splendidly. 'Pack of twittering hens!' he muttered between arrivals. 'The men too. Ignore 'em!'

Benedict said gravely, his eyes twinkling, 'As ever, my brother-in-law shows the greatest good sense. Of course you will carry the thing off perfectly. And since we do not mean to make our life in society, we need not concern ourselves very greatly with its opinion of us.'

Kate thought privately that if that were really the case, she was not sure why they had come to stay in

London at all, but she knew that that was foolishness born of nerves; to have hidden away and made no appearance at all after their marriage must have led to gossip, which could damage her reputation, and therefore one day Lucy's, and that of any other children she might bear.

This train of thought inevitably caused Kate to reflect on her secret, which was in general something she avoided thinking about unless it was forced to her attention. Her courses were now over a month late, and there could be little doubt, she thought, that she was with child. She felt at times not ill, but odd: not quite herself. A little nauseous, perhaps. More than a little, at times. Someone had sent her some bonbons yesterday – she did not know the identity of her benefactor, there was no card, merely a fine beribboned package addressed to her, and Benedict denied all responsibility – and in normal circumstances she had a sweet tooth, a tiny guilty secret, but when she had opened the box and gone to choose a sugared treat, all at once violent revulsion had overwhelmed her, and she had hurried from the room to be excessively unwell. That was a sign, was it not? She knew that such matters were uncertain, especially in the early months, and she would very much have liked to confide in Maria, and benefit from her experience and advice. But it would be wrong to do so before she had spoken to Benedict. It was something that concerned him very closely, and it was wrong to keep it from him. She had to tell him, and without loss of time.

Kate found herself oddly reluctant to do so, and was not quite sure why. She knew he would be pleased: delighted, in fact. To have a child – an heir – was after all one of the main reasons he had married her. To be seized with the effects of matrimony so very quickly was perhaps somewhat embarrassing for a lady, but it was ridiculous to be missish, especially in regard to her husband, in such circumstances. They had discussed – and done – the most extraordinary things in the privacy of their bedchamber, and indeed elsewhere. They had shared their deepest desires and been more intimate than she could have imagined possible. Why was it so hard to tell him this happy news?

Perhaps he would now consider his duty done, and cease spending every night in her bed and in her arms. If their child should prove to be a son, perhaps he might never feel the need to lie with her again. She could not really believe this to be true – she thought his desire for her was as strong as hers for him – but she did not know, and she was fearful.

Loneliness, that was what she was afraid of. It was not the lack of love – she thought she had accustomed herself to that – but to have been so intimate with him, even if only physically, and then to have it taken from her, to wake in a cold bed alone and converse in public as polite acquaintances, that would be hard. She would have a child to console her, she supposed. That would be a great deal. And if her child should be a daughter, he would come back to her again, would he not?

This was no time for such reflections; Kate was being introduced to dozens of modish strangers, some of whom greeted her in a friendly fashion, and some of whom inspected her in a way calculated to put her quite out of countenance. She met again one of the military gentlemen who had been introduced to her at the opera: a major from Benedict's old regiment, his closest friend, a great blond giant of a man with gentle manners and smiling, humorous blue eyes. She could be sure that he at least looked on her kindly, and she was very happy to converse with him, especially as he was a fellow denizen of Yorkshire, and was delightfully familiar with the narrow medieval streets where she had grown up, and the ancient, crumbling city walls she had clambered over as a child.

But here was Mr Silverwood once more, the unwelcome guest, fashionably late and bowing over her hand with exquisite grace and insolent eyes, and enquiring after her health. She was wearing her red velvet gown and her rubies, and before his arrival had felt herself to be perfectly correctly, even fashionably attired; many married ladies who were present were wearing similar deep, rich colours, and their bodices were cut just as low as hers. But as his gaze ran over her – she would swear she felt it, like a chilling, unwelcome touch – she suddenly felt conscious of how much bosom she was exposing, and fought the strong temptation to tug at her gown in a vain attempt to cover herself. She was sure that he was deliberately setting out to make her feel uncomfortable, and resolved that he should not know that he succeeded all too well. She would not give him that satisfaction.

Although she did not turn to look at Benedict's face, she sensed his dislike of his cousin in the stiffening of his posture. She was sure that the antipathy was by no means one-sided. Whatever the cause of it, hostility crackled in the air between them. *One day*, she thought, *there will be a confrontation between these two. Please, let it not be tonight. And let me not be the cause of it.*

Mr Silverwood was complimenting her on her appearance in a manner she could not like, and which she was sure her husband must like even less. 'What splendid jewels,' he said, the direction of his regard leaving it unclear whether he referred only to her rubies, or also to the décolletage that they adorned. 'Quite magnificent. I feel sure my cousin bestowed the gems upon you as a bride gift, for I have an instinct for these things. How generous he is.'

'He is indeed, and I am very sensible of it,' said Kate, conscious of the fatuity of her words, but rushing into speech in an attempt to forestall anything more cutting that Benedict might be on the verge of saying. Once more there was an implication; it was that the rubies could not possibly be Kate's own, for surely someone from such an impoverished background – that refrain again – could never have afforded them. The fact that this was true did not make it any the less unpleasant. She put her hand on her husband's arm, and squeezed it in a silent plea for restraint, and he must have understood her, for he said nothing.

'It is inspiring to behold such husbandly devotion, I do assure you both,' Silverwood responded with another perfect bow, before he took his leave and drifted off to converse with a gaggle of fashionable matrons of his acquaintance; from the giggles emanating from thence, and the sharp looks this group soon began to shoot her, Kate felt sure that she was the subject of malicious tittle-tattle, no doubt instigated by her husband's cousin.

'What the devil does the fellow mean by *that*?' ground out Benedict. 'What business is it of his? And why should I not buy my wife a wedding gift, I should like to know?'

Kate would have liked to know that herself, for there always seemed to be a direction to Mr Silverwood's malice; he did not appear to her to fire his shots at random. But there was no time to fret over it, for the music was soon to begin, and Kate could always lose herself in music well performed, which this was sure to be. She took her seat in the front row of chairs in Maria's music room, and prepared to be transported.

The excellent performances by various ladies and gentlemen of the works of Beethoven, Bach and Arne, as well as some popular airs, indeed soothed her mood and lifted her spirits, and when it came time for her to take her place by the piano – her sister-in-law had placed her last on the programme – she was surprised how calm she felt. It was true, as she had told Maria, that she was quite accustomed to singing in front of others, but she had never stood up in front of so many strangers, nor ones so fashionable and likely to be critical. There was Mr Silverwood, too, eyeing her impertinently through his quizzing glass, and whispering to his neighbour, a thin blonde with prominent eyes and almost no chin. Well, she was determined not to disgrace herself – or, by extension, her new family – in front of him. Let him watch and be amazed!

She was to be accompanied by a lady who had played for some of the other singers, and who was highly skilled; they had met earlier in the day to practise, and Kate was confident that they understood each other. She had chosen to perform only Italian music; everyone else had sung in English or French, and since she had through no particular merit of her own a rarer accomplishment, she meant to display it to advantage. She was to sing two songs, both by Mozart: '*Voi avete un cor fedele*', and to finish, '*Deh vieni, non tardar*', with which she had teased Benedict while they were at the opera. They were both songs of love, and in that sense at least suitable for a bride such as herself, though she doubted another person present would understand them fully. She stood straight and tall, regulated her breathing, and nodded to the pianist, who smiled encouragingly at her and began to play.

CHAPTER THIRTY-EIGHT

Benedict leant back in his chair and folded his arms. He had enjoyed the concert as much as one of his limited musical abilities could be expected to, and he recognised that his sister had chosen performers of rare talent – even he was able to contrast what he had heard this evening with the usual dull, awkward and not entirely tuneful efforts of young ladies at such events. He had, along with the rest of the audience, applauded all the previous musicians with more than the required polite appreciation, but rather with genuine admiration for the skill on display. He only hoped with a sudden fierce concern that Kate would be able to acquit herself respectably in such company; he had never heard her sing, so he could only trust that his sister knew what she was about in putting her last. It would be painfully apparent to everyone present if mere partiality and family feeling had placed her so.

There could be no denying at any rate that she looked quite magnificent, he thought, as his wife left his side with a brief smile and took her place. The red velvet gown became her admirably, clinging lovingly to her lush curves of breast, belly and thigh, and the fire of the rubies complemented it extraordinarily well, contrasting so perfectly with her lustrous dark hair and rich olive-toned skin. Her warm brown eyes were sparkling with anticipation and excitement, and the gems around her throat glinted as her bosom rose and fell. A small smile just curved her sensual lips as she stood waiting for her cue, and he felt a sharp, almost painful stab of desire for her that took his breath away. She looked a queen tonight: not just desirable, though God knows she was that, but statuesque, dignified, impressive. A woman of consequence. And yet in a few short hours – and the moment could not come soon enough for his liking – he would strip her naked, save for the rubies perhaps, and her gloriously responsive body would be his to possess. And she would possess him.

And then she began to sing.

Her voice was extraordinary, was his first thought. It was not merely that she was clearly a very talented and well-trained singer, with a beautiful voice that reminded him somehow of an instrument, because he felt instinctively that she controlled it, and could make it do exactly as she wished; no, what astonished him was that she somehow found the means to pour all the enthusiasm and passion that he of all people knew her capable of into her singing. It was not in the least a wild and undisciplined show of emotion, but rather that she appeared able to harness all the fire of her nature and put it at the service of her voice. Perhaps he was wrong; he could claim no expertise at all in the matter of music. But that was how it seemed to him, particularly in the second song, which he recognised as the one that she had partially translated for him at the opera. It had had an effect on him then that he would not soon forget, and all the more now as her glorious voice caressed the words. It spoke of yearning for a lover, as he knew, but it was not necessary to understand the words at all to be deeply moved by the power of her performance.

As she sang, and it seemed to him that she looked chiefly at him and sang chiefly for him, he began to feel uneasy and, after a little while, ashamed. Maria, he must admit, had taken the trouble to enquire if Kate was accomplished in music, and presumably had asked her to perform for her in private so that she had been able to make an accurate assessment of the extent of her skill. He had not done half as much, and she was his wife. He had been as intimate with her, physically, as it was possible for one person to be with another. It was not just that they had shared the act of sexual congress, for he had shared that before with women and still not felt himself to be particularly intimate with them, nor ever wished to be so; it was the way that they had explored their desires together, had trusted each other to make experiments in the fulfilment of passion that he had certainly never imagined with another person, least of all his wife. It might be that all married couples did so, though his own experience suggested far otherwise. But he was forced in all honesty to acknowledge that, whether their situation was an ordinary one or not, by far the greater trust and the greater courage had been hers, for she had been a gently bred young lady and a virgin, while had been a man with a past. He had, as she said, possessed her utterly. She had given herself to him without reservation, and trusted him entirely, and he had taken what she had given, as if it were his due. And yet he now recognised that he knew almost nothing about her. Had not exerted himself to ask, had not cared enough. She had this extraordinary talent, and he had known absolutely nothing of it. What else did he not know about her?

And, more than that, he had shared so little of himself with her, except the physical. He had expected her to commit herself to him, and she had done so, a lifelong, irrevocable commitment, without his ever thinking it necessary to tell her a single detail of the tragic, shocking events that had ripped his life apart and wounded him so deeply. She knew of poor Alice's death and that of her child, she knew that Caspar had died in an accident, and that Vanessa too had died shortly thereafter, but he had told her nothing else, and it had been egregious folly. She deserved better from him. She deserved his full confidence. Watching her pour all her passion into her singing now, he could not believe that he had been short-sighted enough to imagine that someone so open-hearted, so vital and so brave would be satisfied for long with the tiny part of his life that he had given her. Once passion lessened, as it surely would, even if it took years before they reached that point, what would be left between them if he could not be open and honest with her about every part of his life?

That he must change if this marriage were to have any chance of success was obvious to him now. Whether he could do so, and how Kate would react if he tried – those were quite other matters. He could only resolve to do his best, and for the rest, he could not in all honesty claim to know his wife well enough to say.

CHAPTER THIRTY-NINE

'*Ti vo' la fronte incoronar di rose.*'

Kate sang her last note, and the piano completed its final phrase and fell silent. There was no immediate reaction, and the moment stretched a little. She curtsied, and was about to return to her seat, when the audience began to applaud enthusiastically. Several minutes passed before Maria was able to make herself heard above the hubbub, thanking the pianist, the other performers and Kate herself for the splendid entertainment that they had provided that evening. Kate was surrounded by a crowd of people eager to congratulate her, and she could not help but be satisfied with the reaction her singing had evoked. It was highly gratifying, naturally, to be compared to the great Madame Catalani, and to have a gentleman, albeit clearly a foolish one, kiss her hand almost in a state of ecstasy and address her as La Divina, but there was only one person for whose opinion she greatly cared, and he was nowhere to be seen: Benedict.

At last she saw him at the edge of the group of people who crowded about her, and he made his way to her, responding with smiles and brief thanks to the congratulations he too was offered. In a moment he was by her side, and she smiled at him, exultant. He did not seem to share her exhilaration; he drew her aside a pace or two, his face oddly serious, and she looked up at him questioningly.

He spoke quietly. 'My dear Kate, that was extraordinary. I do not have the words adequately to express . . . I was deeply moved by your performance. I had not the least notion that you were in possession of such a talent.'

In the heat of the moment, she spoke honestly, without thinking. 'I sang for you.'

'I know you did. I felt it. I do not deserve it.'

'Why do you—?'

They were interrupted. It was not merely the intervention of malign fate, for it was Felix Silverwood who stood before them, careless of the intrusion, his eyes glittering with malice, his eyes running insolently over her body once again. 'My dear cousin, I congratulate you. Such skill, such passion! One has hardly seen the like on any stage, and certainly never in a drawing room in Clarges Street. Surely you have considered taking up the opera as a profession. Did you never think of doing so, in your youth? I am sure you would have made a great success of it, for you are so eminently qualified in all respects.'

A young lady who happened to be standing nearby heard all that he said, and let out a small involuntary gasp, which she instantly muffled with a gloved hand. Kate was conscious that a silence had fallen around her; many people must have overheard Mr Silverwood's words, and surely few of them could have failed to appreciate the deadly insults that they contained. Once again it was necessary that she speak, before Benedict rushed to her defence and caused a public scene. It was vital that she keep her wits about her, and above all things ignore the implication of immorality in his words, vital that she answer it, and defuse the situation, without appearing to have understood it at all.

'It is quite true, cousin,' she said coolly, 'that my first music teacher did once represent to my grandmother that my voice was such that I might, with training, become a professional singer. But my grandmother, of course, declared that it was quite out of the question, and should never have been suggested. She said that she would be afraid that her father, the late Count, would immediately return, rather in the manner of the Commendatore in *Don Giovanni*, and drag her off to the infernal regions if any descendant of his were to set foot upon the stage in such a capacity. For you may perhaps not be aware,' she said with what she hoped was a sufficiently supercilious smile, 'that my Italian family are proverbial for their pride of lineage, having some centuries ago declined, so it is said, a most advantageous marital alliance with the Medici of Florence, because of their once having been engaged in trade.' This was of course entirely untrue, for she had made it up on the spot, but Kate was reasonably confident that Mr Silverwood could not possibly know any better.

Several people could be heard to titter politely at this sally, and Silverwood's handsome, disdainful face displayed considerable chagrin at being so bested. 'I had not known your family to be so illustrious,' he almost hissed, his malice more nakedly exposed now. 'I am sure I would never have suspected it.'

Kate dared not glance at Benedict to see his expression, for she felt sure that it was thunderous, but he surprised her by springing to her rescue. 'It is quite true, Cousin Felix, that her English upbringing has given Kate the pleasant, well-bred ease of manner and perfect consideration for others that we so value in English society, though it is not, alas, always to be met with even here.'

He paused for a second to underline the import of his words, then continued urbanely, 'I believe the continental nobility do not in general share such happy, informal social graces. I am sure if my wife had been raised in Italy in her uncle's palace, she would now be so very grand that I would never have ventured to address her, feeling sure that I would be rejected with contempt if I did. I can only consider myself very lucky to have been able to win such a bride.' The suavity of his words was quite at odds with the fact – obvious to her if not to those who knew her husband only slightly – that they were produced from between gritted teeth, but his speech, with the scarcely veiled and perfectly justified criticism of his cousin's manners that it contained, was received with a little ripple of appreciative laughter. It seemed that Mr Silverwood was not universally popular, and that several persons were glad to hear him receiving a well-deserved set-down.

Kate had a sudden lightning vision of her grandmother Albina, grand scion of continental nobility that she was, and entitled by Italian convention to call herself Countess if she so chose, wringing out her stockings, which she had washed in the absence of a maidservant, and hanging them carefully to dry by the fire in their humble, low-ceilinged lodgings in York, but she pushed it away, for this was no time for humour. The danger had not yet passed, and there was no knowing what her adversary – for so he had plainly showed himself to be – might say next.

It seemed that Mr Silverwood was prepared to concede defeat, temporarily at least. His voice still had an edge, but he had recovered a perfect command over his countenance, and said, 'We must all – your family, and no doubt your wider circle of acquaintance – agree that you have indeed been very lucky, Benedict. Perhaps we may call it the triumph of hope over experience. And now, I am desolated to say that I am obliged to take my leave of you, for I have another engagement. Please do make my apologies to your dear sister, cousin, and thank her for a most . . . entertaining evening.'

'Let me do you the courtesy of showing you to the door, Felix,' said Benedict. His words, and even his tone, now that he too seemed to have complete control of himself, were both perfectly civil, but Kate feared that he meant to confront Mr Silverwood once they were alone, and so after a moment had elapsed she followed them from the room, accepting congratulations from all sides and pasting a brilliant and entirely false smile upon her face as she did so.

CHAPTER FORTY

When she managed to make her way through the throng of people to the hall, Kate was just in time to see her husband's broad back disappearing into Mr Singleton's library; she presumed that his cousin preceded him, possibly under some form of duress. She was glad that Benedict retained enough sense to restrain himself from playing out an angry scene in front of the servants, not to mention any guests who should happen to come upon them, but she was still anxious, and was determined to follow them, however unwelcome she would be. She did not care in the least for Mr Silverwood's wellbeing, but if Benedict, under severe provocation though it might be, should do him serious injury, there would surely be consequences too hideous to contemplate.

She entered the room and closed the door firmly behind her. The cousins were standing close together, and, as she had feared, Benedict had Silverwood by the neckcloth, and was shaking him. Two flushed faces turned to her: her husband's full of anger, Felix's betraying what she took to be an odd mixture of fear and a kind of sick satisfaction. It was obvious that Benedict was deeply displeased to see her, and she could not wonder at it, since she supposed that if he meant to offer physical violence he would rather she did not witness it. But his cousin, she thought, was glad to see her, though she did not at first understand why this should be so. Perhaps he was a coward, and misliked the reaction his needling had provoked, and thought that he would be safer from harm with a woman present.

The pair stood frozen for a moment, and then her husband said, 'Lady Silverwood, this is no place for you. Please have the kindness to leave us. This is a private matter between me and my cousin.' He had not released his grip.

'On the contrary, sir,' she replied calmly, 'I consider myself deeply involved. Mr Silverwood has done nothing but insult me with subtle sneers and scarcely veiled attacks upon my reputation since first we met. I have no notion why he should despise me so; I have done nothing to deserve his malice, and I feel I have a perfect right to know the cause of it. I am not weak or helpless, and if I am to be the topic of conversation, I insist on being present.'

Benedict smiled rather grimly. 'Well, I would rather you were not here, madam, but I am forced to concede the justice of your argument. Do tell us, Felix' – and here he gave him a shake – 'why precisely you have set out to cut up my wife's peace and damage her reputation with your foul slurs and malicious gossip. She has, as she says, done you no harm, and you can know nothing to her discredit, for there is nothing to know. I demand that you account for yourself. Here, I will release you – sit!' He let go his cousin's neckcloth and gave him a contemptuous little shove that pushed him into the leather armchair at his back, his legs buckling under him.

Silverwood made a show of nonchalance, but the fingers with which he attempted to adjust his ruined neckcloth were shaking. 'Do you mean to demand satisfaction from me, Benedict?' he said, his voice hardly more than a croak.

'Challenge you to a meeting with pistols, you mean? Certainly not! You are not worth the trouble, and I will not have my wife the subject of rumours, as she surely would be if we fought over her. Such things always come out.'

'How convenient for you!' his cousin sneered.

Benedict laughed incredulously. 'What can you possibly mean by saying anything so foolish? It is you who should dread a meeting. If you are my equal with a pistol, I am yet to hear it, and if you think I would delope when you have insulted my wife so gravely, you do not know me very well at all. Cease this folly and explain yourself, or shall I drag you out of that chair and plant you the facer you so richly deserve?'

'Benedict—' she interjected hastily.

'Do not worry, my dear. My cousin is a coward, and has no intention of pushing me so far that I actually do him serious physical harm. Or do I wrong you, Felix?'

'I am quite sure that you have no intention of carrying out any of your ridiculous threats, Benedict. They are all so much bluster, done to impress your doxy, such as she is. But I suppose you could hardly find a better, this time, with what the world knows of you. It is, as I said, most convenient that you have excellent reasons to avoid gossip. You would hardly care for your bride to be the subject of public scandal once again, cousin. People will start to whisper that the fault – the very grievous fault – surely lies in you.'

Kate saw with something approaching horror that Benedict's face was white and drawn. His impulse towards violence seemed to have left him completely, for he sank down into a chair opposite his cousin, as if his legs would not support him. He did not speak – not a word of denial did he offer, nor would he meet her eyes.

Felix Silverwood was smiling maliciously now, his confidence quite restored, and when he turned to look at Kate's face and took in the confusion that he saw there, his teeth bared in a savage, triumphant grin. 'Oh! I see that my suspicions were correct, poor Lady Silverwood, and he has not told you anything of the dreadful scandal in his past. An understandable omission, I am sure, but a shocking one. I shall not come between a married couple, nor do my dear cousin's dirty work for him – I will only say, ask him, madam. Ask him the precise circumstances in which his last wife died. Ask him what he has kept concealed from you, and insist that he tells you. Oh, Benedict, Benedict, and you dare call *me* a coward?!'

CHAPTER FORTY-ONE

Silverwood seemed to think his words a sufficiently effective parting short, for he rose, straightened his coat, and strolled from the room without another word.

Benedict was left sitting in the chair, shoulders slumped, his head in his hands. And Kate could only stare at him and say, 'What . . . what did he mean? I can see that you are deeply distressed, and I am very sorry for it, but I insist you tell me what he meant, not leave me in hideous doubt and suspense!'

He raised his head and said dully, 'He is quite right, I am a coward. I should have told you long since. I should have told you before we married, and given you the chance to refuse me, as well you might have done. I realised this just now, while you were singing. I realised that I have not treated you as I should, and that I must make amends, if indeed it is possible for me to do so. I meant to take you aside and tell you everything, Kate. I swear I did.'

Kate had no idea what she should say in response to this, but she was given no chance to reply, for at that moment the door opened to admit Maria, who bustled into the room, crying, 'So this is where you are hiding! Please return to the party instantly!' before she caught sight of both their faces, and said sharply, 'Why, whatever is the matter?!'

'I cannot answer you,' said Kate, 'for I do not know. Mr Silverwood has just left, but before he did so, he said some things . . . made some terrible insinuations about Benedict's late wife . . .' She could see from Maria's appalled face that she knew, or feared she knew, exactly what her cousin had referred to; she was the only one in ignorance, and she was torn between a rising anger and concern for Benedict, so silent and defeated.

He said in a low tone, 'Felix called me a coward, and rightly so. He advised Kate to ask me to describe to her the exact circumstances of Vanessa's death, for he divined quite correctly that I had not done so. He indicated, too, that those circumstances are generally known, and the subject of vulgar gossip. Of course I have no means of knowing if this is true.' He gave a sudden, harsh bark of laughter that made both the women jump. 'People are hardly likely to talk of it in my hearing, after all!'

'Oh, Benedict, my dear, I am so sorry,' Maria said, her voice low with emotion. 'I am sure it is not something that is generally known; that is just his malice speaking. He would say anything to wound you, the dreadful creature. And he has no right to call you a coward – no one does. But you should have told Kate, however hard it was for you.'

'Thank you, Maria. I know I should. I had resolved to do so, earlier this evening.'

'But now is not the time!' said his sister, recovering her composure and becoming her usual managing self once more. 'Benedict, I am taking Kate back to the party. Do you follow us in a few moments, when you can regulate your manners and your facial expression as you should. The guests are leaving, or will be soon; we need only make our farewells, and in a short while it will all be over, and you can talk. Kate, I promise you, it is not nearly so dreadful a story as I am sure you are imagining, and not a single thing that happened was Benedict's fault, I promise you, though I am sure he will persist in blaming himself for everything. Come, Kate, and smile!'

Though her thoughts and her emotions were whirling in confusion and threatened to overwhelm her, Kate could see the sound good sense in what her sister-in-law proposed. There was little point in holding a party to introduce her to society if she then disappeared before it was done and made herself the subject of speculation, and if there were any unsavoury rumours in circulation concerning Benedict, it would be dangerous to act in a way that gave the least credibility to them. It was necessary she return to the throng, and her husband too, if he could manage it with anything approaching a normal countenance.

She said, 'Maria, you are right, of course. Benedict, let us talk later. It will present a very odd appearance if people look for us to bid us goodbye, or to offer us congratulations on our marriage, and we are both nowhere to be seen. Maria might as well not have gone to all the considerable trouble of holding the party tonight. I know you perceive that this is so.'

He sighed. 'Indeed. You go, and I will follow in a moment. Thank you, Kate, for not making a scene, as you would be quite justified in doing, or insisting on the full explanation that I owe you at this precise moment. I am conscious of your forbearance, believe me. I promise you the answers you seek will not be long delayed.'

She nodded, and left the room in Maria's wake, once more pinning a false smile upon her face, though she felt it would soon enough be aching with the effort. Before they re-entered the music room, Maria had time only to reassure her that she still looked perfectly charming, and to hiss urgently, 'When Benedict tells you that it was all his fault, I know you have the sense to disregard it, and judge for yourself!' With this she was forced to be content, until her husband should have the opportunity to explain himself to her. She dreaded what he might have to say, but she knew that she must steel herself to hear it, whatever it might be.

CHAPTER FORTY-TWO

The rest of the evening passed in something like a dream; Kate had to presume that she smiled, and nodded, and thanked people for their congratulations, and said all that was proper in farewell, and she saw that Benedict did the same, but his eyes were anguished and his face was strained, to one who knew him. But then, could she say that she knew him at all, when he had been keeping some hideous secret from her for all these weeks, and she had never so much as suspected it?

There could be no question of intimacy between them tonight. Her maid undressed her, and she washed herself and put on a night-rail and dressing gown. For a moment she considered plaiting her hair, as she had not done since her wedding, but she thought it would be a petty act, indicating perhaps that she had already made up her mind that her husband was very gravely at fault, and so she did not do so, but left it loose about her shoulders as usual. There were chairs either side of the fireplace in Maria's luxurious best spare bedroom, and a small fire burnt in the grate against the autumn chill. Kate sat by it and sought to warm herself, for she felt as though the cold had struck deep into her bones, and she would never be warm and comfortable again.

After a short while Benedict came to join her, and sat down opposite her, still drawn and white. Some part of her wanted to reach out to him, to say that she did not care what he had concealed from her, that she loved him, and ached to see him suffering. But a greater part of her felt that that was not right. Once before he had hurt and disappointed her, on the first day of their honeymoon, and she felt now that she had perhaps forgiven him too quickly, made things too easy for him, weakened as she was by her love for him. If she had had more pride, perhaps he might have treated her differently. Perhaps if she had pushed him harder to explain why he had deserted her that morning without a word, he might have reflected on his behaviour more deeply, thought about what he owed her as his wife, and shared with her then the dark secret he still carried. It was impossible to know, but tonight she resolved to be stronger. She said nothing, but merely looked at him. Her face, she hoped, was expressionless: not angry, but not soft and forgiving either.

He said, 'Kate, let me say again that I am sorry. I wish I had not allowed this to happen to you, and spoilt what should have been your evening of triumph. Please believe me when I tell you that I did not intend any of this. I would not hurt you for all the world.'

She made a slight movement with her hand; she did not mean to dismiss what he said, but while she could see that he was truly very sorry, she could also see that once again he was putting off, even if it were only for a moment, telling her the truth. It was surely a terrible thing, to make a man who had faced the enemy in battle countless times fear to speak it. He seemed to understand her, for he sighed and said, 'You are right. I must tell you. There is no escaping it.

'Let me first explain a little about our family, so that you understand what I have to tell you. You might have noticed that we almost never speak of my father, and that my mother has no picture of him in her private sitting room.'

She nodded. She had noticed it, but had not thought a great deal of it; there could be a dozen reasons. She knew that Sir Frederick had died long ago. Her own parents had done so too, and she spoke rarely of them, for the simple reason that she did not remember them at all well. She supposed she had thought that something similar was the case with Benedict's father, but now realised that this could not be so.

'My father was neither a kind nor a good man. He treated my mother badly, and Maria and me scarcely better. We could not love him, all the more because we always took my mother's part. We would have protected her from him if we could, but we were very young, and could find no way to do so. But Caspar . . . Caspar was the heir, and his favourite. They were very close, and if my brother saw how cruelly he bullied our mother, he did not care, or perhaps thought it deserved. There was a crisis, a final estrangement between them, and Caspar urged him to put her aside, send her away from us for ever, and Maria and I hated him for it, even though it never came to pass.

'When our father died a few years later, the three of us were relieved, even happy, Kate. It was as if we were prisoners who had been freed after years of incarceration. What a terrible thing that is to say. But Caspar felt his loss very deeply, and knew that we did not. With few bonds of affection to any of us, and our father not there to check him, he threw himself into a wild, dissipated existence. When he was barely old enough to do so, Felix joined him in that world, and became one of his closest companions. It was with Caspar that my cousin learnt to gamble and drink and live a debauched life – you could with justice say that Caspar ruined him, and caused him to waste what modest fortune he had, and yet he professed to love Caspar and, as you have seen, he hates me, though I have never done him harm. Is that not odd?'

Kate did not think that he expected an answer to his question, and so did not give one, and Benedict went on, staring into the depths of the fire now, as if he could see pictures there of the unhappy events he described.

'But Caspar was saved, or so we thought. He met Alice, and fell in love with her, and gave up all his wild ways. He really did, my mother said. I had my commission by then, so I never came to know her very well, but Maria and my mother told me that she was gentle and frail, but with a strong character, full of fierce love for him. She was not in the least put off by his reputation, but took him, confident that when he swore he would change for her he sincerely meant to do so. And he was reconciled with our mother, at Alice's insistence, and they were happy. I came home when I was wounded, and my brother and I grew a little closer for a time. I married Vanessa, and we were a family as we had never been before. But then Alice . . .'

He sighed. 'She was never strong physically. She had had rheumatic fever in her infancy, and her heart was affected. The strain of carrying a child was too much for her, and as her time grew nearer, she grew weaker still. My mother told me that it was obvious to everyone except Caspar that there was grave cause for concern. I was not here – I had to return to my regiment – but my mother has painted a vivid picture for me of the dreadful day when her pains began, of Caspar pacing the floor, beside himself with anxiety when the doctors would only shake their heads and look grave. The child – a son – was born dead, and then Alice slipped away. She died in his arms.'

Kate murmured some incoherent words of consolation, and Benedict smiled at her, a brief, sad smile.

'My mother believes that Caspar lost his mind after she died, and perhaps it is some consolation to her to think that he was never entirely rational afterwards. He left Silverwood Hall and returned to London, and to all the vicious ways he had given up for Alice.

'Vanessa knew that she was with child by then, and she lived quietly with my mother, and in due course Lucy was born, and all was well. They were both strong and thriving. I managed to get a brief leave to come home to see them both, and it seemed at least that there was some happiness after the pain. But not for Caspar. I see that now, and I can partly understand it. He would not come and meet my child – it was too painful for him. When I went to see him in London, the new closeness between us had entirely vanished. He abused me in a manner hardly rational. Of course, he was very drunk; I believe he was almost always drunk, in those days.'

He said, his voice almost a whisper now, 'It is now that the tale becomes hard for me to tell, Kate. I returned to the peninsula, to what in my foolishness I imagined to be my duty, leaving Vanessa and Lucy with my mother. Safe, as I thought. I never troubled to ask myself if someone as young as Vanessa – she was barely nineteen, and had led a very sheltered life – could truly be happy with such a restricted existence in the country. Of course she could not; of course I should have known it.'

Kate was gazing at him in deep consternation now. She feared that what he was about to tell her was something quite terrible; she even had a faint inkling of what it might be, if her imagination was not playing tricks on her.

After a little while he went on, 'She grew bored and restless, and when Lucy was a few months old it was proposed that Vanessa should go to stay with Maria for a time, to be presented at Court as a married woman and to enjoy the social pleasures that she had so missed while in Berkshire. Where was the harm? And now that she was married, she no longer needed to be strictly chaperoned. She had more freedom. She had never known the least freedom before, I suppose, though I did not realise it then. Her whole life had been prescribed, controlled by others: her parents, me, though I did not mean to, even my mother. No wonder it went to Vanessa's head. It would have been a wonder if it had not.

'And Maria was pleased to see that Caspar began to visit them more. She was glad, my dear sister, to think that he might perhaps be mending his ways, and coming back to the family. She certainly never thought to suspect him of any sinister intentions towards Vanessa. Why should she? Her own brother.'

Kate stifled a gasp. So what she had feared was true. He heard her, and grimaced. 'Yes. He set out to seduce her, my poor young wife, and he succeeded. He was handsome and charming, when he made the effort to be so, and very experienced with women, and she was just a girl, lonely, missing me, abandoned by me, as she must have felt, and with no mother or sister to confide in. She begged me not to go back, you know, after Lucy was born, but I spouted some pompous, arrogant nonsense about my duty – as if the capture of Bonaparte depended on me alone, as if my presence could make the slightest difference. And so I did not listen, did not take her seriously, and left her. If it had not been Caspar, it would have been another, I dare say. But the fault was mine. Is mine.'

She made some instinctive sound of protest, but he shook his head. 'It might be said – my mother has said it – that she married a soldier, and should have been prepared for the life of a soldier's wife. But how could she be prepared? She was only a few months out of the schoolroom when I married her. Not much more than a child herself. I should never have been so selfish as to take a wife, least of all a wife like her. I am well aware of that. I do not blame her, you know. I have never blamed her, nor been angry with her – except perhaps for a few moments when the full horror of what had happened was revealed to me.'

'But your brother . . .' Kate could hardly form a coherent sentence.

'I have found it in my heart to blame him, for I believe he set out to seduce Vanessa only because she was my wife, only because I still had what he had lost. And that seems . . . unkind. Unnecessary, to put it no more strongly. My mother believes that in his twisted mind he was also seeking revenge on her, his own mother, for living when my father died, and for certain actions of hers that are not my secret to tell. I do not know. All I know is that he and Vanessa carried on an affair under my sister's roof for several months, until at last Maria grew suspicious, and charged him with it, hoping, I think, that he would laugh it off, and say that she was grossly mistaken, even grow angry with her. But he did not. He admitted in it, gloried in it, told her that he had never loved Vanessa in the slightest. I admit that that still hurts, when I think of it.

'And they left Maria's house that night. They were running away together – not to be married, for how could they marry? He was determined to ruin her completely, to tear our family apart.' His voice was shaking now, and Kate could not wonder at it.

'Thank God, thank God, Lucy was with my mother, or I am sure Vanessa would have taken her, for she loved her, you know – never think for a second that she did not, Kate – and Caspar might even have encouraged her to do so. It was late at night, and raining, and Caspar was drunk – of course he was drunk. He could not handle his team, and they bolted, and the curricle crashed.'

Kate had her hand over her mouth now as she listened to the relentless words. 'His neck was broken when he was flung from the carriage; he was killed instantly. Vanessa was very gravely hurt. A doctor came to the scene, and tended to her, and she rallied a little. She did not die that day, nor the next. My mother and Maria went to her. But there was no hope that she could live, her injuries were too severe. And the child—'

She let out a tiny cry of horror as she realised what he was saying. 'Yes, there was a child. Not my child, for

I had been gone too long. Far too long. The child could not live, and they both died together. A son, they said it was. Caspar would have had his son.'

She could stay silent and distant from him no longer. All her fine resolutions to be harder on him had fled instantly in face of such a tragedy. She rose to her feet and went to him, and he stood to meet her. She put her arms about him, and after a moment's hesitation he embraced her too, and buried his face in her hair. His body shook, and she realised that he was weeping. She held him, and tried to make her mind blank, and give him the comfort he needed as he wept for his lost love.

CHAPTER FORTY-THREE

It seemed that a long time passed before Benedict stirred in her arms, and pulled away from her a little. He said in low tones, 'I am sorry, Kate. I am deeply embarrassed to have broken down in front of you in such an unmanly way. There is no reason in the world why I should expect you to comfort me, when I have kept so much from you. It is very generous of you. Much more generous than I deserve, that is certain.'

'I am your wife,' she said simply.

He took her hand and kissed it, exclaiming as he did so, 'Your hand is like a block of ice! Shall we not get into bed while I tell you the rest? There is not much more to say, and I can at least hold you and warm you.'

Kate felt herself to be chilled to the bone, and so she agreed, and slipped off her dressing gown to lie in his arms under the covers. He said, 'That is the first time I have told anyone that story in any detail, my dear – the whole sorry spectacle of our family laid out before you.'

She murmured, 'I can perfectly understand why it should affect you so. It is terrible, what you have suffered.'

He tightened his hold on her and went on, 'Somehow in my absence, my mother and Maria, with a great deal of help from Singleton – God bless the man, he was an absolute tower of strength for all of us through this dreadful time – managed to put about a story that Vanessa had heard from my mother that Lucy was unwell, and prevailed upon Caspar to drive her home to Silverwood Hall, on the night of a terrible storm when it was not safe to travel, hence the fatal accident. As far as I am aware, the story was accepted without question. I do not think Felix's insinuation that Vanessa's death is the subject of widespread gossip can be true, now that I reflect upon it more soberly. We would have had some indication of it long before this.

'And I rushed home in response to an urgent, barely coherent message from my mother, to find by the time I arrived Vanessa dead as well as Caspar. Mama tried to keep the worst of it from me, but she could never look me in the eye and lie to me, and I guessed the truth, which she had no choice but to confirm.'

'How utterly devastating. I can scarcely begin to imagine your emotions upon making such a dreadful discovery. I do not know how you endured it.'

'I think after the initial horror I became . . . numb; I suppose that is the word. For a long time I saw the world through a sort of grey fog, and the only thing that made a real impression on me was the thrill of battle. Of killing. I am ashamed to say it, and ashamed to say that I do not think I greatly cared if I lived or died – no, worse than that, I wanted in some way to die. It was the sheerest luck that I survived.'

She felt him sigh, and his breath ruffled her hair. 'Thank God I took no hurt, for Lucy's sake more than my own. She has lost enough in her short life, and it was extraordinarily selfish of me not to have a care for her sooner. I should have sold out long before I did. I have made one mistake after another, compounding my selfish, careless errors with yet more of them. And when I should have realised how unbelievably lucky I was to have a fresh start with you, what have I done but made a mull of everything again, by not telling you all that you deserved to know even before you married me, so that you could make your decision with clear eyes and full knowledge of what you were taking on. You might have chosen not to marry me after all, and I could not have censured you for it.'

Kate did not answer him for a moment. Her mind was in turmoil as she struggled to comprehend the full implications of all that Benedict had told her. So much that she had not fully understood before was becoming clear to her now. The way in which the Dowager had been so quick and eager to welcome her as Benedict's bride, despite the undeniable truth that he could have looked so much higher than a penniless governess. Her deep motherly anxiety about him. Even Miss Sutton's fierce protectiveness towards her employer and friend. The way Sir Caspar's name was so rarely mentioned by his family, and his father's, never.

But most of all, poor Benedict. Her heart ached for him; the pain was almost physical in her breast. What a good man, what a strong man he was to have gone on existing day to day and caring for his family after such a series of disasters. Disasters that might have utterly broken – had broken – a man less resilient. And he had not merely survived; he had somehow managed not to become bitter. He did not appear to blame his young wife in the least for her betrayal of him, and with his own brother, as so many men surely would. She remembered now that when on their honeymoon he had spoken briefly of his previous marriage, he had said something in reference to their intimate life, to their mutual inexperience, and with the benefit of hindsight he had sounded only desperately sad, not angry or resentful.

No wonder he had found it so hard to tell her all that had occurred. No wonder it had taken him so long to marry again; no wonder above all he had chosen her, and not another Vanessa, young and careless and needing so much more than he might be able to give. No wonder he might never love her.

She thought now of the portrait, of how she had stood before it and seen nothing but icy, haughty perfection. It had been what she, what anyone, was meant to see, of course, but she had been quite wrong: nobody was so perfect. Poor Vanessa. It seemed that she too had been a lost and lonely child, playing at grown-ups, with nothing to protect her but her beauty and her fragile armour of silk and lace.

It was deeply wrong to permit herself to entertain selfish thoughts when she had heard such a story, but now that she knew all he had suffered, she was forced to ask herself if all her hopes that he might come to love her one day must always be entirely vain. And at the same time, how worthy of her love he was, so much more than she could ever have known.

He said sadly, 'I suppose I am justly answered by your silence, my dear, though you are too good to reproach me. If your trust in me is shattered and can never be mended, once again I only have myself to blame. I am so sorry, Kate. I know that all this is more than any woman can be expected to bear.'

CHAPTER FORTY-FOUR

'No!' said Kate explosively, sitting up in bed and freeing herself from his arms with a suddenness that made Benedict start.

'No . . . ?' he asked tentatively.

'No, I will not allow you to go jumping to conclusions and imagining you have the least idea what I am thinking. You do not!'

'I'm sorry, Kate,' he said in a tone of mortification. 'I assumed from your silence—'

'Do not assume anything. I was silent for a moment because I was cast into confusion by the painful things you have told me. But you need not apologise for anything. It is true that you should have told me these terrible secrets long since, but now that I know them, I can scarcely blame you. It would be hard indeed to relate all this to someone you barely knew, and how often had we met before you asked for my hand? Three times? Four? And once we were married, I can well imagine that the right moment seemed never to occur, and the longer you left it, the harder it must have been. I was angry for a while earlier, when your cousin shocked me so, but I am no longer.'

He looked at her in astonishment. 'Are you truly telling me that you are not horrified, disgusted, by what I have revealed to you? I cannot credit it.'

'I do not see why anything that you have told me should serve to give me a disgust of you. It is plain to me that none of it is your fault in the slightest, apart from your failure to disclose it to me earlier, and I have already said that I can understand how that came to pass.'

He shook his head, his face a picture of incredulity, and she said passionately, 'I understand why you regret so much leaving your wife alone, and what flowed from it, but it is simply wrong to blame yourself. A thousand soldiers leave their wives every day to go off to do their duty, and I dare say most of those women have infinitely harder lives than Vanessa ever did, many of them living in poverty and terrible loneliness as well as worry for their absent husbands. I do see that it was not easy for her, and that she was lost and confused. But if she was young and foolish, and you understand and forgive her for it, very well – you should also extend the same mercy to yourself. Surely, if there is any blame to apportion, it lies chiefly with your brother. From what you tell me of his early life, his character was never steady, and your father's influence upon him was not a healthy one. Or perhaps he had after all run mad, as you say. In either case, it is not your fault!'

She could see from his expression that she had by no means persuaded him of the truth of her words, and she exclaimed in frustration, 'This is what comes of never speaking of such things with anyone, in this foolish way. I understand why it has all been kept so secret . . .'

He murmured, 'For Lucy's sake. The family's reputation – even her reputation when she is grown – is very far from being my chief concern, Kate. But it is my earnest hope that she never comes to know the manner of her mother's death. I could not endure the hurt that such knowledge would surely inflict upon her once she was old enough to understand it.'

She reached out a hand to him. 'My dear! Of course that is true. Of course your first duty is to protect her in any way that you can. But have you never discussed these dreadful events with your mother, or Maria and her husband, or one of your intimate friends – the major, perhaps, as he is a sympathetic person and seems to esteem you very greatly? I do not mean when it happened, but later?'

He shook his head. 'No. No, I have not done so until tonight. Hence my reaction, I suppose. I could not endure to speak of it at first, and then later I did not wish to revive the painful memories when they had ceased to torment me quite so much. And I think people

– even those close to me – have been reluctant to discuss it too. I certainly would not have wished to add to my mother's distress . . .'

'I doubt you could do so, Benedict. But I am almost sure that if you had spoken of it with one of the people who cares for you most dearly, they would have helped you look at it in a more rational light. I would venture to suggest that all of them have their own views on the situation, and these new perspectives might have tempered yours, which I believe to be distorted, though I do not wonder at it.'

He smiled rather ruefully. 'You are a remarkable woman, Kate. I do not know what I have done to deserve you. While you sang this evening – it seems like days ago now – I realised how little I know you, really, and how much I wish to do so. Is it too late for us, do you think, to try to begin again?'

Once again the urge to confess her true feelings was very strong; once again Kate was tempted to tell him how much she loved him, and how long ago he had captured her heart without having the least idea of it. But once again she resisted. He had never spoken of love to her, and, after all that she had heard tonight, she was even less confident that words of love from her would be welcome to him. He had every reason not to trust a wife again, after the terrible hurt that Vanessa had inflicted on him. Why should he risk exposing his heart once more? And if he were to repudiate her, or fail to conceal his dismay at the nature of her confession, she could not endure it. She must remain silent, however hard it was.

And tonight was not the time to reveal to him her other secret – that she carried his child inside her. There had been too much talk of tragedy and of dead children tonight. She did not believe in ill omens, and yet, and yet . . . They were both exhausted by the emotion of the evening; she would wait for a calmer moment, when both their tongues were more guarded, and when neither of them would feel so tempted to say something they might later regret, and could not take back.

So she said only, 'I am very happy to begin again, Benedict. I welcome it. But I think we should make no grand resolutions tonight, and talk no more now. We are both very tired, and should sleep, and hold each other, and take comfort.'

He agreed, and kissed her gently, gratefully. It was plain to her that, whatever his other feelings might be, he needed her presence in his arms tonight. Perhaps it was merely an animal need to feel a warm, soft body beside him, and know that he was not alone in the darkness. But whatever the reason, he held her close, and soon his breathing told her that he had fallen asleep. It was far longer before she could join him in much-needed oblivion.

CHAPTER FORTY-FIVE

It was a subdued group of people who met in Maria's sitting room late the next morning, having most of them breakfasted separately in their chambers. Benedict had been up relatively early, leaving Kate sleeping, and had taken Lucy and her younger cousins to the park to run off some of their excess energy before their lessons had started. He had slept, though restlessly, and seemed composed enough, but quiet. Kate and Maria, for their part, were both weary and heavy-eyed, though Mr Singleton appeared his usual stolid self, and Kate felt oddly reassured by his air of imperturbable calm. She was beginning to realise that he was a kindly and dependable man, if in general one of few words, and one on whom her lively sister-in-law relied greatly, despite any appearances to the contrary.

Maria said now, 'May I assume, Benedict, that you have shared the full details of what Cousin Felix so maliciously revealed last night with Kate? Because I warn you, if you have not, I shall go into strong hysterics, and will not be responsible for any of my subsequent actions.'

Her brother smiled at her a little wryly. 'I have, Maria. The time for concealment is long past, I am well aware.'

'Well, thank heaven for that, at least!'

Her husband entered the lists now, saying abruptly, 'Been thinking. Was up half the night, mulling it over.'

His family looked at Mr Singleton expectantly, and he went on, 'What do you think your cousin was about? Set against Lady Silverwood from the outset, determined to make her uneasy – saw it at the opera. Question is, why?'

Maria said in exasperation, 'Is it not obvious, John? He must loathe this marriage. His hopes to succeed Benedict, his jealousy—'

He shook his head. 'Not enough, if you ask me. Don't like him, never have, but he's not a simpleton. Not dicked in the nob. How old is the fellow, eight and twenty? Not reasonable to expect to succeed a man who isn't five years his senior, and lives a dashed healthier life than he does, besides. Might have thought to do so when Ben was charging about the world getting shot at on a regular basis and catching fevers; might well have hoped to see him turn up his toes on a dozen separate occasions. But not since.'

'What are you suggesting, John?' said Benedict, frowning. 'I can see the sense in what you say, but what follows from it? Do you mean he has some deeper purpose in mind than mere general malice towards us? I find that very hard to believe.'

'Been thinking that the fellow was used to live in Caspar's pocket. Know you are aware. Thick as thieves, they were. Shared a lodging, on occasion. No wish to cause distress by speaking of painful matters, but I have sometimes wondered . . .' He fell silent, apparently deep in thought, and even his wife did not see fit to interrupt him on this momentous occasion.

'You have to admit,' he said at last, 'that if you're both right and your cousin always had a hankering to call himself Sir Felix, however unreasonable that was, it was dashed convenient for him, Caspar running off with Vanessa like that.'

'What can you possibly mean by saying such a thing, John?' asked his wife, her brows furrowed.

'Well, putting aside the accident, suppose they had succeeded in setting up house together in that dam—er, that dashed havey-cavey fashion, what would have been the result of that?'

When he saw that his audience, though rapt, did not fully apprehend his meaning, he said, 'Mean to say, would you have divorced her, Ben?'

'Citing my own brother in a crim con case and exposing my family to public ridicule? Making sure by my own actions that Lucy would be bound to hear of it one day? No, I most certainly would not!' replied Benedict grimly.

'Didn't think so. Expect your cousin could have worked that out too. Knows you well enough. Don't supposed you'd have challenged your own brother to a duel, either. Not at all the thing. So where would you and Caspar be left, then, regarding the title?'

His logic was irresistible, and his brother-in-law answered him slowly, incredulously, 'With both of us in a situation where we could not possibly beget a legitimate heir.'

'And if you'd then been killed in action, as you easily could have been? Would anyone have wagered a large sum on Caspar living to a ripe old age, would you say, Ben, the pace he was going?'

It was plain to all of them that at a stroke Felix's chances of inheriting would have been substantially increased in such a scenario. It was a chilling thought, all the more because it was only now being brought to the Silverwoods' attention after so many years had passed.

Kate had been listening in appalled silence, but she broke it now to say, 'But this is madness! Even if what you say is true – and it has a sort of horrible plausibility to it, I am forced to admit – how could Mr Silverwood have advanced such an outcome? To say that he might very easily have profited from it is one thing; to say that he somehow helped to bring it about is quite another, surely?'

Mr Singleton's large, honest face was grave as he said, 'You don't know, of course, but very suggestible, excitable fellow, Caspar was. Not a particle of sense in that head of his. Sharing lodgings, thick as inkle-weavers, Felix dripping poison in his ear, nasty insinuations about what he might do to cock a snook at Benedict? Easiest thing in the world. Not the least danger to himself, and no way to prove it happened if it ever were to come out. No way to prove it now, if it comes to that. Clever fellow, you know, always thought so. Mind, I'm not saying he predicted or wanted the accident; don't see how he could have done, and it hardly suited his purposes, leaving Benedict free to marry again if he survived the wars.'

His wife said, 'Which brings us to the present day. Supposing we grant all you say – and I by no means allow that we should – what is his purpose now?'

'Drive a wedge,' Singleton said promptly. 'Dripping poison again, since it worked so well last time. Cause an estrangement between Ben and Lady Silverwood. Separation. Result? No heirs.'

'But that would not in itself ensure his succession. Benedict could still outlive him by thirty years. He must surely know that as well as anyone,' objected Kate.

'True,' answered Singleton, rubbing his nose. 'It may be that the prospect of the inheritance would be enough. Live on the expectation, you know, stave off his creditors. That's one thing. Devilish downy fellows, some of these tradesmen and cent-per-centers. Charge interest, high as they please, be sure to be paid one day. Maybe that's enough. Hope it's just that, to be frank. Not something worse.'

'John, are you suggesting that he would contemplate . . . ?' cried Maria, trailing off before she could complete the sentence, and put into words the quite shocking thing that was in all of their minds.

'Not quite sure what I am suggesting, to be frank. Not by any means easy in m'mind. All I'm saying is, a few years ago two healthy young married fellows – Ben and Caspar, not to mention a parcel of brats they both might have – stood between the fellow and the inheritance. Chance of inheritance? Low, very low. Now? Remarkable thing. Just Ben. And Lady Silverwood, of course. If you was to meet with an unfortunate accident tomorrow, Ben, well, good day to you, Sir Felix. And if Lady Silverwood did, seems deuced unlikely to me that you'd have the stomach to marry again. Not the easiest thing in the world to find another woman to take you either, to be blunt. Dashed Gothic imaginations, these women have. Curse of the Silverwoods, that sort of nonsense.'

No one responded by saying that Mr Singleton too might be said to have a Gothic imagination. As Kate had said, there was a sick, insidious plausibility to the picture that had been laid out before them. She determined to put it into plain words, as her companions seemed understandably reluctant to do the thing – so that they might confront it in all its stark unlikeliness.

'So are we all truly sitting here together imagining that Mr Silverwood – your own cousin – is a potential murderer?' she said baldly.

The word seemed to hang in the air between them.

At last Mr Singleton said baldly, 'Yes. Well, I'm dashed well imagining it, anyway. And . . .' He hesitated, then went on, with a little difficulty, it seemed. 'I didn't want to tell you this – apologies for speaking of it, wouldn't do so if I didn't think it were important. Lady Silverwood, do you recall those fancy bonbons some admirer sent you?'

'Yes, of course,' she said, distracted. What could this have to do with the very grave subject under discussion? 'I did not want them. I do not know what became of them. Surely this—'

'I do,' he said rather grimly. 'Maria don't care for such things, nor do I, and so it seems they ended up in the kitchen. Mrs Croft may have intended to take them for herself, or perhaps give them to her old mother as a gift, for they were untouched, she said.' He held up his hand to stay Benedict's obvious intention to burst into speech. 'At any rate, she forgot about them, in the bustle of getting ready for the party, and yesterday evening she found them on the floor, scattered. She thinks the cat must have got at them, and she's devastated, and very sorry. She was scared to tell you, Maria, in case you might be angry. Told me instead. Known me from the cradle, you understand.'

They gazed at him in puzzlement, and at last he said, 'Thing is, that cat of hers is dead. Great ginger brute, apple of her eye. Stretched out stiff as a board – well, I won't go into details. I've seen it and it wasn't pretty.

Ben, it ate the chocolates intended for Lady Silverwood, and now the creature's dead. Poisoned. Tell me that's a coincidence, if you like, but I won't credit it.'

Benedict said heavily, 'Poison, my God . . . Of course, there can be no proof.'

'There was no card with the gift,' said Kate slowly, in a kind of daze. 'I thought it strange at the time. But oh, I cannot believe this! Anyone might have eaten the sweetmeats – I might have given them to the children!'

It was an appalling thought, and shocked them all into silence.

'Very well,' said Maria shakily at last. 'Suppose we accept all of it, including this quite extraordinary suggestion that our lives are in danger. What then do we *do* about it?'

'Always been practical, you, m'dear. Often said so. Now, that's where you have me at a stand,' he admitted, rubbing his nose in perplexity once more. 'Not the least idea in the world.'

CHAPTER FORTY-SIX

Kate knew that the secret of her delicate condition had great bearing on this present crisis, and that she must share it with Benedict with all possible speed, whatever her qualms. But that could only be done in private. She said now, 'You are right in saying that there is no possibility of proof of any of this – not his past actions, nor his possible designs on our lives.'

'Can't be,' replied Mr Singleton with confidence. 'Fellow's not such a sapskull to be leaving letters lying about like some villain in a novel. Supposing Ben and I tried to force a confession from him? Threats of violence? Enjoyable, I'm sure, but unlikely to work. Knows we wouldn't kill him in cold blood. Only has to stay mum as an oyster. What can we do? Getting ourselves arrested for attacking him would play into his hands. Like I said, fellow's no fool.'

'It is unendurable that you should have to live like this, with the children in danger too!' cried Maria hotly. 'I refuse to believe there is not something we can do!'

'Perhaps there is,' said Kate. 'Have you considered bribery as a possibility?'

'Bribe the fellow not to kill you?' enquired Mr Singleton. 'It's a bold idea, ma'am, but I can't help thinking there's a flaw in it somewhere.'

'Indeed,' said Benedict drily, though he smiled at Kate as he said it. 'What is to stop him taking the money and making the attempt anyway?'

'That's the thing,' agreed Singleton sadly. 'Not as though you'd be in a position to ask for your money back, eh? Being dead and all. Pity. Thought you had something there for a moment.'

'Of course,' said Kate with dignity, stifling an impulse to burst into hysterical laughter, 'I do not mean that you should bribe him not to kill us. That would be ridiculous. I mean to suggest that you bribe him to leave England. Pay for his passage, and have him watched. Offer him a sum – not too large – in advance, to be paid to him on arrival in Paris, say, and then smaller regular sums that he can only draw if he is in a foreign city, not in England. So that he goes abroad, and stays there. And thus you would receive regular reports on his location, so that we might be easy.'

Mr Singleton let out a low whistle of admiration. 'Why, ma'am, what a head you have! I call that an excellent idea, do not you, Benedict, Maria? I know it goes against the grain to give him money, scoundrel that he is, but it's surely a small price to pay for your peace of mind. All the money in the world is no use to you if you've turned up your toes.'

Maria said anxiously, 'I am sure it is an excellent idea, but is it enough? What if he laughs in your face and simply refuses?'

They were all silent for a moment, and then her husband said ruthlessly, 'Make sure he can't. Pockets to let, you know. Not a feather to fly with. Make it clear you repudiate his debts – publish a notice in the newspapers saying that they are no business of yours. Creditors would descend like locusts. Have to flee. Happens all the time.'

'That might work, I suppose, John,' his wife replied. 'But what if he agrees, but then employs someone to . . . to do you a mischief? If he were far away, he could not be suspected. Would we not then have played into his hands?'

Benedict said, 'Now we have strayed too far into in the realms of the Gothic. He is not a villain in a novel by Mrs Radcliffe; John said as much, and he was right. I seriously doubt that he would be hiring assassins. He is too cautious for that, I believe, for it would put him at the grave risk of blackmail. No, I think it is an excellent idea, Kate, and one that we should definitely carry out, with a small addition: that you and I – all of us – go to our lawyer and each swear an affidavit that we believe Felix Silverwood to have been implicated in the tragic accident that killed my brother and my first wife, and furthermore that if one or both of us, or anyone close to us, subsequently dies by unnatural means, we believe that he has had a hand in it. We shall describe what happened with the bonbons, and the poor creature that ate them. We shall do this, and tell him that we have done it – show him a copy, so that he knows that we are not bluffing. This affidavit shall be held in safekeeping and not produced unless one or both of us meets with a fatal or very serious accident. Then it shall be published abroad. Sent to every newspaper in the land. It does not matter that we have not a jot of proof, for we could not be sued . . .'

'Because we would be dead,' said Kate with a shudder.

'Exactly.'

'Do you think it could work?' Maria asked anxiously.

'Sure to,' said her husband firmly. 'The fellow cares a great deal for his consequence. Wouldn't like it at all, to inherit but be the subject of whispers wherever he goes. Shunned by society. Not received at Carlton House. Cut by Prinny. Unwelcome at White's. All of that. Poisoned chalice, it would be. By Jove, that's rather appropriate, ain't it? I consider that a capital idea. What a team you are, the pair of you!'

Kate felt herself flush, and her heart fluttered in her breast as she saw the warmth with which Benedict was smiling at her. 'I do believe we are!' he acknowledged. 'But it is you, John, who chiefly deserves our thanks, I think.'

It was Mr Singleton's turn to blush now, and modestly to disclaim any particular merit whatsoever. But he seemed gratified, none the less, and moved forward to seize his brother-in-law's hand in a manly clasp, and shake it heartily.

'After all,' Maria said suddenly, 'there is no great harm if we are wrong, and if we are right, the greatest peril is now, and over the next year or two. Beyond that, God willing, it will not matter so much.' She saw the men's puzzled faces, and by contrast the full consciousness of her meaning betrayed by Kate, and laughed. 'Ninnies! Because of course by then we hope that Kate will have given you a son, or more than one, so that the danger will have passed! However wicked he is, Felix can hardly hope to wipe out an entire family without attracting the least notice. He cannot for ever be sending poisoned sweets to us, now that we suspect him. Not when he knows that the affidavit is held safe against such a circumstance.'

Kate looked down and tried not to meet her husband's eyes, nor her sister-in-law's, all the while aware that the marked degree of embarrassment she must have betrayed in her reaction to this comment had caused Maria to look at her a little sharply, an expression of the liveliest curiosity dawning upon her face. She did not dare to attempt to ascertain whether Benedict might be reacting in the same manner, or if he was oblivious.

He coughed and said, 'Quite so, Maria. Are we resolved then to act upon this?'

They all nodded solemnly. 'Very good. I shall send a message to my lawyer, and we shall swear our affidavits today. And then you and I, John, shall put our heads together and consider how best to approach Felix.' He smiled rather grimly, his face resolute. 'I confess that that is something I am quite looking forward to.'

CHAPTER FORTY-SEVEN

The rest of the day was all bustle, with a hastily arranged visit to the office of Benedict's lawyer at Lincoln's Inn. He was an elderly, punctilious gentleman, a relic of the previous century, whom Kate had met briefly on her previous visit to London in connection with the formalities regarding her extremely generous marriage settlement. His seamed face was very grave as Benedict recounted his story, and he shook his grizzled head sadly over the revelations of possible villainy on the part of a member of the Silverwood family, although, being as cautious as most of his kind, he refused to commit himself to any definite statement in the absence of proof. He considered the swearing of an affidavit a very grave step – a very grave step indeed – but when he was politely challenged as to what else the family could do in their most unusual circumstances, he had no answer for them.

The separate statements all had to be drawn up laboriously by hand, of course, by Mr Kinghorn's staff of legal writers, and this would take some time, so it was agreed that they would stay only for Benedict's document to be prepared, sipping Mountain Malaga and making rather strained civil conversation with the elderly lawyer in his ancient wood-panelled chamber as they did so. After what seemed an interminable wait, the document was ready for solemn signature and witnessing, and they took their leave with a meticulous exchange of compliments, arranging to return upon the following day, when the remaining papers would have been prepared.

On their return to Clarges Street, Benedict and his brother-in-law withdrew to the library – Mr Singleton's particular den, though it was doubtful whether a great deal of reading of the many venerable leatherbound tomes it held ever occurred there – to discuss exactly how they would approach Mr Silverwood and make their proposal to him. They had firmly declined any feminine participation at this meeting, and, as Maria said to Kate once they were alone in her sitting room, it was hardly necessary, since it seemed likely that they would merely use a great deal of intemperate masculine language, and egg each other on to make vague threats as to what they intended to do, without actually discussing anything of real importance, which had in any case already been decided.

Earlier in the day, Benedict had set his groom Joseph Sykes – his former batman during his years in the army, an individual who, fortunately for the task in hand, bore very little resemblance to a respectable gentleman's servant – to watch Mr Silverwood's lodgings, which was just a few moments' walk away in Mayfair. He had just reported, by means of a street urchin who had carried a message, that Silverwood had not left the house since he himself had arrived; as Pinks of the Ton were not in general known to be early risers, it was to be assumed that – if Silverwood had in fact spent the night in his own bed, and not someone else's – he was safely inside under their eyes for the time being.

Maria and Kate sat down to take tea and lemon cake, both suddenly weary after so much emotion. 'Kate . . .' said Maria, after the tea tray had been removed and they were both feeling somewhat restored.

'Yes, Maria?'

They looked at each other, Maria in enquiry, Kate blushing, and after a moment they both burst into laughter. 'Do not ask me anything!' Kate said. 'I cannot tell you.'

'Because you do not know for certain, or because you have not yet shared the news with Benedict?' Kate shook her head, smiling, and her sister-in-law said, 'I will wager it is the latter. Goodness, men are so very dense sometimes, are they not? You might imagine a husband might notice that his wife had not . . . Well, I will not press you. Once this horrid matter is behind us, I hope we may all be easier, and there will be time to speak of such things. I shall not congratulate you yet!'

They turned the topic by mutual consent, and spoke of the excellent new governess who, with Mrs Singleton's help, had been found for Lucy and interviewed by the Silverwoods a few days ago, and when she would be able to commence her duties. 'I confess,' said Kate at last, 'that although I am most grateful to you for having us to stay with you, Maria, and there is no denying that it has been a most memorable visit, I am eager to return to the Hall.'

'I can certainly comprehend why you might be, after all that has happened,' said Maria, not in the least offended. 'How does my mother say that Mr Waltham gets on? There is no concerning news there, I trust?'

Kate sighed. 'She does not attempt to conceal from me the fact that he is a little weaker even than he was when we left, perhaps even perceptibly weaker with every day that passes. I think we should go home as soon as this wretched business is concluded – perhaps the day after tomorrow, since first we must sign the papers. She is anxious about him, and would feel more secure if I were close by, and I feel that I should be, so that I can spend some time with him, before . . .' She trailed off, and Maria clasped her hand in silent understanding. There was nothing more to be said.

Benedict and Mr Singleton emerged from their seclusion, and informed their womenfolk that, since it was now late afternoon and Felix had still not stirred from his rooms, they meant to go to confront him without loss of time, before he had the chance to depart for some evening engagement. Though it went against the grain to be excluded from such an important interview merely because she was a woman, Kate could acknowledge that there was no point cavilling at it; it was not at all the done thing for ladies to visit gentlemen (unless they should be very close relations) at their single lodgings, and if Felix should surprise them all and offer direct violence to his unwelcome visitors, her presence would be a hindrance rather than a help. She could only trust that his brother-in-law would be able to restrain Benedict from any extreme action if they should come to blows. It was not at all to her taste, nor to Maria's, for that matter, to be left pacing the floor and wringing her hands, but there was no help for it. The men departed, and there was nothing to do but wait, and hope.

CHAPTER FORTY-EIGHT

It was but a few minutes' walk to the respectable house where Felix Silverwood had his rooms, and Benedict and John strode there briskly through the growing autumn dusk, talking inconsequentially. They paused on the doorstep to nod sternly to each other. Benedict felt a little ridiculous suddenly, doubtful all at once that their wild suppositions could really be true, and wondered if his brother-in-law was conscious of the same feeling, but did not care to ask. Were they about to make colossal fools of themselves?

And then it was too late – John was knocking firmly upon the door, and they were being admitted by the woman who had the running of the lodging. She kept them waiting for what seemed an interminable time as she went upstairs to see if Silverwood would receive them, and they stood fidgeting in the hall, but at last she came down to admit them, and they exchanged glances and mounted the stairs together.

The rooms to which they were shown on the first floor were not large, but they were comfortable. Or at least, they were now. Benedict had been there before – he had visited his brother there once, on his brief return to England after Lucy's birth. He had come reluctantly to invite Caspar to his niece's christening, at his mother's insistence. It was a memory he would prefer not to recall, because Caspar had been drunk, and had repudiated his invitation in the coarsest terms, and all but ejected him from the house. He had tried at first to speak softly, to condole with Caspar and to reason with him, but it had been no use, and in the end he too had become heated, and harsh words had been spoken on both sides. It had been the last time he had set eyes on his brother. Scarcely more than a year later he was dead. And then Vanessa . . .

He recalled that the sitting room he had been shown into then, and was shown into now, had been in the greatest possible disorder – clothes and other mingled belongings had been strewn everywhere, along with a prodigious number of empty bottles and glasses. Benedict was quite used to living in exclusively male company in circumstances where order and cleanliness did not always prevail, but even he had recoiled a little at the close, sickly smell of stale liquor and unwashed linens that had greeted him, a sign, if one had been needed, of the careless way in which his brother had been living.

It was far otherwise now. He had partly excused the degradation he had perceived six years ago as a sign of slatternly housekeeping, but he could see now that this was not so, for the place was immaculate – beautifully and tastefully decorated with an expensive Chinese paper that glowed with rich and surely costly colours, as well as gleaming with the care of an excellent housekeeper – and nothing else had changed save that his brother no longer lived here. If the order and nice taste that prevailed in this room was a sign of Felix's preferences as well as his housekeeper's skill, and it could hardly be otherwise, then living with Caspar and all the dirt and chaos he created would have been a daily trial to him, and a severe one. He must have had good reason for enduring it; Benedict himself could not have done so for above a day. John was not privy to these thoughts, and so said only, warming himself in front of the welcome fire, 'Snug little place he's got here. Too much china for my taste. Knick-knacks. But homely.'

There was no time to comment, for Silverwood lounged in, immaculate as ever, though Benedict somehow had the sense that he had only just finished dressing, despite the late hour. Felix raised an eyebrow and drawled, 'Dear me, a family deputation! To what do I owe this rare honour, dear cousin, or dear cousins, I suppose I should say? But my manners have gone begging – I can only apologise, and ask you to set my lapse in courtesy down to the delightful surprise of seeing you both in my humble abode. We have been near neighbours for so long, Singleton, and yet this is the first time you have favoured me with a visit, unless I am badly mistaken. Will you take some Madeira, both of you, and sit down, and tell me what I can do for you?'

They took the offered seats, but did not remove their overcoats, and refused refreshment. They would take no food or drink that came from his hands. There was no sense in beating about the bush, and Benedict said bluntly, 'We have come to offer you money to leave the country at the earliest possible date. There is a packet sailing from Dover in three days' time, and you will be on it. I will pay your passage. I will pay you a sum to be drawn in my bank in Paris, and in addition a monthly sum after that, to any European capital you care to name. But you will leave England and never return.'

There was an arrested expression on Silverwood's face, although he otherwise remained impassive, and the flare of some unidentifiable but strong emotion in his eyes. But his voice was level as he said, 'This too is unexpected. Will you do me the favour of informing me why you have come to make me this generous though sadly vague proposal? Why should I wish to leave all the comforts of home and risk myself upon the seas at this unpropitious time of year, merely because you say it should be so?'

'Because you are done up – so deep in debt that you cannot possibly recover yourself, but will end in a sponging house or worse – and because your position as my heir no longer looks quite so secure now that I am married,' his cousin answered tersely.

It was anger, the flame burning in his eyes. Anger and something more, thought Benedict.

'Assuming it to be so, will my fond and oh-so-wealthy cousin not assist me, for the sake of the august family name?'

'No. I will not. I know Caspar was used to do so, but my patience is at an end. I will repudiate your debts publicly, if it comes to that.'

'And yet you are prepared to make me an allowance, of a sum unspecified.'

'Not if you stay in England. If you are determined to remain here, you can rot in the King's Bench or the Fleet for all I care; in fact, it would suit me very well,' said Benedict brutally.

Felix blinked slowly, and it seemed to his interlocutors that his face grew white and took on a somewhat rigid aspect.

Singleton added stolidly, 'Realised a few things today. Should have done so sooner, I dare say.'

'Oh, have you, now?' said Felix with a rather ghastly attempt at an insouciant smile. 'Setting that aside for a moment, if you will, what is to prevent me from taking your allowance and returning to England all the same?'

'Nothing. But once you have left, your creditors will be alerted to your flight. It will be impossible, therefore, for you to return here, to these rooms, or indeed to appear anywhere that you would care for in Britain under your own name. It is hard to see how you could be comfortable in such circumstances. Whereas in Paris, or Rome, or where you will, you will have an allowance that will enable you to live like a gentleman. Although I must caution you that it will only be paid to you in person, not to others on your behalf.'

'I understand your position, I believe, cousin, and I can quite see that it would be most convenient for you to have me gone.' Silverwood almost spat out these words, and the mask of suavity he habitually wore was beginning to crumble, to reveal quite another creature – a wild, furious one – beneath it. 'But are you sure that you will be . . . quite safe? Can you have thought of all the eventualities that might occur, once I am safely parcelled off to the continent?'

'I believe so,' said Benedict grimly. 'I have today gone to my attorney and sworn an affidavit stating that I believe you to have been implicated in the death of my late wife, and of my brother. I have further sworn that I have reason to fear for my life, and that of my present wife and any children she might bear, at your hands. I have said that if I die, or any of us dies, in any but the most natural of circumstances, I believe that you will be the cause of it, whether directly by your own hand or through paid assassins. I have described the box of bonbons that were sent to my wife, and the cat that died from eating them.' When he heard this, it seemed that Felix grew paler still, and made some effort to speak, but his cousin was relentless as he continued, 'I have said that I believe you to be entirely ruthless, and not sane. My wife, my sister and my brother-in-law are having affidavits drawn up to say the same. And if any of us does perish in such circumstances, or is even injured, our affidavits will be published as widely as can be contrived. I have arranged for money to be set aside for this purpose. It shall be blazoned across every newspaper in Britain.'

Felix found his tongue at last, and spat out, 'You are bluffing. You would never countenance such public disgrace to the name of Silverwood, whether you were alive or dead, just because some accident should befall that whore of yours for whom you do not care two pins.'

'I am not bluffing. And you shall not refer to my wife again, in those terms or any other. If you do so again, I shall knock your teeth down your lying throat. You are very lucky that I have not done so already, for daring to think of harming her, you treacherous cur!'

They had both sprung to their feet, and faced each other across the room, just a few short paces apart. Singleton rose too, and was eyeing them both warily, as if poised to intervene.

Felix Silverwood began suddenly to laugh rather wildly. 'Oh, please, cousin, let us not put on these Drury Lane airs. You are making yourself perfectly ridiculous, without the least cause. I see that you believe all that you have said, and here is stout John to back you. What can I do against two such fine specimens of English manhood? Calm yourselves; it is very poor ton indeed to allow yourselves to become so agitated. I admit nothing, but I will accept your offer, once you have clarified the terms a little. As you correctly suggest, I am . . . somewhat financially embarrassed just at present. I am sure that I will find the climate in Paris or in Rome most congenial. I suppose I should thank you, but I cannot bring myself to do so just yet.'

He turned, as if in dismissal, and Singleton rumbled suddenly, 'Too easy, Ben! Have a care!'

As John spoke, Felix took two long strides towards his cousin – no one who was acquainted with his famously languid demeanour would ever have believed that he could move so fast – and lunged desperately at him with a long, wicked blade that he must have had concealed in his sleeve all the while they had been talking. Benedict had time only to step hastily back, too shocked to take any further action, but Singleton strode forward and stuck out his foot to trip his assailant. He meant merely to avert the danger to Benedict in the only way that occurred to him, but he was far more effective than he had intended. Felix's violent rush of movement carried him over the extended foot, with no chance to save himself, so that he stumbled and fell hard, and struck the side of the marble fireplace with an audible crack, and a force that shook the room and set all the Venetian glass and china on the shelves tinkling. He slumped to the floor, and lay still.

Benedict and John stood over him, silent and frozen in place, and were standing so still when the housekeeper rushed into the room, crying out that she had heard a terrible crash. Singleton collapsed into a chair, but his brother-in-law stepped forward, as the woman stood wringing her hands, and knelt beside his cousin, expecting him to find him stunned by the blow to his head. In a moment he looked up and said tonelessly, 'He is quite dead. There is a great deal of blood – I can only think he fell upon the knife he was carrying. The force of his motion . . .'

'Are you sure, sir?' cried the woman.

'I am,' he replied rather blankly. 'I have been a soldier, and could not mistake it. We must send for the constable – the watch? I do not know who . . .'

'Did he attack you, sir?' She seemed to be recovering her composure remarkably quickly, and did not appear to be deeply grieved by the loss of her tenant. 'He'd been a terrible queer mood these past weeks, last night in particular. Had he run mad, do you suppose?' There was an odd, gloating tone to her voice, as of one who enjoyed trouble, if it was the trouble of others, but her companions were too shocked to make any objection to it.

Benedict gathered his scattered wits and said, 'I think you are aware that I am his cousin, madam, and this is my brother-in-law. We had heard rumours that he was in a great deal of debt, and on the point of being taken into custody for it.' She was nodding avidly, this clearly being no surprise to her. 'We had come to offer help – to say that I would give him an allowance if he agreed to live more cheaply abroad. But he became enraged – full of resentment, and . . . and . . .'

'And he went for you with that nasty, wicked foreign knife of his!' she said, her eyes gleaming. 'Are you the gentleman which he was heir to, if you don't mind me asking?'

Benedict nodded wearily. 'I am. And I have recently married.'

'Ah!' she said profoundly. 'Well, that explains it, then!'

'I suppose it does. Is there anyone you can send to fetch the authorities? I feel we should not delay.'

She nodded, and was about to leave the room, when an unwelcome thought struck her, and her tones became markedly less genteel as she spoke again, saying, 'Here! What about the three months' rent I'm owed? Where will I get that now?!' This loss seemed to grieve and shock her far more than anything else that had previously occurred, not excluding the presence of a dead body under her roof.

Singleton rallied to say shortly, 'We will cover it. Don't suppose you'd have seen a penny of it if he'd fled to the continent. So you won't be the loser.'

She seemed much struck by this, and looked around the room now, cupidity evident upon her thin face. 'And all these lovely things what I've cared for so well for so many years. China and silver and such. What's going to happen to them?'

'I fear his creditors will have first claim on them. But you are not among their number, are you, madam? For we will settle your account privately, without any disagreeable quibbling over shillings, so that you have no need to fear the competing claims of others,' said Benedict. 'Now if you please, the constable . . . ?'

CHAPTER FORTY-NINE

Hours dragged by without any word. Maria and Kate spent some while debating how long such an errand could possibly take, but neither of them could find a way to make it stretch much past an hour, or perhaps two at the outside. Saying good night to the children and telling them a story – Lucy had clamoured for Kate to share her Italian tales with her cousins, and she had been doing so ever since their arrival in London – had been a welcome distraction, and Kate had been hoping that when she left the nursery and came downstairs she would find that Benedict had returned. But she was disappointed, and when three hours had passed and then four, she and Maria began to be seriously concerned. Dinner was postponed, and they did not go up to change, but sat huddled together on the sofa, having fallen silent long since. They were both straining for the sound of the front door opening, and voices in the hall, and some reassurance that dreadful things – they scarcely knew what – had not happened.

At last they heard a bustle, and then a moment later deep, familiar tones. They both sprang to their feet and stood close together, their hands clasped in mutual support, though they were unconscious of it. Benedict and John found them so when they entered the room. Maria ran to her husband and took him by the shoulders, shaking him and crying, 'John, where have you been?! We have been in torment, not knowing what was happening!' She then surprised him, and perhaps herself, by bursting into tears and flinging her arms about him. He staggered a little, but recovered impressively quickly, and returned the embrace with equal fervour.

Kate stood stock still, gazing at Benedict in horror. 'Your waistcoat . . .' she said. 'Your shirt . . .'

He glanced down to see what she had observed, and he had not: blood, a great quantity of it, not only on his waistcoat and shirt, but soaked into the knees of his grey pantaloons too. 'Oh, no, Kate, it is not mine . . .' he began, stepping forward to reassure her, but she did not hear him. Darkness descended on her suddenly, and she slipped into it. He was close enough to catch her in his arms as she fell, and set her gently down upon the sofa just behind her.

She opened her eyes to see three anxious faces hovering over her: Benedict, who was sitting beside her, chafing her hands, and behind him Maria and her husband. She struggled to sit up, and he released her hands in order to help her rise, propping cushions behind her so that she could lean back in comfort. 'I am sorry,' she said weakly. 'I have never fainted in my life. But we have been so very anxious, and when I saw the blood . . .'

'It was thoughtless of me not to consider how it might affect you,' said Benedict. 'But I thought you would wish to know all that had happened immediately, and so did not go up to change.'

Maria was regarding Kate closely, and said, 'You are still very white! Benedict, do you go and put off those frightful things, and I will tend to Kate.'

'But—' he protested.

'Go! She is about to be extremely unwell, and no wonder, with you as close as you are, your hands all . . . I insist that you leave this instant! You too, John! You may both return as soon as you have changed. We shall not dress for dinner.'

She shooed them out, and hurried back to Kate with the first receptacle she had seized upon: a fine Sèvres vase from the mantel, which was promptly used for a purpose for which it had never been intended. Maria held Kate's hair back and made soothing noises until she was done, and when she was sure it was over she rang the bell, thrusting the vessel into her startled butler's arms and desiring him to have it set to rights, and also to fetch Lady Silverwood's maid with warm cloths, and to hasten, because her mistress was unwell.

They waited, Kate apologising feebly and Maria brushing it aside. 'Have you been, er, queasy before this?' she asked.

Her sister-in-law shook her head gingerly. Sudden movements seemed a bad idea still. 'Not like that! I have felt a little nauseous in the morning, but never . . . to such an extent. It was the shock, I think, and the blood. So much blood, as if he had been kneeling in it, and his hands . . . Maria, what can it mean? Neither Benedict nor Mr Singleton appears to be wounded in any way.'

'They do not, though I am sure they deserve to be, frightening us like that! I do not wonder that you were affected so. I could have swooned myself! Could they not have sent word that all was well?'

'Perhaps all is not well,' said Kate faintly, leaning back against her cushions.

'We will find out soon enough!' Maria replied.

Half an hour later, Kate had had her face and hands wiped, and rinsed her mouth out, and her maid had rearranged her dishevelled hair. Tea had been brought, and she had drunk it thirstily. Benedict and John returned, looking much more presentable, though deeply weary, and once they had been reassured that Kate was not seriously ill, but had merely been shocked and was feeling much more the thing now, they all sat down together to discuss the events of the afternoon and evening.

Mr Singleton said gravely, when Benedict appeared to be reluctant to begin, 'There's no more danger. Must tell you that first, ma'am, Maria. The family is safe now. Fellow won't be troubling you any more. Or anybody, come to that. Good thing.'

Maria appeared to be about to burst out with a sharp question, but then took a deep breath, as if to check herself from rushing into speech, and asked slowly, with an anxious glance at Kate's still-pale face, 'John . . . have I run mad, or are you trying to break it to us gently that Felix is . . . severely wounded?'

'He is dead, Maria,' said Benedict heavily, taking Kate's hand as he spoke and holding it tightly.

'But you have not been arrested, either of you? Please explain, Benedict!' whispered Kate, clinging to his hand, determined not to betray weakness again, but unable to let go of him now that he had returned to her.

'There will be no arrests and no charges,' he replied. 'That is why we were so long, dealing with the authorities. It is so very odd to think that the hideous encounter itself cannot have occupied much more than half an hour. It was the aftermath that took so long, giving our statements. I am sorry we could not send word to reassure you, but we were fully occupied, and we feared that a mere message telling you that Felix was dead and explaining no further would come as a great shock to you. But it is almost done with now. There will have to be an inquest, of course, and it will not be pleasant, but I believe it to be a mere formality.'

'They accepted that it was self-defence?' Kate asked anxiously.

'Nothing of the kind!' said Singleton. 'Fellow did it himself!'

Maria and Kate gazed at him in astonishment as he described the interview, its apparently successful conclusion, and then the horror of Felix's sudden mad rush with the knife he had kept concealed.

'John saved me,' Benedict said, as his brother-in-law shook his head self-deprecatingly. 'Truly he did. He was quite splendid, Maria, you should know it. I do not think I was ever in so much danger in my life as in that moment. I stepped aside, but had no time to do more, and Felix was determined to stab me in the heart. I am convinced he would have kept on coming for me in a sort of frenzy. I was not in the least prepared for it. But John reacted quicker than I could have imagined, tripping Felix and preventing him from reaching me, and . . . and he fell, and his own knife pierced him. He was dead in an instant.'

'Every dreadful thing we suspected about his actions was completely true, then. He meant to kill you,' Kate murmured. 'All we surmised – the very worst of it that we scarcely dared imagine – was nothing but the bare truth: he would have killed you.'

'Me, my dear, or perhaps you if he could have found a way. It must be so. His mind was disturbed, surely. No sane man could have hoped to do away with me, and I suppose John too, in his own rooms, in such a manner. And even if he had by some chance succeeded and overpowered us both, what then? How could he possibly have concealed our deaths? The woman saw us enter, he must have realised that you both knew our whereabouts, and we had told him of the affidavit. No, he was past all thought of inheritance in that moment. Past all thought of anything but taking my life. He could not endure that I should leave that room unscathed, whatever the consequences might be for him. Such hatred as he felt for me.' Kate squeezed his hand, and he returned the pressure.

There was a moment of silence as they all contemplated the appalling events that had occurred a few hours ago. Maria broke it. 'What did you say to explain it all? You cannot have told the truth, surely? It could only have served to throw fresh suspicion on you, if you had said what you suspected. They might have thought you came to kill him, in order to ensure your own safety, and conspired together to make it look an accident.'

'Benedict had his wits about him,' replied her husband. 'Dashed impressive. Told them we had heard that the fellow was rolled up, prospect of debtors' prison looming, so we came to offer him the chance to run, said we'd support him on the continent. Help the fellow out to avoid the scandal of his being taken up. Could prove it was so, fortunately – financial papers in Benedict's pocket. Draft on his bank in Paris. Friendly family visit, nothing sinister at all. Perfectly understandable, kind of thing any gentleman would do. They lapped it up.'

'And then how . . . ?'

'How did we explain his attack on me, Kate? A moment of madness. What else could it have been?'

'Woman who kept the house – nasty creature, kind of hag you'd have found knitting under the guillotine, loving the spectacle – said he had been in a dashed queer state of mind ever since his cousin married. She'd known him for years, knew all about the family. Knew he'd counted on inheriting and couldn't accept losing his place. Knew his pockets were to let, too. Rent owing. Then Ben came to see him – offer of assistance kindly meant – couldn't endure it. All hangs together. Shook their heads solemnly, said how sad, sorry to inconvenience you, gentlemen, do be on your way and don't trip over the body on your way out.'

'So it is over.' Kate could scarcely believe it.

'Almost. Once the inquest is done with, it will be over, sweet Kate. And we can go home.'

CHAPTER FIFTY

None of them felt like eating, but Maria was insistent that they should try, and when the few dishes that had not been irretrievably spoilt by the passage of time since the regular dinner hour appeared, they picked at them with varying degrees of appetite. There was a sort of comfort, they discovered, not so much in the food, but in going through the motions of normal life, and so they all felt a little better afterwards. They did not linger, however – the ladies did not withdraw – and all made their way upstairs not long after the table had been cleared.

Kate was in bed when Benedict came to her. She felt very far from sleep; the events of the day were still churning in her mind, and besides she was resolved that she must now share her secret – one of her secrets – with him. If she were to be unwell again, as Maria had warned her she might over the next few weeks, her condition would surely become obvious to everyone around her; she was quite sure that her maid suspected it already, and once they returned to Berkshire the sharp eyes of the Dowager would no doubt be very quick to divine it. Benedict should have been the first to know; he should certainly not be the last. It was time.

'Shall I put out the candles, my dear, so that you can get some rest?' he asked.

She shook her head. 'In a while. I could not sleep quite yet.'

'I am sure you are exhausted, after all the worry you have had today. I am sorry we could find no way to get word to you that we were safe. We did not feel ourselves under any kind of suspicion for very long, once we told our story, showed them the financial papers and were plainly believed, but it did not seem wise to demand to write a note, since we could hardly reveal that anyone had any particular reason to be worried about us or concerned at our absence.'

'I can understand how that could be so. It does not matter now; all that matters is that you both came home safe. It could have been far otherwise.'

He shrugged off his dressing gown and climbed rather wearily into bed beside her. 'Will you let me hold you, Kate? I promise to ask no more of you tonight. I am sure you are scarcely in a frame of mind conducive to passion, and I confess that I am not either.'

She moved into his arms, resting her head on his chest, and he smoothed back her hair, and kissed her forehead. It was tempting just to lie there and enjoy the warmth and comfort of his body, tempting too to fall asleep in his arms, but she had resolved not to do so. She was about to speak, was framing the words that she would use, but he spoke first.

'It is perfectly true that I could have died tonight. I know he shrugged it off, but John's quick thinking undoubtedly saved my life, you know. I underestimated Felix; I always thought of him as a frippery fellow, a mere popinjay. I certainly did not seriously, in my heart of hearts, think him resolute enough to intend to kill me, nor anyone else. I suppose I thought John's suspicions a remote possibility, no more than that. And even if I had credited them, I could not have imagined he was mad enough to attempt to do it in such a reckless way. John had his measure better than I, I think, and so reacted more quickly.'

She shuddered, and his arms tightened about her. He pressed his lips to her hair once more, and when he next spoke his words were a little muffled in it. 'I have had occasion to observe before that a brush with death rather serves to concentrate the mind, Kate. It has certainly done so for me this day. If I had died tonight, I would have died as a fool.'

'What do you mean?' she asked, trying to make her voice cool, though she feared that it might be shaking with suppressed emotion. What was he about to say? She did not dare conjecture. He was kissing her, and holding her – surely it could not be anything so very bad?

He said hesitantly, 'In the moments when I realised how close death had been in that room, before I quite accepted that I was indeed safe, the emotion that almost overmastered me was regret.'

She dared not look up at him. But he was continuing, 'Regret that I had not acknowledged, even to myself, the depth of my feelings for you while there was still time. Regret that I would die without ever telling you that I love you. Regret that you would never know it. There were other thoughts that grieved me too – the loss of a life and a future with you, and children with you, and the deep sorrow that I would not live to see Lucy grow up. But in that moment, that was the strongest.'

She pulled away from him and raised her head so that she could see his face, and he reached out and stroked her cheek. 'I know you may not wish to hear it from me, sweet Kate, and do not think that I am asking you to respond in kind – why should you? – but I shall say it all the same. I love you. I do not know when I fell in love with you, perhaps it was a gradual thing and there was no one moment, but I love you now, with all my heart.'

When she did not reply for a moment, he smiled sadly and said, 'I just wanted to tell you. We need never speak of it again, if you do not wish it. But at least I have told you.'

'Oh, Benedict . . .' When he seemed about to speak, she reached out and put a finger on his lips. 'I have heard you out. Now you must hear me.' She sat up, and leant back against the pillows, and he turned to look at her, hope and confusion warring on his face.

'I shall tell it as if it were one of the stories I tell Lucy. Once upon a time, a few years ago, there was a provincial girl who made her come-out in the London Season. She was not wealthy or fashionable, beautiful or well-connected, so she did not have any great expectations of making a splendid match. But she liked dancing, and parties, and she resolved to enjoy herself. Until one day she happened to dance with a young gentleman. Perhaps he was one among many, although taller and broader in the shoulder than most, but he was certainly very handsome and dashing, and although he had no interest at all in this particular young lady, he spoke kindly to her, and danced like a dream. The young lady began to think about him a great deal, and look for him at the balls and assemblies, and be disappointed if he were not there. At last she told herself that she was in love with him.'

Once again she placed her finger on his lips, to check whatever he had been about to say. 'She was not such a foolish young lady after all, because although in truth she did not know the gentleman very well, she had not just lost her heart to a handsome face and a fine pair of grey eyes. She could see that he was brave – he was an officer, wounded in battle – and kind, intelligent, held in high esteem by all who knew him, and that he was altogether exactly the kind of young man who deserved a young lady's love. But he did not care for hers, sadly, or even know of it. He fell in love, and our poor heroine saw him do it. Stood in the ballroom in his arms and watched him look over her shoulder at another, and saw his heart go out to the beautiful girl in the sparkling blue and white dress, with the silver-gilt curls. Because she cared for him, she noticed the moment where others perhaps did not.'

He stirred a little, and looked her incredulously, dawning wonder in his eyes, but he did not make any further attempt to speak.

She went on, 'She was very sad, of course, our heroine, and it was small consolation to her that the young gentleman did not become selfish or self-absorbed because he was in love, and because very quickly his love was reciprocated. He did not change in the least. He still danced with the less favoured ladies, and spoke kindly to them. And his love was returned, as such a man deserved it should be, and he was able to offer for his choice and be accepted, and very soon they were married.

'And the young lady never saw him again. She received no offers that Season, and when later on she did, she refused them. She told herself that it was not that her heart was broken, you understand, nor even irretrievably damaged, but merely that this gentleman or other did not suit her, for one reason or another. She was very lucky that, despite her lack of fortune, there was no one in her life who would put pressure on her to marry a man she did not care for. And so seven years passed, as in a fairy tale.

'The young lady was then obliged to leave her home and go to live near where the gentleman, now a widower, had his residence. She told herself that she need never see him, and that if by chance she did, he would mean nothing to her now. It had only been a silly infatuation, after all, and it was long past. She became friendly with the gentleman's mother, and with his daughter, but there was no harm in that. She enjoyed their company, and grew to love them both for their own sakes, and if she did find a certain pleasure in hearing them talk of him, no harm in that either. She still had not seen him. Perhaps she never would.'

She stopped for a moment, and Benedict took her hand and held it clasped in his, and said, 'What happened then, my dear?'

'The gentleman returned, and she saw him. And she was overset, for it seemed to her that all her long-buried feelings came flooding back to torment her once more.'

'Did she still care for him, then?'

'She feared she did. She feared her poor heart would be hurt again, and she resolved not to let it be so. Even though she could see that the young man had indeed grown to be someone any woman could be proud to love.'

He raised her hand to his lips and kissed it, and held it to his cheek. 'Oh, my dear . . .'

'But then, as it seemed to her, fate played a cruel trick. Her grandfather told her that the man wanted to marry her. Not because he loved her, for he did not, but for many excellent reasons of his own. She spent a terrible night wondering what she should do. She thought she had no real choice but to refuse him, but she was sorely tempted – not for material reasons, but because she was so very lonely, and to be at his side, and a part of his family, to be a mother to his child whom she loved and perhaps to more children too, was seductive to her. But then to be married to him without love on his part . . . She was not sure she could bear it. She resolved to refuse.'

'But she did not refuse. Thank God she did not, but why?'

'No, she did not. His mother came to her, and told her that she had guessed her secret – that she knew the lady loved her son. The mother pooh-poohed the idea that it was mere infatuation.'

Benedict gave a small involuntary snort of laughter. 'Well can I imagine that scene.'

'And because of that love, the mother begged the girl to marry her son.' He stirred, but said nothing. 'She said that he had been very badly hurt and as if one frozen in misery – she did not tell the half of why – but that he was slowly coming back to life. She thought that he was interested in the young lady, just a tiny spark of interest, she said, but one that might grow. She said, very shockingly, that her son desired the young lady – that a mother can tell such things.'

He swore, briefly but emphatically, but she ignored him, and continued. 'The mother did not promise that her son would grow to love his bride, if she married him, but she hoped very much that he might. She begged our heroine to be brave and take that chance. And so she did.'

He released her hand, but only so that he could take her in his arms. 'She is truly very brave, our heroine,' he said, his lips very close to hers. She shrugged a little, a very un-English gesture, but he persisted, 'Oh, she is. There could be none braver. To marry him, that was courageous enough, but still she could have done that and held a corner of herself separate. Kept herself safe. But she did not.' He kissed her then, at first gently, a mere butterfly brush of the lips, but soon deeply, passionately, and she responded with equal intensity, their mouths open, tongues tangling, their hands clinging tight to each other's bodies. They were both breathless when he pulled away to look down at her and say, 'You gave yourself to me completely. Held nothing back. I was an utter fool and thought that when you told me that, showed me that in all your incredible generosity and trust, you meant only physically. That would have been much. But you did not mean only that, did you, my love?'

'No, no, I did not. I told you once, no half-measures. It is not in my nature to play safe, or I would never have risked marrying you. I held nothing back from you save the fact that I loved you.'

His lips claimed hers again, and they lost themselves in the pleasure of it. When he lifted them, it was only to say, 'To think I held you in my arms once – you wore pink, did you not, and flowers in your lovely hair? I remember now – and danced with you, and was such a

373

blind fool that I did not know all that could have been mine. But I am a fool no longer. Kate, my sweet love, I want you now. I could have died without ever knowing that you love me, but I did not. I am the luckiest man in the world tonight, and I want to be inside you, to possess you. All of you, all of me. Will you take me, right now?'

'Oh, Benedict, my love! Yes,' she said. 'Yes, I will.'

They fumbled with their nightclothes, laughing in their impatience, and then he was in her, plunging into her wetness, filling her, and they were moving together, fast and hard and urgent, their mouths hungry, their hands exploring, eager, desperate for each other.

They came together, in perfect union, the pleasure so intense that they both cried out, almost screamed, careless if anyone in the house might hear, oblivious just then to the existence of anyone in the world save each other.

They lay entwined, afterwards, and he shifted so that he could kiss and caress her breasts, burying his head between them, and her arms cradled him close to her body.

'Do you remember, love, a few nights ago – I cannot say when it was, it seems like months – I said that I desired a fresh start?' She stroked his head in assent, since he was in no position to see her nod, his face buried in her flesh as it was. 'I was beginning then to suspect the depths of my feelings for you. I have been uneasy, I think, ever since that I heard you sing – feeling that we should be closer, that I was in the wrong, somehow, in my relations with you. Knowing that I was keeping secrets from you, of course, but more than that. I am greatly relieved, Kate, that there shall be no more secrets between us.'

'Ah,' she said.

CHAPTER FIFTY-ONE

'Benedict, I do have another secret. I meant to tell you tonight, but . . . events overtook us.'

He raised his head a little, a tiny frown between his eyes, and she smiled down at him. She took his hand from where it lay cupping her breast, and placed it on her belly, and held it there. 'Can you guess my secret, my love? Our secret, I should really say.'

'Kate . . . Is it true? My dearest love, that is marvellous! Are you sure?'

'I have no experience to guide me, but I have not bled since we were married. I am in general very regular in my courses, and they were due perhaps two weeks after our wedding. It was a month ago now, that they should have arrived. More than that, in fact. Too soon to be secure of it, perhaps. But I thought I must tell you. Maria has begun to suspect.'

He moved so that he was no longer putting his weight on her body, and lay close beside her, taking her hand and kissing it fervently. 'Oh, my dearest! To learn of new life on a day such as this! You were unwell earlier, was that . . . ?'

'Yes, I think so. I have been feeling queasy in the morning, and when I saw those wretched bonbons, and the same nausea overwhelmed me all at once when I saw the blood on your clothes and feared that you were injured. Maria was an angel, and said nothing, when I told her I could not speak of it.'

'Are you happy, my love? So quickly . . . is it what you wanted?'

She caressed his face, and he turned his head to plant a kiss on her palm. 'Benedict, it is all that I could have wanted. To be loved by you, to have your child . . . I could not have dreamt it possible, a few short months ago.'

They kissed again, murmuring endearments, lying wrapped in each other's arms. 'I was used to think myself a spinster for so long, I expect I will find it a little difficult at first to have everybody look at me, so newly married, and know . . . that we have . . .'

He chuckled. 'I am sure that everybody assumes it in any case. It is the common fate of those recently married to be the subject of such speculation, even if it is not voiced in polite society. And then again, you are so very desirable, Kate, and your body is so fitted for sensual pleasure, that no one will be in the least surprised, I am sure, that I have been a most eager bridegroom. It is, of course, also a tribute to my virility, as well as your fecundity.' He looked quite boyishly delighted with himself as he said it, and she could only laugh.

'Not voiced in polite society! Are you forgetting your mother? She all but came out and asked me if I was increasing yet on the day after we returned from our honeymoon! You may imagine my reaction. I could only blush and say it was far too soon to speak of such things.'

'I cannot wonder at it. She is incorrigible. But she will be delighted. And so will your grandfather, I am sure.'

'Oh, Benedict, he will be so happy! I am anxious to return home and see how he does, and tell him our news. When will we be able to leave?'

'After the inquest and the funeral. Three or four days or so, I should think. I shall go to Mr Kinghorn, too, and see the affidavits destroyed. No one must know of their existence.'

'Of course; I had forgot about them. So much has happened in so short a time.'

'Indeed it has. Oh, my love, my sweet Kate. I am so very lucky to have your heart, and to have you by my side, and now this news to crown it all. Kiss me again, and then let us sleep. You need to rest now. I insist you stay in bed tomorrow, and recover your strength . . .'

She lay on top of him and kissed him, long and

slow, holding his face between her hands, pressing her body close to his and murmuring at last, 'Talking of recovering one's strength, sir, I perceive . . .' and it was long before they slept, but when they did it was very soundly, and in each other's arms.

CHAPTER FIFTY-TWO

Kate and Maria were of course not present at the inquest, nor at the very quiet funeral that soon followed it, but both passed off well enough, with a verdict of accidental death brought in for Felix Silverwood; it was plain that he had not intended to take his own life, and certainly nobody else had laid a hand upon him. The coroner turned out to be something of a sycophant, which in the circumstances was most fortunate, as it meant he was deeply sympathetic to the illustrious Silverwood family and the troubles that had descended upon them. The details of Felix's death were very quickly glossed over, so that only those actually present – a small number, which most fortuitously, due to some misunderstanding regarding the appointed hour, did not include the gentlemen of the press – were aware of his sudden, murderous intentions towards his cousin. There was no mention of poison. The family wore black armbands, but did not go into deeper mourning, and the funeral was very sparsely attended. It seemed Mr Silverwood was greatly missed by almost no one in the society he had so revered, and risked so much to remain a part of. If he had had any intimate friends, they had not thought to pay their respects in person. Only two carriages were sent, and of their noble owners there was no sign.

Benedict, Kate and Lucy left London as soon as they were able. Kate and Maria had spent a great deal of time in private conversation while the men were absent, and Kate now felt herself to be furnished with more information about her condition, and what she might expect in the coming months. They had become fast friends over the last few days, an outcome that she would never have expected, but that she welcomed. She was part of a family now, and it was a comfortable feeling, she found.

She had also written to her grandmother to share her news: a joyful letter to write, but also a sad one, for it made her wonder when she would see Nonna Albina again, or if in fact she ever would. She knew that she soon must part with her grandfather – that was inevitable – and it was sad to think that her grandmother too was effectively lost to her. There was no prospect of Kate herself travelling so far in the foreseeable future, and it was not to be expected that her grandmother would ever leave Italy again. She shared her sorrow with Benedict and with Maria, and they consoled her as best they could, and after a little while she grew more cheerful, and put it from her mind to dwell on more pleasant things. She was conscious of a great desire to return home to Silverwood Hall, and to settle into her life with Benedict and with Lucy, and prepare for the future.

Lucy was sorry to leave her cousins, but she had missed her home, her grandmother, and above all Wellington, and was eager to see them all again. She and Kate had kept up their Italian lessons – apart from unavoidable interruptions caused by such events as visits to lawyers and sudden deaths in the family – and she was eager to demonstrate her progress to the Dowager and to Miss Sutton, not to mention Wellington. Her new governess, the young and vigorous Miss Morgan, was due to arrive in a few days, and her bedchamber and sitting room must be made ready to receive her.

Kate felt a great sense of relief when the travelling carriage swept between the pineapple-topped gateposts and up the gravelled drive to the Palladian front of the Hall. The autumn evening was drawing in, and there was a brisk chill in the air; it was dusk, a mist was rising from the river, and the house was a blaze of warm light that contrasted pleasantly with the growing darkness outside. Lucy jumped down, scorning helping hands, and Benedict sprang lightly down too, and held out his hands to help Kate to join him. 'Welcome home at last, my dearest love!' he said, and seized her about the waist and kissed her soundly on the lips, careless of the presence of Lucy, his mother, Miss Sutton, the excited, wildly barking puppy, and all the waiting servants.

Blushing, but not greatly displeased, Kate found herself embraced by the Dowager, who whispered in her ear, 'I am sure you have a great deal to tell me! Let us take tea tomorrow and have a comfortable coze!'

Even Miss Sutton shook her warmly by the hand and said gruffly that she was glad to see her, and before she could draw breath she was inside, divesting herself of her bonnet and travelling pelisse and handing them to the smiling butler. It was a true homecoming indeed.

Kate took breakfast in her bedchamber the next morning and then rose and dressed, eager to see her grandfather, yet dreading to perceive a great change in him. Benedict walked with her across the demesne – they paused for a brief but enjoyable dalliance by their gate, which left her pink and a little dishevelled – and came up to greet Mr Waltham and shake his hand, but shortly left them alone so that they could talk in private.

She found him thinner still, perceptibly weaker after the passage of only a fortnight or so, but serene and content. She had not written to him to tell him of Felix's betrayal and all that they had discovered of his shocking past actions – she had discussed it with Benedict, and they had agreed that the Dowager and Miss Sutton, who had of course been informed by letter, should break the news to him in person, lest he should be very greatly shocked and suffer some reaction to it. They had done so, and he had been horrified, but had borne it well, with no ill effects that they could see, once he was reassured that Kate and Benedict were quite safe and all danger was past.

They spoke of it now, and Kate said, 'I realise now that when you talked to me of Benedict and all he had suffered, before we were married, you were fully aware of all the dreadful things that happened with Sir Caspar, and the manner of Vanessa's death.'

He sighed, and his thin hands worked upon the coverlet. 'I was, my dear. Charlotte told me everything at the time; she was in the greatest distress, as I am sure you can imagine only too well, and we are very old friends, after all. I hope you do not blame me for concealing it from you, for it was not my secret to tell. I thought Benedict should share it all with you, for I knew you would not think of blaming him for any of it, but instead would give him comfort, if comfort still were needed. But that was up to him. There was not the least thing there to his discredit – quite the reverse, or I would never have encouraged you to marry him.'

'We have spoken of it now, dear Grandfather, and I do agree with you most emphatically. If blame there is, it lies with Sir Caspar, and more justly with his cousin, who was, we now suspect, dripping poison in his ear all the while and encouraging him to reckless, immoral action when he was half mad with grief and unable to judge wisely. What a cruel, wicked man Felix Silverwood was.' Mr Waltham muttered in agreement, his language regrettably unclerical for a moment, and she pretended not to hear. 'We should not speak of that, for it was all very shocking, but it is done with now. And indeed I have some much happier news for you.'

'Do you, my dear?' he said, smiling fondly at her. 'I cannot for the life of me imagine what it might be!'

She told him, and he was overjoyed, and kissed her, and shook Benedict warmly by the hand, when he was summoned up from the parlour to be congratulated. 'If it is a boy – and for my part I care not a jot whether it be boy or girl – I had meant to ask Kate if we should name him Theodore,' said Benedict.

Kate nodded vigorously in agreement, unable to speak for a moment, her eyes brimming with tears at the suggestion, and the loving thoughtfulness it revealed, and Mr Waltham too was greatly touched; perhaps there was not one person in his bedchamber who was entirely dry-eyed at that moment.

'Well,' he said at last, 'that is very gratifying, I am sure, but I hope it does not mean that if you have a girl, you will feel equally obliged to name her Albina to please your grandmother. I am sure she is an excellent person, but I cannot think it a suitable name to inflict upon a child.'

'I have not thought too deeply on the matter,' answered Kate, smiling, 'nor have we had a chance to discuss it. There is plenty of time for that.'

'I am sure Lucy will have an opinion on the matter, when we have told her, which will not be for a little while,' Benedict said. 'Not that I mean to say that we will necessarily need her suggestions, for all they are bound to be highly amusing.'

They left him when he became tired, promising to return upon the morrow, and strolled across the park together, Benedict making Kate laugh with ridiculous and fanciful suggestions of names for their daughter or son. And then it was time for Lucy's Italian lesson, then nuncheon, and some time later tea with the Dowager. Kate knew that her husband had taken breakfast with his mother that morning while she had slept in and rested after the journey, and he had told her that they had discussed Felix very thoroughly, but he had not, he said, shared her news, thinking it more appropriate for his wife to do so. More likely, thought Kate fondly, he had feared a grilling as to dates and who knew what intimate matters from his mother, and thought that she might as well endure it instead. She did not mind; she was too happy to resent it in the least.

She found the Dowager alone, Miss Sutton having tactfully absented herself on some errand or other, and once the tea tray was set before them, they regarded each other across it, both of them smiling a little, each waiting for the other to speak first.

The Dowager asked her to pour the tea – now that the autumn cold was setting in, her joints had begun to pain her sadly, she said, and she could not well lift the pot. Kate did so, and her mother-in-law thanked her, and took a thoughtful sip. She said at last, 'I am sorry you had such a terrible time with Felix, my dear.

I was quite shocked by the revelations in Benedict and Maria's letters. Although . . .' She sighed deeply, and shook her head. 'If there is any shred of a silver lining in the whole appalling episode, it is the thought that poor Caspar was perhaps not quite as bad as we had imagined him. If he had someone very close to him, whose evil intent he had no cause to suspect, egging him on to rash actions, when he himself was not quite in his right mind and very often sodden with drink besides, it makes me feel rather less angry with him for what he did, though it is still very terrible to think of it. Am I being a foolish old woman, or can you understand that in the least, my dear?'

'I can. I do not think it foolish at all. Did you suggest as much to Benedict too?'

'I did, and he agreed with me, or pretended to. He tells me that he has shared the whole sorry tale with you, as I always hoped he would, although indeed I understand that he had small choice in the matter, since Felix revealed a part of it to you.'

'I understand why he did not tell me sooner, you know, ma'am. I can well imagine that a propitious moment for such a painful account could hardly ever arise. He said that he had never spoken of it at all since the first time you were forced to reveal it to him.'

'He had not, and I am so glad that now he has. And I think that, now there are no more secrets between you, I must share one of my own. The one that lies at the root of all our troubles.'

'Please, ma'am, I beg you, do not feel it necessary to tell me anything that causes you distress. Benedict has said that . . . that your husband did not treat you well, and this caused a rift in your family, which you feel led to all the rest. I am very sorry for it, and for you, and I do not need to hear more of the cruelty that you have undergone. I am sure I could never blame you for anything.'

The Dowager shook her head, and said, 'That is kind of you, my dear. Perhaps it is foolish of me, and perhaps I will regret it, but I find I would like to tell you. Ben has said that he and Maria took my part, while Caspar cleaved to his father?' Kate nodded and her mother-in-law continued, 'I tried to do my duty as a wife, you know, for a long time. I had never wanted to marry Frederick when my parents told me I must, for all he was handsome, and not greatly advanced in years, and of course had all the social advantages that anyone could wish for. My family and all my acquaintance considered me very lucky, and I tried to feel the justice of it, but all the while I shrank from the prospect. It was years before I realised why. Certainly I was not the wife to Frederick that he wanted, and as a result never as close to Caspar as I should have been, though I did better with the younger ones. And then there was an incident. I was careless, and suffered for it. I had . . . a friend, and I allowed myself to . . . act unwisely, and Frederick, Frederick saw us. He beat me, he . . . But I will not speak of that. He shared the details of what he had discovered with Caspar, which was unkind in him, I think. Caspar judged me very harshly – he was only fourteen, too young to hear such things, and he urged his father to put me aside, to send me away, ensure I never saw the children again.' Her voice wavered, and Kate reached out and took her hand, and held it.

'It was not mercy that prevented Frederick from doing so. He felt himself to be perfectly justified, and most men would have agreed with him. It was nothing more than fear of scandal that stayed his hand. We lived apart, without any formal separation, but then, so many couples do in our rank of society, and nobody remarks upon it. But then of course he died just a couple of years later, of the influenza, and Caspar was devastated. He blamed me for his death, and because of it I could not offer him any comfort, nor temper his wildness.

'It was not until he fell in love with Alice years later that things grew easier between us. When he told her what I had done, hoping to shock her and enlist her to his side, you know, against me, she called him a hypocrite. I wish I could have seen his face! He had confessed all his wild ways to her, and she threw them back at him, and asked why it was acceptable for him to act in such a fashion, and yet he could not forgive me one mistake. "Why should women always be judged more harshly than men?" she told me she asked him. I wish you could have known her, Kate.'

'I wish it too.'

'And then of course we lost her, and you know what followed from that. All the catalogue of disasters, even up to the events of this past week and Felix's very shocking attack on Ben. For I cannot believe that Felix would ever have been tempted into wickedness as he was if Alice and her son had lived. What would have been the point? So many lives stood between him and the title then. It was the sudden, enticing prospect of his inheritance coming within his grasp that was irresistible to him, I believe.'

'I think you are right – how can I say? I scarcely knew him. But none of this is your fault, just as it was not Benedict's. You both have a great propensity to blame yourself, it seems to me, for things that have been done, and even for the actions of others. You make excuses for them, and not for yourselves. I partly understand it, ma'am, for I too am formed in such a way that I will always be thinking too much on my past actions, and wishing I had behaved differently. Benedict sometimes tells me I think too much, and that I should stop, and I am trying to act on his words, and would urge you to do the same. Can we not put the past behind us, and look to the future?'

The Dowager smiled a little mistily, and said, 'It would be good to do so, if we could, my dear.'

Kate said, 'Shall I give you a reason for it?'

'I wish you would.'

'When you suggested to me on our return from our honeymoon that I might have some news for you, you were correct, though it was too early then to say. I am with child, ma'am. There is no doubt of it.'

'Oh, my dear Kate, I am so happy! What wonderful news! I am glad that Ben did not share it with me, but left you to tell it.' They found they were both crying, and they embraced, and mopped their tears, and Kate told her the date that Maria had helped her calculate: the middle of May.

When they had composed themselves, the Dowager said, 'And that is not the only reason for celebration, is it, my dear girl? For my son tells me that he has come to his senses – and it only took the prospect of imminent death to bring this about, so I suppose Felix performed one action of merit in his life, even if by accident – and realises that he loves you. And you have told him of your love for him.' Kate blushed and smiled, her eyes shining. 'This is better news even than the other. It is all I could have hoped for!' And once more they shed a few tears, and then laughed at their foolishness.

When Kate had taken her leave, Miss Sutton at last emerged from the adjacent chamber, where she had been listening shamelessly to all that had passed through a crack in the door left for that purpose. 'I like that girl,' she said in her usual abrupt way. 'Good head on her shoulders. Your doing. Benedict could not have done better. Fond of Lucy, fond of all of you.'

'Of all of us,' the Dowager corrected, smiling.

'And yet, you did not tell her quite all, Charlotte. Thought you meant to. Sure you could have trusted her.' She spoke gruffly, as usual, but there was hurt behind the words, and Charlotte could not fail to be aware of it.

'Oh, my dearest Dotty, I am so sorry. You know it is not that I am in the least ashamed. All that is behind me. It was just that . . . in that moment, my courage failed me. I could not endure that she should look on me with horror or disgust, or somehow fail to understand me.'

Dorothea sighed, and shook her head, and they embraced, and after a while she said sadly, 'Perhaps you will tell her one day. Like to think so. Can't criticise you, can I? Haven't told my own brother.'

'Oh, well, men! Your brother has such a commonplace mind, after all,' said Charlotte dismissively. 'We are very lucky that Ben and Theodore are quite exceptional persons.' Miss Sutton agreed grudgingly that it was so, and their talk turned to happier things, and presently they went to change for dinner, which they were to take with Benedict and Kate that evening. Dorothea fussed a little at having to put on what she described as finery, but Charlotte cajoled her, and at last she did so, and they walked across to the other part of the house together, arm in arm.

EPILOGUE

It would be a subdued Christmas at Silverwood Hall that year, for Mr Waltham had slipped away at the start of December. He had not suffered the least pain, but had merely sunk into a deep sleep from which he had not awoken. Kate had been present at his bedside, for Dr Crew had warned her that the end could not long be delayed, and so she had slept in her own old room for a few nights, so that she could be sure to be with her grandfather in his final moments. Before he had slipped into his final coma, he had spoken of his dear wife, and Kate's mother who had died so young, but he had done so calmly, in the anticipation that he would soon be with them again; his only regret was that he would not live to see Kate's child.

It would be wrong to feel any extravagant grief for his passing, as his end had been so very peaceful and so much what he would have wished, but still Kate found it rather difficult to enter into the celebrations as much as she would have liked. Benedict was most understanding, and held her when she cried, and shielded her from the exuberance of Lucy and her cousins as much as he was able.

Kate was almost five months gone now, and her condition was quite obvious, especially in day gowns with their slightly lower waist, so that they had been obliged to share the news with Lucy, who was greatly excited at the prospect of having a little brother or sister; it was not by any means usual to be an only child, and she was delighted that she would not be one for much longer, but instead an older sibling, which seemed to her a splendid thing, rather than the youngest in the family as she had been all her life until now.

The Singletons were staying at the Hall for Christmas Day, before leaving – weather permitting – to make their way to Mr Singleton's own estate near Oxford, where they would celebrate the New Year. The children had been put to bed, with some difficulty in the case of the younger ones, and the adults all sat around the dinner table now, on Christmas Eve: Benedict at the head, handsome in his dark evening coat; Kate opposite him, in a black velvet gown that showed her mourning, but, as her husband assured her, and had demonstrated emphatically on the first occasion on which she had worn it, became her excessively too. He had bought her a string of lustrous, exotic black pearls, and they glowed against her skin. He smiled at her down the table, and raised his glass to her. The Dowager sat on her son's right, with her daughter opposite her and Miss Sutton on her other side, and Mr Singleton sat on Kate's right, next to his wife, to complete the table. Miss Morgan, Lucy's excellent new governess, had been granted a holiday to visit her parents in Bath over the festive season.

There was a bustle outside – an extraordinary thing, for who could be visiting them at this hour, and on Christmas Eve? There was a confusion of voices in the hall, and rising above it one that Kate recognised at once, though she had thought its owner a thousand miles away. It seemed impossible, but it was so; there could be no mistaking the tones, and indeed the language. She rose to her feet, and started towards the entrance, as the rest of the party looked at her in puzzlement. The door swung open, and before the affronted butler could announce her, a tall, magnificently dressed lady with abundant silver curls made a dramatic entrance, crying, '*Mia cara nipote! Lascia che ti guardi, carissima!*'

'Nonna!' she exclaimed. They embraced each other, laughing and crying all at once, and Benedict beckoned to the slightly stunned butler, and indicated that he should set another place for his mistress's grandmother.

'Three places, sir,' that worthy man suggested with a discreet cough. 'The foreign lady has brought a young lady and gentleman with her, whom I understand to be relatives of hers. They are waiting in the hall, not wanting to intrude, as I understood.'

'Three places,' agreed Benedict. He had heard a great deal about his wife's grandmother, and now he perceived that not a word of it had been an exaggeration. She was plainly akin to a force of nature; he wondered idly if Kate would be so too, when she was older. The idea did not displease him.

There was a little confusion for a while, but at last the table was rearranged, and Mrs Moreton and her young nephew and niece were seated, and served with food and wine. It was discovered that they spoke excellent English, which was a relief to many present, and they were both excessively handsome young people, with a strong resemblance to Kate, and excellent manners. It was obvious that neither of them had in the least wished to impose themselves, and at such a season, upon a family who were, after all, complete strangers to them, and equally obvious that they had been unable to resist Mrs Moreton's extremely forceful personality. She had meant to cross Europe, and desired their company, and they had had no choice in the matter.

Benedict looked down the table at his wife and thought how magnificent she looked in her black velvet and pearls, her dark hair shining and her face glowing with joy as she sat clasping her grandmother's hand, spilling out to her, as she so clearly was, all the events of the last months – both happy and far otherwise – that it had been so hard to convey in letters. He tapped his glass sharply, and the room fell silent, his family and guests all turning to look at him enquiringly.

'I am very glad to see us all together on this Christmas Eve,' he said. 'I am happy that you received my letter, Mrs Moreton, inviting you to come to us without delay, and delighted that you acted upon it so promptly, with the result that we now see you here at our table. I know Kate has missed you greatly, though I am sure that she bravely attempted to conceal it from you.'

Kate looked at him in astonishment at the subterfuge that he had practised with such success, and he grinned at her unrepentantly. Such happy secrets were permissible, surely? If he had told her and her grandmother had been unwilling or unable to come, she would have been downcast. A surprise was better. And family should be together at this time of year above all other.

He went on, 'It has been an extraordinary year – one with deep sadness in it, but also a great deal of joy. I do not in the least wish to belittle the losses and the grief we have suffered, nor is it possible to forget the unhappy events that have taken place, but for me this year will always be remembered as the year in which I found Kate, the love of my life, and had the great good sense to marry her. And so I would like to propose a toast to my dear wife, and to say – you will tell me if I have this right, Kate, but I hope I do – *buon Natale* to you all!'

'*Buon Natale!*' they chorused, and raised their glasses.

Merry Christmas.

ACKNOWLEDGEMENTS

I wrote this novel in my kitchen in lockdown. I'd never have developed the confidence to do it without the encouragement of all the complete strangers who commented so positively on my Heyer fanfic on A03. But the real inspiration came from my good friends in the Georgette Heyer Readalong on Twitter. I'm particularly grateful to Lucie Bea Dutton, who spent many hours of her precious time setting up and running the readalongs. I can't possibly name everyone – there are too many of us – but thank you all, amazing Dowagers.

Like many people in the writing, publishing and reading communities, Twitter has been a wonderful place for me. As someone who's always been a back-room sort of person, I found it helpful and freeing in more ways than I can possibly describe. So I'd like to thank all my

Twitter friends for the years of chat and mutual support, especially the very talented Katy Moran.

I've been obsessed with Georgette Heyer's novels since I first read them when I was eleven. They have their faults, but they've provided solace and escape for millions of people in tough times, so thank you, Georgette, even though you would have absolutely hated this book.

Thanks also to my family, Luigi, James and Anna, for putting up with me while I wrote this. Luigi did not sign up for having a late-onset author in the house, but has been immensely patient and helpful (and came up with a really good solution when I was stuck on the plot at one point), although some of his alternative title suggestions were truly terrifying. Jamie, Annie: I love you. Please don't read it.

My lovely work colleagues Amanda Preston, Louise Lamont and Hannah Schofield have also been extremely supportive throughout: thanks, Team LBA!

I am very lucky to have a superb agent in Diana Beaumont of Marjacq. She has believed in this book from the first time she read it, and made the hellish process of being on submission (and not being able to tell anybody about it) as bearable as it could be. Her editorial suggestions were brilliant, and she's just an all-round star.

Many thanks to Lesley Crooks and everyone at Allison and Busby, including Becca Allen for the fantastic copyedit. (I thought she'd mess with my punctuation, and she didn't. I have strong views on punctuation.) All of Lesley's inspired edits have made the novel so much better, and it is a pleasure to be published by her. It's been a long journey to publication for me, as a debut author in her fifties, and I can't express how much it means to me that Allison and Busby have given me this opportunity.

Finally, if you're reading this because you've bought the book: THANK YOU!

Read on for your chance to meet
The Runaway Heiress
coming autumn 2023

CHAPTER ONE

A ragged cloud blotted out the sliver of moon. It was suddenly darker in the elegant square of fashionable houses, and Cassandra scurried down the shallow steps in front of her. Once at the bottom, she huddled in the shadows at the far end of the paved semi-basement area, panting. She was trespassing on some gentleman's private property, but that was the least of her concerns in this moment. Her heart was pounding in her chest, and she was dizzy with terror. It was good to stop running for a moment, to try to collect her thoughts. But she dared not relax, for there was no safety here – there was nothing at all to prevent her pursuers from finding her in her makeshift hiding place and dragging her away by force. There was not the least point screaming and hoping that passing strangers might come to her aid; the men who were chasing her had already demonstrated that they had a ready answer prepared for any passer-by who should question their actions. She had thought that the gentleman she had stumbled into a few hundred yards back might assist her, but her pursuers had caught up with her and told him some plausible tale, and he had shrugged, and gone on his careless way. She had barely escaped them then, only her desperation, her youthful speed and their drunken state allowing her to evade their grasp.

The streets of London in the dead of night were a perilous place for a woman alone, and she was well aware that in running out of her uncle's house at this hour she had forfeited any claim to respectability in the eyes of the world. There was no help to be found, only more danger. She was entirely alone. She must *think*.

There was a faint light inside the mansion, spilling out from a small, barred window and coming, she presumed, from the servants' quarters in the basement. What little she had seen of the house in her headlong flight did not suggest that it was currently occupied by its aristocratic owners, which was why she had made the snap decision to seek refuge here. Cassandra had noticed in a single, desperate glance that the doorknocker had been taken down and the tall windows at street level and above were all securely shuttered. She supposed that the noble family who owned such a large and imposing building in the most exclusive part of Town were away. The Season was coming to an end, so it was reasonable to think that they had joined the rest of the polite world in some fashionable seaside resort, leaving a skeleton staff of servants to ensure the safety of their home. She was in danger from the servants too, of course – perhaps they would not molest her, but if one of them should have occasion to come out here, and saw her lurking where she had absolutely no business to be, they would undoubtedly raise a hue and cry which would attract the attention of her pursuers. And if a commotion should instead alert the patrolling Watch, she would be in no better position. She could surely expect no aid or sympathy from them. They might – she was ignorant of these matters, and hoped to remain so – apprehend her for vagrancy and lock her in some dreadful gaol, and if they should ascertain her identity they would merely return her to the care, for want of a worse word, of her uncle and guardian. And then she would be back where she started.

Cassandra stiffened as she heard voices, angry male voices, in the square above her. Her uncle, and . . . him. Clearly they had not given up seeking for her yet. Of course not: too much depended on finding her.

The best thing would be to gain entry to the mansion somehow, and hide there till daylight. The streets would be less dangerous then. It was not much of a plan, but it was all she had. If she could somehow attract the attention of the people in the house, so that they came out, she might perhaps slip inside while their backs were turned – how, though? – and be safe from her pursuers for a while. She could not think beyond that. She felt hot panic rising inside her, and pushed it down. Losing her head would not help. She must plan, and then she must act.

She crept towards the stairs that led up to the street – she had been huddling like a frightened animal in the darkest corner of the area – and strained to hear her uncle's voice. It was close, but if there was any chance of her desperate plan working it would need to be much closer.

The wait seemed interminable, but at last she could hear him cursing not far away. She judged that he was probably directly in front of the neighbouring house. She slipped back towards the basement door and picked up a wooden pail that had been left there; she had almost fallen over it a moment before, and that had given her the germ of an idea.

No time to hesitate. She flung the pail with all her strength against the lighted window and shrank back into the shadow of her former hiding place, close to the basement door but – she hoped – invisible. The wooden bucket clattered against the iron bars – a loud, shocking noise in the relative quiet of the deserted square – and she heard a shout of angry surprise from inside and, a moment later, the screeching of bolts as the door was unfastened. Meanwhile, a triumphant cry of, 'Got her!' came from the pavement above, and heavy, urgent footsteps pounded towards her, then slowed a little as they descended the steps in the darkness. She had been counting on that: that they would follow the sound, confident that they had run her to earth at last.

The basement door was wrenched open, and a man emerged into the area. He was so close to her that she could have reached out and touched him. A servant, she supposed. He was an African. Silhouetted against the light inside, he made an impressive figure; he was tall and powerfully built, and his posture was belligerent, his fists raised in front of him in what Cassandra imagined to be a boxer's stance. There was a woman close behind him, almost as tall and broad. A formidable pair, and their attention was not focused on her, but on the men who had just reached the bottom of the steps. 'Oi!' bellowed the manservant, moving nearer to the intruders, his fists still held ready for action. His companion, as bold as he was, followed him. 'What d'you mean by trespassing on a gentleman's property and making this racket?! If you've come to mill the ken, you'll have me to deal with, and you'll soon regret the day, my bully boys!'

'My good fellow . . .' began her uncle in the unctuous tones she so hated.

She did not stay to see how their altercation resolved itself; she edged closer and closer to the open door, still hidden in shadow and blessing her soft slippers for their silence, and then slipped inside, entirely unobserved by any of the participants in the scene playing out behind her. It was dangerous – there could be others present in the basement rooms, and if anyone saw her now she was lost – but she was wagering everything on the chance that, if there had been anyone else there, they too would likely have been drawn outside by the commotion and the impulse to protect their master's property. It was a risk she was prepared to take. She had no choice.

Her gamble paid off: the stone-flagged corridor was deserted, and the room opening off it – a kitchen – appeared to be empty too. She did not stay to make sure, but penetrated deeper into the house, resolved to seek the upstairs quarters where she thought she might be safer from discovery.

The layout of a gentleman's town mansion generally followed a set pattern, and Cassandra had no difficulty finding the servants' staircase. She crept up it to the green baize door that must lead to the ground floor of the house, opening it a crack and poking her head cautiously around it. A grand entrance hall, paved in squares of black and white marble. A little chilly moonlight crept in from the large fanlight above the door, enough to see her surroundings. She thought for one awful moment that she saw a tall, motionless human figure, standing there in the alcove, watching her, and let out an exclamation of surprise that she muffled hastily with one ungloved hand. But she realised in the next second that it was a classical statue: a fine marble copy of the Apollo Belvedere, some part of her brain noted irrelevantly. She felt hysterical laughter bubbling inside her. Apollo could do her no harm, and just at this moment the prospect of being transformed into a tree as the nymph Daphne had been while he chased her was not at all unattractive. No, it was living, breathing men she had to fear, not ancient gods.

She opened the door fully and slipped through it, closing it with agonising but necessary slowness behind her. She could hear no sounds of pursuit coming from below, and it did not seem to her from what she had seen of him that the burly servant who had accosted her uncle so confidently was the kind of man who would meekly allow two complete strangers to enter and search the building that was under his care. But still, it would be the highest degree of folly to stay here. She must find a more secluded place to hide. And do it very, very quietly. She crept forward. She was a criminal now, she supposed. A house-breaker. But she was committed to this course of action, and could not turn back. Which door should she choose . . . ?

CHAPTER TWO

Hal cursed as he struggled to insert the key in the lock. He could hardly blame the darkness for the difficulty he was having, for the midsummer dawn was just breaking over the square behind him, and he could see perfectly well. And yet he was damned if he could get the blasted key – which was large enough, in all conscience – into the confounded lock. He was, of course, drunk. Very, very drunk. Drunk, he reflected hazily, as a lord. Which, of course, he was. So that was perfectly in order.

At length he managed what should have been a simple task, and the door swung open in front of him. He entered. With exaggerated caution he closed the heavy front door quietly behind him and stood in the marble-tiled hall, swaying slightly on his feet and considering what he should do next. Apollo Belvedere – evidence that his grandfather, like most of his generation, had in the previous century undertaken the Grand Tour and spent at least some of his money in the approved fashion – studiously ignored him, gazing off towards the library door with sightless eyes and outstretched marble arm, almost as if pointing the way. Perhaps the god of . . . all the things that he was god of, things which Hal couldn't quite recall at that precise moment, was disapproving of his owner's sadly inebriated condition, although from what Hal recalled from his schooldays all those Greek deities were what his friend Tom Wainfleet would call devilish smoky fellows. 'Not at all the thing!' said Hal with a crack of slightly wild laughter. The sound echoed in the hall, and all at once the big house seemed very empty. As it was, of course. He was not supposed to be coming home, but had returned on a whim, and most of the indoor servants had been given holiday. Some of them were still here, naturally; a house like this could never be left entirely unprotected. Hal's head groom Jem Oldcastle was somewhere in his private fastness, and presumably his wife Kitty too, but they were not expecting Hal's return tonight – this morning. Nobody was. Georgiana was in Brighton, Bastian was on a reading tour with some friends from Oxford, and the younger children were in Lyme Regis with Aunt Sophia, heaven help her.

After the trials of the Season, Hal had been looking forward to some peace and quiet with a fierce intensity, but now that he had finally obtained his wish he found the idea unaccountably depressing, as he followed the direction of the statue's stony gaze and made his rather erratic way into his private sanctum and favourite room. The rest of the house, apart from his bedroom, would be done up in Holland covers, but he insisted that the library always be left ready for his use, and he was glad of it now. No doubt his sudden gloom would lift when he was in less chilly surroundings. Altogether too much marble in the hall: floor, wall panels and statues. Enough to make anyone blue-devilled.

He sighed with relief as he entered his library. That was better; much cosier. With the ease of long familiarity he threaded his way between the furniture in the darkness and found the tinderbox that was always left ready in its accustomed place on the mantel. He fumbled a little as he attempted to light a candle by touch alone, but by the exercise of a prodigious concentration he achieved the feat in the end, and turned, momentarily dazzled, to pick up a candelabrum and light yet more.

He stopped. Something was wrong. He was not alone in the room.

There was a girl.

In his foxed state, Hal was not perhaps as surprised as he should be to find a perfectly strange young female in his library. Perfectly strange young females had, if truth be told, occasionally been a feature of his life in the years since he had left Eton. He certainly had no objection to them on principle. Especially not if they were pretty, which this one appeared to be, from what little he could see of her.

Vague thoughts that she might be some friend of his sister's flitted through his mind, but he retained enough sense somewhere in a dim recess of his brain to realise that that was nonsense; his sister Georgie was not here and, even if she had been, there was no earthly reason why one of her innumerable bosom bows should be huddled on his library sofa at – he squinted at the gold mantel clock, but it had stopped – some unconscionable hour of the morning.

Asleep. She was fast asleep, entirely unaware of his presence.

He moved a step or two nearer, and raised the candle to have a closer look at her as she slumbered. Yes, very pretty. The fair unknown was curled up in the big Knole sofa, with one hand pillowing her cheek. She was wrapped in a voluminous black cloak, and against its darkness her vivid colouring stood out dramatically, even in the flickering candlelight. She had cropped hair of flaming red, and her short nose was scattered with the freckles that often accompanied such locks. Long lashes brushed her cheeks, and her skin was very pale. She had a heart-shaped face, and her pale pink mouth, which was slightly open as she slept, was rather appealing. Kissable, was the word that popped into Hal's fuddled brain. Yes, kissable. She looked to be about Georgie's age, it was true – perhaps eighteen or so. He could see a glimpse of very crumpled white muslin under the voluminous cloak, and small feet in dusty silk evening slippers peeped out from under the hem.

But what the devil was she doing in his library?

He must have made some sound, for suddenly her eyes sprang open – they were green, he noticed – and she looked at him blankly. And then screamed.

He swore, and dropped the candle, and the room was plunged into darkness.

EMMA ORCHARD was born in Salford. She studied English Literature at the Universities of Edinburgh and York, before working behind the scenes in publishing and television for many years. Her first job was at Mills & Boon, where she met her husband in a classic enemies-to-lovers romance. She now lives in North London.

@emmaorchardbooks